PRETEND YOU'RE MINE

CRYSTAL KASWELL

COPYRIGHT

ABOUT THIS BOOK

This is the worst idea in the history of the world.

Leighton is my best friend. My subordinate.

My girlfriend.

That's the story we're selling. To our co-workers. To our friends. To everyone who's anticipating the breakdown of the year at my ex's wedding.

It's a terrible idea.This ruse is going to f*ck shit up. Losing her is out of the question.

Touching her is all kinds of wrong.

And right deep in my bones.

Then Leighton slides her hands into my hair and presses her berry lips to mine.

And all that wrong fades to right.

I stop pretending.

I forget about the woman who broke my heart. I forget about our rules. I forget I'll be lost without her.

I kiss her back like I'll never get enough.

I won't.

But I can't risk losing my best friend.

Even if she's the woman who might finally unlock my heart.

PROLOGUE - RYAN

She cuts through my bullshit with six words. "You need to kiss me now."

My body takes over. My eyelids flutter closed. My fingers dig into her soft hips.

I pull her closer. Let my lips brush hers.

It's soft. Slow. Sweet.

Then it's harder.

She tugs at my hair.

I pin her to the wall.

My head spins.

She wants me.

It makes no sense.

And it makes every lick of sense in the world.

She sighs as she pulls back. "Inside. Now."

I shift my hips to release her.

Her ass brushes my crotch as she presses the door open and steps inside.

I follow. Lock the door behind us.

Her eyes find mine.

They beg for love, trust, satisfaction.
I still don't know shit about the first two.
But I can make her come.
I need to make her come.
Now.

2

RYAN

Four Weeks Ago

My keys clink against the plastic table.

It's too quiet today.

Way too fucking quiet.

I tug at my t-shirt. Close my eyes. Let my thoughts drift back to the way this place used to be. The mass-produced paintings on the walls, the carefully arranged photos on the fridge, the decorative pillows on the leather couch.

I should have known shit was gonna end like this the second she brought home one of those pillows.

That was the type of thing we hated. The type of thing we mocked together.

No. I'm not doing this. Not tonight.

Not ever.

She's gone. And I'm going to get over it.

One day.

I toss my bag on the couch—right where that ugly *Home, Sweet Home* pillow used to rest—then I shuffle through the mail.

Bill. Credit card offer. *Rolling Stone*.

Thick, square envelope. Handwritten address. Familiar stamped return address.

I peel the envelope open.

It's there, in curvy silver letters.

You are cordially invited to the wedding of Penelope Winters and Francis Hobbs.

My stomach drops.

My throat tightens.

The air gets heavy. Hot. Suffocating.

This isn't fucking happening.

There's no way my ex-girlfriend is getting married in six short weeks.

There's no way she's walking down the aisle with the guy I caught her fucking in our bed.

There's no way she's inviting me to watch this train wreck.

FOR THREE DAYS, I SHOVE PENNY'S WEDDING TO THE BACK OF my mind.

I focus on my routine.

I perfect every link of ink. I run. I spar. I cook dinner, for myself or for Leighton. I drown myself in tattoo mock-ups, at my desk, alone, or on my best friend's couch.

My illusion of normalcy shatters the second my phone sings with *Maneater*.

Penny's ringtone.

She's calling me to—

I don't know. Or care. I don't want to hear her excuses. Or her apology.

I'm sorry, but I don't love you anymore.

It echoes through my brain. She was right there. In our bed. Only the sheets were pink.

My eyelids flutter closed. I can see her, hugging the Egyptian cotton to her chest. Pushing her dark hair behind her ear. Staring at the ground to hide the shame in her honey eyes.

Or was it the lack of shame?

She never apologized for hurting me. For fucking him behind my back. For lacking the guts to leave.

Only for falling out of love with me.

The air gets hot again. It's ridiculous—I'm naked, freshly showered and sopping wet, and the air conditioning is set to high. The room is freezing. Freezing enough my dick is shrinking.

And my dick—

It's a been a year since I've fucked anyone. I get hard at the drop of a hat now. Especially around Leighton.

Which is fucking ridiculous.

She's my best friend.

And I'm not fucking that up.

One nine-year relationship in flames is plenty for one lifetime.

I wrap a towel around my waist. Cinch it tight. Stare at my cell as the call goes to voicemail.

My phone sings again.

She's still infecting the air. Robbing my life of every ounce of pleasure.

My last drop of calm evaporates. I need another shower. I need a thousand showers. I need to scrub away every memory of her.

No, I need more than that. I need to step out of my skin and find some new body. One that won't react to Penelope Winters.

I take a deep breath and exhale slowly. Whatever her bullshit reason for calling, I'm not letting her believe I'm a mess without her.

I answer the call. "Yeah?"

"Oh. Ryan. I thought I'd get voicemail." Her voice is soft. Sweet.

The same voice she used to whisper *I love you* the first time.

Then to whisper *I'm sorry, but I don't love you anymore.*

My stomach twists.

My chest gets heavy.

Her voice undoes me. Sends me right back to the moment where my heart shattered into a million tiny pieces too small for anyone to see.

A million tiny pieces that tear up my skin anytime I get close.

It bounces around my brain.

I'm sorry, but I don't love you anymore.

I press my back against the wall, but it doesn't do shit to steady my thoughts. "Is this important? I've got a lot to do."

"It will only take a minute."

It's been nearly a year since I've heard her voice. I can still hear the Penny I fell in love with. But there's something else too. Some person I don't recognize.

"How's the shop?" she asks.

"Good. We bought it from Manning."

Her voice perks. "Really?"

"Yeah."

"That's amazing, Ryan. Perfect for you."

"Thanks." My voice wavers. I press my palm against the wall. Owning the shop is perfect for me. It's what I've always wanted. Hell, it's the only thing besides her I ever really wanted.

But why the fuck is she happy about that?

The last year, she kept dropping hints about how I needed

to find a "real job." Never mind that we used to stay up all night talking about how we'd never fall into that bullshit trap.

Yeah, we were kids. But it's not like she was ever idealistic. She meant it.

"I'm guessing you got the invitation?" Something creeps into her voice. Regret. Remorse. Or maybe pity.

In her eyes, I'm still a loser tattoo artist. Not like her respectable finance bro fiancé. My hair is too long. My arms are too inked. My jeans are too ripped.

I don't own a suit much less wear one to work every day.

"Yeah." Memories flood my mind. The two of us sitting on the swings at the park by her place. Marveling at our sneakers and pinkie promising we'd never get jobs where we had to wear anything else.

Promising we'd never let each other give up on our dreams.

The rubber padding under my feet.

The bright moon against the dark sky.

The sprinklers hitting the grass.

And that watermelon ChapStick on her lips.

I can't get anywhere near the fucking fruit without thinking of her.

"Ryan…" Her voice drops back to that soft, sweet tone. *I love you.* "I'm so sorry." *But I don't love you anymore.* "I told Mom a million times. I told her it was rude to invite you. But she doesn't get that you aren't over me."

Words tumble from my lips before I can stop them. "I am."

"Oh." She barely manages to hide her surprise.

No, I'm not over Penny. Not even close. But fuck her for assuming that. It's not like she's around to watch me slice my fingers trying to pick up the pieces. "I'm seeing someone."

This is bullshit. Even I can't sell it.

7

I don't *see* anyone. All my clients look the same—skin stretched over bone, grunts of pain, nervous smiles.

Women flirt with me constantly. It's something about getting ink. Some rush of dopamine. Some desire to get that *hot tattoo artist* notch on their bedpost.

Women go apeshit for my wavy hair and my inked arms. But that does nothing to thrill me. It's only a knife in my chest, seeing women gaga for the shit Penny hated.

My ex-girlfriend's voice shifts to some tone I can't place. "That's great, Ryan. Really. What's she like? Pretty?"

"Yeah." Of course, that's her first question.

It's all appearances with her now.

Or maybe she was always like this. Maybe I was blinded by how much I loved her.

"What does she do?" Her voice pulls me back into the moment.

The air conditioner hums. The black curtains ruffle against the window. The black sheets soak up the light from the fluorescent bulb.

I swallow hard. Push away all the images forming in my mind. Of times when shit made sense. "Why'd you call, Penny?"

"I'm going by Penelope now."

Of course she is. "Question stands."

"I wanted to apologize. For Mom. The wedding planning is making us both crazy. It was insensitive."

Yeah. It was. But fuck her for that condescending tone in her voice. Fuck her for thinking I can't handle this. Even if she's right. "It's fine."

"Really?"

"It's been a year. It's not like I'm waiting by the phone."

"Oh. Do you… Do you want to come?"

I'd rather tattoo *I'm still in love with Penelope Winters* on my dick. "Of course."

"Really?"

"Yeah."

"It's not a problem, the hotel and airfare? Maui is expensive in August."

I bite my tongue. Has she always been this condescending or is it new? "No. We're doing great. But thanks for the concern."

"So, uh… I guess I'll mark you down for a plus one?"

"Yeah."

"Mom wanted to invite Dean."

Of course she did. "It's your wedding. Do what you want." My younger brother despises Penny. I'd never admit it to the smug bastard, but I envy his easy hatred. I wish I could turn off the part of me that still loves her.

"That's true. I… I think I will. Does he need a plus one?"

"You know Dean."

She laughs. "Yeah. How is he?"

"Same as always." I push off the wall. Focus every bit of my attention on my bare feet against the hardwood. Half a dozen steps and I'm at my desk.

I sit in my eight-hundred-dollar ergonomic chair. Press my palms into my black wood laminate desk. Stare at the sketchbook left open to a mock-up.

It's lyrics from some song about wanting your ex to die in a fiery car crash.

I even envy that violent bastard of a lyricist.

I wish I wanted Penny to die in agony.

That would be so much easier than wanting her to live by my side forever.

My stomach churns. This conversation is torture. How the fuck am I going to survive watching her walk down the aisle? "You want cash or something off your registry?"

"Ryan…" *You're not supposed to ask that.*

I need some way to get through this. A shield. Someone

that will convince her I don't need her. Someone who will get how fucked-up this is.

But the only person who gets this is Leighton.

There's no way I'm using her as—

There's no way I'm using her, period.

She's my best friend.

The only person in the entire world I trust.

The only sliver of light in most of my days.

No fucking way I'm risking that.

I force my voice to steady. "I gotta go. Congratulations, Pen."

"Thanks. Ryan, I—"

I end the call before she can finish her thought.

LEIGHTON

E ven with the beach breeze blowing over my shoulders, the July heat is oppressive. Sun beats down on my back. It warms my hair. Fries my tender, just bleached scalp.

The six-block walk to the shop—it's a miracle I found parking this close—is enough to get my dress sticking to my chest.

The bell rings as I press the Inked Hearts door open.

Fluorescent light replaces the glow of the sun.

The warm air dissipates. It's freezing in here.

Then my eyes catch Ryan's, and the coolness disappears. Heat spreads to my fingers and toes.

He looks so good.

He always looks good, but it's been an entire day and a half since I've seen him.

He really is that beautiful. Those strong shoulders and inked arms aren't figments of my sexual fantasies. They're all him.

"Hey." He nods hello from his suite, the one on the right, next to the window.

"You're here early."

"I'm always this early."

"No. Just usually." I pull my arms over my chest. How can I be hot and cold at the same time? It defies explanation.

His eyes find mine. "You want my hoodie?"

My toes tap together. My tongue slides over my lips. Ryan offers his hoodie almost every day. And I always say yes.

But not because I'm cold—my cardigan is in my purse, and it looks a hell of a lot better with this outfit.

Because it smells like him.

Because it's *his*.

He bends to pull it from his backpack. His fingers brush mine as he hands it over.

It's black, of course.

His entire world is black—his jeans, his t-shirt, his backpack, his car, his sketchbook, his pens, his attitude toward humanity.

You'd think the whole constant brooding, still not over his ex thing would be enough to convince me to stay away.

Not that I've ever had good taste in men.

I fell for the wrong guys for so long that I gave up on guys entirely.

Then I met Ryan.

And I tried to get over him. Really. When I started working here, he was still with Penny. I'm a lot of things, but I'm not a home-wrecker.

I had no intentions of stealing him from her.

I have no intentions of claiming him.

He's been single for a year now. We've been friends all that time. More.

But that's all we are.

That's all we'll ever be.

I'm okay with that. Really, I am.

Being his friend is a lot better than being his nothing.

I slide his hoodie over my shoulders. Turn as I inhale the scent of him. Lemon soap, rubbing alcohol (the shop reeks of it), and something distinctly Ryan.

"You want coffee?" he asks.

"I can do it."

"Sit. I'll fix it."

"If you tell me why you're frowning."

"I'm not frowning." His lips press into a smile. It's genuine. It lights up his eyes. Softens his brow.

God, he has a nice smile. "Okay, why you were frowning."

He shrugs like nothing has ever bothered him before—a hard claim for anyone to make.

But for someone as broody as Ryan? There's no way he's selling that.

He motions to the Keurig in the lobby. "It's happening."

"I have to restock it."

"Already did it."

I bite my lip. He does this all the time—gets to the shop early or stays late, does my job for me.

It's nice, having less to do. It frees up my time. Lets me focus on graphic design instead of busywork.

But—"That's my job."

He shrugs. "I was here."

"Thanks." I guess.

He crosses the room and fills a pod with French roast.

The smell of coffee fills the room as I set up. Purse under the counter. Computer on. *Come In, We're Awesome* sign turned. Schedule printed.

He sets my coffee on the counter along with one container of half-and-half and another of Sugar in the Raw.

"Thanks." I tear the fixings, pour, stir. Mmm. Sweet, creamy, rich perfection. "You're weird today."

"I'm always weird."

"True." But he's being extra weird. "You miss karate or something?"

"Aikido."

"You realize you're the only person who cares about the difference."

"It's my cross to bear." His voice stays dry.

But the joke still warms me everywhere. Ryan hides his sense of humor from most people.

I get it.

I get that side of him.

I get so much of him.

But, still, my heart wants more. Even if my head knows better.

I take another long sip. There's something in those baby blues, something hurting him, but he isn't going to tell me.

He isn't the sharing feelings type.

Not that I can talk.

My heart is locked up tight. It's easier that way. Safer.

You can't fall for guys who pretend they love you if you keep them at arm's length.

You can't buy into yet another *I'll change, I promise* if you don't believe in someone in the first place.

And you'll never, ever suffer the rejection of being someone's second choice, if you don't care about being first.

Yes, I'm crazy about Ryan.

Yes, we're best friends.

We hang out. We run. We mock bad TV and eat dinner and tease each other about how we fix our coffee.

We don't pour our hearts out.

"You sure you're okay?" I ask.

His gaze goes to the bright blue sky outside the windows then it's back on me. "I'll get there."

"You want to talk about it?"

"Maybe later."

My stomach twists. That's a no.

I hate that he won't let me in.

I hate that I don't get every thought in his head.

I hate that he isn't mine.

But I'm not about to unlock the vault around my heart.

How can I ask him to do the same?

"YOU'RE WHAT?" DEAN'S VOICE ECHOES AROUND THE ROOM. It's free of his usual *aren't I an adorable troublemaker?* tone. He's genuinely concerned.

That's weird. And worrisome. Dean only drops the pretenses when shit is bad.

And with that way Ryan's shoulders are at his ears…

This is bad.

I'm quitting the shop and moving to Siberia; it's the only place as cold as my soul bad.

I take a deep breath and exhale slowly.

There's no way he's leaving.

That's absurd.

I try to focus on the computer screen. To actually finish double-checking these records. To pretend as if I'm not eavesdropping.

I fail.

My gaze stays on Ryan's back.

He runs a hand through his wavy hair.

He shrugs, completely failing at aloof. "You're invited too."

"Fuck." Dean's sandy hair falls over his bright eyes as he shakes his head. "She's such a bitch."

"Don't talk about her like that."

"I'll say it as much as I want." Dean steps sideways, into the lobby. "Penny is a bitch."

Ryan's brow furrows as he turns and follows Dean. "I said I'm going, not 'I'd like your opinion.'"

"You're not going."

"Yeah, I am."

Ryan is going somewhere. Doing something Dean objects to.

But Dean doesn't object to anything.

Unless—

Fuck.

Dean continues. "All right. Go. Get wasted. Stand up in the middle of the ceremony and scream 'here's a reason why these two can't wed. Because she fucked him behind my back. And what the hell do you think that means for you, Francis? You think she's gonna be loyal to you after that?' Then drop the mic, get wasted, sleep with a bridesmaid, and come home the victor."

"Fuck off."

"You're gonna make a fool of yourself either way. Might as well do it right."

"She thinks I'm not over her," Ryan says.

"All you're gonna do is prove you care enough about her opinion to drop two grand on plane tickets and a hotel in Maui."

Penny's getting married.

And Ryan's going.

What the hell is he doing going to his ex's wedding?

And what the hell is he doing telling Dean instead of me?

Ryan's black-on-black Converse squeak against the hardwood floor as he takes a step toward the counter.

Dean shakes his head *what the hell is wrong with this guy*. "If you show up single, she'll think you're a loser."

"He's right." The words tumble from my lips. So much for pretending I'm not eavesdropping. But this is my business.

Ryan is my best friend. I care about him more than anyone does.

Ryan shakes his head *kids today*. "I'm not showing up single."

Dean laughs. "You didn't—"

Ryan turns back to him. "I'm still not interested in your opinion."

"Yeah. You are." Dean shakes his head *you're an idiot for this*. "Or you wouldn't have brought it up."

"I was letting you know my schedule." Ryan slides his hand into the front pocket of his black skinny jeans.

"It's sweet. You care." Dean presses his hands to his heart —he's the opposite of Ryan, in his bright blue t-shirt, light jeans, and navy and white checkered Vans—and feigns catching a hug. "You can admit it."

"Right back at you," Ryan says.

I laugh. "He's got you there."

"Love you too, babe." Dean blows me a kiss. He laughs as he turns to Ryan. "Have I ever told you not to do something?"

"Well..." Ryan brushes another wavy lock behind his ear. Again, it fails to stay in place. It falls to his cheek. Frames his blue eyes in a perfect shade of brown. "She thinks I'm never gonna move on."

"You aren't," Dean says.

"Fuck off." Ryan moves forwards. Until he's only a few feet away.

His eyes find mine.

They fill with vulnerability. Then he blinks, and his expression is steel again.

"You really told her you're bringing someone?" Dean asks.

Ryan's shoulders climb to his ears. "Not someone." He tries to keep his voice even, but he doesn't quite get there. "My girlfriend."

Dean shakes his head harder. *Fuck, you're stupid.* "You

17

don't even look at chicks. Where are you gonna find a girlfriend?"

"I'll do it." Words leap from my throat.

I do nothing to stop them.

I'm powerless to stop them.

This is crazy. But it's also perfect.

I press my lips into a smile. A calm *this is a great idea* smile, not a lovesick *anything to be close to you* one. "I'll go to Penny's wedding. I'll pretend I'm your girlfriend."

Ryan's eyes fix on me.

It's not a good look.

It's not a *yes*.

It's not even a *that's a ridiculous idea, but points for trying*.

More like a *not in a million years*.

But it's not over until it's over.

4

RYAN

No.

Fuck no.

A million times no.

Leighton is better than this bullshit.

I need to be better than this bullshit.

I stare into my best friend's blue-green eyes, but I can't find her intentions.

Hawaii is gorgeous. I get that. Penny used to mock me for wanting to go someplace so "basic" for our honeymoon. The insult never made sense.

Basic is good.

Simple is good.

Easy is good.

Fuck knows I need easy.

Like me and Leighton.

Our friendship is easy.

So what the hell is with her intense stare?

Nobody wants to see the Aloha State that badly.

I shake my head. "I don't want shit to get weird."

My brother looks from me to her. He tries out that shit-stirring smile of his, but it doesn't land.

He's worried about her.

This *is* a stupid idea.

It must be the worst idea in the history of the planet if Dean's concerned. The only thing he's serious about is work. Even then, he pretends like everything he does is effortless.

"Yeah. Right. Of course." She twirls a short, purple strand around her finger. "But what if it didn't make things weird?"

"How could it not?"

"It's just acting." She taps the counter with her shiny silver fingernails. "I was Abigail Williams in *The Crucible*. I've performed more difficult roles."

"More difficult than pretending you can tolerate Ryan?" Dean's voices jumps back to bouncy. "Is that possible?"

"Not for most," she teases. "But I'm a true thespian."

"This is getting interesting." He motions *go on*.

She rolls her eyes. "Are you fourteen? Even you are better than that."

I shake my head. "He's not."

His smile jumps back to playful as he flips me off.

Leighton laughs. Her eyes find mine. They're greener today. It must be that purple makeup. Or the teal and black cat-print dress. "I, uh. I do agree with Dean. It's a stupid idea. But if you're going to do it, you might as well do it with someone you trust."

It's a fair point.

But it's not enough.

There are only three times my world brightens: when I'm doing a tattoo, when I'm working out, and when I'm with her.

I'm not risking that.

Not for something as stupid as proving I've moved on.

I stare into her eyes. "I'll find a way to call it off."

She nods *sure*, but her expression screams *you won't*.

My client shows. I sit her down, clean her up, talk her through the first line of the day.

The world fades away as I fall into the piece—an epic sleeve of produce. This girl loves fruits and vegetables so much she wants them on her body forever.

It's weird in a charming way.

She's going against the grain.

Same way I did when I first walked into a tattoo shop. I never managed to please my parents, no matter how hard I tried. My B.A. in business is useful (not that I'd ever admit that to them), but it didn't do anything to get them off my back.

I started apprenticing halfway through college. I always wanted to do tattoos but as soon as I actually put ink to skin —a spade on my ankle—I fell in love.

This is where I belong.

This is the place where everything makes sense.

Always.

For three hours, I work to the buzz of that gun and the breathy groan of Leighton's favorite band.

Technically, no one is in charge of music. Technically, me, Dean, Walker, and Brendon each own a quarter of the shop.

We each get a quarter of the say.

Really, I'm the boss and Brendon is second in command. I do the books, I make the schedule, and I veto the music.

Only I let her listen to whatever.

It's not altruistic.

I love the way she hums along with the music, tapping her toes, smiling as she swoons over some damaged lyricist.

Hell, it's not just her reaction.

I love her miserable taste.

It's comforting. Somebody else out there is as fucked-up as I am.

Thousands of screaming women adore this singer for all the pain in his breathy, raspy voice.

They love that he's hurt.

They want to save him.

I guess I'm still a romantic at heart.

Deep down, I still believe in all that shit. Even if my head knows better.

The album shifts to the next as my appointment ends. I walk my client out, schedule our next session.

Leighton is still sitting behind the counter. She's staring at something on her laptop, humming the melody of the angsty anthem flowing through the shop.

We have an understanding. As long as she does everything she needs to do for Inked Hearts, she's free to use her time to work on whatever.

Like homework for her summer school class.

Her eyes flit from her computer. "Unless you're about to show off my first-class ticket to Hawaii, save it. This is due at midnight."

"The design?"

She nods. "Design 201." Her eyes fix on the screen. She adjusts something with her mouse. "I don't see tickets."

"Leigh—"

"It won't be weird. But suit yourself." Her brow furrows as she leans back. Takes in the design again. She bites her lip.

I know that look.

It's almost there.

But something is off.

"Let me see," I say.

"It's not done."

"That's why I can help."

Her eyes meet mine. She stares at me, assessing my intentions.

I don't get it. I don't fuck with her the way Dean does. I don't play everything cool the way Walker does. I... all right, according to Leighton, I "brood all over the place," even more than Brendon does.

But I don't do it *at* her.

I'm always clear about what I want.

"It's not good enough," she says.

Unlikely. Leighton is amazing. A better designer than I am. She does all the shop's graphics. She slays them, but she never takes credit.

I press my palm against the counter. Stretch my fingers. I love this job like my life depends on it, but it's too sedentary. I need to move. "I'm gonna go for a run. If you don't want help—"

"I do. Thank you." She turns the laptop to me to show off a green on white logo design. *Health Express*. "It's a fictional fast casual restaurant. I want it to look healthy. Is the green too obvious?"

"Obvious is good."

Her shiny silver nails tap the counter. "You... you aren't saying anything."

"It's good."

"Good?"

"Yeah."

"Just good?"

"Great."

"But?"

She taps the counter with her pointer finger. "Something's missing."

"I know that. I need to know what."

I blink. Stare with fresh eyes. It's a great design. Bold. Classic. But too busy. "Pick one, the eggplant or the name."

"No name? All eggplant. Is that really—"

I chuckle. "That's what you're going for."

"I'm not sure what you mean." She plays coy. "It's a simple vegetable."

"That's shaped like a dick."

"Never considered that." She holds her poker face for a few moments.

It cracks.

Her laugh bounces around the room, drowning out every other sound.

I can't help but smile. It feels so fucking good, seeing her like this. "Send it to me tonight. After you revise it."

"Really?"

"Yeah. I'll let you know what I think."

"Thanks."

There's nothing left to say, but I don't want to tear myself away from her. I want to linger at the counter, helping her with the design, teasing her about her taste in broken musicians, talking about nothing.

But there's something in her expression.

Something that says *leave me alone*.

So I do.

WITH EVERY STRIDE, MY THOUGHTS UNFURL. THE MESSY LINES straighten. Arrange themselves in order.

Fail to offer clarity.

Bringing some woman to Penny's wedding is a terrible idea.

Pretending she's my girlfriend is worse.

But there's this voice in my head screaming *you have to do this*.

My phone buzzes against my thigh. I tell that voice to quiet and wish for distraction.

Leighton: It's done. Just emailed you. Tell me it's not horrible.

Ryan: On a run. I'll check it out after I shower.

Leighton: It's a million degrees.

Ryan: And?

Leighton: Are you dying?

Ryan: Yeah.

Leighton: You are not. You walk in here like you're fresh from a shower after half your runs.

I snap a picture of my surroundings—the ocean, the Santa Monica pier, the busy Venice street, the bright lemon sun—then I turn my phone to selfie mode, and snap a picture of my sweaty shirt.

It's hot as hell today.

But I don't feel the embrace of the sun. I don't see the brightness. I know it's there—I always end these runs dripping sweat—but I miss the comfort of it.

Ever since that day I walked in on Penny under Frank, I struggle to find the comfort in anything. Drowning my thoughts in work, booze, or exercise is as good as it gets.

Besides Leighton.

But that—

I'm not thinking about that.

I send her the photo.

Leighton: Barely sweating.

Ryan: I went nine miles.

Leighton: How can I get some of this infinite endurance?

Ryan: Join me next time.

Leighton: You're too fast.

Ryan: I'll slow down. Call it a rest day.

Leighton: Asshole.

Ryan: You just figuring that out?

Leighton: It's a constant revelation.

I can't help but smile. There's something about the way she teases me. It warms me the way the sun used to.

I slip my cell into my pocket, fill my bottle at the nearest fountain, run the half a mile back to Venice, then the twenty blocks to my apartment.

A hot shower washes away the day, but it's not enough.

The invitation is still sitting on my desk.

Without my contacts, it's a blur of white and silver. An anonymous reason for celebration.

When I slide my glasses on, the words come into focus.

You are cordially invited to the wedding of Penelope Winters and Francis Hobbs.

It's still happening.

There's still no way I can stomach it alone.

And it's still a terrible idea finding a fake girlfriend.

I am gonna figure this out. Somehow.

I push it aside as I pull up Leighton's design on my laptop. It's perfect.

I grab my cell and shoot her a text.

Ryan: Fucking amazing.

Leighton: There's nothing you'd change?

Ryan: Nothing.

My chest warms. It feels good, helping Leighton. Everything feels good with Leighton.

There's no way I'm risking that.

I let the thought bounce around my brain as I prep dinner —a simple, sautéed lemon chicken.

Usually cooking calms me. But, today, it isn't working.

Memories of Penny threaten to flood my mind. Her standing in the kitchen, in her ironic pink and white apron, joking about how she's a perfect homemaker.

That smile as she perfected penne *arrabiata*.

The intense look in her honey eyes as she watched me take my first bite.

She's been in the corner of my mind for the last year and change. She's been a ghost in my thoughts. A watermark on a perfect photo.

There.

But easy to ignore.

Now, with that fucking invitation sitting on my desk—

A million memories of her crash together.

I'm sorry, but I don't love you anymore. It echoes around the silent room.

I plug my cell into the knockoff iHome. Boot up one of Leighton's most miserable playlists.

Penny drifts from my thoughts as heavy guitar fills the room.

I only see Leighton's plum smile. Her blue-green eyes crinkling as she laughs. Her hand on her hip as she defends the song from Brendon's "I'm not listening to that emo shit" complaints.

I finish cooking. Place the chicken on a salad. Drizzle it with oil and vinegar.

It's not gourmet, but it's my hard work.

That makes it perfect.

My phone buzzes as I bring my plate to the dining table.

Leighton: I hear Hawaii is beautiful in August.

Ryan: Don't.

Leighton: At least think about it.

Ryan: I am.

Penny's wedding owns my thoughts.

I'd kill to erase it from my mind.

But Leighton—

What the hell does she get out of this?

Ryan: This is all for Hawaii?

Leighton: You don't know how badly I want to zip line.

Ryan: When did zip lining become part of it?

27

Leighton: You think I'm gonna go all the way to Maui and not do everything I ever wanted to do there?

Ryan: Don't make me say no again.

Leighton: Okay. Fine. But I want to state, for the record, that you won't find anyone better.

Ryan: Agree.

Leighton: And that it won't make things weird.

Ryan: You agreed to drop it.

Leighton: Okay. Dropping it. I should go soon. I have class at eight.

Ryan: You get up early enough to get somewhere at eight?

Leighton: Go to hell.

Ryan: Already there.

Leighton: Well that takes the sting out of hurting you.

Is she pissed or teasing?

I don't know. I never do with her. With the guys, it's easy. They annoy me all the time, but it's 'cause they wear their irritation on their sleeve.

Ryan: Why are you taking that class?

Leighton: You gave me shit all spring about how I should go back to college and now you're asking me why I'm taking this class?

Ryan: You're better than this 201 shit.

Leighton: Maybe. But it's a requirement if I want to do a design program at any UC or Cal State.

Ryan: You could skip that. Charge for your shit. It's good.

Leighton: Not that good.

Ryan: It is. Trust me. I know what I'd pay for your designs.

Leighton: Doing Facebook graphics isn't a career.

Ryan: It is. But you do a lot more. Logos. Websites. Book covers. You could do any of it.

Leighton: Well...

Ryan: Well?

Leighton: Can you keep a secret?

Ryan: Who am I going to tell?

Leighton: True. Nobody else listens to you.

Ryan: Bane of my existence.

Leighton: I know.

I can't help but laugh.

Leighton: I designed a cover for Kaylee's book.

Ryan: It has a title?

Leighton: Something like "Forbidden." I have one with that title. But my best mock-up is titled "I Love Fucking Brendon."

Ryan: With a picture of him naked?

Leighton: If only I had one *sigh*

Ryan: You're hot for him?

Leighton: Ew.

Ryan: You don't find him attractive?

Leighton: He's good-looking, yes. But I'm not interested.

Ryan: Why?

Leighton: He's been in love with Kay the whole time I've known him.

Ryan: If he wasn't?

Leighton: Hard to imagine. And I'm done with this subject. You want to see the cover or not?

Ryan: Yeah.

My phone flashes with a new picture message. A mock-up for Kaylee's book.

The eighteen-year-old college student/aspiring author is Brendon's girlfriend. He's one of the co-owners, and the oldest guy at the shop after me.

It should be fucked-up—their eight year age difference, him being her best friend's older brother—but it's not.

They love each other.

Everything else is irrelevant.

My cell buzzes as two more mock-ups join the first.

One is a silly throw back—a buff, shirtless guy clutching a woman in a fancy dress.

The next image is simple. *Forbidden* carved into a black

background, revealing the lush red rose beneath it. *Kaylee Hart* at the bottom in a simple sans font.

It's beautiful. Something my mom would buy.

The third isn't nearly as classy.

It's a shirtless guy, from the waist up.

It's—

Ryan: What am I doing on your book cover?

Leighton: Saving me the stock photo credit.

Ryan: What the fuck, Leigh?

Leighton: You have a certain something.

Ryan: Tattoos?

Leighton: Yeah. And something else.

Ryan: Abs?

Leighton: You're proving my point.

Ryan: This is weird.

Leighton: Look at it again. Pretend it isn't you.

Fuck that. There's no way I belong on a book cover. Even if it's a pointless mock-up. I have nine years of Penny complaining about our pics to prove that.

But when I blink, I see it. Not in some *damn, look at my hot bod* kind of way.

There's an ache there. Not just exhaustion and sweat, but something else.

It's like I'm screaming *I'm never gonna be okay.*

Ryan: Am I really this hopeless?

Leighton: Isn't that what you're going for?

No. I just don't know how to be anything else.

5

LEIGHTON

My cell is flush with texts from Dean.

Dean: You're not doing this.

Dean: It's too stupid. Even for me.

Dean: He's still in love with her.

Dean: He's gonna break your heart without even realizing it.

Leighton: I want to help him.

Dean: You want to kiss him.

Leighton: It can be both.

Dean: No. It can't. 'Cause he doesn't want to kiss you.

Leighton: Ryan's your brother. You should look out for him.

Dean: I am. After he breaks your heart, you'll leave, and he won't have anyone.

Leighton: And you'll miss me?

Dean: Don't do this, Leigh.

Leighton: I'm not. He's still saying no.

Dean: But you'll convince him to say yes.

Leighton: How do you figure?

Dean: You convinced me to hire you.

Leighton: It wasn't hard.

Dean: 'Cause I was desperate to replace Ally. He's desperate to prove this shit. Same deal.

Dean was a regular at Rock Bottom forever. We weren't friends, exactly, but we were friendly. I knew he needed help. When he found out I needed a new job, he hired me right away.

At the time, I thought it was because he wanted to get in my pants.

But now...

Well, I'm still not exactly sure of his intentions.

Leighton: You can admit you'll miss me.

Dean: Course I'll miss you. You have great tits.

Leighton: You'll miss me. Not my tits.

Dean: No, I'll definitely miss your tits. That top you were wearing yesterday was ridiculous. They were about to pop out.

Leighton: Thanks?

Dean: You looked hot as fuck.

Leighton: And?

Dean: Did Ryan say anything about how he wanted to motorboat you?

Leighton: I'm rolling my eyes now.

Dean: Trust me, Leigh. Any normal guy looks at your boobs and thinks "I need to come on those."

Leighton: You're so gross.

Dean: And if Ryan pushed you against the wall and whispered "I want to come on your tits?"

My cheeks flush. I press my knees together. I, Uh...

Leighton: Your point?

Dean: He doesn't want to fuck you.

Leighton: Okay. I'll concede that. I'm not doing this to fuck him.

Dean: You have no idea what Penny and her friends are like. You don't know what you're getting into.

Leighton: I don't care. I'm doing this.

Dean: You're smarter than this.
Leighton: I'm doing it.
Dean: Promise you won't leave if he breaks your heart.
Leighton: He won't.
Dean: He will.
Leighton: No, he won't.
Dean: Then it will be an easy promise to keep.
It's bizarre seeing Dean worried.
But sweet.
I cross my fingers.
Leighton: Okay. I promise.

———

USUALLY, I LOVE MY DESIGN CLASS. TODAY, IT'S A SLOG. THE lecture on typography goes in one ear and out the other. My thoughts are all tuned to Ryan.

To the possibility of kissing Ryan.

I try to pay attention by making him the centerpiece of my homework—a book cover, my favorite—but it isn't enough to keep my head in the game.

The entire drive, I think of him. As I park and walk to the shop, I think of him.

As I enter the door, I think of him.

He's thinking of me too.

Lunch is sitting on the counter. Grilled chicken and cherry tomatoes over arugula. A lemony vinaigrette on the side. Wonderful cool food for another sweltering July day.

Ryan nods hello. Motions to the salad.

"I can't take your food."

"Had my own."

"Still."

"Then don't." He disappears into his suite.

I sit at the counter and log into the shop computer. There

isn't much to do today. There isn't much to do most of the time.

Technically, I work the counter. I help customers check out. I keep the shop clean, keep the schedule organized, keep the snacks stocked.

And, yes, I wear figure-flattering outfits that attract the attention and tip-money of our male clients.

The guys are plenty charming. They don't need help extracting money from women.

Even Ryan... well, he is charming in that tortured bad boy kind of way.

Not that I actually think of him as a bad boy.

More that I'm acutely aware of the stereotypes of many of our customers. The clean-cut ones who want tattoos to show off their rebellious streak.

No judgment. I only have a little ink—the cherry blossom on my forearm, the cartoon dragon on my wrist, the Latin quote on my ribs.

alis volat propriis

She flies by her own wings.

It meant something to me when I got it.

Now...

It's another ugly reminder of why I needed to ink encouragement onto my skin.

Of how impossible it is to trust anyone.

At least *that* convinced me to stop schilling booze. I'd never have quit bartending without extra motivation. The money was too good.

The money may be worse at Inked Hearts, but everything else is better.

I love this place. The big windows, the smell of the ocean air, the red and pink heart string lights, the friendly smiles from Walker, the paternal glances from Brendon (currently in his suite, working on some equally quiet guy's tattoo), the dumb jokes from Dean.

And Ryan.

Everything from Ryan.

I keep half my attention on him as I catch up on book-keeping. And lunch.

It's amazing. Tender, crisp, lemony. The best lunch he's made me in a while—he always brings me his leftovers.

I nearly inhale the food. Then I get back to work. Schedules. Social media. I don't have to do much—even Ryan posts his work on Instagram regularly.

They make my job too easy.

I miss feeling needed. I'm sure it helps business, having a warm smile and a little cleavage behind the counter, but I want to be more than a prop.

I want to do work that uses my brain.

I love design, but I'm not good enough to strike out on my own. Not yet.

Maybe I'll get there one day.

Until I do, I'm staying here.

The money is good. The company is great. So what if the work itself is boring? There's more to life than creative fulfillment.

Besides, working on designs for myself is fulfilling in its own way.

After I double check everything twice, I pull up my laptop and start my homework: a flyer for a fictional concert.

There's a ton of information to convey on one sheet of paper: three headlining bands, a dozen others, two charities supporting the event.

There must be some way to streamline it.

I play around with mock-ups until Ryan walks his client to the counter.

A cute Hispanic guy. Dark eyes, tan skin, devilish smile.

Total fling material. If I had any interest in a guy who isn't Ryan.

I flirt anyway. Help Ryan earn a forty percent tip.

He nods goodbye to his customer then turns to me. "Really?"

"Really?" I point to the tip on the receipt.

"You're stealing my credit."

"Show off your boobs. Steal it back."

His chuckle is soft. "Aren't you cold in that?"

My high-waisted shorts, key-hole white crop top combination is perfect for the eighty-degree weather outside. But in here? "Thank you. I'd love it if you turned down the AC."

He shakes his head. *No way is that happening.* "How's the homework?"

"Good. Thanks."

"Show me."

I check that the *Ryan Maddox* tab is closed, pull up the best mock-up, turn the computer to him. "What do you think?"

His gaze fixes on the screen. His brow knits with concentration. His hand slides into the front pocket of his black skinny jeans. "Good. Clean."

"But…"

"You're good at this."

My cheeks flush. "You don't—"

"Yeah. I do." His eyes fix on mine. "Good enough to charge."

"Maybe." Definitely not.

"Those covers you showed me—"

I clear my throat. Motion to Brendon, still in his suite in the front of the shop.

Ryan's hair falls in front of his eyes as he leans over the counter. "Why's the title *I Love Fucking Brendon* with a picture of me?"

Because it's actually *I Want to Fuck Ryan*. I press my lips together. Force a poker face.

It falls apart as I look him in the eyes.

"Explain." He straightens himself as he stands. "Or I can tell—" He motions to Brendon's suite.

"You won't."

He shrugs *won't I?*

No. But I need to keep his guard down. "It may have said *Ryan*. Just Ryan. Like Cher."

He shakes his head *you're ridiculous*.

I close my computer. Slide off my stool. "You meant what you said last night? About the run?"

"Of course."

"You ready to go?" I pick my backpack off the floor. Set it on the counter. "I can change now."

He nods. "Meet you here in ten."

"Sure."

I INHALE THROUGH MY NOSE AS I PUSH THE GROUND AWAY. MY next breath is easier. My body takes over. I fall into step next to Ryan.

We're doing an eight-minute mile. Faster than my usual pace. Slower than his.

We're already such a good fake couple, compromising on our running speed.

My thoughts drift away as my sneakers hit the ground.

Pounding the pavement clears my head. When I run, it doesn't matter that I have no idea what I'm doing with my life.

It doesn't matter that my mom chooses booze over me.

It doesn't matter that Ryan barely knows I'm female.

Running is like sex. When it's good, it's the only thing that matters.

I forget about my plan. I forget about Ryan's ex. I forget about everything except my body.

We stay like that for two miles, breathing and moving together.

The sky streaks red as Ryan stops at a water fountain. He pushes his hair behind his ear, bends, drinks.

His messy waves fall to his shoulders as he stands.

He fills his bottle then steps aside. Motions to the fountain.

I place my hands on the stone. My ass brushes his hip as I bend.

My body buzzes. The water is cold on my lips, tongue, cheeks, but it does nothing to temper the heat racing through me.

He runs his hand through his hair. "You good?"

I'd be better if we were naked. "Yeah."

"You're welcome."

I flip him off.

He chuckles.

This is it. He's relaxed. We're sweaty and half-naked. And losing the light.

I pull out my cell. "Let's take a picture."

He raises a brow.

"Life doesn't happen unless you document it on social media."

"I don't do social media."

"You post all of your tattoos on Instagram."

"That's for work."

"You have a Facebook. You just ignore it." Or, more accurately, he's ignored it since he and Penny broke up.

But that's an ugly technicality.

He pulls out his cell. "I'll do you first."

Yes. Strip off my shorts and panties then plant your head between my legs. I want to tug on your hair as I come. "I'm a mess."

"How?"

I motion to my flushed, sweaty face.

"You look just fucked."

"I'm wearing too many clothes."

He shakes his head. "You're wearing nothing."

"Uh… Okay." This is good. I'm wearing nothing. I look just fucked. If I post this, write something sexy, Penny will see it.

Text him.

Like it.

Somehow goad him into doing this.

I smile, attempting a casual pose.

He stares at the cell screen.

I press my lips into a smile.

Click.

I cock my hip. Muss my hair. Shoot the camera *fuck me* eyes.

Click.

There's a picture of me on his phone. There's a picture of me in a sports bra and tiny shorts on his phone.

My blush spreads over my chest. I force myself to look up at the sky. Throw my hand over my eyes. Pretend as if I'm endlessly fascinated by a plane flying overhead.

Click.

I brush my sweaty hair behind my ears. "I look terrible, don't I?"

"You're better than baiting for compliments."

"You don't understand the insecurity a girl feels posing for photos without makeup."

"You call this without makeup?"

Okay, so I don't leave home without winged eyeliner and dark lipstick. That isn't a crime. "With less makeup."

"You look perfect, Leigh. Like a punk rock princess."

"You know that's a Something Corporate song."

"I knew the first time you told me." He stares at the screen. "Still suits you."

I shake my head *you're ridiculous*, even though I love the nickname.

I love that he thinks I'm a punk rock princess.

I love that he notices my hair, clothes, and makeup.

I turn back to Ryan, uncap my water bottle, suck the last drop of water from the mouthpiece.

Click.

"Not sure I get this, Leigh."

"It's fun." I pull my cell out. "Your turn."

He shoots me that *you're ridiculous* look, but he still straightens his t-shirt.

He stares up at the sky like all his hopes and dreams are in the sunset. *Click.*

He turns to the camera. His piercing blue eyes fill with this gorgeous mix of hurt and frustration. *Click.*

Then he blinks, and it's garden grade exhaustion. *Click.*

I move closer. "Take one with me."

His eyes light up with epiphany. "No."

"Why not?"

"You're better than this."

"Than posing during a run with my best friend?"

His expression softens. It means something to him, being my best friend.

It's my chance to strike. "I'll post it on Facebook. Tag you. That's it." I cross my fingers behind my back. "Maybe make one little suggestive comment."

"'Just finished fucking my boyfriend. His ex is missing out on his generosity.'"

"I was thinking 'massive cock,' but that's good too."
Generosity. He's generous. As in he wants to eat me out. I
mean, not me, but...

"Leigh?"

"Are you generous?"

"Not discussing this."

"I'm going to take that as a no."

"Your call." His eyes narrow. It's a *drop it, now*.

Fine. Pushing him is only going to push him away. "Just
come here and pose for the proper picture with me." I
motion to the ground *on your knees*.

He laughs. "Subtle."

"Thanks." I motion to the ground again. "I'm waiting."

His smile spreads over his cheeks. He moves closer. Joins
me on the selfie side of the phone. "What's this accomplish?"

"A reaction."

"Yeah."

I rest my head against his chest. Look to the camera with
a smile.

He stares at the cell.

Click.

I look up at him. Stare into his eyes like he's the only
thing I want.

No, he is the only thing I want.

But he can't know that.

He stares back at me, his blue eyes curious, his
expression soft.

Click.

"One more," I whisper.

He nods. Leans forward. Brushes my hair behind my ear.

My eyelids press together. My head tilts to one side. I let
out a soft sigh.

Click.

His eyes find mine. "You doing this now?"

"No time like the present."

He watches as I pull up Facebook. Pick the perfect three pictures—the hottest one of him, the most flattering one of me, the cutest one of us together—and add a caption. *Ryan always makes me sweat.*

I show it to him. "Okay?"

"All right."

"Put it on your Instagram too."

"She doesn't check—"

"Then what's it hurt?"

6

RYAN

Red, orange, yellow, and green hit the pan with a sizzle. I grate ginger over sliced bell peppers. Add rice vinegar. Stir.

The shower turns off.

Footsteps move into the hallway. "I left my change of clothes at the shop."

Leighton is standing in the hallway, wrapped in only a black towel.

She holds it closed with one hand. Pushes her short hair behind her ear with the other.

She's dripping wet.

But I don't care that she's dragging water all over the hardwood floor.

Only that she's naked under that thin layer of cotton.

She looks so much like the Leighton I know.

Her hair is still hanging at her chin.

Her eye makeup is that same seamless line.

But her lips are bare.

Her tits—

I shake my head. Push away the mental image of her

without that towel, my hand between her legs, her lips parting with a groan of pleasure.

My heart thuds against my chest.

My back tenses.

The thought of Leighton coming is hot as fuck, but it's confusing.

Penny was the last person I touched.

She's the only person I've touched.

Sex and lies are a tangled mess in my brain. What I have with Leighton is the opposite of that.

That's why it works.

We're honest with each other because we aren't making each other come.

"Ryan?" She cinches her towel tighter. "Clothes?"

"You can grab a t-shirt from my dresser. Top drawer."

"Boxers?"

"Might have a pair in the bottom drawer."

"Is it laundry day?"

I shoot her a *really* look.

"Oh." Her eyes light up. "You go commando."

"Yeah."

Her gaze shifts to my crotch. Her pupils dilate. Her cheeks flush. "I, um, maybe sweat pants. Or a parka. It's freezing in here."

"Like my soul."

She laughs. "That was good. You're improving."

"You think I can't make you laugh?"

"No." She spins on her heels. "I think you choose not to."

Maybe. I've never been a happy-go-lucky guy. I've always tried to have a sense of humor about myself. At least about how fucking miserable I am.

But I used to enjoy a lot more shit.

I used to smile at the guys' stupid jokes, even when I had to keep up that *I'm the boss* poker face.

I move to the kitchen. Drown the images flitting through my head—Leighton stripping out of that towel, lying on my bed, spreading her legs wide and motioning *come here*—in fixing dinner.

I combine the chicken and vegetables, add sauce, stir, turn the pan to simmer.

Sesame oil for the finishing touch.

My bedroom door opens. Footsteps move through the hallway, into the kitchen.

Leighton smooths my black Inked Hearts t-shirt. "You're too fit."

"Am I?"

"Yeah." She tugs at the pajama pants she's wearing. "They're tight on me."

"Guys have narrower hips."

"Still."

"You gonna tell me something about how you don't like your hips?" I force myself to stare into her eyes. "That's ridiculous, Leigh. You know you're hot."

"I do?"

"You wearing those tight dresses for your health?"

"It's hot."

"Exactly."

She laughs. "Another joke. I think I might be corrupting you. Tell me you're thinking dirty thoughts."

You have no fucking idea. "Grab your laptop. We'll start setting up after we eat."

The playfulness fades from her voice. "I don't remember agreeing to this."

"Then don't." I shrug, playing coy. "Grab drinks. I'll bring the food to the table."

She rises to her tiptoes to open the top cabinet. "Bourbon or water?"

"Water."

"Me too."

"You don't drink bourbon."

"But you keep Belvedere here for me."

I do. I keep a lot of shit here for Leighton, even though we do most of our hanging elsewhere.

"It's wrong when it's too hot for vodka."

"I thought it was as cold as my soul in here?"

"It is." She smiles. "There's this vodka lounge in Vegas where everything is made out of ice."

"Is there?"

"Yeah. Even the glasses. They give you a parka so you don't freeze to death."

"And?" I play the straight-man.

"It was much warmer than your apartment."

I laugh. It's a cheesy, obvious joke. It wasn't funny the first time. Or the second. But the fiftieth time? It feels like home. "Still don't believe this place exists."

"We can go right now." She looks to the time on the microwave. "Be there by midnight."

"Is it open?"

"It's a bar."

"That isn't a yes."

"If not, we can wait until tomorrow." She grabs two glasses from the shelf. Her ass brushes mine as she moves to the sink, fills the cups with water. "We can one-up Penny. Get married there."

"Crash her bachelorette party to announce it?"

"Yes. Perfect." She brushes against me as she moves out of the kitchen. Into the main room. She sets the glasses on the table, slides into a dining chair, sits cross-legged. "Is she having a bachelorette party?"

I shrug like I don't know.

"Ryan Maddox." Leighton laughs. "You stalked her, didn't you?"

"No."

"You did." She shakes her head with a faux *tsk tsk*. "And you say you're better than all this pretending bullshit."

"Dean informed me."

"Is that reverse psychology?"

"He's not smart enough for that." I scoop food onto ceramic plates, grab silverware, bring everything to the table.

"He's smarter than he acts."

"Would it be possible for him to be stupider than he acts?"

Her laugh lights up her light eyes. "True." She smiles as I hand over her fork. "This looks amazing."

"Thanks." I sit next to her.

"No." She stabs a piece of chicken, brings it to her mouth, chews, talks with her mouth full. "Thank you."

My cheeks flush. It's weird, accepting gratitude.

I'm not used to it.

I can't wrap my head around the idea of deserving it.

Making Leighton dinner is a selfish decision.

I want her eating with me. I want her groaning over how good the food is.

I want to fall asleep tonight, knowing she's eating actual food.

Knowing someone is taking care of her.

I want to be that person.

"You're welcome." The words are awkward on my lips.

"God." She lets out a soft moan. "You're too good at this."

I shoot her a curious look.

"I'm going to have to kidnap you." She brings a slice of red pepper to her lips. "Force you to cook for me."

"You could just ask."

"That's less exciting than kidnapping."

"You want to go?" I motion to the empty area between the TV and the couch. "See if you can overpower me?"

Her teeth sink into her lip. "Is this where you invite me to karate again?"

"It's aikido."

"Will people hit me?"

"You spar, yeah."

"I'm out." She leans back in her seat. Exaggerates a sigh of defeat. "I guess I have to ask nicely."

"I'm waiting."

"I'm thinking about it." She takes a long sip of her water. "Are you?"

"Leigh—"

"Was it that awful, posing for a picture with me?"

No. It felt good. Too good. "Drop it or leave."

"You wouldn't kick me out."

"Try me."

She stares into my eyes, picking me apart. She must decide I'm willing to make due on the threat, because she drops the subject in favor of taking another bite.

We eat in silence for a while. It's not like the quiet when I'm alone. It doesn't suffocate me.

It's comfortable.

Easy.

Dinner is perfect, but it's not the taste that thrills me. It's the satisfaction spreading over her face.

I want more of it.

I want it in ways I shouldn't.

I grab the easiest distraction I can find.

"Let's get started." I motion to her laptop.

"I didn't agree."

"Then don't do it."

She presses her lips together. "I run the Inked Hearts website."

"And?"

"I know how to do this."

"If you don't want help—"

"I don't want to do it at all."

"You're stubborn."

"And you're not?" She opens her laptop, types her password, turns it to me. When I don't respond, she nods with triumph. "There are too many options."

"Use what we use for Inked Hearts." I type the website into the search bar. "You have a name in mind?"

"Even More Inked Hearts?"

I chuckle. "Really?"

"Inked Wing Designs."

"That's your tattoo." I check that the domain is available.

"Yeah." Awkwardness drips into her voice. "It, um… It's alis volat propiis."

"She flies by her own wings."

"You know Latin?"

"Only the most popular quotes."

"Are you calling me basic?"

I shoot her a curious look.

"What?"

"Penny used to say that."

"Oh." Her lip corners turn down. "Sorry. I didn't mean to—"

"No. I don't get it. What could possibly be bad about something being basic?"

"It's dumb Internet culture stuff."

"You're saying it." I fill the domain registration form with Leighton's info then turn the computer to her.

"You know those girls who come into the shop in their sheepskin boots, toting Pumpkin Spice lattes, asking for kanji tattoos?"

"Yeah." It describes a certain type of customer.

"They're basic."

"And?"

"Nobody wants to be ordinary."

"It's underrated."

"Maybe." She hits *submit* on the form then reaches over to the couch to grab her backpack. "How am I already doing this?"

"It's what you want."

She finds her credit card in her wallet, uses it to fill out the payment form. "It's what *you* want."

"Yeah."

"You're desperate to get rid of me."

"I offer to teach you to do ink every day."

"Why?" She looks up from the computer. "Why does it matter so much?"

"I want the best for you."

"Even if it means me leaving the shop?"

"You can't work our counter forever."

"What if I want to?"

"Do you?"

Her eyes meet mine. "Well…"

"I still remember that day Dean brought you in."

"Pointed to my cleavage and said *wouldn't you pay anything for this.*"

"He's such a fucking pig."

She laughs. "It worked."

Yeah, it did. But not because of her tits. "I hired you 'cause I liked you."

"Dean hired me. You just didn't veto it. Which is actually a lot. Now that I know you."

"You must make less here."

"You sign my W-2s. You know how much I make."

More than I'd figure. But less than she deserves. She's the only tolerable person at the shop.

A ray of sunshine on a dark night.

The warm smile that welcomes everyone.

Keeps them coming back for more.

I stare into her blue-green eyes. "How much less?"

"I don't know. Thirty, forty percent."

"That's a huge pay cut."

"I like it here."

"That can't be it."

"I didn't like it there." Her gaze goes back to her laptop. "I was done working at a bar."

"Dean did your rib tattoo, right?"

"And you did the dragon. And Brendon did the cherry blossom. What's your point?"

"That was right after you quit Rock Bottom."

"Ryan, I—"

"Why'd you leave?"

"I wanted to."

"Can't be the hours. You groan every time you get in at nine thirty."

"It's early."

"Assholes still leer at your tits."

"I appreciate the attention."

I shoot her my best side-eye.

"Not all of us look like—" She looks to her computer. Taps the mouse a few times. "Romance cover models." She turns the screen to me. Shows off the cover mock-up with me. Only now its title is *Ryan* and the author is *Leighton Black.*

"You think I can't play this game?"

"Maybe."

I grab my cell. Pull up my favorite graphics program. It's a lot more streamlined than Photoshop, but it's enough to prove my point.

She stares, tapping the table with her shiny fingernails, as I whip up a design.

I show off my finished work—a book cover with her as

the model. It's an older picture. One of her staring into the distance, her then pastel pink hair blowing in the wind, her blue-green eyes contemplative.

Same title concept. *Leighton* with *Ryan Maddox* as the author.

"Mine looks better." She motions to her computer. "You're a better model."

"Or you're a better designer."

She shakes her head. Turns her attention back to her computer. "Domain acquired."

"We still have to set it up."

"Later."

No. Now.

I need to find the source of her resistance and destroy it.

I will—she's too good not to do this full time.

My phone's buzz pulls me out of my thoughts.

It's a notification from Instagram.

@P3nnyForYourThoughts likes your post.

The one of me and Leighton at the beach, close enough to touch.

"Oh. Is that her?" Leighton leans over. Her eyes go wide as she takes in my screen. "I knew she followed you."

I guess she did.

"How does it feel?"

"Weird." My throat is tight. The same as it was when Penny called.

But there's this warmth in my chest.

I want to throw up.

And I want to revel in my victory.

I may be wasting my time and energy obsessing over her wedding.

But she's wasting hers thinking of me.

She's keeping tabs on me.

Wondering if I've found someone.

If I know anything about Penny, she's asking herself if Leighton is prettier. Cooler. Smarter.

Kinkier.

She's asking herself if I fucked Leighton behind her back.

If she somehow missed all the signs.

That's one thing I learned about cheaters—they project their deceit right back on you.

Start accusing you of the shit they're doing.

Looking for cracks in your story.

Digging for lies.

"Look at your face." Leighton claps her hands together. "You want to do it. I can tell."

I shake my head. Part of me does. But the other part is struggling to breathe.

"Let's make a deal."

"I have a bad feeling about this."

She presses on. "We take another set of pictures. See how Penny reacts."

"Leigh—"

"I let you set up my entire website."

I shake my head. "You start accepting clients."

Her silver fingernails tap the table. "Sure."

She's too relaxed. There's some loophole here. I need to close it.

"You start advertising. Actively looking for clients," I say.

Her blue-green eyes fill with worry. "I don't know."

"You're good enough."

"And if I'm not?"

"You are."

"Not an answer."

"You offered a deal. I countered. Take it or leave it."

She stares into my eyes. "Okay. Yes."

She's going to actually pursue design.

Fuck, that warms me everywhere.

It opens up my airways.

I suck a deep breath through my teeth. "You're not gonna find some bullshit loophole?"

"No. I promise." She offers her hands. "You let me help you. I let you help me."

"You tell me why you took the job at Inked Hearts?"

She smiles wide. "No way in hell."

It's still a good deal.

I take her hand.

Shake.

Let the warmth of her touch fill me everywhere.

7

RYAN

L eighton's phone clicks as she snaps a picture of her lunch.

We spent the last few days ironing out the details of our arrangement.

She gets one day of photos with free rein over what we do and how we pose.

I get one night to put her website together.

And one month of her actively seeking out and accepting clients.

"What happened to fries?" She glares at the sautéed kale that comes with her burger. Nudges her iced coffee into place.

"Less disturbing than coffee with a burger."

"No. This is America. You're unpatriotic."

"You wore all black at Walker's Fourth of July Barbecue."

"So did you." She looks to my plate of shrimp curry. "The food. Then you. Then both of us."

I nod *sure*.

She arranges the food just so, snaps a picture, turns the

camera to me. "Look natural. No. Smile. No. Natural." Her finger slides over her cell. "Your call."

I pick up my water, take a sip, stare at the hotel across the street.

It's modern, expensive, beachfront. The kind of place to spend your wedding night after a ceremony by the pier.

The kind of place Penny and I would have—

Click. "Contemplative Ryan. Classic. I'll add a caption about how the beautiful weather is making us think about our big day."

I shake my head.

Not going there.

Not letting Penny infect my thoughts.

Even if this expedition is to… to make my ex feel something.

Leighton is after something specific.

But why? She keeps insisting she should play my girlfriend at this wedding.

There must be a reason.

More than her wanting to help me.

"Ahem." She clears her throat.

We have a deal. I need to hold up my end of the bargain.

I settle into my chair.

Stab a shrimp with my fork.

Leighton moves around the glass table and takes the seat next to mine.

She rests her head on my shoulder and turns the camera to selfie mode. "What do you see for your wedding?"

Penny.

I still see her. In a flowing gown, holding a bouquet of pink flowers.

Staring into my eyes.

Smiling like she's so happy she could die.

I blink and it's gone.

Replaced by the lemon sun bouncing off the glass tables.

The planters of succulents lining the patio.

The bright green umbrellas casting shade over the busy restaurant.

"Ryan?" Leighton's fingers brush my stomach, pressing my t-shirt into my skin.

"Yeah?"

"I guess that's a no on the wedding planning."

I nod.

"You ready to do this?" She motions to her cell.

"Yeah." I slide my arm around her. Settle into the pose.

Click.

She turns to me. Pushes my hair behind my ear. Laughs as the wind blows it over my eyes.

Click.

"One more." Her palm plants on my neck. "Like this."

She leans in.

Brushes her lips against my cheek.

She's soft.

And she smells like cherry ChapStick.

It fills someplace that's usually empty.

My eyelids press together.

My heartbeat picks up.

My body screams for more.

But that isn't happening.

It's going to have to get over it. "Your lunch is gonna get cold." I motion to the burger on the other side of the table.

"Oh. Right. This first." She loads the first pic—the one of her kissing my cheek—to Instagram. Types. *He's the only thing sweeter than dessert.* "Too cheesy?"

"You don't mean it like that."

Her cheeks flush. "I should add an eggplant emoji."

"And the water drop emoji."

"And lips." She laughs. "Spell it out."

Fuck, the places my head is going—

Her laugh is rich. Full. She shows off her Facebook. It's right there. *He's the only thing sweeter than dessert.* Lips. Eggplant. Water drops.

An *I'm talking about his cum* story in three images.

I shake my head.

"You're no fun."

"Good."

She erases the emojis and replaces them with a winky face. "Compromise?"

"Fair."

"There." She hits post, sets her cell down, moves back to her seat. "What is this?" She stabs a leaf of kale.

"You suggested this place."

"Still."

"You love kale."

"But with a burger?"

"Someone else tell you to order this burger?"

She laughs as she points at me.

I shake my head *you're ridiculous.*

"You think we'll get a reaction?"

"You gonna edit it with that *I love cock* story if you don't?"

"Is that a dare?"

"I know better."

Her phone buzzes. She grabs it. Stares. "Not her yet." She chews. Talks with her mouth full. "Okay. This is good."

I bring a spoonful of curry to my lips. Creamy coconut, ginger, lemon, gangal, crunchy carrots. "Fucking amazing."

She picks up her knife and cuts her burger in half. "Please."

"Please what?"

"It's so… healthy." She motions to my plate. "Vegetables, shrimp, brown rice."

"You only pretend to like that orange chicken?"

"No. I…" She twirls a purple strand around her finger. "But don't you ever want something bad for you?"

"What do you call this—" I motion to her cell.

"You don't want to do this. I had to talk you into it."

No. I want it too. There's a monster in my gut dying to make Penny jealous. To show her how little I need her. How much better off I am without her.

But that's an ugly impulse.

One I should reject.

"You do want it." Her eyes light up. "Ryan Maddox. Desperate to make your ex jealous." She smiles. "You've finally come to your senses."

"I'm thinking about it."

"Good." She looks to my plate. "Now, we can work on your lunch."

"I ordered this 'cause I want it."

"But what about french fries—"

"It's a travesty. This place doesn't serve french fries."

She laughs. "Ice cream?"

"Sure."

"Sure? All ice cream rates is 'sure'?"

I shrug. "It's not sex. It can only be so good."

"What about sex?"

I arch a brow. "What about it?"

She takes a bite of her burger. Talks with her mouth full. "Oh my God," She chews. Swallows. "This is amazing. Not sex. But—" She takes another bite. Offers me what's left of the half. "You want some?"

I shake my head.

"Your loss." Two more bites and she's done. "Have you been with anyone since Penny?"

59

"No."

Her eyes go wide. "You've gone a year—"

"Fourteen months."

"Fuck." She licks aioli from her pointer finger.

"You?"

"It's been… not fourteen months. But awhile."

"Why?"

She shakes her head. "We're not having this conversation."

"You've been single—"

"For two years."

"There must be a reason."

She traces the outline of her fork with her thumb. "It's not one we're discussing."

"Yeah, it is."

She shakes her head.

"You want me to agree?"

"Of course."

"Then I need to know what the hell you get out of this."

"Helping you isn't enough?"

"No." It needs to be something else. Something that will convince me this won't fuck shit up.

She stares into my eyes.

I stare back.

"Fine." She taps her fork against her plate. "You're incredibly annoying. You know that?"

"Of course."

She presses her lips together. "There's someone I want. But he's not available."

My shoulders relax.

She's getting something out of this.

Shit isn't going to get weird.

This is good.

But there's another part of me, one that hates the idea of her with this guy who—"You're the other woman?"

"No. He's just... You know what. It's none of your business."

"And my tragic love life is yours?"

"Well..." She takes a long sip of her coffee. Stares at the glass. "Okay. Yes. I want to do this because of him."

"To make him jealous?"

"No... to make him see I'm an option."

"Dean offers to fuck you ten times a day."

"It's not Dean." She takes a long sip of her drink. Lets out a soft moan. "He's nothing like Dean."

"Walker?"

"How is Walker nothing like Dean?"

"Brendon?"

"You're not gonna guess."

"I know him?"

"Does it matter?"

"Yeah." I stare into her eyes. "You deserve a guy who will move the stars for you."

She stares at her plate. Pushes her kale to its rim. "He would. If he was mine. But he's not."

"Tell me you're not as hopeless as I am."

Her laugh is sad. "Is anyone?"

"True." I study her expression. Her brow is furrowed. Her eyes are turned down. She's frustrated. And she's off somewhere else.

Who the fuck is this idiot who can't see how amazing she is?

I have to know.

"He, uh..." She takes a long sip of her iced coffee. "He's the only person for me. I've tried to get over him, but I can't. Is it the same for you?"

"I don't want her anymore."

She stares into my eyes. "I'm not sure I believe you."

Me either.

She lets it slide. "He's not like Penny. He's a good guy. He deserves it."

"How do you know?"

"How do you know you want to do tattoos?"

"That's a stupid question."

"Exactly." She sits back. Brushes a purple strand behind her ears.

"No offense, Leigh, but he sounds like an idiot."

"Why's that?"

"He can't see how amazing you are."

Her eyes turn down. "He has his reasons."

"How good could they be?"

Her smile is sad. "Good. But he... it doesn't really matter. He's not interested."

"You sure?"

"A hundred percent."

"Leigh, you're hot as fuck."

"I am?"

"We went over this yesterday."

"I don't recall."

"Look at your tits."

She makes a show of tilting her head down. "Can't see them."

"Here." I grab my cell, pull up a photo of her from our run. She's wearing nothing. Shining with sweat. Flushed. Staring at the camera like she's begging it to make her come.

"They look good in this picture, yes."

"You're smart. Funny. Talented."

"I put up with your bullshit."

I chuckle. "So how the fuck do you know he's not interested?"

"I just do."

I hate this jerk for the way she's frowning.

This guy doesn't realize she's amazing.

He doesn't deserve her.

But she's my friend.

I'm gonna help her figure out shit with this idiot.

Even if I want to punch him in his stupid face.

8

RYAN

"What's he do?" The words fade into the chatter. This is the hippest coffee shop in the area on a Saturday afternoon. It's packed.

"Huh?" Leighton takes a long sip of her coffee—the mint mojito that shouldn't be good, but is—and lets out a heavy sigh. "Fuck. How did I not know this existed?"

Somehow, her moan cuts through the room. It bounces off the concrete floor, the high ceiling, the uncomfortable metal chairs.

Her lipstick stains the white lid.

Her black fingernails scrape the brown paper cup.

Some guy in slacks and a dress shirt turns toward us. He gives Leighton a long once-over then shoots me a *nice* look.

Fuck that, asshole.

And the asshole occupying her thoughts.

There's no way he deserves her.

Not if he can't see what's right in front of his face.

I wrap my fingers around her wrist. Lead her outside.

She squints as she looks up at me. "What did you say?"

"This idiot. What's he do?"

"Uh-uh." She digs her sunglasses from her purse. Slides them on. "We're not talking about that."

"You want me to agree to this plan?"

"Yes. But we're still not talking about that." She moves forward, toward the beach. "You're mine today. And I'm ready to escalate."

"Tell me one thing about him."

"He's tall."

"Leigh—"

"That's all you're getting."

"Taller than I am?"

"Are you threatened?"

"No." That's ridiculous. My gut is churning. But it's not jealousy. It's concern for my best friend. Concern that she's wasting her time on someone who doesn't deserve her.

"About the same."

"That's all you like about him?"

"That's all you're getting." She stops at a red light. Takes a long sip. Looks to me. "How are you drinking hot coffee? It's a million degrees."

"It's better hot." I take a long sip of my medium roast.

"Black like your soul?"

I chuckle. "Joke only works if I take it black."

"It still works."

"Tell me something else."

"Tell me yes."

"No."

"There's your answer."

"If you tell me, I can help."

"How?"

"I could kick his ass," I offer.

She laughs. "Probably, yeah. But he hurts enough."

"Leigh—"

"You want to talk about Penny?"

I say nothing.

"Then follow me."

———

MY BLACK BLANKET FLUTTERS AGAINST THE WIND. WE BEND, lay it on the ground, secure it with our bags.

Leighton drops to her knees. Looks up at me like she's about to groan *come here, baby, I want you in my mouth.*

No.

That's my head.

She's into some guy she can't have.

Some idiot who doesn't appreciate her bright smile.

The oblivious motherfucker doesn't even appreciate her lush tits.

She's wearing nothing—three scraps of cherries on black held together by red nylon.

Technically, it's a bikini. Really, it's a *look at my tits* sign.

I want to smash this idiot's smug face.

For *not* seeing her.

And for looking at her.

Who the fuck does he think he is turning her into a piece of ass?

She pulls her sunscreen from her backpack. Looks up at me with that same needy stare. "I'll do you if you do me."

Take off that bikini. I want you naked when you come on my face.

Blood rushes south.

I throw up the brakes.

Things are good between us. I can't fuck that up. I can't lose her.

But that tiny swimsuit is making this hard.

The bottoms barely cover her cunt. Their strap hugs her round hips. Show off her long legs. Invite my hands.

She laughs. "I know." She motions to her tits. "It's kind of slutty."

"Suits you."

"I'll take that as a compliment."

"I mean it as one."

"No offense, Ryan, but you should work on your sweet talking." She laughs. Motions *take it off*.

All right. We're at the beach. It's a socially acceptable excuse to strip to almost nothing.

To take *look at us, practically fucking* pictures in almost nothing.

I kick off my sandals, toss my t-shirt over my head, do away with my shorts.

Leighton lets out a soft sigh.

Her eyes go wide. "I didn't think you were a Speedo guy. But uh… You, uh…"

"It's comfortable."

"Really?"

"And that?"

"Aren't we shallow?" She bends at her waist and digs through her bag.

Fuck, that swimsuit is tight.

I can see every line of her folds.

My eyelids press together.

For a second, I see it—that bikini on the ground, my fingers in her cunt, her hands around her ankles.

I force myself to avert my eyes. Wait for her to find her phone, up the brightness, decide exactly how she wants to frame this.

"There." She motions toward the ocean. "I'll get all that blue in the background. Bring out those beautiful eyes."

I move to my right. Turn toward her. Cop my best *I'm at the beach and I'm happy to be here* pose.

She laughs. "Just… do your thing. Stare. Smile. Whatever inspires you."

"You sound like a photographer."

"I considered that." She moves closer. Stares at the viewfinder as she frames a picture. "But I like being inside, in a quiet room, by myself." *Click*.

"I get that."

"You choose to work with people."

"'Cause it's fucking amazing."

"It is." She moves behind me. "You help people. I know you don't see it. But I do." *Click*.

"Thanks. You could—"

"You already won this round." *Click*. "I'm letting you set up that website. Stop gloating."

My chest warms. I stare at the bright blue sky. Follow the horizon south, past the Santa Monica pier, past the curve of Marina Del Rey, all the way to the smog of Long Beach Harbor. "I'm proud of you." The words aren't enough. I need more.

I need to touch her.

Hold her.

But not the way I want to congratulate the guys.

And not quite the way it was with Penny.

It's something else.

Something I want more of.

Something I can't have.

AFTER AN INCREDIBLY LONG PHOTOSHOOT, LEIGHTON convinces me to join her in the water.

She laugh-shrieks as a wave smacks into her stomach. Grabs my arms. Pulls me under the water with her.

We run around the beach forever.

Mostly, I stare out at the horizon.

She jumps around in the waves.

The Pacific Ocean is freezing, same as every summer.

But there's something about the cold water and the salty air.

Something familiar. Comfortable. Warm.

For the first time in forever, I want to stay somewhere besides work. I want to hang here with her. I want to hang with her, period.

Maybe that's enough of a reason to say yes.

To buy me six weeks—five now—of Leighton all the time.

This guy is gonna come to his senses. Realize she's amazing. Scoop her up.

Then she'll be his.

And not mine.

It doesn't matter how platonic we insist we are. Mystery Man isn't gonna be okay with me making her dinner, driving her home, spending the night on her couch.

Shit is gonna change.

The thought steals my oxygen.

It's as bad as the memory of Penny groaning Frank's name.

Worse even.

It bounces around my brain as we dry off, pack our stuff, drive back to Leighton's place.

A shower fails to wash it away.

It fills the room with the scent of her shampoo. Leaves me smelling of her. Like we slept in the same bed.

Like we fucked all goddamn night.

Orange light floods the tiny space as I pull the blinds.

This is a nice apartment—all the touches of her are perfect—but it's tiny.

And without air conditioning.

I push the windows open. Let the breeze fill the room. We're far enough from the beach that it only barely smells of salt.

But that's enough that it doesn't smell of her coconut shampoo.

The shower turns off.

The blow-dryer turns on.

She's in that tiny bathroom. Changing—I'm sure into something tight. Doing her hair. Putting on her makeup.

It's too domestic.

Too familiar.

Too inviting.

I pull out my cell. Get lost in answering messages on Instagram. Mostly people asking about tattoos. A few *damn, your new girl is hot* "compliments."

She looks fucking amazing in that bikini.

And we look like we're about to fuck in half these pictures.

There's a heat there. A need. An urgency.

It's weird.

But right too.

Our latest post is drowning in likes and comments.

One from @P3nnyForYourThoughts.

I always thought you'd look good together.

Like hell.

I can see Penny's fake smile. The worry in her honey eyes. That look she's shooting Frank—the one she always shot me—*does she have something I don't?*

And it feels good.

It feeds that beast inside me.

But it's more than that.

It's knowing Leighton's plan is working.

Knowing it's me and Leighton driving her crazy.

Driving the whole fucking world crazy.

I must be out of my mind.

I want to do this.

I want to risk my friendship with the most important person in my life.

The blow-dryer turns off.

Leighton steps out of the bathroom in a tight grey dress. Her eyes light up as they find mine. "Does that mean what I think it does?"

"You really want to do this?"

"No, I keep asking because I hate the idea."

"You really want to make Mystery Man jealous?"

"That's a wordy nickname."

"How about Austin Powers?"

She laughs. "How about him?"

"He's an international man of mystery."

She looks at me funny. "You enjoy *Austin Powers* movies?"

"Who doesn't?"

"They're stupid."

"So's my younger brother."

"Aww, I can see you and Dean watching movies together as kids. I bet you were cute."

"Tell my mom that. She'll love you forever."

"She hates me."

"She hates everybody at Inked Hearts."

"Even Dean?"

"No. He's got some youngest kid advantage."

"She blames you for corrupting him."

"Ridiculous?"

"Maybe. He's more obvious about being a perv. But you... You've got that in you."

She has no fucking idea.

She moves toward me. "I guess we can call him Mr. Powers."

"Sure." I already hate him.

"Yes, I want to make Mr. Powers realize I exist. But I mostly want to help you." She offers her hand. "Let's make this official. Celebrate with dinner."

"I'll cook."

"I don't have food. We'll get street tacos. They're amazing."

"I grew up in SoCal—"

"In Beverly Hills."

"I know street tacos."

She wiggles her fingers. "Okay. You can pick the taco truck. Just agree. Officially. I'll take care of the rest."

"I get veto power on everything."

"You pay all our expenses."

I nod. I was always gonna insist. I make three times what she does. And I don't trust her to treat herself.

"How long do we keep this up?"

"Through the wedding."

She shakes her head. "Until a month after. Otherwise, it seems fake."

Fair enough. "I'm still finishing your website."

"I know."

"And asking you how it's going every day."

"I know."

"And offering you advice on every design question you have."

"Are you just giving me information I know?"

"I need you at the wedding. Even if Mr. Powers wants to snap you up first."

"I know."

"But I don't want shit to get weird."

73

Her cheeks flush. "Me too. We're adults. We'll discuss it like adults."

"That possible?"

"I can do it. Can you?"

Maybe. "Yeah." I take her hand.

Shake.

Watch as she pulls up Facebook, changes her relationship status.

Do the same with my cell.

There it is.

We're official.

This is either the smartest thing I've ever done or the stupidest.

One of the two.

9

RYAN

Leighton smiles as she hands my client a receipt. Then a pen.

She presses her palms into the counter, leans forward, squeezes her arms to push her tits together.

She always does this shit.

Usually, I shrug it off.

Today, it's making my jaw crick.

My fingers curl into fists. Words form on my tongue. *Keep your eyes to yourself, asshole.*

As far as clients go, this guy is great. Receptive to my ideas. Honest when he needs a break. Good at keeping still.

But I want to deck the motherfucker and tell him to keep his money.

He could be the guy who has Leighton's heart.

It could be anyone.

Fuck, she looks good today. Hot pink sundress with a black dinosaur print. Lacy black bra peeking out from the neckline. Purple hair in that perfect straight line.

Purple makeup bringing out the green in her eyes.

Berry lips drawing every ounce of my attention.

The guy chuckles at some compliment. "Me too." He pushes his shirt up his shoulder, showing off his now finished sleeve.

Leighton giggles. Leans in to whisper in his ear.

He nods. Scribbles a tip. Signs on the dotted line. Writes something below it.

His phone number.

I bite my tongue.

This is part of her job.

She's better than it. But we all have to stoop to shitty stuff sometimes. It's part of making ends meet.

No matter how badly I want to punch this asshole, I'm not going to steal her tip money.

The customer turns back to me. He offers his hand. "Thanks, dude. It's perfect."

I shake. Nod *no problem*.

He leans in to whisper. "Put in a good word for me with the babe with purple hair."

"Can't."

"Cruel."

"She's my girl." The words are unpracticed. But they're easy on my tongue. Natural.

"Fuck. Really?"

"Yeah."

"Didn't realize." He shrugs at me. "Sorry."

She smiles that wide *nothing is a problem* customer service smile. "Keep it our secret." She winks.

His chuckle is nervous. "Forgive me enough to do my next one?"

"Yeah."

He nods *sweet* then makes his way to the door. The bell rings. It nearly screams *the asshole is gone*.

Leighton's tits fall forward as she leans over the counter. "Can you believe that guy? Apologizing to you for wanting to ask me out? Like I'm your property or something?"

"Asshole."

"Not with the times." Her eyes find mine. "Are you really pissed about that?"

No. I'm worse. I'm pissed he's looking at my girl when she isn't even mine. "You're gonna pop out of that dress." I try to make it matter of fact, but it's not. It's weird, her on display. Inviting in a way it shouldn't be.

"Sorry. Next time, I'll wear something that will get you less than a thirty percent tip." She waves the receipt like it's a first-place ribbon.

"My talent had nothing to do with it?"

"It's canceled out by your attitude."

"Not everybody wants to chat."

"Uh-huh."

Dean steps into the lobby. "What did I hear about Leigh's tits?"

She rolls her eyes. "Why are you always here to offer commentary?"

"Your tits." He makes a show of leering at her chest. "Why else?"

She cocks her hips to one side. "Don't you have clients?"

He motions to the clock. "Ten minutes until my next appointment. Enough time to talk you into keeping 'em on display."

"You couldn't talk me into a cup of French roast with extra half-and-half." She sighs in the direction of the Keurig. Waves at the coffee maker like it's her favorite thing in the entire world.

I slide my hand into my pocket. Wrap my fingers around my cell. The shit on it is good news. But it still makes my throat tighten.

I look to my younger brother. Raise a brow *you mind?*

He folds his arms. *Yeah, I do.*

I ignore him. Take three steps to the counter. Until my thighs are pressed against the black plastic.

I pull my cell from my pocket. Pull up my texts. "It worked."

I show her the display.

Penny: Why didn't you tell me you were seeing Leighton?

Ryan: I didn't?

Penny: I always thought you'd be good together. Frank and I are going to a cake tasting Saturday morning. You should join us. Make it a double date.

Leighton's eyes stay glued to the screen. "She thought we'd be good together? What the hell is that?"

Passive aggressive bullshit. "It's what we're going for, yeah?"

Dean clears his throat. He's still standing behind me.

"Yeah?" I keep my back to him.

He moves forward. Until he's next to me. "Leigh, tell me you're not."

She looks to him. "You already know the answer."

"You're smarter than this," he says.

She motions to me. *He's right here.*

"Fuck this. I'm not gonna be the voice of reason. Ruin your lives if you want," he says.

Leighton's eyes turn down. She presses her lips together, fighting a frown.

I hate the frustration in her brow.

I want to wipe it away.

I want to destroy all the pain in her life.

But that isn't different. She's my best friend. I've wanted the world for her for a long time.

This isn't changing shit.

It's just not.

I turn to my brother. Find the first change of topic I can. "We need to hire help."

Dean shakes his head. "What about the dozen artists you rejected?"

"What about them?" I ask.

He laughs. "Half of them were better than you."

"No." Some of them were good, but none of them were better than me. No one takes their shit as seriously as I do.

"All right. But they were plenty good."

"And?" I ask.

"You're transparent." He turns to Leighton. "Isn't he?"

She shrugs. "All four of you turn down appointments. You need to hire more help."

"Set up some appointments," I say.

"Sure. But I'm holding you to hiring someone." Dean turns. Looks to Walker, who's currently in the middle of a back piece. "You eavesdropping, Williams?"

The hum of his gun ceases. He whispers something to his client. Then said client pushes himself up with a *thank fuck for the break* sigh and moves to the bathroom.

Walker stands. Moves into the lobby. Studies the three of us like he's an anthropologist encountering an entirely new civilization.

His dark eyes fix on Dean. "What did you do?"

"Ryan wants to hire help," Dean says.

Walker shakes his head. "Bullshit. Ryan turned down every artist on the Westside."

"You for this plan?" Dean asks.

"Hell yeah." Walker runs his hand through his dark hair. "I don't want to keep working while Iris is off."

"Don't you need money?" Dean asks.

"I'm gonna be a trophy husband once she gets her PhD," he says.

"In, what, five more years?" Dean asks.

"About that," Walker says.

Leighton shakes her head. "I'm not letting her date a loser."

"It's gonna be for her." He leans against the half-wall to his suite. "So I can cook her dinner every night."

"And eat her out the second she gets home," Dean suggests.

Walker laughs. "Great fucking idea." He pulls out his cell. Smiles as he taps a text to his girlfriend.

"You need dirty talking tips from Dean?" Leighton sits on her stool. Crosses her legs. "Sad."

Walker raises a brow. "Twenty bucks says I can make you wet in under a minute."

"You can't." Her pupils dilate as she tugs at her dress.

"That's a challenge." He stares into her eyes. "Now I'm gonna have to fill you in on every dirty detail of what I did to Iris last night."

"What did you…" She clears her throat. "Not interested."

"Bullshit," he says.

Leighton blushes. Stammers her way to a response. "No comment."

"Drop it," I say.

She pulls her dress down her legs. But that only pulls it down her chest.

Shows off more of her lacy black bra.

Walker looks to me. Raises a brow. "What are you all pissed about?"

"He's an idiot," Dean says. "That's the crux of the issue."

"Strong words from Dean." Walker looks from his best friend, to me, to Leighton, back to me. "You all right, Ryan? By your standards?"

"Don't talk to my girl like that." The words are still easy on my tongue. Even though it's a million times weirder calling Leighton my girl to Walker.

"Your girl?" Walker's gaze goes to Leighton. "You and Ryan…"

She nods. Presses her lips together.

I shoot her a look. *Play along.*

She nods *of course.*

Walker's expression screws with confusion. "Did I step into a time warp to April Fool's Day?"

Dean looks to me. "Really?"

I nod *yeah.*

He turns to Walker. "Penny's getting married. Ryan told her he has a girlfriend. So Leighton volunteered."

"This is the kinda shit you'd crucify me and Dean for," he says.

She presses her lips together. "So?"

"What's the point of making your ex jealous?" Walker looks to me. "You're better than that."

"Nah. He's not. But at least he's gonna do it right." Dean jumps in. "You're gonna whip it out on the dance floor, show her what she's missing." He motions to his crotch. "Massive cocks run in the family." He winks.

She laughs. "Methinks the lady doth protest too much."

Dean makes a show of scratching his head. "Not following."

"You're gonna have to break it down for him, word by word," Walker teases.

Her tits shake as she laughs. "You're always going on about how virile—"

"Virile? Babe, you know I only read at a third-grade level," Dean teases.

"You do not." She slides off the stool. Adjusts the dress. Her eyes catch mine for a second then they're on Dean. "You're always talking about your cock. Like you're compensating for something."

"Babe, you bait me so well." He blows her a kiss. Reaches

81

for his zipper. "Let me prove it." He unbuttons his jeans. "Take out those tits. I'll be hard like that—" He snaps his fingers.

She presses her arm to her stomach, doubling over with laughter.

I don't get it.

She and Dean are always flirting like this. He's always being disgusting. She's always pretending to hate it, but smiling anyway.

She says he's not Mr. Powers.

But he must be.

The way she laughs with him—

I've never been jealous of my brother before. But this—

My fingers curl into fists. When I close my eyes, I see red. I want to hurt someone. Anyone who's ever hurt her.

I'm not this guy.

I don't get pissed like this.

Dean is a fucking slut, yeah. But he's a good guy, deep down. He'll treat Leighton well.

If he is Mr. Powers, I'm gonna have to find a way to be okay with that.

"I hate to be the Ryan, but Greg doesn't want to see your dick." Walker motions to the bathroom in the back.

"All right. Let's go to my suite." Dean winks at Leigh. "You can give me a little manual help."

"You make it sound so enticing," she teases back.

"I'll reciprocate." He falls to his knees. Presses his hands together. "You know I dream about making you come."

"You do not." She laughs. "You don't want to fuck me."

"Leigh, how could you say that." He tugs at the waist of his jeans. "Come with me. See how *massive* my desire for you is—"

"All right. I'm out. I'm gonna ask Iris to explain it to me." Walker turns and moves into his suite.

Leighton's still shaking her head at Dean.

Still smiling at his crude advances.

Not that I can talk.

I said a lot dirtier shit to Penny.

But Leighton claims she finds Dean repulsive.

Is she sparing my feelings?

Worried I'll buy into that blood is thicker than water bullshit and rat her out to my brother?

It has to be him.

It's the only thing that makes sense.

The bell rings as the door swings open. A short woman with long hair steps inside. She looks to Dean, who's still kneeling on the floor, and laughs. "You're always in a compromising position."

He jumps to his feet. "Sounds like an invitation."

She laughs.

He motions to his suite, then follows her into it.

Leighton's eyes find mine. Her cheeks stay pink. Her smile stays wide.

"Sorry you got cunt-blocked." I try to unpeel my shoulders from my ears, but it's a struggle.

She sticks her tongue out in disgust. "Ew."

"You don't have to bullshit me."

"No. It's…" She presses her fingers to the counter. Stares at her black fingernails. "I'm your girlfriend. There's not gonna be anyone else."

"If you're into him—"

"I'm not."

"I won't tell him."

"I know. It's someone else." There's something in her eyes. She's hiding something.

It must be her lust for Dean.

What the fuck else could it be?

She picks up my cell—it's still sitting on the counter. "You mind?"

"It's got a password."

"I know it."

I arch a brow.

"Sorry. I spy." She punches in the code—the date we officially bought the shop—unlocks my phone, and pulls up Penny's texts.

She taps a reply.

Perfect. Tell me where and when.

She looks to me. "Okay?"

No. This isn't even close to okay.

But it's necessary.

I nod.

She taps send.

A moment later, my cell buzzes with an address.

I'm gonna help my ex pick out her wedding cake.

Fan-fucking-tastic.

1 0

LEIGHTON

I step into my nicest dress. Pull the zipper. Check my reflection for panty lines.

None. Good.

This is good. I think.

What the hell do you wear to taste cakes with your fake boyfriend's ex?

This fit and flare dress must be close. It's a grey and black checkered print. It hugs my chest, but not in a *look at my boobs* way. In more of a *I've got a waist and I'm not afraid to flaunt it* way.

I take a seat at my desk. Fall into my makeup routine. Concealer. Foundation. Blush. Brow pencil. Eye shadow. Eyeliner. Mascara. Lipstick.

It's not a vanity thing. Yeah, I want to look pretty. But, more than that, I want to cover all the cracks in my armor.

I learned this back in high school, the first time shit got bad with my mom.

If you look tired, people worry.

If you look alert and rested, people believe it when you say *I'm fine.*

If you look tough and untouchable, people don't bother to ask questions.

There. Perfect. Pretty and *don't fuck with me*. Enough to convince Ryan I'm fine with this. To convince his ex I'm… something.

I barely know Penny. I'm not sure what I want her to believe about me. Only that I want her a million miles away from Ryan.

The doorbell's ring interrupts me.

It's early. What is Ryan—

"Open up." Iris's voice flows through the door. "Or I'll knock this door down."

"You're capable?"

"I've been working out."

She's here to talk me out of this.

It's not happening.

I was a little impulsive, offering to play Ryan's girlfriend without thinking it over. But I have thought it over.

It's a good idea.

I'll help him get over Penny.

We'll spend two glorious months together.

Then we'll go back to being friends.

No hurt. No rejection. No risk of coming in second place.

Because how can he choose her over me if he doesn't know I'm an option?

I move toward the door. "Can it wait?"

"You know the answer to that."

I let her in.

She smiles as she steps inside. Pulls me into a hug.

My shoulders relax. My chest gets warm. Even knowing she's here to lecture me, the embrace feels good.

Iris and I met a few months ago, when she and Walker started a fuck buddies thing (they swore it was casual, now they're practically engaged). We became fast friends. She's funny, sweet, tenacious, up for anything.

Concerned.

Which I appreciate.

Really.

But this idea isn't nearly as tragic as everyone's making it out to be

"I've already made up my mind." I close and lock the door.

She smooths her sundress. "No. You've lost your mind."

"Even so."

"Are you really pretending to be Ryan's girlfriend?"

"Yes."

"And he's aware you're in love with him?"

"I'm not in love with him."

"Right."

"I have strong feelings. But love?"

She tilts her head to one side, assessing me. "He's aware of your feelings?"

"Well…"

"This plan gets stupider?"

"He knows I'm into someone."

"Someone?"

"Mr. Powers."

"Austin Powers, International Man of Mystery?"

"You know it?"

"Everyone knows it." She stares into my eyes. "And he thinks this guy is…"

"All he knows is that Mr. Powers isn't interested in me."

"Wow. That's…" She taps her toe against the hardwood floor. "You're technically not lying to him."

"Thanks."

"You know how that worked out for me?"

"You're now happy with Walker."

"Uh-huh." She rolls her eyes. "You're skipping over something important."

"You ended up with him. Who cares about a few bumps in the road?"

She shoots me some serious side-eye. "Remember that night you took me out because I was miserable?"

"Sounds vaguely familiar."

She tilts her head to one side, assessing my bullshit level. "How many eighties nights have we gone to?"

"We go every month."

"We've gone to two."

"Is it only two?"

"You're full of it." She laughs. "You said the only thing worse than being his best friend and not his *everything* is being his nothing."

"It was profoundly less poetic, but, yes. That was the general sentiment."

"Has that changed?"

"No."

She takes another step toward me. "So what happens if this ends your friendship?"

"I won't let it."

She folds her arms. Stares at me, daring me to justify my claim.

My eyes go to my shiny patent heels. They're three inches. So I'm eye to eye with Ryan.

"I have all day," she says.

"Don't you want to hang with Walker?"

"He's working until four."

"Oh." I move past her. Sit at my desk. Pretend as if I'm fascinated by re-applying my lipstick.

She stays behind me.

Continues staring.

Finally, I break. "You're right. This might ruin everything.

But it might cure him of his tunnel vision too. And I have to try."

"What if he falls for someone else?"

"I can live with that."

"Really?"

No. But he won't.

The doorbell's ring cuts through my thoughts.

"That's him." I push myself to my feet. "I already promised. And I want to do this. Even with all I'm risking."

Her sigh is soft. "Call me if... if you need to talk. No matter what time it is. Promise?"

"I promise." I move to the door. Pull it open for Ryan.

He's standing there in his usual outfit. Snug black t-shirt. Snug black jeans. Black on black converse. Black Wayfarers.

His fingers brush mine as he hands me a takeout cup. "French roast."

"Thank you." Warmth spreads through me as I take a sip.

It's perfect. Just enough half-and-half, just enough sugar.

I take another sip. Let it warm my throat. Jump start my thoughts. "Come in. Iris stopped by to..." Talk me out of this. "To say hi."

"No," he says.

"No?" What the hell?

The apartment dims as he pushes the door closed.

It brightens as he slides off his sunglasses.

God, those blue eyes...

"I asked her to come." Ryan nods hello to Iris. "To help us practice."

"Oh." I shoot my friend a *how could you* glare. "She didn't mention that."

"You know how it is? Sometimes, important details slip your mind." She shrugs and shoots back the same glare.

"Yeah." Ryan runs his hand through his wavy hair. He looks to me. "I guess we should try this out."

"We have time to chat." She looks to me and raises a brow then turns to Ryan. "You brought Leighton coffee. That's sweet."

"She always forgets to make it," he says.

"This is that Philz place." She stares at my brown cup. "That's primo stuff."

"You must drink it ten times a day when you're at Walker's."

"They don't have cold brew." She shakes her head. "But if I really want something hot, it's great."

"You have one?" I ask him.

"In the car. It's yours if you want it," he says.

"Generous too." She stares into Ryan's eyes. "You're already a model boyfriend."

"Thanks." He shifts his weight to his other foot. "How's school?"

"It's July," she says.

"Your—"

"Internship. It's good."

"You and Walker?"

Iris lets out a dreamy sigh. She presses her hands together. Looks at the plain white ceiling like it's a sky full of stars.

"You really do have the obnoxious happiness down pat," I say.

"Thank you." She smiles. "You try it. Leighton first." She turns to me. "How are you and Ryan?"

I let my head fill with beautiful mental images—the two of us walking along the beach on a starry night, his hands around my waist, his lips on my neck, his words in my ear. *I need you more than I've ever needed anything.*

My hand goes to my heart.

My lips part with a sigh.

"Amazing." My gaze goes to Ryan. To his piercing blue

eyes, his long wavy hair, his soft lips. I get nearly two months of this. How can I turn that down?

"You go, Ryan." Iris nods to Ryan. "How's everything with Leighton?"

"Good." His voice is less dreamy. More awkward. He looks to her.

She shakes her head. "Try again."

He turns back to me. Shrugs his shoulders. Slides a hand into his pocket.

His lips curl into a half smile. "Shit with Leigh is perfect." He stares into my eyes. "She's the sun in my sky."

My cheeks flush.

"The silver lining on a rain cloud." He moves closer. His hand skims my hip. "She's everything."

I stare up into his eyes.

I get lost in those beautiful eyes.

He leans in like he's going to kiss me.

Moves closer.

Closer—

"Ahem. Let's try another." Iris shoots me a *be careful* look.

My body goes cold as Ryan releases me.

He isn't mine.

He isn't going to be mine.

I have to get used to that.

11

LEIGHTON

Kurt Cobain mumbles over heavy guitars as Ryan turns onto a cozy Beverly Hills street. We park under the shade of a lush tree. It's as green as anything gets around here.

He turns off the car, ending Kurt Cobain's wail.

"Better." He presses his back into his seat. Fidgets with the keys in his right hand.

"Who doesn't like Nirvana?"

"It's fine."

"Fine?"

"Doesn't do it for me."

"Playlist on the way back. Trust me. You'll feel positively normal compared to how fucked-up some of these guys are."

"Just guys?"

"And girls. But when it's a guy... I don't know. Maybe it's because I'm a girl, but women tend to have more of an *I'm better off without you* attitude. Whereas guys can be very—"

"I hope you die in a car crash?"

"I've got one like that."

"Did a lyric tattoo the other day."

"Someone wanted that on their body forever?"

He nods.

"And you say you're hopeless."

His laugh is more sad than anything.

My stomach twists. My fingers slide over the center console. I want to touch him. To stop him from closing off.

But there's something about his expression. Like he's screaming *leave me alone.*

I unclick my seatbelt. Slide my purse onto my shoulder. "You ready?"

"No." He undoes his seatbelt. "But I'm not gonna be."

"We don't have to—"

"I do."

"Okay." I reach for the door, step onto the pavement, smooth my dress.

Sunlight falls over Ryan as he gets out of the car. It bounces off his light skin. Sinks into his dark clothes.

He offers me his hand as he steps onto the street.

I intertwine my fingers with his. My skin buzzes from the contact. My body fails to understand we're pretending. My pulse races. My stomach flutters. My breath catches in my throat.

It's hot today.

And with Ryan this close—

God, I'm on fire.

I move closer. Fall into step next to him.

We turn the corner, walk past a lingerie shop, a yoga studio, a cafe.

There it is, the bakery chain doing the wedding's catering. The shop is all white and pink, lace curtains, soft colors, three, four, and five tier cakes in the windows.

Ryan pulls the door open and motions *after you.*

The room buzzes. Conversation. Clinking forks. The hum of the air conditioner.

Two kids are sharing a cookie in the corner. The family next to them is tearing into a tiny purple cake. And the short, thin woman in an orchid cardigan—

Penny.

Ryan's hand squeezes mine.

I pull him closer. Not for him—though I can *feel* how much he needs that. For me. Because her curious stare is draining every ounce of my warmth.

The guy sitting next to her is handsome. I'll give him that. He's tall, with neat dirty blond hair and green eyes. His relaxed t-shirt hugs his broad shoulders. His tanned arms are ink free.

He looks like a Dockers advertisement.

Like a guy who wears boat shoes.

He *is* wearing boat shoes.

It's three steps to the ground floor. A giant display case of pastries is in front of us. A sign, with prices and coffee specials, is behind that. The tables are to our right.

Penny and Boat Shoes are sitting at the table next to the pastry case.

They're sipping coffee from pink mugs.

She's staring.

He's oblivious.

Ryan drops my hand. Slides his arm around my waist. "You ready?"

I turn to him. Peel his sunglasses from his face, fold them, hang them on his shirt.

He stares down at me.

Hurt fills his blue eyes. I run my fingers over his cheek. I need to do something to wipe his pain away.

But that's hopeless.

The best I can do is—

His palm plants on my lower back.

His eyelids flutter together.

95

Slowly, his lips brush mine.

My knees go weak.

My fingers dig into his t-shirt.

It's a stage kiss.

It barely last two seconds.

But I still feel it everywhere.

The mint of his toothpaste. And something else. Some taste distinctly Ryan.

He unpeels his body from mine. Brings his mouth to my ear. "You look amazing in that dress, baby."

My cheeks flush.

"I want to rip it off," he stage whispers.

I bury my head in his chest.

"You wearing anything under that?"

"Maybe," I stage whisper back.

His fingers skim my waist. My hip. He presses the cotton into my skin, feeling for the fabric beneath it.

I suck a breath through my teeth.

He's really going for this.

He's really touching me.

I... I...

"Over here," Penny calls. Her voice is bright. Like she's happy to see us.

Or happy to rub her new beau in our faces.

Ryan releases me.

But I'm still floating. I squeeze his arm. Focus all my attention on placing one foot in front of the other.

Somehow, I get to Penny's table.

She stands. Smooths her off-white dress and offers her hand. "It's been a while, Leighton."

I shake. "It has."

She motions to her fiancé. "This is Frank. I'm not sure if you've met."

"No." I offer him my hand. "Nice to put a face with a

name." Okay, so the name in my head is *douchebag who helped destroy Ryan*, but it's still nice to have a face for my virtual punching bag.

"Ryan, you remember…" Penny presses her lips together. "Thank you for coming." She motions to the chairs. "Please. Sit. I'll check on the cakes."

I nod. "Thank you."

Ryan pulls out my chair for me.

I sit.

He follows.

Frank folds one leg over the other. For a second, his eyes meet Ryan's. He opens his mouth to speak.

But Penny cuts him off. "It's coming!" She takes a seat next to him. Sets her left hand on the table like she's making a point of showing off her massive rock.

Ryan's gaze goes right to the two-carat ring. He pulls his hand to his side. Curls his body away from mine.

I scoot closer. Rest my palm against his thigh like I'm used to having my hand this close to his cock. "How did you decide on Maui?"

"I always wanted something on the beach." Penny smiles. "And Daddy insisted on hosting it somewhere his business partners would want to visit." The confidence in her voice wavers. "Since he was paying. You know how he is."

Ryan nods. He knows what Mr. Winters is like.

They're sharing some intimate history.

I hate it.

Penny pulls her hands to her lap. "Ryan, I… I'm really glad you're here. I… I hope there aren't any hard feelings."

He looks to his ex-girlfriend. Forces his frown into a neutral expression. "It was for the best."

Her sigh is heavy with relief. "Good. You… um, I sometimes worried you two were…" Her laugh is hollow. "You look good together."

"Thanks." I squeeze him tighter. "But this is nothing."

She blinks. "Oh."

"You should see how good we look naked," I say.

"They can." Ryan smiles wide. "Unless you deleted those pics, baby."

"Never." My cheeks flush. Me and Ryan naked. In a photograph forever.

His bare torso against my back.

His hands on my hips.

His cock driving into me.

The mental image burns into my brain.

Boat Shoes chuckles.

Penny nudges him. Frowns. *That isn't funny.*

I let my cheeks flush. "We, uh… Sorry. We lost track of time this morning. Stopped before we could finish." My smile is a *fuck you*. "You know how it is when you can't keep your hands off someone." Like when you want some khaki wearing asshole so badly you sleep with him even though you're in an eight-year relationship.

"Here we go." An older woman in a pink apron spares Penny my vengeful stare. She sets two plates of cake between us, then goes over each flavor. They're all impossibly fancy. Earl Grey with grapefruit frosting, vanilla bean and lavender, poppy seed and lemon creme, etc., etc.

Penny looks to Ryan. "Can I buy you a coffee?"

Yeah. A coffee is going to make up for cheating on him.

My nails dig into my thigh.

She's so…

Who the fuck does she think she is, inviting him to her wedding?

To this cake tasting?

To this half-assed attempt at an apology?

"I'm good." Ryan's eyes meet mine. "You good, Leigh?"

"Great. Thanks." I hate her expensive cardigan. I hate her *I'm gonna be a bride* ivory dress. I hate her perfect smile.

I need her to be wrong.

I need her to hurt.

I need her to cry herself to sleep wishing for his forgiveness.

Does she even realize how thoroughly she broke him?

Like a reflex, my hand goes to his chest. I tug at his t-shirt. Pull him into a kiss.

My lips brush his.

My other hand slides into his wavy hair.

My knees knock together.

I suck on his bottom lip. Groan against his mouth.

He presses his palm against my thigh.

He kisses back.

Not like it's pretend.

Like he needs me as badly as I need him.

My anger dissolves.

I don't care about Penny. Or Boat Shoes. Or whether or not the sun rises tomorrow.

I only care about Ryan's teeth scraping my bottom lip.

Fuck.

The room spins as he pulls back. I blink, but that does nothing to steady me.

I'm buzzing.

I'm floating.

I'm riding a wave of the deepest, purest bliss.

"I… Uh…" I need to say something. To convince him I know this is fake. To convince them it's real. "You're so sweet. It makes me…" I turn back to Penny. At least, I think that's Penny. The room is still this blur of pink and white. "You know what a good kisser Ryan is."

"That was a long time ago." She picks up her fork. "Shall we?"

Boat Shoes whispers something in her ear.

She shakes her head. Digs into one of the slices of vanilla bean. "Be honest. Tell me if you hate it."

Hate. It's such a funny word.

Who could hate anything?

The world is so beautiful and bright.

Sweet, like spearmint.

Like lemon.

Like Ryan.

———

WHEN I FINALLY COME DOWN FROM MY HIGH, PENNY AND Boat Shoes are debating between Earl Grey lavender and lemon poppy seed.

It's an easy choice.

Lemon.

Like Ryan's soap.

Like…

Okay, I'm still floating. But fifteen minutes of wedding small talk cure me of that.

There will be a hundred guests. And a reception at a hotel ballroom. And have Penny and Boat Shoes picked their song? Oh, they have, and it's something as douchey as his face…

I'm about ready to stab them both with my fork, when Ryan excuses us.

He helps me up, slides his arm around my waist, pulls me close.

We stay like that as we leave the restaurant. As we walk down the sunny street. As we step into Ryan's car.

His pretenses fall away as he pulls the door closed.

He turns to me. "You have—"

"Huh?"

"Here." His thumb brushes my lip.

The pad is rough, calloused, but his touch is so soft.

He stares back at me as he catches a drop of frosting on his digit.

Slowly, he brings it to his mouth.

His lips curl around his thumb. He sucks icing off it like it's some part of me.

Heat pools between my legs.

God, he's sexy.

I need to focus on anything else. "You hate it?" I'm not even sure what *it* is. The morning. The meeting. The bakery. The too sweet cakes.

"No."

"But you hate her?"

"No."

"How can you not? She barely apologized. *Oh, sorry about fucking this asshole. Have some free cake. How about a coffee? That should make up for it.*" I dig my cell from my purse. "Sorry. I shouldn't get pissed on your behalf—"

"It's fine."

I try to place the tone of his voice, but I can't.

"Trust me. The breakup playlist will help." I reach for the aux cable.

"I trust you, but—"

"Good."

"Is he awful or is it me?"

"Boat Shoes?"

His laugh bounces around the car. "Frank, yeah."

"I refuse to call him anything but Boat Shoes. And yes. He is. I'm sure he has some redeeming qualities. A fat bank account. Or a massive cock. Or ungodly oral sex skills—"

He stares at me like I'm crazy.

My cheeks flush. "I don't mean, uh... I'm sure you're also incredibly talented. But I... uh... I don't get it. I know that doesn't help, that it probably hurts worse—it did for me. But I don't get why she'd—"

"Leigh—"

"Sorry."

"I need to wash that taste out of my mouth."

Yes. With your lips. Or your neck. Or your cock. Right here is fine. As long as you promise to pull my hair... Ahem. "Me too."

He nods. "You want lunch?"

No. I want you to unzip those jeans and pull me into your lap. "Sure."

LEIGHTON

"Fuck." I let out a soft groan.

Lean back in my chair.

Savor every ounce of eggplant Parmesan. Tender, umami eggplant. Rich, tangy marinara. Fresh mozzarella. Sharp garlic.

It's not as good as Ryan in my mouth.

But it's still fucking good.

"You eating that or fucking it?" He brings a slice of his—well, our, we're sharing two dishes—white fish to his lips. Chews. Swallows.

"It is an eggplant."

"That really why you ordered it?"

I'm not sure. It's burnt into my brain, the idea of Ryan in my mouth, his hand knotting in my hair, his groans filling the room—

Uh.

"It's delicious." I take another bite. Let out another soft moan. Maybe I'm overdoing it, but I don't care. This is amazing. The perfect antidote to Penny's saccharin smile.

"Nothing is that good."

"This is." I cut a slice of eggplant. Offer it to him.

His hair falls in front of his eyes as he leans forward. Sucks the eggplant from the fork.

It falls back to his ears as he settles into his chair. Chews. Swallows. "Amazing."

"Told you—"

"But not that good."

"But being here—" I motion to the cozy dining room. This Italian restaurant is a tiny place. And it's empty. We're well before the usual lunch rush. "And not there. It's that good."

He nods *it is.*

And being with him, with *my* Ryan, the guy only I know…

It's amazing.

Even if his heart is still locked.

And I'm still desperate to unlock it.

I find my cell in my purse. Motion to the table. "Should we?"

"Are we gonna document every meal together?"

"Yes."

"Why?"

"I'm in charge—"

"I have veto power."

"Just get over here and pose with me."

"You get over here."

"I'm gonna sit on your lap."

He pushes his chair back. Drops his arms to his sides. Pats his thighs. *Do it.*

"You know better than to dare me."

He nods *of course.*

I wipe the tomato sauce from my lips, leave my napkin on the table, move to Ryan.

Lower myself onto his lap.

He goes commando.

There are only three layers of fabric between us.

We're so, so close to being exactly where we should be.

I fight my blush. Suck a breath through my nose. Press my knees together. "You ready?"

"Yeah." He slides his arms around my waist.

I frame the photo. Relax into his chest. Rest my head on his.

Click.

"A few more. Just in case." Every part of me goes warm. He's holding me like he'll never let go.

I need that.

I need it to be real.

I let my eyelids flutter closed. I let myself believe it. I let myself fall harder.

My eyes blink open. I stare at the camera. Smile.

Click.

Click.

There. I force myself to rise. Fight the urge to wrap my body around his forever.

"These look good." I focus all my attention on picking the perfect photo. There. The second looks the coziest. Even if it's obvious my lipstick is long gone. I show it to Ryan.

"What's the caption. *Wish I could suck my boyfriend's dick. I've got to settle for a phallic vegetable instead.* Nice and subtle?"

"You think I won't post that?"

"You'd make it dirtier."

I laugh. "Yeah." I take a seat. Avoid his intense stare.

He's picking me apart.

Examining all my secrets.

That's a non-starter.

I'm not telling him how I feel about him.

And the rest...

Nobody knows about the rest.

"No caption." I hit post. Pull up Instagram. Repeat the process. "How long until she likes it?"

"Don't know." He stabs a green bean, brings it to his lips, chews, swallows. "She saw us together. She gets it. We can ease up."

"No. We have to go harder. We have to make her hurt."

"Leigh—"

"Don't tell me not to hate her. I hate her."

"I know better than to talk you out of anything."

"Thank you."

"Wasn't a compliment."

"Don't care." I eat another slice of eggplant Parmesan. It's still delicious, but it doesn't thrill me the way it did a few minutes ago.

It's nothing compared to Ryan's body against mine.

Compared to all that concern in his piercing blue eyes.

"Here." Ryan pushes his plate toward me. "Take what you want."

"You aren't hungry?"

"Still feel like throwing up."

"She does that to you?"

"Worse."

"Tell me about it."

He shakes his head.

I fight a frown. I can't ask him to talk if I won't. But, God, I want him to talk so badly. "I can't eat all this."

"Take it home. Eat it for dinner."

"Maybe." The white fish flakes against my fork. Melts on my tongue. Tender. Buttery. Lemony.

It's delicious, but I'm not eating his lunch.

I push the plate back to him. "No."

"No?"

"You insist on making me eat."

"Not like that."

"Yeah, like that. You give me shit about not eating."

"Someone has to take care of you."

Warmth spreads to my fingers and toes. He wants to take care of me. God, does he have any idea what he does to me?

What that means to me?

I feel it *everywhere*.

My eyelids press together. My head fills with images of a life together. A real one. Waking up in his bed. His arms around me as he scrambles eggs. The two of us arguing about coffee roasts, opting to use the French press so we each get exactly what we want. The smell of java filling the air.

Those soft lips on my neck.

Those calloused fingers between my legs.

That hard cock—

His cell's buzz pulls me from my dirty thoughts.

He pulls out his phone and checks a text. "Fuck."

"What?"

"Dean." He taps a reply into his phone. "He's throwing us a pool party."

"Why?"

"To celebrate our anniversary."

"How long have we been dating?"

"Six months."

"Not bad."

"All bad." His brow furrows as he stares at his cell. "He's inviting their mutual friends. His friends. Everybody."

"It's a chance to rub this in Penny's face. That's good."

"It's Dean. It's bad."

"Does he even have a pool?"

Ryan's eyes fix on mine. They fill with confusion. "You've never been to his place?"

"Why would I?"

"You hang all the time."

"At the shop. At bars. With Walker. And sometimes with you and Brendon. But never alone."

"Never?"

"Okay, sometimes." It's only natural for us to talk a lot. There are slow times, between appointments, where there's nothing else to do. Dean is nosy, obnoxious, and over-the-top, but he's also entertaining. "But not at his place."

His eyes bore into mine. "You and Dean haven't?"

"Haven't what?"

He stares back at me.

"No. God no." I would never sleep with Dean. Ever. He's a good friend. But he's so…

He's a slut.

And that's good for him.

But I don't want to wonder where his dick has been.

That was it at first. But now…

He's like a brother. It's weird even considering the possibility of kissing him.

"Not even when you were drunk?" Ryan presses his palm against his thigh.

"Never."

"Nothing?"

"Nothing."

"Not even a kiss?"

"What about nothing is confusing to you?"

"The way you flirt."

"We don't."

"He offered to make you come."

"He was kidding."

"Didn't bother you."

"Because he's just being stupid."

"He asked you to take out your tits and give him a hand job."

"He's just proving a point."

"What the fuck point is that?"

Something about how Ryan isn't into me. How I need to get over that idea.

But Ryan's jealous.

His brow furrows. His jaw cricks. His palm rises, curls into a fist. He blinks, and it's flat on his thigh again.

People are only jealous of things they want. There must be a part of him that wants me.

Somewhere.

"You can tell me if it's Dean," he says.

"It's not."

He nods *okay*, but it's clear he doesn't believe me.

Maybe I should let him believe it's Dean. It will be easier doing this if he isn't pressing me for details every three seconds.

I turn over my options until a buzz cuts through my thoughts.

Ryan's phone.

His brow furrows as he stares.

"Dean?"

"Penny likes our photo. *Aww, young love. How sweet.*"

"God, her nerve." Anger courses through my veins. I forget about Ryan's jealousy. About Dean. About everything but how badly I want to put a million miles between Ryan and his ex.

"She's trying."

"You trust her?"

"No." He sets his phone on the table facedown. "But I want to."

"She can't make amends better than asking you to do her a favor."

"It's not for her."

My heart pounds. He's sharing something with me. I need it. All of it.

"It costs me too much energy hating her."

"But she deserves it."

"That doesn't do shit for me."

It's a valid point.

Incredibly mature.

Incredibly unappealing.

"I still hate her." My stomach churns. I should get over it, for his sake, but I can't.

"You don't have to."

"How could I not? She destroyed you, Ryan." My voice rises to something much too loud for the family restaurant. "You were about to fall apart. For months."

He stares back at me with those piercing blue eyes.

"You barely got through it. And she doesn't even care. She doesn't care that she destroyed you."

"I'm here."

"But you're—"

"Hopeless?"

"No, I—"

"That's what you think of me."

"It isn't." I press my palms against the table. "Stop telling me how I feel."

"Stop making me guess."

My fingers dig into the table.

"You make me guess everything, Leigh."

"And you?"

He ignores the question. "It's been two years. You still haven't told me why you left Rock Bottom."

"And you're always sharing your feelings with me?"

"You don't ask."

No. I must. I want them so badly. I must ask. "I do too."

He shakes his head. "You think I won't talk to you?"

Yes. "I don't know."

"I will."

"Then tell me about Penny. About how it ended."

"Tell me who this guy is."

"I thought you'd talk."

"I will."

"That's a fucking ultimatum, Ryan. Sharing isn't quid pro quo."

His eyes fill with frustration. "You talk to Dean about why you left Rock Bottom?"

"No."

"You two laugh about how hopeless I am?"

"I DON'T THINK YOU'RE HOPELESS."

He stares at me.

I stare back.

"Why can't you admit it's Dean."

"That's ridiculous."

"It's not."

"Yes. It is. I know how I feel."

"But I don't."

We return to our staring contest.

His expression screws with confusion.

It's my fault.

Of course he's confused. He's looking for Mr. Powers' identity. There are only two obvious possibilities. Ryan and Dean. But Ryan is never going to see that it's him.

I want to tell him the truth. I want to do whatever it takes to erase the hurt in his eyes.

But I can't.

If I tell him, he'll leave.

Maybe I can tell him the rest, but I sure as hell can't tell him this.

13

LEIGHTON

We finish our lunch in silence.

Pay the bill in silence.

Walk back to the car in silence.

Ryan says nothing when I plug my cell into the aux, boot up my breakup song playlist. It's a modified version of the one I made after things ended with Dave.

Destiny's Child's *Survivor* fills the car.

Ryan pulls onto the sleepy street. Cuts through the neighborhood to our left.

I watch five-bedroom houses and lush green lawns blur together until the song fades into the outro.

Our breath fills the car. Then the next song kicks in. Drowns every other sound.

He keeps his eyes on the road. His hands on the steering wheel. His attention elsewhere.

I want it back.

I want him back.

But there's no way I'm telling him who Mr. Powers is.

And there's no way I'm getting him back without peeling back the walls around my heart.

It's only fair to hand him the key if I want to unlock him.

Ryan is wrong.

I trust him.

But I've placed my trust in the wrong people way too many times. What if I'm wrong about him too?

It seems impossible.

I'm not a naïve high school girl anymore. I'm not falling for *I love you, sweetie, let me show you with my body* anymore.

I'm smarter.

Or at least less stupid.

Ryan isn't going to run away if I tell him why I left Rock Bottom.

But it's still a terrifying risk.

He stops at a crosswalk. Watches a young mom walk her twin sons across the street.

"Is this where you grew up?" I ask.

"Close, yeah."

"I've never seen the house."

"You will."

"Oh?"

"Dean's pool party's at my parents' place."

"Really?"

"They're out of town."

"How high school." I play with my seatbelt. "So he doesn't have a pool?"

"It's a shitty apartment complex pool."

"But he still sits out there in his swimsuit, flirting with all the women who walk by."

"Leigh—"

"What?"

"Don't bullshit about this." The family steps onto the side-walk. Ryan looks left. Then right. He taps the gas, moving the car forward. "I'm not gonna fall apart over you wanting to fuck Dean."

"I know."

"I'm not gonna tell him."

"I know."

His blue eyes find mine. "Why won't you admit it?"

"Why won't you believe me?"

He settles into his seat. Turns back to the road.

Ugh.

Fine.

I guess we won't talk.

He's so…

UGH.

I pick up my cell. Check my emails. My texts. My social media. Sure enough, our post is popular.

What a cute couple!

OMG, girl, your hair looks amazing.

That eyeliner. Muy caliente!

I knew you two were doing it.

Gwen Stefani's breathy vocals fills the car. *Ex-girlfriend.* The ultimate *I should have known better* anthem.

Ryan and I are still trading cold shoulders.

Still silent.

Still running from every chance at vulnerability.

Am I going to be playing this song in two months?

Tonight?

This silence is stupid.

He's my favorite person in the entire world.

I take a deep breath and exhale slowly.

I've spent the last half a dozen years running from intimacy.

If I want more of him, I have to let him in.

Ryan turns onto Santa Monica Boulevard. The car zooms over the empty street.

Thoughts bounce around my head as Gwen fades into Kelly Clarkson.

I'm tired of keeping this to myself.

I want to show him my scars. Even if they're ugly. Even if they scare him.

He might think less of me.

But that's a risk I have to take.

My fingers curl into my seatbelt. "I left Rock Bottom because of my mom."

He turns to me. "You've never mentioned her."

"Because I hate her."

"You hate a lot of people."

"I know."

"That shit is bad for your soul."

"You want to hear this or not?"

"Yeah." His voice softens. "Of course."

"I started working at restaurants in high school. For extra cash. And a way to get out of the house. I wasn't a great student. The only class I liked was art, and everybody told me that was a good way to live in a cardboard box."

"That's bullshit."

"I know that now. But then... I wanted my own money. So I wouldn't have to ask my mom."

He nods *I get that*.

"My dad's never been in the picture. I know I told you. But maybe you forgot."

"I remember everything you tell me."

My stomach twists. This is confusing.

He remembers everything I tell him.

He's jealous of some idea of me and Dean.

But he doesn't want me.

It's just...

He's so...

I take a deep breath. Exhale slowly.

I'm inventing this confusion.

Ryan and I are friends.

Just friends.

Period.

I tug at the soft fabric of my dress. "I started as a host. Eventually became a waitress. Then a bartender. I skipped around bars for a while. Until I settled in at Rock Bottom."

"Dean talked about you all the time."

"Bragged about how he was gonna bang the bartender?"

"Yeah." His nails dig into the steering wheel. "He ever try?"

"Can we not?"

He nods *fine*.

"I liked it there. It was busy. The time went fast. My tips were great. Lots of hot guys left their numbers."

"You slept with them?"

"Dated some, yes. Is that a problem?"

"No."

"It was a great place to work. But there was something about selling booze all night then going home to…"

He stops at a light. Turns to me. Stares deeply into my eyes.

I don't want to say this.

We're nearly to my place. I can get out of the car, lock myself in the apartment, never admit to this again.

Never let him into my heart.

"I didn't like that I made a living getting people drunk. But I was okay with it. Until one day, I wasn't."

I cross my legs. Smooth my skirt over my thighs. Ignore the intensity of Ryan's stare.

I want to tell him this.

I want to show him my ugly parts.

If he thinks less of me…

That's a risk I have to take.

My shoulders relax as I exhale. "There was this regular who always had the bar in stitches. She was on her third gin and tonic. Laughing. Telling the bar this epic story about how she met some famous actor. How he begged her to go back to his hotel room and she shot him down."

"It was bullshit?"

"Maybe, but that didn't matter. It was an epic story. Entertaining even if it wasn't true."

The light flashes green. Ryan turns to the road. Taps the gas. The car moves forward.

Houses and businesses blur together.

"She had the bar hanging on every word. At least, every time I checked. It was a busy night. I kept fixing her drinks. Didn't pay much attention." My stomach churns. This happened two years ago, but the pain is still fresh. The wound is still there. "Closing rolled around and she was still there. Slumped over the bar. Drunk. But holding her own."

"You could have got in trouble."

"Yeah, but I didn't care about that." I suck a breath between my teeth. "It was when someone came in looking for her."

"Isn't that a good thing?"

"It was her daughter."

Ryan's attention turns to me.

"You're driving."

"You're talking."

"I want to live to see tomorrow."

He looks at the road. "I want to hear this."

A snappy comeback dissolves on my tongue. I want him to hear it too. I want him to see my scars. "She was young. Eleven. Maybe twelve. But that wasn't the worst part. It was how weary she was. Like she did this every night."

"Did she?"

"Probably. I did. That was why I made sure to work nights. So my mom couldn't count on me to clean her up and put her to bed."

"Leigh—"

"I saw this look in her eyes. An acceptance. Like she knew her mom would never change. Like she knew she'd be doing this forever. And I thought: why is a twelve-year-old smarter than I am?"

"Your mom—"

"Yeah. I went home. Told my mom I was moving out unless she quit drinking."

"And—"

"She stared at me, all glassy-eyed, laughed it off."

"She called your bluff."

"Yeah."

"You moved out the next day?"

"Yeah." My laugh is sad. "How'd you know?"

"I know you."

He does. He knows me better than anyone. Just not as well as I want him to. "I moved out. Quit my job. Begged my way to… well, I guess you know the rest."

"Your mom is that bad?"

"She was. Now… I don't know. We don't talk anymore." I press my lips together. "I know, it's fucked, leaving her to drink herself to death—"

"She's the parent. She should be responsible."

"But…"

"That's it."

Maybe.

"You did the right thing."

"I spent years shilling booze."

"You made ends meet."

I shake my head. "I didn't need to work. She has a good job. She's high functioning at work. Waits until she's home to really get wasted. Waits until I can clean up her mess."

"Fuck. Leigh. I'm sorry."

"Thanks." My shoulders relax. He isn't running away. He

119

isn't staring with judgment. He isn't kicking me out of his car.

His voice is soft. Sweet. The kind of voice you use to whisper *I love you.* "I thought shit was fucked with my parents. But it's nothing. The usual *are you sure you don't want to go to business school* thing."

"You did."

"Yeah."

"Did it make them happy?"

"Until I started apprenticing."

"Was it worth it?"

"Don't tell them, but yeah. I learned a lot." The car slows. Pulls to a stop.

We're here.

Ryan unclicks his seatbelt.

I do the same.

He moves closer. Wraps his arms around me.

I let my eyelids press together.

Let my fingers dig into his t-shirt.

He's warm and he smells good. Like lemon soap and like Ryan.

I feel him everywhere. In my lungs and my bones and my soul.

It's deeper than usual.

More intimate.

Ryan never holds me like this.

Never.

"I'm sorry, Leigh." He pulls me closer.

"Do you… do you want to come in?" *Hold me all afternoon. Fall asleep in my bed. Make me forget the world.* "I'm still working on my portfolio. I could use your help." Even if I'm not planning to start taking clients for a long, long time.

He runs his fingers through my hair. "Whatever you want."

I want you.

I swallow the thought. Push it as deep as it will go. "We could get that amazing mint coffee first."

"Anything."

Not anything. Not by a long shot.

But something all the same.

14

RYAN

We spend the afternoon walking along the beach. Spend the night eating street tacos over hours of work on Leighton's portfolio. Her shit is amazing, but it's unfocused. She needs to pick a niche and own it.

I keep arguing she should do book covers.

She keeps resisting.

I don't know why she doesn't want to go after this.

But I'm going to figure it out. I'm going to convince her to do this.

It's late when she gives up on work. But she doesn't ask me to leave and I don't offer.

Instead, she puts on *Austin Powers* and pats the spot on the couch next to her. "Promise you won't ask again?"

I will.

But not here.

Not tonight.

I nod and take the spot next to her.

She pulls her knees into her chest. Rests her head on my shoulder.

She falls asleep in my lap halfway through the movie.

If feels right having her this close.

Intimate.

Terrifying.

Like she's going to rip my heart from my chest and leave it beating on the floor.

That can't happen.

Shit can't change.

No matter what, I can't lose her.

BRENDON TAKES A SWIG FROM HIS WATER BOTTLE. HIS DARK eyes fill with that paternal *I know best, and it's not this* look of his. "You really want to hand her more of your thoughts?"

"It was Leighton's idea."

"You're an adult. Take responsibility for yourself."

The water sloshes against the side of the pool as Leighton does a cartwheel.

There are another dozen people in the pool—Dean went all out—but I only see her.

Her purple hair sticking to her forehead.

Her lips parting with a laugh.

Her ass bouncing as she jumps, straining the straps of that so-called swimsuit.

"What did you tell me when I was trying to get over Kay?" He takes another swig.

We're standing in the shade, under the patio umbrella, the enormous backyard in front of us.

The grill to our right.

Dean's fixing burgers. Flirting with a mutual friend.

Leighton insists he isn't Mr. Powers.

But who else could it be?

"Nobody fucking warns you good advice comes back to haunt you," I say.

"Be less insightful."

"I'm trying."

"See somebody. Do something. Anything that's not about Penny."

"I am."

"Pretending to date your best friend—"

"I'm seeing her, aren't I?"

"You're fucking her?"

"No." My voice is incredulous. "That's ridiculous."

"Then you aren't seeing her."

Maybe not romantically. But I am *seeing* Leighton. When I close my eyes, she's there. Pressing her berry lips into a smile. Running her fingers through my hair. Shifting into my lap with a sigh.

"You like her?"

"She's my best friend."

"You want to fuck her?"

"Look at her."

He chuckles. Takes another swig. "Beyond that?"

"Not looking for your advice about getting over someone."

"Fair enough." He finishes his water, tosses it in the recycling bin. "But I know not getting over someone."

"And?"

"Proximity doesn't help." His dark eyes fix on something to our right.

Kaylee. His still eighteen-year-old girlfriend.

She's wearing an Ariel bikini with a purple top and a flared metallic green skirt. Her long blond hair hangs over her shoulders. Powder blue glasses frame her green eyes.

She's too young for him.

But the way they're looking at each other—

125

Anybody can see they belong together.

She turns to me. Waves. Spares me the torture of a hug from an acquaintance. "Hey, Ryan. How's it going?"

"Good." I take a long sip of my tequila and lime. It doesn't hit the spot, but everything else makes me feel like I'm being boiled alive. "How's work?"

"The new restaurant is great. Down to two days a week for the same money as four." She wraps her arm around Brendon's waist. Rests her head against his chest. "Are you and Leighton seeing each other?"

Brendon chuckles. "You're gonna field this question all day."

"How hard is it to say yes?" I ask.

"I don't lie to my girlfriend," he says.

"All that lying to your sister and your friends use up your quota for deception?" I try to make my voice teasing, but it's more of an attack.

She looks to him. *Huh?*

He brushes her hair behind her ear. Leans in to whisper.

She nods *oh*.

He keeps whispering.

She blushes.

"Dirty talk somewhere else," I say.

She laughs. "I guess that answers my next question."

I arch a brow.

"If you're sleeping together." She pulls her boyfriend closer. "Sorry. That was rude. You can still be cranky after sex."

"Bad sex." Brendon pulls her frames from her eyes. Folds them and sets them on the glass table next to us.

She nods *true*.

They share a look. Something like *oh, that's Ryan's problem. He needs to get laid.*

No arguments here.

I need the sweaty exhaustion that comes with sex.

I need soft thighs against my cheeks.

I need a woman's groan in my ear.

But I can't handle the intimacy of that.

"You look good, Ryan… Happy." She nods *goodbye*, wraps her hands around her boyfriend's wrists, pulls him toward the pool.

He nods his own goodbye. Jumps in with her.

Fuck, this backyard is the size of most houses.

My parents are too rich.

Their story is always something about *buying when the market was right*. But then rich people never think they have money. Even when they have MBAs and six-figure salaries.

"You do look happy." Walker plops on the lounge chair next to me. Surveys the pool. "It's weird. But good."

"That a compliment?" I watch Leighton do a somersault. Jump to her feet. Wrap her arms around Iris and pull her into the water with her.

"She really wearing that?"

"And Iris?"

"Fuck." He lets out a low groan. "She's too good at torturing me."

Her deep purple swimsuit is nearly as tiny as Leighton's.

She looks good.

Like she's gonna drag Walker to an empty bedroom and tear off his swimsuit.

Her eyes find his.

She blows him a kiss.

He catches it and press it to his chest.

She blows another.

He presses that one to his crotch.

She blushes.

Leighton laughs. Her eyes find mine. They promise something, but I'm not sure what it is. Only that I want it.

With a wave, she turns back to the pool. Drags Iris under the water again.

"You and Leighton talk a lot?" I ask.

He nods.

"You know if she's into anyone?"

He shoots me a curious look. "Isn't she into you?"

"It's pretend."

"You sure about that?"

"Yeah."

"You know a lot more about relationships than I do, Ryan. But I know one thing."

"Yeah?"

"You want to know something, ask her."

"I have."

"Then believe her."

It's good advice.

I want to believe Leighton isn't head over heels for my younger brother.

But there's something about the way her voice wavers. The way her eyes fill with dread.

There's some reason she's dead set on keeping this a secret.

Walker peels off his sunglasses. "You need anything, you know who to call." He pushes himself up, nods goodbye, makes his way to the pool.

He jumps in, finds Iris, wraps his arms around her like he's never gonna let go.

He isn't ever gonna let go.

It's weird, being surrounded by all these happy couples. Seeing the guys settling down.

I'm happy for them.

Usually, it pokes the *she's gone, and my entire future is gone with her* bruise.

But that doesn't hurt as badly today.

I move to the grill. Refill my tequila. Wait for Dean to finish flirting with his blond friend.

He turns to me. "You want a burger?"

"Sure."

"Medium rare?"

I nod.

He pulls a patty from the ice box. Sets it on the grill.

"You went all out."

"You're welcome."

I take a long sip. Let the booze dissolve my inhibitions. He did this for me. It's sweet. In a Dean kind of way. "Thanks."

He picks up his beer. Holds it up to toast.

I do the same.

We clink glasses.

He laughs. "You look fucking ridiculous in those black board shorts."

"More or less ridiculous than Brendon?"

"Tough call." He turns to the pool. "The fucker corrupted Kay too thoroughly. She barely responds to my teasing."

"And Leighton?"

"What about her?"

"You offered to make her come."

His blue eyes light up as he laughs. "You're gonna have to be more specific. I offer to make her come all the time."

"Why?"

"Why do you wear black every day?"

I see his point. Asking Dean why he teases Leighton is like asking a fish why it swims.

It's just what he does.

But—"Have you two ever?"

"I tried. Believe me. But she's not interested."

"You do want to fuck her?"

He motions to Leighton in the pool. To the tiny swimsuit hugging her tits. "Of course I want to fuck her. Look at her."

"Said the same thing to Brendon."

"Great minds think alike."

"That's terrifying." I take another swig. "Do you actually want to fuck her?"

"Don't understand this *actually* word. She's hot. And she plays hard to get. What else is there to consider?"

"You like her?"

"Yeah. I am capable of friendship."

"You want to be with her?"

"You're going in circles, Ryan." Dean uses a spatula to scoop the burger onto a paper plate. "You want a bun?"

"No."

He hands over the plate. Nods to the condiments.

I grab mustard and a fork. Drown the patty in Dijon.

Dean scoops a second burger onto a plate. Piles it high with toppings.

He turns the grill down and plops in the blue patio chair.

He looks over the glass table to me. "Be careful with her."

"Leigh is tough. She doesn't need—"

"Yeah. She does. Don't let her forget it's pretend."

"She's into someone else."

"And you're hung up on Penny."

The sound of her name threatens to close my airways.

But I'm not *hung up on her*.

I don't want her.

I want her out of my thoughts.

And now.

"I'm getting over it." I bring a slice of my burger to my lips. "This is good shit. Thanks." The word is awkward on my tongue. My brother and I have never had an earnest relationship. And our parents aren't exactly the *thank you, you did great, we're proud of you* types.

"You're welcome." He takes a messy bite.

"You hate this idiot as much as I do?"

"I know a lot of idiots. You'll have to be more specific."

"This guy who doesn't see how great Leighton is."

Dean laughs. "He's an idiot, but what matters is how he treats her. Right?"

Fuck, he knows something.

But he's not gonna tell me.

I nod. Settle into my chair. Finish half my burger.

Footsteps pad against the concrete.

The sun falls over Leighton's soft skin.

Dean shoots her a look.

She waves him off.

Slides into my lap and wraps her arms around me.

Fuck. That feels good.

Too good.

She leans in to whisper. "They're here."

And for a second I thought that was for me.

Maybe Dean is right.

I need to be careful with this.

I need to keep my head on straight.

Leighton slides out of my lap, offers her hand, helps me up.

Sure enough, Penny and Frank are standing at the side gate.

Smiling.

Stealing the warmth from the air.

Stealing my oxygen.

15

RYAN

"What a cute swimsuit." Penny hugs Leighton hello.

Leighton presses her berry lips—somehow, her lipstick is still perfect—into a smile. Squeezes Penny, wetting her breezy white sundress.

She always wears white now.

It's like she's screaming *I'm about to get married.*

I'm not the girl you fell in love with, the one who rolled her eyes at the idea of a Maui wedding, who only wore jewel tones, who refused to take Daddy's money.

She turns to me. Spreads her arms to offer a hug.

I stare back at her.

Her honey eyes soften. "Of course." She fights a frown as she offers her hand.

I take it. Shake.

"You look good, Ryan. Happy." She wraps her arms around her fiancé. "Aren't they a cute couple, Frank?"

He nods *for sure.*

She still prefers quiet guys.

I'll give her that much.

133

"It was sweet of Dean to invite us." She tugs at Frank's white t-shirt. "Should we go over and say thanks?"

Dean is still on the other side of the backyard, sitting in a blue and white striped lounge chair, staring at Penny like she's the devil incarnate.

"Later." I motion to the sliding glass door to the house. "Bathroom's inside if you need to change."

Her lips curl into a frown. "I know."

"How long was it you and Ryan were together?" Leighton copies Penny's gesture. She slides her arm around my waist, pulls my body into hers, rests her head on my shoulder. "I forget."

Penny fails to fight her frown. "Nine years. But Ryan only lived at home for the first few."

"Oh. Of course. So that means the two of you started dating when you were—"

"I was sixteen. He was seventeen." She tugs Frank's arm. "Will you get me a drink, sweetie?"

He shoots her a curious look. *Are you okay?* Or maybe *do you really expect me to trust you with your ex after the way we started?* "You want anything to eat?"

"No. We have dinner with my parents." She finally manages a smile. "Daddy has been really supportive."

"I imagine." He must be jazzed about Penny upgrading from tattoo artist to finance bro. "How's work?"

Her honey eyes fill with frustration. She blinks and it's gone. "Great, actually. I just got a promotion."

"Oh? What do you do?" Leighton asks.

"Ryan never mentioned it?" Penny asks.

"No." Leighton pulls me closer. "We don't really talk about the past. Well, most of the time, we aren't exactly talking."

My laugh dissolves the tension in my shoulders.

She's too good at this.

I rest my hand on Leighton's hip. Right over the strap of her tiny bikini. "Baby, you're insatiable today."

"Look at what you're wearing." Her fingers skim my bare stomach. She draws circles on my skin.

My eyelids press together.

That feels too fucking good.

Too fucking real.

I pull every soft inch of her body against mine.

Lean down to press my lips to hers.

Her hand knots in my hair. She holds my head against hers, sucking on my bottom lip.

Groaning as I scrape my teeth against her lip.

My body wakes up.

Desire races through my veins.

Blood flows south.

Finally, I feel the warmth of the sun.

No, it's her. Every soft inch of her.

Then she pulls back, and Penny is there, and clouds are everywhere again.

Fuck, this is confusing.

I shake it off. Step into my role.

Acting isn't my strong suit. But I know Penny well enough to do this.

She's standing there, her wide-brimmed straw hat casting a shadow over her pretty face. She's as beautiful as she was the day we met. Still a head shorter than I am. Still model thin. Still polished.

"I work in marketing." She digs a French manicured nail into the tip of her thumb. "My father works with Ryan's."

"Oh." Leighton's blue-green eyes bore into mine. "At the 'anonymous' MBA job."

"They introduced us when we were kids," Penny says. "Mom used to tease me about how I was going to marry Ryan one day."

"Her parents lost interest in that idea after I got my first tattoo." My fingers go to the Latin quote on Leighton's ribs. Trace the letters.

Her lips part with a sigh. Her knees press together. Her head turns to one side.

This is doing something to her.

Something that isn't pretend.

I should stop.

But I can't.

It feels too good, my hands on her skin.

"No." Penny's gaze goes to my hand. She watches as I trace the lines of Leighton's tattoo again and again. "Mom always loved you. She still does." She turns. Watches Frank laugh at something Dean is saying. "She's had a lot of unkind words for me."

"She wasn't big on you cheating on Ryan? Imagine that?" Leighton snaps.

The anger in her voice wakes me from my trance.

We're not doing this to send blood to my cock.

We're not doing it to fill that gaping hole in my gut.

She's doing this to protect me.

I need to protect her too.

Dean is an idiot, but he's right about one thing: I need to be careful with Leighton.

The sun fades behind the clouds as I pull my hand from her skin.

Her sigh is heavy. Needy. She shakes it off. Turns to Penny. "I'm sorry. That was—"

"No. You're right." Penny smooths her sundress. "I shouldn't have done that to you, Ryan. I am sorry. I understand if you don't believe me. But I hope you do. I really want us to be friends." She looks to Leighton. "Would you mind?"

Leighton clears her throat. "Would I mind what?" Anger

drips into her voice. Her eyes narrow. Her heels dig into the concrete.

"If I spoke to Ryan alone?" Penny's smile is soft. Disarming.

The girl I fell in love with.

But it doesn't mean shit to Leighton.

She looks to me. "It's up to you. I'd rather we go up to your room." Her fingers trail the waistband of my board shorts.

Fuck.

I want her hands on my skin.

I want these clothes gone.

I want her naked in my bed.

Thoughts of baseball do jack shit to cool me down.

"Give us a minute, baby." I brush Leighton's wet hair behind her ear.

Leighton frowns. "Are you sure?" Concern fills her blue-green eyes. She folds her arms, glares at Penny. *I'll kill you if you hurt him.*

Or maybe *I'll kill you if you touch him.*

"Yeah." I need her gone or I'm gonna touch her. I'm gonna forget this is pretend. I pull back. "Go. Eat. You look starved, baby."

"I am." Leighton makes a show of giving me a long once-over. Her gaze lingers on my crotch. "But food isn't going to satisfy." She shoots Penny a forced smile. "I'm sure I'll see you soon."

"You're both coming to the joint bachelor, bachelorette party, aren't you?" Penny's voice is soft. Sincere. She really does want us there.

To rub her marriage in my face.

To make amends.

To prove something to herself about how over me she is.

All of the above, maybe.

Leighton looks to me. Raises a brow. "It depends."

I return her gesture.

"Will there be cock lollipops?" She smiles.

Penny laughs. "Mom is planning it."

"So yeah." I can't help but laugh. Mrs. Winters is fun. Sarcastic. Punk rock. Everything Penny was when we fell in love.

Now…

I'm not sure who the hell my ex is now.

Leighton nods *your call*, spins on her heel, saunters to the grill.

I watch her ass sway as she walks away.

Fight my urge to go after her.

To bend her over the patio table, roll her bikini bottoms to her knees, and drive into her again and again.

"She hates me, doesn't she?" Penny presses her French manicured nail into her middle finger.

"You blame her?" I ask.

She shakes her head. "I would hate me too."

"Do you?"

"Hate myself? Is that what you want?"

Part of me does.

The rest just wants to be done with her.

"When I first saw the two of you together…" Her honey eyes fix on mine. "There's something about the way she looks at you."

"What's your point?"

"Does she treat you well?"

"Excuse me?"

"What?" She runs her fingers through her dark hair. "I know I hurt you, Ryan. I know what I did was shitty. But it wasn't because I stopped loving you."

"Then what the fuck was *I'm sorry, but I don't love you anymore.*"

Her eyes go to the floor. "I'll always love you—"

"Spare me the bullshit about how you love me but you aren't in love with me."

"I am. I mean, I was." She bites her lip. "Hate me if you want. Kick me out of your house. It won't change how I feel." Her fingers curl around my wrist. "I want the best for you. I always have."

"Like walking in on you with the kind of guy we used to mock?"

"I made a mistake."

"You made *a* mistake?"

"I should have left as soon as I realized it. But it wasn't just me."

My jaw cricks. We had rough patches, same as everyone, but I always tried to smooth them.

"After I took that job with my dad..." Her eyes meet mine. "You lost respect for me." Her gaze goes to the patio tables. Frank is sitting at the one on the left. Mutual friends fill the one on the right.

Leighton is M.I.A.

Probably pissing or something.

Or fucking Dean in his bed.

My fingers curl into fists.

I need to step back. Cool off. Destroy the part of me that cares.

A deep breath does nothing to offer clarity. Penny is still standing there, staring at me like I'm a horse with a broken leg.

Like she's so, so sorry she's gonna have to put me down.

Fuck that.

Fuck Dean's vagueness.

Fuck Leighton's secrets.

I stare at my ex. "You looked me in the eyes and asked me to strangle you if you ever decided to work for your dad."

"When I was sixteen."

"So?"

"People change."

"I didn't."

"You ever consider that's why this happened?"

"You decided to fuck some finance bro. Don't put that on me."

"He's more than that."

"Tall?"

"Ryan." She folds her arms. "I'm barely five three. You think I really notice that?"

"Blond?"

Her lips purse. "No. It's not because he's more attractive than you. He's not."

There's no victory in her admission.

Only another twist of the knife in my gut.

"He's not better in bed. He's not blessed with a bigger cock. Or more stamina."

"Then what—"

"He talks to me."

"I talked to you."

"When we were kids, yeah. But one day, you stopped. I still remember it. I still remember coming home to you with this glum look on your face, asking you what was wrong, and getting nothing."

I shake my head.

I offered her everything I had.

Everything.

And it wasn't enough.

I always suspected that, but now I know for sure.

"He listened. He cared. He didn't stare at me like I was the enemy for taking the job my dad offered," she says. "He didn't expect anything of me."

"I only wanted the best for you."

"Your best."

"No. Our best. What we both agreed on—"

Regret streaks her honey eyes. "I'm not here to fight."

"Then why'd you pick one?"

"I just want to know you're okay."

No. I'm not okay. But fuck her for asking.

For caring.

For looking at the cracks.

Her lip corners turn down.

Her eyes fill with frustration.

Her perfect posture slumps.

She's miserable.

And there's still a part of me that wants to promise her it's going to be okay.

LEIGHTON

I t flashes in my head for the hundredth time—
Penny's French-manicured nails digging into Ryan's tattooed forearm. Her laugh filling the air as she leans closer. Whispers some memory about old times. About how thoroughly he fucked her. How much she misses his lips, his fingers, his cock.

I suck the last drop of Grey Goose from my straw. Unscrew the cap on the bottle. Fill my glass to the brim.

That's enough to knock me out all afternoon.

This is complete hypocrisy.

It's pathetic, drowning my feelings in booze.

But I don't care.

I need these awful mental images gone.

The two of them in *this* bed, him tearing off her pretty cardigan, her unzipping his tight jeans. Sliding them off his hips. Trailing her lips down his stomach.

His hands in her long, dark hair.

It's so long. And dark. And pretty.

She's gorgeous. In that striking way. In a New York City kind of way. In a *she had nine years in his bed, and she's already a cheater, she's probably not going to keep her hands off him* kind of way.

I suck vodka through my straw. It's crisp. Clean. Clear.

But it fails to ease the tension in my shoulders.

I drain the glass. Leave it—and the bottle—on the black dresser.

Ryan hasn't lived here for nearly a decade, but this room still screams of him. Posters for gritty thrillers and indie bands cover the black walls. White string lights line the ceiling.

When I pull the blackout curtains—black, of course—the sun disappears.

The room goes dark.

I flip the switch and the string lights glow like stars.

Mood lighting.

Lighting to fuck by.

Or fuck yourself by.

I press my eyelids together. Attempt to destroy my mental images of Penny and Ryan with much more appealing ones.

It doesn't work.

I see them. Here. There. Everywhere.

The room spins as I fall onto the black bedspread. It smells like him.

It's not him.

But it's warm and comforting all the same.

I wrap myself in the blanket, close my eyes, try to convince myself to stop imagining Ryan and Penny's conversation.

I fail.

LIGHT FLOODS THE ROOM.

The door presses closed.

"Fuck, Leigh." Ryan's voice flows into my ears.

I wipe my eyes. Pull the blanket tighter.

"This is healthy."

"Fuck off."

The weight on the bed shifts as Ryan sits behind me. His fingers trail my upper arm. My shoulder. "What are you doing in my bed with a half-empty bottle of Grey Goose?"

"You're out of Belvedere."

"That's why you're trying to destroy your liver?"

No, I'm trying to destroy my mental images of the two of them together. "It's a party."

"You look like you're having fun."

"Are you here to berate me?"

"No."

"What do you want?"

His voice gets soft. "I was looking for you."

"Why?"

He makes that *what the hell* noise.

His fingers curl into my shoulder. He tugs at my skin. *Turn around. Look at me. Offer me everything you have to give.*

My breath is shaky. "I don't feel good."

"Wonder why." He nudges me again. *Look at me.*

I don't. "If you want fun, let's go outside. Swim. Why don't you swim?"

"The chlorine fucks with my contacts."

"Take them out."

"Nobody sees me in my glasses."

He's right. Somehow, he's spent the night at my place a dozen times, and I've still never seen him in his glasses.

"Okay. Fine. We can dare someone else to skinny dip," I say.

"Dare?"

"What's wrong with a dare?"

"You Dean all of a sudden?"

145

"Good idea. We'll get Dean to start a truth or dare game. You can ask Penny if Boat Shoes has a bigger cock—"

"I don't give a fuck about his cock."

"What if that was why she left?"

"It wasn't."

"How do you know?"

"Really?"

"Yeah." I hug the blanket. Every petty, immature impulse rises in my throat. I'm a teenager again, crying at a party because the guy I like is never going to like me back.

Because there's no one waiting at home to wrap their arms around me and promise it will be okay.

I grew up taking care of myself.

I can do it again.

But it feels so good, letting Ryan take care of me.

Letting him in.

I can't give that up.

He brushes a wet hair behind my ear. "You need to know something, Leigh."

"Yeah?"

"I have an exclusive on crying in this room."

"Is that right?"

"I'm the only person allowed to be miserable in here."

"Scribble *no one understands me* in your sketchbook?"

"Exactly."

"Draw *I hate my parents* on your arm?"

He shakes his head. "Angry lyrics."

"Linkin Park?"

"Everybody my age screamed Linkin Park at some point."

"You're forty, right?"

He chuckles. "You want to know a secret?"

"Of course."

"I'm a vampire."

146

My laugh breaks up the tension in my shoulders. "Is that right?"

"Yeah. I'm four hundred."

"Is that why you avoid the sun?"

"People would see me sparkle."

"You do sparkle."

"That a compliment?"

"Yeah."

His fingers skim my neck. Shoulders. Arm.

His touch is impossibly soft. Impossibly sweet. Impossibly loving.

But he doesn't love me. He's still wrapped up in her. It's obvious in the way he looks at her.

"Leigh." He tugs at the blanket. "Look at me."

"I'm not sure what that could accomplish."

"I'll tell you what Penny said about Frank's cock."

"She didn't tell you anything about his cock."

He's quiet for a long moment.

"Ryan?"

"I'm making a face. You can only see it if you look at me."

"You don't make faces."

"I don't have facial expressions?"

"That's not the same."

"You want to see, you have to look at me."

Fine.

I force myself to turn around.

He's sitting there—now in black jeans, only black jeans—his piercing blue eyes fixed on me.

"She did not say anything about Frank's cock."

He nods.

I shake my head.

Again, he nods.

"We're going in circles."

"Yeah."

147

"What did she say?"

"He's not bigger." His lips curl into a half smile.

"I knew you cared." My gaze fixes on the hollow of his neck. His bare shoulders. His chest. His stomach. Those soft hairs beneath his belly button. "You're such a guy."

"And you're apathetic?"

"Totally."

"Then why'd you ask?"

"Because…"

"You want to know why she left."

"How could anyone leave you?" My cheeks flush. "I don't mean…" Yes, I do. I don't understand how anyone could leave Ryan. But I can't admit that. "I… I saw you together. You were good to her."

"Her story's different."

"What? That's ridiculous."

"Parts of it."

"You want to talk about it?"

"Not with you drunk."

"I'm not drunk."

He motions to the half-empty bottle on the dresser.

"It wasn't a fresh bottle."

"How many shots have you had?"

"Not enough to be drunk."

"This is a sober conversation."

"Then just go."

"Fine." His shoulders tense. "You can sleep this off."

"With Dean?" I bite my tongue. I'm better than cheap shots to make him jealous. Even if his envy is thrilling—it means a part of him wants me.

His jaw cricks, but he shakes it off. "I have an exclusive on coming in this room."

"That's selfish."

His eyes light up as he chuckles. "Guess I should say, nobody can come in this room unless I'm here."

"You know you're daring me to masturbate in your bed."

He arches a brow *would you*.

"Dare me again. See what happens."

"Is it still masturbating if I'm here?"

Tug at this blanket. Untie my bikini. Demand I fuck myself for your viewing pleasure. Please. "It depends."

"On?"

"If it's giving you sexual gratification."

"You really think I could watch you come without—" He shakes his head. "You're insane."

Every part of me goes warm at once. "You don't mean…" I swallow hard. I can't stomach a no. Better not to ask. "Was that all she said?"

"You're drunk, Leigh."

"Not that drunk." Not drunk enough to forget how much I want him. How much that hurts.

"I didn't need her to tell me I'm bigger."

"Oh."

"Dean was right."

"That's a scary sentence."

He nods.

Oh.

It clicks. Dean was right about how massive cocks run in the family. He's… Uh…

Ahem. "How do you know about Dean's—"

"You haven't seen it?"

"No. Why would I?"

"He used to fuck chicks in the backyard all summer. I wish I'd never seen him."

"And he… he's seen you?"

"He walked in on me and Penny a few times."

"Oh." I take a deep breath and exhale slowly. The thought

of Ryan naked sends heat to my fingers and toes. But the thought of him naked *with* her steals every ounce of my warmth. "Was that all she said?"

"He's not a better lay."

"Is that actually comforting?"

"No."

"What if he was a better lay?"

"I don't know."

"You should say *hard to imagine. I'm just so good.*"

He laughs as he lies next to me. "I don't brag."

"You're right. Show don't tell. That's the first rule of a good story."

He looks at me like I'm crazy.

"Are you generous?"

"Stop it."

"What? Talking to my best friend?"

His hair falls in front of his eyes as he shakes his head.

"Ryan…" My fingers curl around his wrist. I'm not sure what I'm asking for, only that I want it.

His voice is soft. "You look miserable, Leigh."

"But hot?"

"You're wrapped in a blanket."

I unpeel the layers of cotton and polyester. Let the comforter fall at my sides.

His eyes glide over my body. Slowly. Like he's savoring every inch. He takes in my breasts, my stomach, my hips, my thighs, my calves, my painted red toenails.

Then he works his way back to my eyes. "I lost one relationship because I didn't understand what a woman wanted."

"Oh?"

"What do you want me to say to that?"

"Whatever you're thinking."

"You know you look good."

"But I don't know what you think."

"You're my best friend."

The four words are an explanation. *You're my best friend. It wouldn't matter if you were the hottest woman in the world. I can't look at you that way.*

I press on anyway. "But you want to fuck me?"

"You're drunk, Leigh."

"No. I'm not."

"Yeah. You are. And you're pissed at me and I don't have a fucking clue why."

I shake my head.

His eyes bore into mine. "She said I didn't talk to her."

"Did you?"

"I thought so..." His gaze goes to the string lights. "But maybe I didn't."

"Oh."

"You think I talk to you?"

"A little. But not really."

Understanding fills his eyes. "I listen?"

"Yeah. But I don't talk."

"You trust me?"

"Of course."

"But not about Mr. Powers."

"Ryan. God." I grab a pillow and hide behind it. "We were starting to get somewhere."

"We weren't."

"Maybe not." I hug the pillow to my chest. Look up at him. "I'll prove I'm not drunk." I bring my finger to my nose. Raise my right leg.

His fingers curl around my ankle as he pins my leg to the bed.

Fuck, this is so, so close to where we need to be.

Just slide these bottoms to my knees. Unzip those jeans. Forget about talking and show me what you're feeling.

"You want me to go?" he asks.

I shake my head.

"Then tell me why you're crying in my room."

"I can't stop picturing you together."

"Leigh—"

"Not like that." Okay, not *just* that. "You're still in love with her. And I hate it. I hate that she gets any of your heart. I hate that you're giving her the chance to hurt you again."

"This was your idea."

"Maybe it was a bad one."

"You want to call it off?"

"No. Do you?"

"No." He lies next to me. Looks up at the stucco ceiling. "I'm not in love with her."

"At all?"

"There's a Penny shaped hole in my gut, yeah. But I don't want to fill it with her."

"But…" I swallow hard. "The way you looked at her. You… Are you sure?"

"No."

"Oh."

"I don't have a fucking clue what it's supposed to feel like, loving someone. Not anymore. Not after that."

"After what?"

"The look in her eyes when I caught her."

"Guilt?"

"No." He lets out a heavy sigh. "Relief."

17

LEIGHTON

Moonlight flows through the windows. It casts soft highlights and shadows over the stairs. Melts into the yellow glow of the den's fluorescent bulbs.

The house is quiet except for the sizzle of a pan.

It's late. The party's over. It's just me and Ryan.

My feet pad the plush beige carpet. Then the slick equally beige tile.

Oh.

That isn't Ryan.

Dean's standing at the stove, in jeans and a t-shirt, his attention on a grilled cheese sandwich, his back to me.

He turns from his spot at the stove. His blue eyes meet mine. They're so much like Ryan's. Lighter. Brighter. Filled with playfulness instead of frustration.

He folds his arms over his chest. "What the fuck did you do to him?" His voice is teasing, but it still feels like an accusation.

I try to make my response playful. "I sucked him off."

"No offense, babe, but you need to work on your technique."

"Is that right?"

"You did something wrong to put that look on his face."

"Okay. I admit it. He likes it rough. I got carried away."

Dean shakes his head *in your dreams.*

"How do you know?"

"I know what a satisfied woman looks like."

"Maybe you don't." I grab a blanket from the couch, wrap it around myself like a cocoon. "Maybe they've all been faking it."

"I know faking it." He turns back to the stove. Flips his sandwich to one side. "You want one?"

Bread and cheese are the perfect antidote to my pounding headache, but I want to eat with Ryan. "No thanks."

He shrugs *suit yourself.*

"What time is it?"

"Time for you to stop drinking your feelings."

I fake laugh. Flip him off.

He returns the gesture.

"You know, I could have sucked him off and refused to let him make me come."

"You get off on making up this bullshit?"

"No."

"Then stop wasting your time."

"How do you know—"

"You didn't get anywhere near his cock."

I take a seat at the dining table. Pull the blanket tighter around my chest. "How are you sure of that?"

"You look desperate."

"Fuck you."

He turns to me. Unbuttons his jeans. "Sure. Let's go. Right now."

I roll my eyes.

He motions to the couch. "Fifteen minutes of anonymous sex. Nobody has to know."

"You're not even offering seriously."

He shrugs. *Maybe I am. Maybe I'm not.*

"You aren't." I feign disgust. It's a game Dean and I play. He pretends he wants to fuck me. I pretend I find him revolting. I'm not sure how it started, but it's our regular routine.

Dean doesn't want me. He did once—he offered to "let me ride Prince Albert" a dozen times. Until, one day, he stopped offering.

Well, he stopped offering seriously.

He laughs. Buttons his jeans. "Yeah. But don't get your hopes up it means I respect you."

"I don't want your respect. How disturbing."

"What the fuck did you do to him, Leigh?"

I'm not sure if I want to smack Dean for the implication or hug him for finally looking out for his brother. "Nothing."

He turns the stove off. Slides grilled cheese onto a ceramic plate.

"Where is he?"

"On a run."

My eyes go to the time on the microwave. Nearly midnight.

"That means you fucked with his head."

"And Penny?"

"I saw his face after he talked to her. Then again after he came downstairs. You did something to him."

"Maybe he should take some responsibility for his mood."

"Maybe you should take some responsibility for lying to him."

That's a fair point. But what's Dean doing on a high horse?

"I'm not gonna tell you to be responsible or honest or some shit like that."

"Good."

He takes his plate, brings it to the table, sits next to me. "I told him to be careful with you."

"Really?"

"Yes. Guess the devil gave back some of my soul."

My anger fades to something warmer. Dean is being earnest in such a Dean way. It's sweet. Weird. But sweet.

"Thought that was my only concern."

"Are you admitting to having feelings?"

He shoots me a look. *Get real.* Offers me half his sandwich.

"I'm not hungry."

"You're drooling."

"Because I'm thinking about Ryan naked."

"Yeah." He leaves the half in front of me, picks up the other half, takes a monster bite. "But that's a constant thing for you."

I laugh. "True."

"I thought he was still in love with her."

"He isn't?"

"I don't know. But I know the look on his face after he left you alone in his room." He takes another bite. Chews. Swallows. "Something hurt him."

"Was she still there?"

"Yeah. They had an awkward goodbye. She left with Mr. Khaki Pants."

I laugh. "I call him Boat Shoes."

"Fuck, that's better."

"Thanks."

"What could anyone see in him?" he asks.

"A six-figure salary and a white picket fence."

"Ryan makes plenty."

"How do you know?"

"We're partners. We all make the same."

"How plenty are we talking?"

He laughs. "Enough for a white picket fence."

"And all the boat shoes you could dream of?"

"And then some." He finishes his half of the sandwich. Licks his pointer finger clean. "It wasn't her, Leigh. It was you. Something you did. Or said. Or something he thought about you." He licks his middle finger clean. "I wasn't worried you're gonna hurt him—"

"I'd never."

"I know. But you are."

My teeth sink into my lip. "That isn't fair."

The front door swings open. Rubber soles squeak against the tile foyer. Then the soft pad of socks on tile. On carpet.

Ryan steps into the dining room/kitchen/den. His brow furrows as he surveys the scene.

Dean and I are eating together.

We're trading secrets.

I know how it looks.

But it's so not that.

I place the half grilled cheese on Dean's plate. Push myself to my feet. "Good run?"

"You were gone forever," Dean says.

"Needed to clear my head." Ryan's blue eyes fix on me. They bore into me. Beg for an explanation for my proximity to his brother.

I know he struggles to trust people.

I get that.

But there's no way for me to explain without giving myself away.

"I just got up." I unwrap the blanket. Drape it over the dining chair. "I need to move."

He gives me a long slow once-over. His pupils dilate. His tongue slides over his lip.

But there's something else. Something that isn't sexual.

Like he's trying to decide if I fucked his brother.

Hurt flares in his blue eyes. He blinks, and it fades into confusion.

His brow furrows. His lips press together.

"I'm gonna go for a swim." I motion to the sliding glass door. "Join me."

Ryan looks to his brother. Stares at his expression like it holds all the secrets to the universe.

Dean looks to me. Raises a brow. *You see what I'm talking about.*

I do.

But I still don't know how to fix this.

———

COOL WATER RUSHES PAST ME. IT PRESSES MY HAIR AGAINST MY cheeks. Tests the straps of my bikini.

Swimsuits have an unwritten rule: you can choose cute or practical, but never both. Four years on the high school swim team filled my quota for one-pieces.

I can live with my boobs threatening to pop out of my bikini.

I press off the shallow end of the wide lap pool. Cut through the water to pull my arms to my sides. My fingers slice the surface. They glue together to push water behind me, propel me forward.

My feet hit the surface with a light tap. But it's enough my legs and ass burn.

It's been forever since I've really swam.

It's as comforting as it used to be.

But it's too familiar. I squeeze my eyes closed, blocking out the aqua sheen, saving my retinas from chlorine.

And there it is—the image of my mom at a swim meet,

smiling at my coach, sipping from a flask she kept in the front pocket of her blazer.

My coach's concerned stare the next day. Her hand on my shoulder as she lowered her voice to that *you can trust me, really* tone and asked if things were okay at home.

My squeaky lie. *Yes, of course.*

Mom, on the couch, sleeping off her drunken stupor, empty bottle of vodka next to her.

Like mother, like daughter, I guess.

If I keep running from my feelings, I'll end up like her.

That isn't happening.

I guess that means I have to woman up and face my shit.

I blink my eyes open as I surface to breathe. Night falls over the backyard, casting the concrete in a beautiful, dark blue.

The kitchen glows with yellow light.

The tiny white string lights lining the backyard shine with a ghostly glow. They make the pool look haunted.

Maybe it is.

By all my baggage. And all of Ryan's.

Maybe Dean's right. I should tell Ryan the truth. Let him decide if he wants to stay or walk. Let him decide if he wants anything to do with a Leighton who's crazy about him.

My hands hit the wall. I close my eyes, dunk my head, do a flip turn.

I get halfway across the pool before I blink my eyes open. Chlorine stings. But it's not nearly as bad as that feeling in my gut.

Mom would rather drink than be there for me. Than have me in her life at all.

And Ryan...

Am I second choice again?

The backup if making Penny jealous doesn't work?

He says he doesn't want her back, that he doesn't love her anymore.

I want to believe him.

I really, really want to believe him.

My hand finds the wall. I do a flip turn, glide halfway across the pool, slice the water with my hands.

I go like that for ages.

Until I see legs. Ryan's calves. He's sitting on the edge of the pool, his eyes on me.

He motions to the plate next to him. "Dean said you didn't eat."

I brush my wet hair behind my ears as I egg beater my way to him.

"Showing off?"

"You do."

He arches a brow.

"How many miles did you run?"

"Don't do it to show off."

"Then why?" I move closer. Until he's five feet away. Three. One. My hands curl over the edge of the pool. This is the deep end. I have to tread water to stay afloat. I have to struggle to stay upright.

"I had to clear my head."

"But why?"

"Why were you miserable all afternoon?"

It's a fair question, but he's still dodging mine.

I stare up at him. "Do you trust me?"

"What are you talking about?"

"I want to explain something to you, but I can't fill you in on all the details. And I need you to trust that I have good reasons for that."

"Leigh…"

"Are you jealous of me and Dean?"

His brow furrows. His eyes turn down. He looks to the

den. Finds only yellow light and clean furniture. "I don't know."

"Is that why you went on a run?"

"Not exactly."

"Then why?"

"My head's a mess." He's eyes find mine. "I can't explain it better."

"Dean isn't Mr. Powers."

"Leigh…"

I stare back into his eyes. "I can't tell you who he is. And I know you won't believe me until I do. But it's not Dean. He's my friend, but that's it. That's all I want."

"He makes you laugh."

"So do you."

"Not the same way."

"No. But I like the way you do it better."

He motions to the plate—a stir fry that smells of ginger. "You should eat something."

"Ryan." I can't reach his face, so I settle for his leg. My fingers curl around his calf. My other hand stays on the cement. "Don't do this."

"What?"

"Lock me out."

He runs a hand through his hair. "I'm not trying to."

"But?"

"I don't know how the fuck to handle this."

The cool evening air nips at my nose, my chin, my shoulders. But he's warm against my fingertips. My palm. "What about it?"

"You're too good at pretending."

"Isn't that the point?"

"It's fucking with my head."

"Oh." The words gnaw at my gut. I keep my hand on his thigh. I keep my eyes on his. "It doesn't have to. I got carried away today."

"You didn't. You were going with it."

"So you… you want to stop?"

"I don't know." He stares at my hand. "I don't want shit to change."

"It doesn't have to."

His fingers brush mine. "It does."

I swallow hard. "What do you mean?"

"Mr. Powers is going to realize you're amazing. He's gonna scoop you up. And then you'll be his."

"We'll still… We'll still be the same."

"Shit can't stay the same."

"It can."

"No. I'm starting to get it, why Penny left."

"Oh."

"You seem sober."

"I am. Mostly."

He motions to the plate. "You should eat."

"Later." I tug at his leg. "Come in. Let the water wash everything away."

"How's that gonna help?"

"It just does. Trust me."

He stares at me for a long moment. Then he pulls his t-shirt over his head and slides into the pool.

Water sloshes against the concrete as he surfaces. He treads water, his eyes on me, his body turned toward mine.

"I want to trust you about this, Leigh. But I don't know how." He dives under the water. Swims to the shallow end. Surfaces with his mane of waves sticking to his head.

I dive under the water. Follow him. Join him at the steps.

His hand brushes mine. "You knew me when it happened."

"Last June."

He nods.

"But you said it's been fourteen months since you've—"

His lips curl into a half smile, but his eyes stay sad. "That's the detail you noticed?"

I nod.

"Yeah. Penny was right."

"Huh?"

"Sorry. I keep forgetting you're not in my head."

"I wish I was."

"It's a mess."

"So's mine." I sit next to him. Follow his gaze to the dark sky. "So's everyone's." The stars are tiny white dots. They're dull. Faint. "You're not a lost cause. I don't think that."

"I know."

"But the other day—"

"I was pissed."

"You were?"

"Yeah." He leans back on his elbows. "Penny wanted to ask if you were good to me."

I can't help but laugh. "Compared to her?"

"Compared to what I deserve, I guess."

"And she knows?"

"Shit was good for a long time. I loved her. She loved me. Says she still does."

My stomach leaps into my throat. "Don't tell me—"

"That usual *I love you, but I'm not in love with you* bullshit."

The tension in my shoulders unfurls. Thank God. "Oh."

"But it wasn't bullshit." He turns to me. "She meant it."

"She really wants you to be happy?"

"Yeah. I want to get there. To wanting that for her."

"Me too. I mean. I want that for you too." And for me too. I want both of us to forget she exists.

"You're good to me, Leigh. Better than I deserve." His eyes fill with vulnerability.

I want to wipe all his pain away. I need to reassure him. I

163

need more than words. But words are all I've got. "You really believe that?"

"I don't know." His gaze shifts to the sky. "I just know I can't lose you."

"You won't."

"I might."

"Anything is possible, yeah. But I'm not going anywhere."

"When this guy realizes how great you are—"

"I'm still going to be by your side." I'm going to be there. With him. Forever. "What was she right about?"

"Two years ago, three now, she gave up on starting her own website."

"The punk one?"

"It was supposed to be an edgy women's interest site, yeah."

"XO Punk Jane."

He looks at me like I'm crazy.

"It's a big women's site. But, carry on."

"Your hair looks silver in the moonlight."

"The chlorine washed out all the dye."

"I always wonder what it's gonna look like."

"I'm pretty settled on purple."

"That's what you said about pink."

"I gave it six months."

He brushes my wet hair behind my ear. "You're afraid of commitment?"

"No. I just like seeing a different person in the mirror sometimes."

He nods *I get that.* Shifts back to telling his story. "Three years ago, she took a job at her dad's company."

"Your dad works for hers?"

"Yeah. The media conglomerate that buys out good websites and turns them into generic pop-culture shit with a theme."

"Oh. Yeah. They're the worst."

He laughs. "Her dad offered her a job at the women's interest one. She took it. When she told me, I couldn't believe it. That was a betrayal of everything we believed in."

"Why?"

"I was never quite as punk rock as Brendon. Hell, Penny was the one encouraging me to rage against the machine. We promised each other we'd never work for the man."

"You were kids."

"That's how she saw it, yeah. She thought we were naïve kids. That things had changed now that she was twenty-three and broke."

"And you?"

"I told her I understood, but I didn't. It became this wall between us. Every time she mentioned the site's name or blurted out a buzz word, I lost a little respect for her. Until I had none left."

"Oh."

"I didn't realize it. I still saw her as the sixteen-year-old who scribbled *Testify* on my arms. Who giggled as we traded promise rings. Who begged me to get ink with her."

"You have matching tattoos?"

He shakes his head. "She chickened out."

"But you—"

He shifts to the right, rolls his shorts down his left hip. There's a locked heart in greyscale.

"Can I?"

"Yeah."

Under the water, my fingers brush his smooth, slick skin. "You loved her with your whole heart, huh?"

"Of course."

"I've never loved anyone like that."

"Your mom?"

"Of course. But not romantically." I press my lips

165

together. "I guess it's easy to explain it like that. Alcoholic mom taught me love is enabling someone. Thus, I have no interest in love. I'm sure Iris would have a better explanation—"

"That's not what I meant."

"Oh."

"It feels good, letting your guard down."

I nod. I want to get there with Ryan. To trust I can spill my guts without him leaving. To trust I can tell him everything.

"But she was right. After she took that job, I started throwing those walls up. I stopped talking to her. Stopped listening."

"Stopped loving her?"

"I kept loving that sixteen-year-old girl. But that wasn't her anymore."

"Now?"

"Part of me still loves her, the old her. But that girl doesn't exist anymore. People change. Maybe I haven't. But I should."

"She's still the one who fucked him."

"Yeah. But it was gonna end either way."

Probably.

"If she'd had more guts or I'd been less oblivious…" He turns toward me. "It was for the best, but—"

"That doesn't make it easier to trust anyone?"

He nods.

"Do you trust me?"

"I want to." His eyes bore into mine. "I want that so fucking badly."

"Me too."

"You're such a good friend. I hate asking for more."

Friend. What an ugly word. It's a knife in my gut. It's acid on my tongue. It's a raincloud on a sunny day. "Asking is the only way you'll get something."

He nods. "Promise me something."

"What?"

"That you'll tell me if I'm about to lose you."

"You won't lose me."

"Promise anyway."

I stare back into his blue eyes. "Okay. I promise."

18

LEIGHTON

W hite light falls over the dresser.

Over the black bedspread.

Over Ryan's inked arms.

Those arms are around me. His hands are on my stomach. His chest is against my back.

There's a thick blanket between my ass and his crotch.

But it's not enough.

I can feel his morning wood.

Every part of me goes warm. I press my eyelids together. Let myself believe his erection is more than a biological response.

The weight on the bed shifts as he stirs.

He pulls his arms to his sides, pushes himself to a seated position, reaches for something on the dresser.

His glasses.

Black rectangles frame his blue eyes as he slides them on.

They're so…

He's so…

I'm fucking melting.

"Shit." He checks the time on his phone. "We're due at work in an hour."

"I know." But I don't care. Not when he's right there. Not when the room smells like him. When I smell like him.

We're in the same bed because Dean invited some woman over. Occupied the living room and thus the couch.

Because Ryan was unwilling to sleep in either his parents' or Dean's bed.

But there's still an intimacy to his body next to mine.

Nobody sees me without makeup.

Nobody sees him in his glasses.

He stretches his arms over his head. The gesture pulls his shirt up his stomach, showing off inches of taut abs. "You want eggs?"

"Yeah. Thanks. I have time to shower?"

"We need to leave in thirty or we'll be late."

"You're an owner. You can be late."

He smiles. "Yeah. But you're an employee. You can't."

"You won't put a word in with my boss?"

"No. He's too much of a dick."

"True." I roll onto my side. Memorize every line of his face. "Did you make sure to get me time off to go to Maui?"

"He threw a fit, but I made it happen."

"Did he?"

Ryan smiles as he nods. He tosses his t-shirt over his head. Finds another in his dresser. Bends to grab a pair of jeans and black socks.

No boxers.

He doesn't wear boxers.

He's not wearing anything under those jeans.

Is that ever going to get old?

"You need to know something, Leigh." He turns back to me.

"Yeah?"

"This—" He taps his glasses. "Is between us."

"Lots of people wear glasses."

He shakes his head.

"They look good."

Again, he shakes his head.

"Really. They're smart. Sexy."

His cheeks flush for a hot second, then they're back to their usual sand tone.

THE BELL RINGS AS I PUSH THE SHOP DOOR OPEN. BUT THE next sound isn't my wedge sandals on the tile.

It's hands smacking together.

Dean is leaning against the counter, doing a slow clap.

Walker is standing next to him, shaking his head *you're ridiculous.*

The guys exchange a look, the kind only best friends understand. Something about me and Ryan.

Ryan rolls his eyes, but it doesn't wipe the smile from his face. He's enjoying Dean's teasing.

That's curious.

I hug my messenger bag to my side as I make my way to the counter. "You're taking up my domain."

"Babe, you can't roll in here in yesterday's clothes without a story." He shoots Walker a look. *Right?*

"Can't say I'm following this." He motions to Ryan, now setting up in his suite.

"You call that pressing for details?" Dean shakes his head *pathetic.*

I feign irritation as I take my spot behind the counter. It's Sunday. The last day of our pay period and schedule. That means extra administrative work.

Dean leans over the counter. "Tell me somebody finally came in that bed."

"I thought I was supposed to… What are you hoping to accomplish?" I ask.

"Accomplish? Why would I do that?" He makes a show of scratching his head.

Walker chuckles. "He's like the Joker. Lives to cause chaos."

"Mission accomplished."

"There's that ugly word again." He mimes wiping something disgusting from his shoulders.

Walker turns to me. "You need me to take him outside? Rough him up?"

"Would you really?" I press my hands together. "If I asked nicely and promised to do something sweet for Iris?"

"Only one way to find out." Walker shrugs *try me*.

"Dicks before chicks." Dean shakes his head. "Cold."

The bell rings as a customer steps inside. She must be Walker's eleven o'clock.

She waves hello. He nods goodbye to us, then goes to greet her.

Dean waits until they're settled in Walker's suite. "Anything I should know about?"

"Did you really fuck some girl so Ryan couldn't sleep on the couch?"

"I don't need motivation to fuck a hot woman."

"That's a yes." I stare into his eyes. "I don't get it, Dean. Do you want me with him or not?"

"I want that."

"Huh?"

"I want you with him or not. None of this pretend bullshit."

God, being with him… That would be everything. "If you want that, help instead of—what are you doing?"

"You're asking for my help?"

"You're right. That's a terrible idea. I take it back."

"Too late. That's a bell you can't unring."

"I have work to do."

"I love you too." He blows me a kiss, spins on his sneaker-clad heel, makes his way to his suite.

Slowly, everyone settles into work. The shop fills with the buzz of tattoo guns, the grunts of customers, the lull of conversation.

The morning passes quickly. I update our social media. Reply to emails and PMs as necessary.

Walker finishes first. Then Dean. I flirt with his customer as I hand him his receipt. Stare at Ryan to see if it's making him jealous.

But he's lost in his own world, the way he always is at work.

It's a thing of beauty—those strong hands on the gun, those blue eyes filled with determination, those soft lips pressed together in concentration.

Dean catches me staring. Laughs as he walks his customer to the door.

It's time for coffee. Mass amounts of coffee.

But Dean is back at the counter, staring at his phone, shaking his head. "Inked Wing Designs, huh?"

"Don't." My cheeks flush. No. My site is not ready for anyone's eyes. It's really, really not ready for Dean's eyes. "It's a work in progress."

"Don't what? Compliment you on this shit?" He shows off one of my cover mock-ups—a stock photo of two half naked people kissing with the title *Desire* in a curvy font. "Fuck. This is like porn. But classy." He turns to Walker's suite. "You see this shit?"

He's fucking with me, but he's being earnest too.

He means the compliment.

He really does think my designs are amazing.

Walker looks up from his sketchbook. Brushes a wavy strand behind his ear. Shoots Dean a knowing look. "I'm sure you're gonna show me."

Dean motions *come here*.

Walker looks to me. "Is that necessary?"

"No. You should stay. Work. We should all work." And not look at my mock-ups. It's bad enough that they're looking at my work. The—

Oh.

Fuck.

"Give me that." I reach for Dean's phone.

He holds it over his head. "Shit. This must get good." He jumps backward. Taps the screen.

I slide over the counter. Follow Dean into the lobby. "Stop it."

"It's a public site. I can pull it up anywhere."

"It's not supposed to be." I agreed to let Ryan design my site so he'd agree to let me play his girlfriend.

No one is supposed to actually look at it.

Even if they're complimenting it.

Is it really good enough they're complimenting it?

Walker rises from his chair. Steps between us. He studies my expression. "Fuck, this really must be good."

Dean nods. "So much better than you could imagine."

Fuck. That must be it.

Dean motions to Walker *come here*.

He does.

The two of them stare at the screen. Then at me.

Dean shakes his head *you didn't*.

Walker nods. "It's pretty good actually." He looks to Ryan's suite. "You have a future ahead of you."

Ryan's concentration breaks. The buzz of his gun ceases. He turns to us. Shoots Walker a *what the hell* look.

Dean turns the cell to face Ryan.

Ryan doesn't scream profanities.

He chuckles.

Smiles.

He's… happy about this.

He whispers something to his client, who nods, happy for a break, then he rips off his gloves and joins us in the lobby.

"Was this your idea?" Dean asks.

"Leighton's," Ryan says.

"Nice job, Leigh." Dean winks at me. "This is good shit. I can see women everywhere spanking themselves to it."

"Can you?" Walker laughs. "Or is there some *Flowers in the Attic* shit I should know about?"

"Some what?" Dean makes a show of scratching his head. "Is that a book or something?"

"Or something." Walker laughs. He checks the cell screen again. Really studies the picture. "Book covers suit you."

"I know." Ryan runs a hand through his wavy hair. "You two wish you looked this good."

"Wish? Please." Dean pulls his t-shirt up his stomach. Pats his six-pack. "Make me your next cover model, babe. Please."

"Sorry. I can only capture inner beauty." I force a smile. These guys are my friends. They're idiots, but they're talented designers. If they think my stuff is good, it's good.

Maybe even good enough for me to go for this.

"You're fucked," Walker says.

Ryan laughs. "Beyond fucked."

"One of you must know outer beauty." Dean tosses his t-shirt on the ground. Strikes a model-worthy pose. "Please." He turns to Walker. Presses his hands together. "It's all I've got."

"Sorry, but I don't see it," Walker shrugs.

Dean turns to Ryan. "Me and you, bro. Let's be a matching set."

Walker looks to me. "You into this *Flowers in the Attic* shit?"

"Where did you pick up that reference?" I ask.

"Where do you think?" He joins me on the other side of the brotherly… uh… love.

Dean slides his arm around Ryan's shoulder. Strikes another pose. "Let's call it *Fucked By Both Brothers*."

"Is this a fantasy I should know about?" Ryan's tone stays dry. But there's a lightness in his eyes. He's teasing.

"Depends on how much you're into it." Walker laughs.

"Zero," Ryan says.

"The fantasy isn't for me. It's for the ladies." Dean winks at me. "Tell me you wouldn't let us double-time you."

"Ew. Ew. Ew. I'm going to throw up." I make a show of gagging.

"How about one at a time?" Dean offers.

"How about I don't want your dick anywhere near me. God knows where it's been," I say.

"That's slut-shaming, Leigh. You're better than that," Dean says.

The bell rings and Kaylee steps inside.

She surveys the scene with a curious stare. Decides it's normal. Cuts through us to go to the counter.

Walker laughs. "She could not give less fucks about you."

"Kay, you wound me," Dean calls out.

She nods *okay*.

He mimes being stabbed in the gut.

"Dean has a new concept for you," Walker calls to her.

She shoots him a curious look. "Does he?"

"Yeah. *Fucked by Both Brothers*." Walker motions to Dean—who's still posing—and Ryan, who's standing there, pretending he isn't amused.

"Hard pass," she says.

"How about just me?" Dean drops his arm. Moves toward her. "Model for your next book?"

"I don't have a model for my first book," she says.

"Will you let me read it?" Dean asks.

"You don't read," she says.

"Will you give me a play-by-play of all the good parts?" he asks.

"Sex isn't the only good part of a book! God!" I roll my eyes.

Kaylee nods to me. "What she said."

"All right. How about we play Truth or Dare. You fill me in on all the dirty details of Brendon tying you up." Dean raises a brow.

"Is one of you going to explain why you're being extra weird?" Kaylee asks.

"I'm starting a cover design business." My limbs get light. This is really happening. I'm really doing this.

I'm admitting it aloud. To all my friends. While they mock me.

It's absurd, but it's right too.

I love these idiots.

"That's awesome." Kaylee's smile is bright. "Are you using Dean as a cover model?"

"If he's willing to pose for free." I turn to the guys. "You're all welcome to pose for free."

Ryan shakes his head. "My model fee is outrageous."

I can't help my laugh. "What is it?"

"Fifty percent royalty," he says.

"That is steep." Kaylee pulls her computer from her backpack. Sets it on the counter.

"Leigh designed a cover for your book," Ryan says.

I shoot him a cutting look. *How could you say that?*

He mouths *you'll thank me later.*

Kaylee blushes. "Oh, really? It's, uh... Can I see it?"

"You don't mind?"

"No. It's awesome. I have no design skills." She plays with the edge of her pastel pink cardigan.

I join her at the counter. Open my laptop. Pull up my designs—the simple abstract one, the one of Ryan, the sexy couple that reads *Desire*.

We start with the rose.

"Oh my God." Her green eyes go wide. "That's amazing."

My cheeks flush. Kaylee is always earnest. There's no way she's messing with me.

"Like something I'd see on a New York Times bestseller."

"Show her Ryan," Dean calls.

She turns to me. "Ryan?"

"Yeah, I, uh… he makes a great model." I tab to Ryan's design.

Kaylee studies it carefully. "Yeah, he does. That first cover is gorgeous, but I think this one would sell more books."

Ryan's eyes go wide. "You're not—"

"Can we?" I press my palms together. "Please."

"Ryan, come on. You're too beautiful to stay anonymous." Dean nudges his brother.

"You're indie publishing?" Walker asks.

"If I had a cover this hot, I'd have to." She giggles as she studies the guys' reactions.

I turn to Ryan. Push him with a bluff. "You wouldn't deny a young woman her dreams?"

"You heard my fee," he says.

"Let's cut that down to a flat rate." She motions *show me the next one*.

I do.

Her eyes glue to the screen. "This one is gorgeous too. Leighton, you're good at this."

My blush spreads over my cheeks.

"Really. I look at expensive covers sometimes. Consider

how much it would cost to put a book together. This—this is top-tier."

"I'm just..." I swallow hard. "Thanks."

Dean interrupts my moment. "What do you say, Kay? Need a model for book two?"

"I'm not offering a fee," she says.

He laughs. "Cold-blooded negotiator. I can see why Brendon likes you."

"That must be it," she says.

Dean turns back to Ryan. "You want more good news?"

"I'm terrified," Ryan deadpans.

"I set up interviews for new artists. A few are coming in tomorrow." Dean smiles wide. "Gonna be great."

"Yeah." Ryan runs his hand through his hair.

The shop quiets as Dean pulls him, and Walker, into a private conversation.

Kaylee settles onto a stool next to mine. Catches me staring at Ryan. "I'm not clear on your relationship with Ryan."

"His ex is getting married. I offered to pretend to be his girlfriend."

"Oh. That seems—"

"Foolish?"

"A little."

"It is."

She looks to me. "You like him, huh?"

I clear my throat.

"A lot."

"Maybe."

"It sucks, wanting someone you can't have."

"You have him now."

"Yeah." She pulls up something on her computer. "But I didn't for a long time. And I hated every minute of it."

"It would be worse, not having anything."

"Yeah. It would."

"He's good to you?"

"He's everything."

I try to focus on my design, but I can't. Ryan is whispering about something. And Kaylee is here.

She got Brendon to unlock his heart.

He's not quite as miserable and brooding as Ryan.

But he's in the same tier.

Fuck, it's embarrassing asking an eighteen-year-old for advice. But I know when I'm outclassed.

"How did you do it?" I ask.

"Hmm?"

"Get him to open up to you?"

"I'm not sure. But I'm glad I did." Her pink lips curl into a smile. "I wish I could be more helpful."

"I think you might have been."

"Really?"

"Yeah." I tap my heels together. "He's not coming in for another hour."

"I know. I had to get out of the apartment. Emma was driving me bonkers."

"Trouble in paradise?"

She laughs. "More like trouble with my headphones' soundproofing."

"She's having sex this early?"

Kaylee laughs. "Her music was too loud."

"Emma has great taste."

"But I can only take so much of it."

Ryan breaks from the conversation. Moves toward the counter. "You really gonna take Leighton's cover?"

"Not this one. But I'd love if she designed one." She looks to me. "I can pay you."

"No. It's on me." My lips curl into a smile. It feels good, being appreciated.

180

"We should finish your portfolio tonight," Ryan says.

I nod, even though it's nearly finished.

"My place. At seven. We can walk over after work," he says.

"I'll be here." I watch him return to his suite.

Kaylee turns to me. "You're sure it's one-way?"

"I was." But now…

Now it seems like there's a chance.

19

LEIGHTON

"I still say we should get street tacos."

Ryan shakes his head *you're ridiculous* as he locks the front door. He kicks off his shoes and tosses his keys on the dining table. "I'm cooking."

I slide out of my sandals. Set my messenger bag on the floor. "What if I want street tacos?"

"When's the last time you ate a home cooked meal?"

"You made me breakfast."

"That I didn't make you?"

Uh… It's been awhile. "I don't cook."

"Exactly." He slides his backpack off his shoulders, sets it on the plain black dining chair. "I want to know you're eating food."

My chest gets light. He's insisting on feeding me. It's some deep seated, primal love.

I argue anyway. "Tacos are food."

He makes that *get real* sound.

"They're a balanced meal. Meat, bread, vegetables."

"Vegetables?" He moves into the kitchen. "Really?"

"Avocados."

"Are a fruit."

"Salsa."

"Tomatoes too."

"Onions."

His eyes light up as he chuckles. "Whatever you want to believe, Leigh." He grabs a pan, sets it on the stove, turns the burner on. "Come here." His voice drops to this demanding tone. One I never hear.

My sex clenches. "Oh?"

"I'm gonna teach you how to make stir fry."

"I'd rather you make it for me."

"Me too." He coats the pan with oil. "But we're not gonna be able to do this forever."

"We're not?"

His eyes tinge with disappointment as he turns back to me. "Don't make me bring him up."

"Who?"

He shoots me a *really* look.

Oh. He means Mr. Powers. Because he still doesn't know I'm actually head over heels for him. "Why would that matter?"

"Let's not do this again."

"Yeah, but…" I bite my lip. I want Ryan to know. But only if he wants me back. Only if he wants more.

If he doesn't…

There's too much risk of losing him forever.

I follow him into the kitchen. "I don't see why you can't cook me dinner if I ever decide I'm dating again."

"'Cause it's fucked."

"How?"

"'Cause it is." He points to the fridge. "Get out the chicken breast."

"Do we have to use chicken breast?"

He arches a brow.

"It's slimy and weird."

"You like eating it."

"Thus proving my point about how it's better if you cook. You love cooking. I love eating. It's a perfect arrangement."

He shakes his head.

"Why not?"

"I'd never let some guy cook for my girlfriend."

"You're not some guy."

"I'm your best friend. It's worse." He taps the fridge with his sock-clad toes.

"Oh. Yeah. Sorry."

"We can use shrimp."

"Yes please."

"It's fussier."

"I'm used to dealing with you. I can handle it."

His chuckle wipes away that last hint of frustration. His eyes brighten. His posture softens. He turns toward me, inviting me into…

Into something. I'm not sure.

I press my lips together. "Where's the shrimp?"

"Freezer."

I reach into said freezer, find the package on the top shelf, next to a dozen packages of frozen spinach. "You're ridiculous."

"You get to be my age, you have to watch what you eat."

My laugh dissolves the last hint of tension in my shoulders. Playful Ryan is a rare treat. And he's all mine.

He's happy.

"You're right. That was insensitive of me." I set the package on the counter between us. "Forgive me?"

"If you ditch the sass."

"Not sure I can promise that."

His smile spreads over his cheeks. "Don't I know it." He

185

brushes a wavy strand from his eyes. "What do you want in this?"

"Whatever is the easiest."

"Carrots and broccoli are hard to overcook."

"Perfect."

He motions to the fridge. "Bottom drawer on the right."

"I know." I pull the door, crouch, dig through said drawer. I look up at Ryan as I hand over a bunch of carrots and a head of broccoli.

He looks down at me with a lazy smile.

The same as this morning.

The same affection.

The same intimacy.

The same easiness.

My head spins as I rise to my feet. But it's not my head. It's the world tilting on its axis.

There's a chance he'll be mine.

It didn't seem possible before, but now it's clear as day.

His eyes bore into mine. "You okay, Leigh?"

"Tired. I sat too much. I should have gone for a run." *Or we could go to your room and get our hearts pumping the fun way.*

"Not too late."

"I don't have my stuff." My cheeks flush as my eyes meet his. A giggle rises up in my throat. I try to distract myself by grabbing the cutting board, but I'm a nervous school girl. All thumbs.

"Maybe I should lead."

"Good idea."

"Hang back and watch."

I nod *sure.*

Ryan fills a small pot with water. "Easiest way to cook frozen shrimp is by boiling." He sets the pot on the stove, turns the burner to high. "You want to cook them until they're a light pink."

"How light?"

"Like a flamingo."

This could be our life—the two of us making dinner together, relaxing in *our* apartment, fucking in *our* bed "They eat shrimp, right?"

"That gives them the color, yeah."

"Oh. Duh." I trip over my tongue. "We... uh... we need rice, right?"

"Yeah. You need a play-by-play for that?"

My cheeks flush. He's teasing me. I feel it everywhere. "No. I know that much." I find the rice in the pantry, scoop a cup into the rice maker, add two cups of water. "I used to cook for my mom."

His voice softens. "Yeah?"

"Well, cook isn't the right word. I'd make her TV dinners. Or sandwiches. I got about as far as mac and cheese. But not the stovetop kind. The microwavable kind."

"You still fed her."

"I guess."

"Don't guess. You did." His eyes meet mine. "You were a kid. You weren't responsible for taking care of her."

"It felt like it. It has since I realized how out of it she was."

"But it wasn't."

I bite my tongue. "I didn't do a great job. We ate like shit."

"That why you love junk food?"

"No." I press my ass against the counter. "I hate junk food. It tastes like wondering why my mom wasn't there. I guess that doesn't make sense."

He shakes his head *it does*. "Still can't eat penne *arrabiata* without thinking of Penny."

"Penny making penne. That's—"

"It's Penelope now."

"Of course it is."

He chuckles. "That's what I thought."

187

"Did you eat it together a lot, or…"

"It was the dish she always wanted to perfect."

"She was the cook?"

He nods.

"Oh. Is that… is there some sort of *I don't need you anymore* to you learning to cook."

"Maybe." He stirs the shrimp. "It was more a distraction at first."

I nod.

"I gotta eat."

"You didn't for a while. I thought you were gonna disappear."

"Me too."

"I'm glad you didn't."

His eyes fill with something I can't place.

"I, uh, I've never had that problem. Of not eating when I'm miserable. If I did—"

"I don't want to hear any more shit about how you aren't a solid ten, Leigh. You know you're hot."

"But not thin."

"Your body is perfect."

I dig my fingers into the counter. Between the matter-of-fact tone of his voice and the freefall of discussing my mom…

This is weird.

I try to find something solid to grab onto. "I've always liked to eat. But I hate preparing stuff too. So I…"

"Eat nothing but street tacos?"

"Eat at restaurants a lot, yeah." I bite my tongue. "I'm sorry, we—"

"Don't apologize for sharing shit with me."

"We were having a nice conversation."

His eyes bore into mine. "We still are."

"Oh." The intensity of his gaze makes my knees knock

together. There's a possibility of me and Ryan. That changes everything. "What about you? Your parents cook?"

"The maid."

"You were that rich?" I swallow hard. "Never mind, I saw your house."

He nods. "They both worked too much."

"You love them?"

"Of course. They're assholes sometimes, but they mean well."

"I'm not sure you've ever admitted that."

"It's between us."

"Of course. My, uh, my hair this morning is between us too."

"It looked good."

I shake my head. "It was a mess. It's still a mess. And it's practically platinum."

He gives me a long, slow once over. "Looks good on you."

"Oh. Thanks. But I... uh... I prefer the lavender. Platinum is kinda trashy."

"Looks punk rock on you." He brushes a hair behind my ear. "Guess I should be used to that by now, Punk Rock Princess."

My blush spreads to my chest. "You, uh... what kind of stir fry are we making?"

"Craving anything?"

You. "Ginger. Like last night."

He nods to the fruit bowl. "Grab it for me."

I do.

He shows me how to peel the ginger with a paring knife. How to grate it into tiny pieces and warm it with the oil.

How to chop carrots and broccoli and set the pan at just high enough to cook without burning.

How to test the shrimp is done, drain it, add it to the pan.

189

We add rice vinegar, garlic, fish sauce, sesame oil, scallions.

I don't hate it.

Not even close.

Then we bring the plates to the table, and we taste our perfectly imperfect dish, and I fall completely in love.

With cooking.

And with Ryan too.

20

RYAN

Finishing Leighton's website takes until nearly two a.m. Not that we're on task. We spend half our time talking about nothing. Or teasing each other. Or trying to prove some point about each other's cover model worthiness by doing mock-up after mock-up.

I nail her bright smile.

She nails my "broody blue eyes."

She drags me to the couch to watch *Gone Girl*, spends the entire movie talking about how the cheating husband got what was coming to him, and falls asleep in my lap.

I carry her to the bed, brush my teeth, wash my face, take out my contacts, lay down next to her.

Fall asleep next to her.

An obnoxious beep fills the room.

It goes again. Again. Again.

Fucking alarm.

I blink my eyes open. Squint at the bright light flowing

through the window. Not that I can make anything out. I'm blind as a bat without my glasses.

Leighton's fingers dig into my t-shirt as she stirs. Her eyelids flutter open. Her blue-green eyes meet mine. A dopey smile spreads across her face.

Then she snaps up, blinks, shakes her head like she just woke from a weird dream. "Shit." She pulls her hand to her side, pushes herself up, slides out of bed. "What times is it?"

I reach for my cell. "Seven."

"You get up at seven?"

"Not normally."

"You set an alarm for me?"

What else would I do? "You have class at eight."

"Oh. Thanks." She smooths her sundress. "Am I really doing the walk of shame again?"

"Some of your shit is here. Check the closet."

"Really?" Surprise drips into her voice.

"You're the one who left it."

"Thanks." She moves to the closet, pulls the door open, pores over her options. She decides on something, but I'm not sure what it is beyond a black blur. "I'm gonna shower super-fast."

"You want breakfast?"

"No. I should leave now."

"Coffee?"

"I can get some on campus."

Fuck that. But I don't have time to object. She's already out of the room. The bathroom door—the one across the hall —presses shut.

Clothes hit the floor.

The shower turns on.

I move through my morning routine, dress, fix her favorite French roast.

The shower turns off.

I press my back against the counter. Then my palms. There's something about Leighton coming out of my shower, some intimacy there.

Different than before.

Fuck, last night was the first time another woman slept in that bed.

It was just sleep.

And we're just friends.

But my head keeps blurring that line. It keeps begging for more. For shit that can't happen.

She steps into the hallway in a tight black dress. Her hair is dry but messy. Her face is bare.

She looks just as gorgeous without makeup.

But knowing no one else sees her like this…

Her cheeks flush as her eyes meet mine. She smooths her dress. Adjusts its straps. "It smells like coffee."

"I can fill a thermos."

"Thanks." She moves to the dining table, takes a seat, digs through her messenger bag for her makeup. "I have more clothes here than I thought."

"You want a drawer?"

"Oh." She flips a compact mirror. Stares at her reflection as she lines her lips in red. "Yeah. If you don't mind."

I don't.

But then I can't offer her this either.

Not when she's after some other guy.

Not when—

Fuck, my head hurts.

I stay busy filling a thermos with coffee, fixing it the way she likes. I find a second, fill it with what's left, add a hint of cream and sugar.

It's warm, rich, sweet, but it's not satisfying.

Leighton swipes purple over her eyes. Outlines them in grey. Coats her lashes in black.

There's an intimacy to this too.

Like she's inviting me into her world.

I watched Penny get ready a million times. In the beginning, it felt like this.

Like she was mine.

But Leighton isn't mine.

She isn't gonna be mine.

I need to destroy that idea.

I down half my coffee in three gulps. Move to the table to hand Leighton hers.

She looks up at me with a blissful smile. "Thanks." She takes a long sip and lets out a soft groan. "Mmm. Perfect."

"We should go."

Her gaze goes to the clock on the microwave. "Shit. You're right."

"You could have eaten breakfast instead of putting on makeup."

"Girl's got to have priorities."

"Here." I find one of those individually packed bags of nuts in the pantry. And a banana. Hand both to her.

"What do I do with this?"

"You want to get creative with it?"

"No. I…" Her cheeks flush. "You're pushy."

"That news?"

"No. But I didn't realize you were this obsessed with feeding me."

"Someone has to do it."

She slides the snack into her bag, pushes herself up, slips on her shoes. "I'm glad it's you."

I want it to be more.

I want to keep waking up next to her.

To keep fixing her coffee, and cooking her dinner, and wrapping my arms around her.

I try to shake it off as I slide into my shoes, but the idea sticks in my head.

It gets brighter, bolder, bigger as we climb into my car.

I turn the key, let the latest pop hit masquerading as rock fill the car, pull onto the street.

Leighton takes another long sip of her coffee.

Her moan fills the car.

It drowns out the music.

And every one of my thoughts.

It takes every ounce of my attention to focus on driving. Santa Monica College is close, but traffic is already clogging the roads. It's not as bad in the morning, especially not this early, but it's enough to slow us down.

She lets out another low moan.

I stop at a light. "You fucking that or drinking it?"

"Can I really?" She draws a heart on the thermos. "Or could I skip right to marriage? This is like sex, Ryan."

"It's been too long since you've had sex."

"That hurts coming from you."

"Even I know coffee can't compare to sex."

"Maybe. Or maybe sex is overrated."

I shake my head. "No fucking way."

Her eyes meet mine.

"Nothing is better than sweaty, exhausting, can't stop until she's coming so hard you think she's gonna pass out sex."

Her cheeks flush. Her tongue slides over her lips as her eyes glide over my body.

It's an *I want to fuck you* look.

I grab the nearest distraction. "Still say you're wasting your time with this class."

The lust in her eyes fades to something I can't place. "I still say you don't know what it's like to start a business from scratch."

195

That's fair.

"Without rich parents to fall back on."

"I haven't taken their money since—"

"Who paid your tuition?"

"You want me to admit I have advantages having wealthy parents?"

She nods.

"Of course I do. And, yeah, there's a safety to knowing they'll bail me out of shit. But I haven't taken money from them since I graduated."

"I like working at Inked Hearts."

"Forever?"

"Until I'm ready to leave. Not until you think I'm ready." Her voice gets defensive.

My fingers curl around her wrist. "You're right."

"I am?"

"Yeah. I shouldn't push so hard. But you're so fucking amazing, Leigh. I hate seeing you waste your time."

"Even if it means I'm in your life more?"

"Even then."

"Oh. Well. Thanks, I guess. But drop it."

"All right. I won't tell you to leave."

"Good."

"You can start designing while you work at Inked Hearts. You can moonlight forever."

She shoots me a *get real* look. "That isn't dropping it."

"We made a deal. One month of you taking clients."

"And?"

"And advertising. We posted on three forums."

"I'm aware."

"You get any interest?"

"I may have had some."

"Leigh—"

"One person. That's all."

"You have to take it."

"Maybe."

"You already agreed to take it." Though that isn't going to buy me shit. If Leighton doesn't want to do something, she won't. End of story.

"But…" She takes a long sip of her coffee. "What if they hate my work?"

"They won't."

"What if they do?"

"You're amazing."

"You're amazing. You still have unsatisfied customers from time to time."

That's true. Sometimes, you never manage to communicate with someone no matter how hard you try. "Give them a refund and refer them to someone else."

"Maybe."

"They'll love it. I promise."

"What if you're wrong?"

"I'll tattoo *bigger than Frank* above my dick."

She laughs. "You will not."

"Will too."

"No, I can't allow you to mar your perfect body. But… Oh. How about this? You have to wear your glasses to work for a month."

Fuck, that is a horrifying idea, as far as mildly horrifying ideas go. "All right. Fine." I offer my hand.

She shakes. But she doesn't look triumphant. More scared.

"We should celebrate this. And you finishing your class." I want to celebrate her twenty-four seven. I want to celebrate everything she does.

"Maybe. Penny's party is the next day."

"You have it memorized?"

"Yeah. What's with having a joint bachelor, bachelorette party?"

"It's an excuse to get drunk."

She laughs. "But isn't the whole idea of a bachelor party so you can lament how awful it is to be tied to one woman forever?"

"You're asking me?"

"You are a man."

"All I wanted was to be tied to her forever."

Her eyes turn down. "And now?"

"I want that with someone. One day."

"With her?"

"Fuck no." The light turns green. I focus on the road. Two lanes all full of cars. Bright blue sky. Brown lawns and beige store fronts. "Someone else. Someone I can trust."

"Are you ready to trust someone?"

"I don't know."

"You're honest with me."

"I try."

Her fingers brush my wrist. "That means a lot."

"Same for you. I mean me. I mean—"

"I know." She traces the lines of the ink on my forearm. "I think I trust you more than I trust anyone."

"Yeah?" Traffic stops me. I turn to her. Stare into those blue-green eyes. She's back to the Leighton everyone knows —dark makeup, fierce hair, tight dress, *I'm friendly until you fuck with me* smile.

But there's something in her eyes.

A promise of more.

Or maybe a plea for it.

Or maybe I'm imaging shit.

I don't know how any of this works anymore.

A car honks behind us.

"Oh. Ryan." Leighton motions to the road.

Traffic is zooming. I hit the gas. Focus on driving the dozen blocks to school.

I pull up to a side street.

She lifts her bag into her lap. "Is it a fancy party?"

"Dean's wearing a suit."

"You have one?"

Somebody behind us honks. We're parked in the loading zone. We're the assholes fucking with the flow of traffic.

But I can't bring myself to drive away.

I shake my head.

"You want my help picking one out?"

"Yeah. Thanks."

"Saturday. After work." She pushes the door open, slides out, sets her bag on her shoulder. "I'll see you tomorrow, Ryan."

"You too."

I watch her walk away.

I think about her every second of my drive home.

A ten-mile run does jack shit to clear my head.

Leighton isn't gonna be mine.

Hell, as soon as this is over, she's gonna be someone else's.

I need to deal with that.

Whatever it takes.

LEIGHTON

I hold up a powder blue suit. "Color isn't going to kill you."

Ryan's hair falls in front of his eyes as he shakes his head.

"Really?" I wave the menswear back and forth. "This is fatal?"

"I'm not going to an eighties prom."

I point to the black slacks folded over his arm. "It's a beach wedding."

"You ever see me wear anything but black?"

"Once you wore grey."

"Black shirt that got faded."

"I've seen your closet."

"No shit. I gave you a drawer."

"In your black dresser, yes. Next to your black desk. And your black sheets. And your black blackout curtains. And if there were black lights that weren't actually purple stoner lights, I'm sure you'd have those."

"Black absorbs light," he deadpans.

The joke knocks me off course. It warms my chest. Sends butterflies to my stomach. "So not my point."

"Yeah." He chuckles. "But the truth."

"You have non-black clothes in there."

"Prove it."

"You sound like Dean."

"Where do you think he learned that shit?"

I can't help but laugh. "There were bright colors in there."

He shoots me a look *get real*.

I set the powder blue suit on the rack. It *is* a little eighties. Okay, really eighties. "How about navy?" I move to the next rack. Pick up a classy suit in a perfect soft navy. "It will bring out your eyes."

"So will black."

Like his glasses. Mmm, Ryan in glasses. Ryan in nothing but glasses. Ryan in nothing.

Ahem.

I shake it off. Move to another rack. The air conditioner's hum drowns out the elevator music. It's quiet in the menswear section. We're the only customers here.

"This is perfect." Ryan holds up the black suit.

"You'll look like you're going to a funeral."

"Maybe I am."

"Oh." Frustration slips into my voice.

"Not like that, Leigh."

I swallow hard. "Like what?"

The guy behind the counter motions to us *need help?*

I wave him over.

Ryan shoots me a look. *Was that necessary?*

I nod.

He moves close enough to whisper. "I feel a little less sick every time I see her." He runs his thumb over the soft black wool. "Part of me wants her to marry him."

"Part?"

"More every day." His breath warms my ear. "Three weeks and it could be all of me. This could be the end of her hold on me."

Or he could stand up during the ceremony and say *I know why you can't wed. I still love you.* And they could ride into the sunset together.

"Can I help you find anything?" The salesguy flashes us a serene smile.

"Yes, thanks. Can you convince my..." What the hell do I call Ryan? "Can you convince him he shouldn't wear black to a beach wedding?"

"It's whatever the bride wants," the salesguy says. "You must be used to that by now."

"No, we're not." I swallow hard. "It's not our—"

Ryan laughs at my nervousness. "All right. If you insist, baby. I'll try a grey suit."

"Excellent." The salesguy turns to me. "Please, have a seat. I'll make sure he's taken care of." He whisks Ryan toward the dressing room.

I settle onto the plush blue couch. Stare into the three-panel mirror. Between the smoky eye, the soft purple hair, and the raspberry lips, I do look every part the punk rock princess.

But it doesn't satisfy me the way it usually does.

Looking hot and tough isn't enough.

I want to *feel* safe, strong, desired, competent. My website is finished. It's ready. But I'm not.

I'm not ready to leave the security of Inked Hearts. To ask people to part with their money for my designs.

To give up seeing Ryan every day.

"Ms. Black, he's ready for you." The salesman offers me his hand.

I nod a thanks and follow him into the dressing room.

"Usually, we don't allow women in here, but seeing as

how we're empty, I can make an exception." He winks at me. *Keep this between us and buy something really expensive to thank me in commission form.*

I shoot him my best smile then step into the dressing room.

My jaw hits the floor.

Ryan.

In.

A.

Suit.

He...

I...

Uh...

He runs a hand through his wavy hair. "That bad?"

"No." I shake my head. Study every detail of him—the grey jacket hugging his shoulders, the white oxford shirt snug against his chest, the black belt securing his slacks to his hips.

The shiny black dress shoes.

Like he's ready to stand at the altar next to me.

I mean...

He...

Uh... "You look perfect."

"Yeah?"

"Yeah." Too perfect.

He picks up the lilac tie draped over a hook. "Can't remember how to put this on."

"I do."

"An ex?" He hands over the tie.

My fingers brush his as I take it. "My first serving job." I slide the short end under his collar and loop it twice.

"Bet you looked adorable."

"Definitely not."

"Too bad I can't beg your mom for pics."

I wrap the short end around the long end. "You can. She'll give you anything for a bottle of vodka."

"Leigh—"

"I'm not going there. Don't worry."

"That's not what I mean." His eyelids press together as my fingers brush his neck. "You want to talk, I'm here. Always"

I tie the knot. Slide it up his chest. "Another time." We're close. Barely inches apart. My palm stays flat against his chest. My other hand goes to his hip. "I don't like talking about her." My fingers curl into his belt loop.

"When'd you rock a tie?"

"High school?"

"What were you like then?"

"Younger."

His chuckle is soft. "Not what I mean."

My fingers climb up his chest. Brush his shoulder. "I was the same as I am now. But more naïve. Worse with my makeup. Shit at bleaching my hair."

"I can't imagine you naïve."

"I wanted to believe in people. Guys who said they loved me, mostly."

"You love any of them?"

"I thought so. But now… no. I know what love feels like and it's not that."

His eyes turn down. "You love…"

I swallow hard. "That's not what I mean."

"Yeah, it is." He brushes my hair behind my ear. "Don't handle me with kid gloves."

I shake my head.

He nods. "You've changed in the two years I've known you."

"How?"

His fingers skim my neck. "You don't walk around with the weight of the world on your shoulders."

"I guess not."

"You smile a hell of a lot more."

"Or maybe I smile more around you."

"Maybe. But when we first met you were the Ryan."

I laugh. "You have a good sense of humor about being miserable."

"I have to."

My voice drops to a whisper. "You smile more too."

"Yeah."

"You're happier?"

He nods.

"Because you're getting over her?"

"I am. But that's not it."

I stare up into his eyes. "Then why?"

"Leigh…" His fingers curl into my hair.

My eyelids press together.

He cups my cheek with his palm. Runs his thumb over my temple.

"Say it."

"Leigh…" His other hand goes to the small of my back. He pulls my body into his. "You know I can't."

"Please." I lean into his touch. "Please, Ryan."

"You." His voice is sweet. "It's all you."

I rise to my tiptoes.

His lips find mine.

It's soft.

Then harder.

My lips part to make way for his tongue.

He backs me into the wall. Holds my body against his as he pins me.

As his tongue dances with mine.

He tastes good.

Like mint and like Ryan.

It's different than our other kisses. Deeper. Realer. Better.

So much better.

My fingers dig into his skin.

His hips rock against mine.

His hard-on presses against my pelvis.

He pulls back with a heavy sigh.

I blink my eyes open.

But he's not staring back at me with joy or need or animal lust.

Those beautiful baby blues are filled with one thing:

Regret.

RYAN

Every molecule in my body is begging for Leighton.
I want to tear off that dress.
I want to plant my face between her legs.
I want to pin her to the wall and fuck her senseless.

But none of that is in the cards.

She isn't mine.

I'm not about to fall for a woman in love with someone else. Not again.

Her blue-green eyes fill with hurt as she stares up at me.

But there's nothing I can say to fix that.

Nothing I can say to change things.

Even so, words find their way to my lips. "I'm sorry."

She blinks and a tear catches on her lashes. Her gaze goes to the floor. She steps sideways. "I'll let you get dressed."

"Leigh." *Stay. Talk to me. Tell me it's me. That there isn't another guy. That there's only me.*

She responds by pulling the door open.

Her footsteps move through the hall.

I strip, hang the suit, change into my street clothes, pay.

But she isn't in the main room.

She isn't in the department store.

She isn't in the parking garage.

She's gone.

Ryan: Talk to me.

I spar until the dojo closes. I shower. I fix dinner.

My cell stays silent.

All night.

All morning.

She's there, behind the counter, when I get to Inked Hearts. Her eyes meet mine for a second then they go to the shop computer.

Dean shoots me a *what the fuck did you do* look.

I wave him off. Wash my hands. Wait impatiently for my eleven o'clock. Turn all my attention to his classic pinup tattoo.

But she's there when he checks out.

She smiles her usual *oh, please do go on about whatever you'd like to discuss, you're just so interesting* smile. Twirls her purple hair around her pointer finger. Presses her tits together as she hands over his receipt.

I walk him out.

Go back to the counter. "Leigh."

Her eyes stay on the computer.

"We're supposed to be adults about this."

"You're sorry. I'm sorry. What else is there to say?"

"Are you?"

"What?" Her voice is curt.

"Sorry?"

Her lip corners turn down. Her eyes scream *no*. But still, she nods. "I let the line blur. I won't do it again." She turns her entire body away from mine.

She might as well scream *leave me alone*.

I know her well enough to know there's no sense in arguing.

She's hurt.

She's insisting it was a mistake.

She's in love with someone else.

Fuck, something doesn't add up.

I try to find an explanation in my suite, but there's nothing. I'm still cursed with an inability to understand women.

Or maybe I'm just unable to understand women I care about.

We're quiet all day.

She leaves without saying goodbye.

It's the same all week. All business, no pleasure. No teasing her, or watching her eyes light up as she smiles, or laughing at the way she roasts me at every fucking opportunity.

I still bring her lunch.

And she still eats it.

And taking care of her still satisfies me in a way nothing else does.

But everything else stays fucked.

23

LEIGHTON

After I get off work Friday, I run until my legs are aching. I get home. Shower. Grab street tacos from my favorite truck. Eat them at my desk.

This is design round three. There are little things that need changing, but it's nearly done. It's a few tweaks from perfection.

And the client is happy.

It feels good, creating something out of nothing, meeting a challenge.

My hands move by instinct. I reach for my cell. Tap a text to Ryan.

Leighton: I finished my first design. What do you think?

But we aren't talking.

I… I'm not talking to him.

I'm running from my feelings again.

I delete the text. Consider calling Iris. But that also means facing my feels. Putting them into words. Figuring this out.

I will do that.

Eventually.

I turn off my cell and drag myself to the couch—it's too

far from the window and its amazing breeze. But there's nothing I want to watch.

Streaming bad TV is no fun alone.

Romantic comedies are salt in the wound.

I settle on a juicy thriller, but it's not the same without Ryan here.

I used to spend all my free time watching movies and TV. But now it feels like I need him here to enjoy pulpy twists and turns.

Maybe I just need him.

I fall asleep on the couch. Wake up to two more requests for covers.

After a run and a shower and a cereal breakfast, I pour myself into work. And I don't stop until I absolutely have to get ready for Penny's party.

I have to face my feelings.

I have to fix this with Ryan.

I have to tell him.

But, fuck, I have no idea how to do that.

RYAN

Moonlight bounces off purple hair as she steps onto the concrete.

She looks fucking perfect with her fancy updo and her soft makeup. It's not a Leighton I see often, a formal version of the punk rock princess.

She's as beautiful as always.

And as irresistible. Her black dress hugs her curves like it was made for them.

Her silver nails dig into her black bag. "Someone had to do it."

I arch a brow.

"Wear all black."

My shoulders relax. I need her smile. I need her teasing me. I need this awkwardness gone. "You look gorgeous."

"Thanks." She moves down the walkway. "You look great too."

"Thanks."

"Really. It's weird though, seeing you in a suit."

It's bizarre, being in a suit.

But it can't compare to the distance between us.

To the memory of her lips on mine.

Of that groan bouncing around the dressing room.

We still haven't talked about the kiss.

That's a million times weirder than dressing like someone else.

I tap the key fob to unlock the door for her. She moves around the car, slides into the passenger's seat before I get the chance to open the door for her.

I get into the driver's seat, click my seatbelt, turn the car on.

Melancholy music fills the car. I've been listening to this shit all week.

I've been a mess all week.

I can't stand it.

She clicks her seatbelt. Sets her purse in her lap. "It's in Beverly Hills?"

"Yeah." I pull onto the street. "Shouldn't be much traffic at this time."

She nods *sure*.

The singer croons about the agony of lost love.

I try to focus on the street and the wall between us. By the time I cross the freeway, it's helpless.

It's a perfect summer night—seventy and breezy—but the car is freezing cold.

"It's making me sick." I stop at a red light. "That you aren't talking to me."

"I'm just busy."

My eyes find hers. "Bullshit."

"No." She refuses to hold my gaze. "I did that first design."

"That's amazing."

"Yeah. Thanks. I'm just working really hard to make it perfect. And then I got my second client. And my third one. And I, uh… I'm busy."

"You didn't tell me."

"I didn't want to bother you."

"Leigh—"

She presses her lips together.

"You asked me not to lock you out."

"I know."

"Don't lock me out either."

She turns to me. For a second, her eyes meet mine. Then they go to my chest. She reaches over the dash to undo my tie. "You didn't quite—" She pulls the knot tight. "There."

"Leigh."

"The light's green."

It is. I turn to the road. Tap the gas. Glide down Santa Monica Boulevard.

Her voice is soft. Frustrated. "I don't know what to say."

"The truth."

"I will. later."

"Later?"

She nods. "Soon. I promise."

What the hell? "Let's go somewhere. Talk. I have all night."

She motions to the road. "We're almost there."

"I can blow this off. You're more important."

"Than your closure?" She crosses her legs. Smooths her dress. "I don't think so."

She's more important than closure.

Than anything.

That hole in my gut isn't as deep. I can think of Penny without my throat closing. I can picture her and Frank without going numb.

But thinking of losing Leighton—

My fingers curl into the steering wheel.

I breeze through a green light. Stare at the clear road. Suck a shallow breath between my teeth.

Things were good last month.

217

Sex always fucks shit up.

And this was just from a kiss.

I need to make sure it doesn't get worse. I need to draw that line between *real* and *pretend.*

To make sure none of it goes below the waist.

Hell, below the neck.

She breaks the silence. "I… I shouldn't have kissed you. I'm sorry."

Is she apologizing to me or to this guy who's her first choice?

I guess it doesn't matter.

She wants him.

I'm not gonna be the other man.

And I'm not gonna lose her.

"Me too." The words feel like a lie.

"Anything I should know about this crowd?"

"I'm not sure I know shit about this crowd."

"Oh?" She lowers the mirror on the visor. Checks her lipstick—still perfect. "You don't know her friends?"

"The old ones, yeah. But I can't imagine anyone who liked me is showing up."

She presses the visor to the roof. Presses her back against the fabric of her seat. "Yeah. You're the innocent one."

"I'm not innocent."

"But you didn't fuck someone who wears boat shoes."

"I'd never do that. I'd never be the other man."

"I know." Her lip corners turn down.

Is that regret or something else?

I don't know.

But I want to.

I want every thought in her fucking head.

It's different than it normally is.

Deeper.

More impossible to ignore.

I turn my attention to the road for the rest of the drive. Leighton taps something into her phone. Work or play or Mr. Powers, I don't know.

I park.

She slides her cell into her purse. Turns every ounce of her attention to me. "You ready for this?"

No.

But I'm tired of waiting for shit.

I'm tired of watching the world slip by my fingers.

STEPPING THROUGH THE WINTERS'S OAK DOOR FEELS LIKE stepping into the past. The living room is the same spacious paradise. White walls. Plush carpet. Sleek red couch. Cherry table.

Penny's life—from her birth to some vacation a few years ago—is on the wall, right above her younger sister's.

The room is packed. A dozen of Penny's friends. A dozen of Frank's—I assume the guys in khakis are his friends. And a dozen of her parents' business partners.

She must hate that she needs Daddy's money. That it comes with strings.

It doesn't satisfy me.

I'm not smirking over how far she's fallen.

I know her well enough to get how much it sucks.

Leighton's fingers intertwine with mine. Her heels tap the tile as she crosses the foyer. They sink into the carpet of the living room.

Her eyes narrow on something.

Penny and Frank in the corner of the room, clinking champagne glasses with her dad and some guy his age. A friend. Or Frank's dad.

Whoever it is, he's happy for them.

He's beaming.

She is too.

Her honey eyes light up as she laughs. She tilts her head back, downing the champagne in one go. Shakes her head *damn, that was a lot.* Looks up at Frank the way she used to look at me.

Asking for his approval.

His praise.

His love.

He gives it to her. He brings his glass to her lips. Smiles as she takes a long swig.

She rises to her tiptoes.

He wraps his hands around her waist.

They kiss like no one is watching.

Like they'll never get enough of each other.

"Ryan." Leighton's nails dig into my wrist.

She's trying to take the hit for me.

But she doesn't need to.

It still hurts, seeing them together. It's quick, like taking a hit during sparring.

It stings.

But it's already fading.

They're happy.

They're good together.

He's giving her something I couldn't. Something I don't want to give her.

Someone steps in front of them, blocking the scene.

Leighton pulls me closer. She raises a brow *you okay?*

I am. But I don't know how to put it into words. I don't know how to do anything but stare into her blue-green eyes.

They're beautiful.

They've always been beautiful, but they've never hit me this deep.

"Oh babe, I'm so glad you took my advice." Dean's voice booms through the room. It turns a dozen heads.

Casts attention on us.

It feels like time fucking stops.

Like everyone is staring.

No, everyone *is* staring. *Did the jilted ex really show?*

"Take your advice?" Leighton makes a show of shuddering. "How disturbing."

He hands a short, clear glass to her. "That's all vodka."

"Shit." Her fingers curl around the glass. "Thank you."

That must be three shots worth. I stare at my brother. Try to figure out his intentions.

Leighton says there's nothing between them.

I want to believe her.

But she's only close with a few people. Dean and I are the only guys.

One of us must be Mr. Powers.

It's not me.

That leaves him.

"About your tits." He slurps his Jack and coke. "They look fantastic."

She adjusts her straps. "Thanks. I think."

"Your ass too." He winks at her.

She rolls her eyes, but she still smiles. Until her eyes catch mine, and her lips curl into a frown. "What do you want?"

"Why do you keep assuming I have complex motivations?" He takes another sip. "I have a drink. I have tits to ogle. I have a train wreck to anticipate."

"Fuck off," I say.

"Shit, it's gonna be good." Dean's voice gets bouncy. "You want to bet on yourself? I'm giving five to one odds on you not causing a scene."

"Don't be an asshole," Leighton says.

"He can't help himself." I pull my wallet from my back pocket, grab two twenties, hand them to Dean. "You're on."

He chuckles as he slides the money into the pocket of his slacks—he's wearing a suit. Navy. Like the one Leighton was pushing. "What do you say, Leigh—"

"Don't call me that." She slides her arm around my waist. "Wasn't it bad enough betting on Kaylee's virginity?"

"That was nothing compared to some of his shit," I say.

Her fingers dig into my sides, pressing the fabric of my shirt into my skin. "You jealous she's having better sex than you?"

"Those are fighting words, babe." He tugs at his belt. "Don't make me prove how good—"

"How would that prove *you* enjoy it?" She rolls her eyes.

"You'll know by the way I groan." He winks.

I'm not sure if I want to laugh or deck him. "He is loud."

She scrunches her nose in disgust. "Too vivid of a mental picture."

"That's sound," he says. "Not image."

"It's an expression." Leighton shakes her head. "I'm gonna take that whole thing as a yes."

He shrugs. "Nobody's having better sex than Kay."

"What about Iris?" she asks.

He laughs. "Yeah. She was really fucking loud at Walker's birthday." He turns to me. "Who's your money on?"

"You," I say.

"Me?" He raises a brow. "Shit. Blood *is* thicker than water—"

"You're that in love with fucking yourself," I say.

Leighton pulls her arm over her stomach, doubles over with laughter. Vodka sloshes over the sides of her glass. Lands on the carpet.

Dean chuckles. "That was good." He raises his drink to toast "Didn't think you had it in you."

He leaves with a smug grin. But it's his usual smug grin. It's his default expression.

Slowly, she straightens herself. "Oh my God." She licks her glass clean. "That was so good."

"Thanks." I unpeel her fingers from her glass. Take a long sip.

"You hate vodka."

"Yeah, but I'm not gonna hold your hair back while you unload a bottle of Belvedere."

"My hair is too short to get in the toilet." She laughs. "But point taken."

I take another sip. I don't know the subtlety of vodka the way she does, but I can tell this is good shit.

Her fingers brush mine as she steals her glass back. "He deserved that."

"Just speaking the truth."

She locks her arm with mine. "You want a drink?"

"Yeah." We move to the bar.

She wipes her glass. Refills it. Finds my favorite brand of bourbon—did Penny really buy this for me?—and pours.

I take my glass.

Leighton holds up hers. "To—"

"Masturbation?"

Her cheeks flush. "Sure."

We clink glasses.

Drink.

Her cheeks flush. Her lips curl into a smile.

The rest of the room fades away. I forget about Dean's flirting. About the possibility of another man. About the reason why we're here.

I forget until I hear her voice. "Ryan, hey." Penny's fingers brush my wrist. "You look great."

Leighton fights a glare.

I nod *it's okay*.

223

She rests her head on my shoulder. "Oh, Penny—"

"Penelope."

"Sorry, Penelope. Great party. You look nice." Leighton forces her frown into a smile. "Not as nice as Ryan though." She turns to me. Runs her fingers along my cheek. "You look amazing in that suit."

My eyelids flutter closed. I lean into her touch.

This is for Penny's benefit.

But it feels so fucking real.

Penny's laugh is soft. "It is something, seeing you in a suit, Ryan."

"Thanks." My fingers curl around Leighton's wrist. If she keeps touching me, I'm gonna have my lips on hers in two minutes flat. Then I'm gonna have that dress at her waist, and her panties at her knees and—

"Would you mind if we had a moment?" Penny asks.

Leighton shoots Penny a serene smile. "I'm not sure I'm ready to leave Ryan alone. Not when he looks this good."

"I can imagine." Penny's voice is impossible to read.

I nod to Leighton *it's fine.*

She bites her tongue. "I'm gonna find a snack."

"There's a tray in the kitchen." Penny's smile is soft. Sincere. She watches Leighton walk away with that same friendly expression.

Then it's the two of us.

Her in a short ivory dress that screams bride.

Me in the kind of suit I swore I'd never wear.

She looks like the woman I fell in love with.

Like she's prepping for our wedding.

But I don't want that.

Not anymore.

I'm not sure what the fuck I want, but I know it's not that.

RYAN

"She's protective of you." Penny's fingers curl around the stem of a champagne flute. "It's sweet."

"She doesn't trust you."

"I wouldn't either." She takes a small sip of bubbly.

"You think you have to tell me that?"

"I trusted you."

That's not how I remember it. Not the last few years. It didn't make sense then. I was always loyal to her.

But that didn't matter.

Cheating wears down your trust. If you see a cheater every time you look in the mirror, you start to look for them other places.

If you realize you've been sleeping next to a cheater for two years...

I want to be able to trust Leighton completely. But, fuck, it's hard.

"I didn't trust other women. I knew how they looked at you," she says.

"What are you getting at, Pen?"

"She's lucky to have you."

"I'm lucky to have her."

"Both can be true." She taps the bar with her French-manicured finger. "I thought about what you said."

"You're the one who said shit."

"Okay. About what I said. I was too harsh."

"You're taking it back?"

"No. I meant every word. But it's not fair for me to blame you for what I did. It was innocent with Frank at first. We were friends. But I realized I was falling for him and I kept meeting him for lunch. I kept crying on his shoulder. I kept soaking up every one of his secrets." She sets her glass on the bar. "I knew what I was doing when I went to his place the first time. Deep down, I knew I needed to end things with you first. I really am sorry about that. I'm sorry I made you feel like it was your fault."

I bring my glass to my lips.

"It wasn't. We weren't meant to be, but that was my fault, not yours."

I shake my head. "You were right. I stopped respecting you. I started putting up walls."

Her shoulders relax. "Thanks for saying that."

"It's not for you, Pen. It's for me."

"It seems like it worked out."

"Yeah."

"She's fiery."

I laugh. "She is."

Penny laughs. "I guess that's always been your type." She brings her glass to her lips and takes a sip. "Are you happy with her?"

My jaw cricks. It feels good, accepting her apology, offering mine. But I can't have Penny in my head or my heart anymore. "Don't ask me shit like that."

"I care about you."

The words twist something in my brain. They're too

familiar and too different. I want every ounce of them and none of them. "Then stop."

"Ryan." Her nails dig into the stem of her flute.

"You lost the right to say my name that way a long time ago."

She sinks into her heels. "I'm sorry."

"Then prove it by respecting me—"

"I do."

Bourbon warms my throat. Sends my thoughts swimming.

"Mom is watching us." Penny nods to her mom, sitting on the couch with her dad. Mrs. Winters looks the same as always—pretty, well-dressed, some mix of classy and grown up wild child. "She's glad you're here."

"Me too."

"Really?"

"Yeah." I swallow another sip of bourbon. "You look happy."

"I am."

"Good."

She looks up at me. "Really?"

"I always wanted that for you."

"Even after I—"

"Not at that moment." But now, I do. I want to let go of that last bit of hate in my gut. I want to be free of her. "You love him as much as it looks like you do?"

Her honey eyes light up. "I really do."

My throat tightens, but a deep breath opens my airways. "Good."

"But the wedding stuff is driving me crazy."

"That's normal, isn't it?"

"I guess so." She takes a long sip. "I didn't realize Dad was going to be this hands on. I get he wants to use this as some bullshit write off, but it's still a wedding, not a business meeting. I try to tell Frank that, but he just reminds me Dad's footing the bill."

"He is."

"I know. And I know I'm lucky. But I wish he 'got it.'"

I arch a brow.

"Working at his company is a headache. Dad nixed my idea about a feminist column. He thinks it will alienate half our demo even though we're a women's interest site. When I told Frank, he took Dad's side—"

"That's just stupidity."

She laughs.

"Every guy knows better."

"Maybe. I'm glad he's honest with me, but—"

"Nobody's perfect."

"Yeah." She takes a long sip. "It felt good, being pissed about the injustice of it. But it would have felt better doing something other than dealing with makeup advertisers." She looks up at me. "Sorry. I know you hate hearing about my job."

I do. But that's not what's weird about this.

It's how much I see the Penny I fell in love with.

She's still there, under the layer of business casual. At least, a part of her is.

And a part of me wants her.

But it's smaller than it used to be.

Quieter.

"I can't believe I let Mom talk me into this party." She finishes her glass and sets it on the bar. "It's as bad as my eighteenth birthday."

"Can't be that bad."

She laughs. "No. I guess not. But it's pretty bad. This is my first interesting conversation all night."

"You don't show it."

"I know how to play Daddy's girl, I guess."

I nod. She fought with her dad a lot when we were younger, but she always knew how to get him on her side.

"It's all bizarre and formal." She smooths her ivory dress. "Not how a bachelorette party is supposed to feel."

"You need to tuck some ones into a stripper's g-string?"

She laughs. "Pretty much."

"Dean's somewhere."

"Dean hates me."

"Use reverse psychology. Tell him you hate strippers. He'll call one to ruin your night."

"I'll consider that." Her fingers brush my wrist as she brings her hands to her side. "But what if he starts stripping?"

"Not sure there's any way to prevent that." I scan the room for my brother, but he's not in my eye line. "You had to know that was a risk with inviting him."

"True." Her eyes linger on me. There's an affection in her gaze, but it's not an invitation. It's something else. "It really is good to see you happy."

"Thanks." I finish my last sip of bourbon. "I better find my girl."

Her smile is soft. "Don't let her mess it up."

If only I had any fucking control over that.

My shoulders relax as Penny turns and walks away. It's easier talking to her, but it still steals the warmth in the room.

I replace it with bourbon.

Leighton isn't in the living room—her purple hair makes her easy to find. I check the hallway. The bathroom. The kitchen.

There.

She's sitting at the dining table, dipping carrots into hummus, nodding along to whatever Penny's best friend Kristen is saying.

229

Kristen's dark eyes light up when she sees me. She leans in to whisper something to Leighton. From her posture, it's clear it's some gossip about me.

"There you are, baby." I move to the dining table with confident steps. "I've been looking everywhere."

Kristen's face goes ghost white. She stutters something. Shoots Leighton an apologetic stare. "Ryan, hey. It's been forever." She pushes herself to her feet. Moves in for a hug.

I offer her my hand.

She shakes with a nervous laugh. "I forgot you aren't big on touching."

"He's not like that with me." Leighton pats the chair next to her. "I was worried I was going to have to save you from a boring conversation."

"But weren't you just talking to Penny?" Kristen clears her throat. "I mean. Um. Are you two good? You and Penny? Don't tell her I said this, but it was awful the way she ended things."

The world is upside down today.

Penny is admitting wrong doing.

Kristen is apologizing.

Leighton is... I don't fucking know what.

"Thanks." I sit next to Leighton.

She slides onto my lap. Curls her arm around my neck and rests it on my shoulders. "Doesn't he look amazing in this?" She fingers the collar of my suit jacket. "I can't get over it."

"Like high school graduation." She smiles. "But more hair."

"Ryan had short hair?" Leighton runs her fingers through my locks. "Really?"

"Oh, yeah. A buzz cut. And the glasses—do you still wear those?"

Leighton runs her fingers along my cheek. She looks down at me. "A buzz cut?"

"Penny likes short hair. She was really upset when he grew it out. Which is kind of ridiculous. Honestly, you look way hotter with long hair, Ryan." Kristen blushes. "I mean…" She clears her throat. "Don't worry. I have a boyfriend."

Leighton turns back to her. "I'm not. You'd have to be blind to miss how smoking hot Ryan is."

Kristen smiles. "Where'd you find someone so fun, Ryan? I expected to see you with someone more like you."

Leighton laughs so hard she doubles over.

I slide my arms around her waist. "Baby, that hurts."

"I know. I'm such a bitch for laughing at that. But—" She bursts into another fit of giggles. "You know what vodka does to me." She turns back to me. Stares into my eyes with every ounce of earnest in the world. "You're fun. You just don't let anyone else know it."

Her eyelids flutter closed.

She leans in.

Brushes her lips against mine.

It's soft. A kiss for show.

But my body demands more. My palm plants on her soft thigh. My fingers dig into her skin. My tongue slides into her mouth.

She tugs at my hair as she kisses me back.

Fuck, I feel her everywhere.

The taste of her. Vodka and lemon and something distinctly Leighton.

The smell of that coconut shampoo.

Her nails against my skin.

I need more.

I need all of her.

I need her naked under me.

She pulls back with a sigh. "Fuck."

Fuck is right.

In too many ways.

Kristen stares at us dumbfounded. She clears her throat. "I guess that's one way to make it up to him."

She's still as tactless as ever. I'll give her that much.

Leighton squirms in my lap as she laughs. Her cunt brushes against my cock—there too much and not enough fabric between us—and her cheeks flush.

Her eyes bore into mine.

They beg me to rip off her clothes.

But this is still fucked.

She's still not mine.

Even if it feels like she is.

Even if every fucking second of this feels real.

"You, uh… how's the shop?" Kristen snaps a potato chip in half.

"Good. Ryan's a co-owner now." Leighton slides onto her seat. Presses her knees together. Fights a blush. "He's basically the boss."

"Oh, wow. Good for you. I always thought you were a good fit for tattoos," she says.

"Feels like I should take offense to that," I say.

"It's clearly a compliment." Leighton looks to Kristen. "Though I'm not sure what it means."

"You're just so… counter-culture, I guess. I could always tell you wanted to be somewhere besides our stuck-up school. And you have that look. Like a damaged musician or something."

"I love damaged musicians."

"Oh my God, what about that one guy who moans twenty-four seven? With the blue eyes? Kind of like Ryan's. But hotter. No offense, Ryan."

"I know exactly who you mean." Leighton winks at me then turns back to Kristen.

"He's so hot, isn't he?"

"And so damaged."

"He's a recovering drug addict, you know?"

Leighton nods *oh, I know*.

"Did you hear their latest album? It's dedicated to his wife. And it's just so... OMG." Kristen fans herself.

"Fuck. I miss something good?" Dean's voice booms through the kitchen.

"Yeah. We just finished a threesome. It's too bad. We were desperate for a fourth. So desperate we considered you." Leighton winks at Dean.

Kristen laughs. "It's good to see you too, Dean. You're so tall now."

"I was this tall last time you saw me," he says.

"Really?" She taps her shoes together. "Maybe I'm shrinking. It sucks being short."

Dean nods *maybe* and moves closer. "You want to do something fun tonight, Kristen?"

She beams over him remembering her name. "Sure."

"Twenty minutes. Out front. Limo." He smiles.

"Do I even want to ask?" Leighton shoots him a cutting look.

"You don't have to come to the real party if you'd rather go home," he says.

I'd rather take her home and fuck her senseless.

Which is exactly why I need to go.

"What's the real party?" I ask.

"There's one thing you need to have at a bachelor party." Dean smiles. "Everyone's coming. And maybe some people will be *coming*. It's supposed to be a classy joint, but you never know." His smile gets wicked.

Leighton whispers in my ear. "He doesn't mean—"

"Yeah, he does."

233

26

LEIGHTON

There's a limo idling in the street.

An actual stretch limo.

I suppose there's nothing strange about a limo on a Beverly Hills street, but this…

Dean is insane.

He smiles wide as he slides his arm around Kristen. His eyes catch mine. He nods to her like he's showing off his conquest.

I stick my tongue out in a show of disgust. I don't object to Dean's manwhoring ways. But bragging about a conquest? Gross.

A chauffeur steps out of the driver's seat and pulls the door open for us. He motions *after you* and extends his hand. "May I help you, madam?"

I let him whisk me inside. Purple lighting casts the maroon velvet seats in an eggplant glow. But that hardly matters when Iris and Walker are sitting on the bench in the back.

My shoulders relax.

I've been swallowing this for a week. I can't take it

anymore. I need to talk to her. To explain everything. Even if it comes with a *just tell him the truth*.

I plop on the bench next to her and throw my arms around her.

She squeezes tight.

"This something I'm gonna want to watch?" Walker chuckles.

"You're not invited." I release her and settle onto the bench. Turn to the door to watch Kristen, then Dean, enter. "Aren't we going to a bar?"

Dean takes a seat on the bench on the right. Pulls Kristen onto his lap. "Sorry, but this is the end of your vodka train. California law. Booze or full nudity."

"Good. I won't have to cart your plastered ass home." Ryan steps into the limo and takes a seat on the bench to the left. His eyes meet mine. They ask for something, but I'm not sure what it is.

Iris leans in to whisper. "What the hell did you do?"

I break eye contact with Ryan to whisper back. "I kissed him."

She mouths *fuck*.

I nod. Fuck is right.

"Guessing it didn't go well," she says.

"Not really," I whisper.

"You could have called."

"I know. I…"

"Wasn't ready to talk about it?"

"How do you know me so well?"

She laughs. "It's a curse."

The driver presses the door closed.

"Is this it?" Ryan asks.

"Penny and Frank are meeting us there." Dean laughs. "They probably want to fuck first. Or after. You're all gonna want to fuck after."

"He got this guilty look in his eyes then said he was sorry," I whisper.

"Does he know you're in love with him?" Iris asks.

I clear my throat. "I…"

She shoots me a *get real*.

"No. He doesn't."

She pushes me toward him. "Sit with your boyfriend."

I move to the bench next to Ryan. Shoot my best friend an *I hate you* glare.

She smiles back *I love you too*.

Walker whispers something in her ear.

She whispers back.

Then he's not quite whispering. I only catch the word *come*. But I'm sure it's dirty from the way she's blushing.

"I texted Kay to invite her. Since we're finally hitting an eighteen plus club. But she texted back something about not bothering her with my bullshit at work." Dean shrugs *how ridiculous*.

"Brendon's gonna deck you," Walker says.

"He still hasn't," Dean says.

"That's shocking." Ryan wraps his arm around my waist then stares at it like he's not sure how it got there.

Dean shakes his head. "I know. I need to up my game."

Kristen looks around the car confused.

Dean leans in to whisper something in her ear.

Her dark eyes light up.

They're dirty talking too.

The limo pulls onto the street.

I let my eyelids flutter together as I rest my head on Ryan's shoulder.

He says nothing as he draws lazy circles on my forearm.

It's a sweet, intimate gesture.

But I don't know what it means.

BRIGHT WHITE LIGHT BOUNCES OFF A SHINY POLE. A WOMAN'S manicured hand wraps around the silver cylinder. Then it's the inside of her knee.

She spins until she's a blur of bare skin and lingerie.

The hip-hop song shifts to the next. She dismounts. Looks out to the crowd—there are a dozen people seated *at* the stage and another two dozen at tables and booths.

The crowd looks back. Claps and hoots as the woman in red unhooks her bra and drops it beneath her.

Dean motions to an empty table in the back. Cuts through the room as the dancer leaps onto the pole. Upside down. Her hair hangs off her head. Her boobs fall toward her face.

It's an awesome trick—she's upside freaking down—but it's weird watching her do it topless.

I follow Dean to the table. Ryan pulls out my chair for me. A gentleman even at a strip club. That's so Ryan. And this whole thing is so Dean.

The dancer dismounts, struts around the pole, grabs onto it and spins.

"This place is classier than I expected." Ryan sits next to me. "For you."

Dean chuckles. "I have exquisite taste."

Iris looks to me and raises a brow. "She is really acrobatic." She looks to the stage curiously.

Walker chuckles as he wraps his arms around her. "Getting ideas, sweetness?"

"Maybe." She slides onto his lap.

He pulls her closer. Presses her lips to her neck.

"Shit. We didn't have to come here. We've got a free show." Dean claps.

"You shouldn't upstage her." Ryan chuckles.

"What if we get her blessing?" Walker murmurs into Iris's neck.

She mumbles some sort of *yes, please, don't stop*.

"Fuck, we lost 'em." Dean shakes his head. *How wrong*. His eyes light up as a blonde in a school girl outfit approaches us.

"Would you care for a dance?" She tugs at Dean's tie.

"Later. I'm waiting for the guest of honor." He shoots her a sweet smile.

She looks to the rest of us with invitation.

Kristen stares with curiosity.

Walker and Iris continue necking.

Ryan shakes his head *no thanks*.

Her eyes fix on me.

I clear my throat. "Maybe later."

She nods, spins on her Lucite heel, and leaves.

I scoot closer to Ryan. "It won't hurt my feelings if you want a lap dance."

His blue eyes narrow. "Think about everything you know about me and reconsider that statement."

"Most guys enjoy attractive women in their laps," I say.

Dean nods *true that*.

I roll my eyes.

"Am I most guys?" Ryan asks.

"No, but you are a man," I say.

"I don't hug people."

"Most people aren't naked women."

Ryan's nose scrunches with distaste. "Kristen's as cute as that dancer was."

She beams. "Thanks, Ryan. I think."

"Didn't hug her," he says.

She nods *yeah, that is weird*. She looks up at Dean *isn't he weird?*

Dean laughs. "You have no idea."

"But." I bite my lip. Where the hell am I going with this? Ryan

239

doesn't like touching. I know that. Of course he doesn't want a lap dance from a stranger. But he... and I... and... "You hug me."

"You're my girlfriend." He plays into our ruse.

I don't. "But there's a reason—"

"It's different with you, Leigh."

"Why?"

"You know why."

"Damn," Dean interrupts. "Look who the cat dragged in." He waves to Boat Shoes and Penny as they walk past security.

He smiles, completely at home.

Her eyes go wide with surprise. But the good kind of surprise.

She pulls him closer. Leads him to our table.

Iris dismounts from Walker's lap, but she stays pressed against him. Her eyes meet mine. She offers me that same *are you okay?* Look.

I nod. I am. Maybe. Sort of.

"I'm going to powder my nose." She pushes herself up. Her eyes find mine. "Join me?"

And leave Ryan alone with the ex from hell?

No fucking way.

"I'll be right there," I say.

Iris's eyes narrow *no, now*.

I wave her away.

She frowns, but she does leave.

Penny sits in one of the black metal chairs.

Frank sits next to her. "Thanks for the invite." He squeezes her hand. "Didn't think I'd ever talk you into this."

"Me either." Her laugh is tipsy. "I'm so glad to not be at that party. Thanks for coming. Sorry it was so dull."

Ryan looks to Dean. "You owe me two hundred bucks."

"Night's not over yet," Dean says.

A cocktail waitress in a black bikini stops at our table. Asks for our orders. Though I guess she isn't a cocktail waitress in a place that doesn't serve alcohol.

How do women strip in clubs that do serve alcohol?

Drunk people are obnoxious enough when you're clothed. When you're naked and they think twenty bucks gives them permission to grope you?

I shudder at the thought.

We order sodas and iced teas then share that *oh my God, how much is this going to cost* look.

"Aren't you joining Iris in the bathroom?" Walker scratches his head. "What is that code for?"

Penny laughs. "Girl talk. Of course." She smiles at me. "Don't let me stop you."

"No, I'm good right here." I force a smile. I know Ryan's trying to forgive her, but I just can't. She destroyed him. And his heart still beats for her. It's unfair. Wrong. Awful.

Dean raises an imaginary glass to Penny. "Glad you finally found someone who suits you."

She stares at him, assessing his words. "Thanks."

Boat Shoes squeezes her.

She giggles.

I whisper in Ryan's ear. "You think she knows that was an insult?"

"Probably." His breath warms my neck.

Penny's giggle gets louder.

Ryan's lips brush my neck. "I tell you how fucking amazing your hair looks like this?"

"No." My cheeks flush. "Not yet."

"It does." He plants a soft kiss on my skin. "Like you're offering me your neck."

I break character. "You're into—"

"Yeah." He pulls back with a heavy sigh. His eyes trace my

body. They light up with desire. Then he blinks and they're full of confusion.

"You do look cute," Kristen says. "Like a princess."

"My punk rock princess." Ryan's fingers intertwine with mine.

"Is that an actual nickname?" Kristen rests her hand on her chest. "That's adorable. I'm in love."

"They are a cute couple." Jealousy drips into Penny's voice.

It fills me with a deep, pure sense of victory.

She has a lot. She has his head.

But she doesn't have his body.

The waitress interrupts to drop off our drinks. Diet coke for me. Club soda for Ryan.

I suck the dark liquid through a straw. Bubbles burst on my tongue. Mmm. Fake sugar.

It's the same as pretending with Ryan—it satisfies for a minute but leaves me craving sweetness.

Another dancer approaches the table. She smiles as she struts. "Celebrating?"

"Our friends are getting married." He stands. Puts one hand on Penny's shoulder and the other on Boat Shoes's. "Can you help them make it special."

Boat Shoes's eyes light up.

Penny bites her lip. Excitement flares in her eyes.

"Congratulations." She trails her fingers over the straps of Penny's dress. "I'd be honored."

"How much for three songs?" Dean asks.

She unfurls her palm as she whispers in his ear.

He pulls a stack of twenties from his wallet and hands them over.

She slides them into a tiny purse on her wrist without counting. All her attention turns to the happy couple. "Follow me."

Dean winks *attaboy* as the engaged couple stand and follow the dancer across the room then through a sheer black curtain.

"What I'd pay to watch that." Dean shakes his head *too bad*.

Walker chuckles. "They make this thing called porn."

"Sounds like you're offering a performance. Walker, take it off. Surprise your girl when she gets back." Dean winks.

Walker laughs. "Don't think I won't."

Dean turns to his brother. "How about you? Ready to bare it all?"

"In front of you assholes?" Ryan shakes his head *no way*, but he's not really here. His attention is on that sheer black curtain.

"You want a dance? It's on me." Dean shakes his wallet. "But I insist on watching."

"You're not even looking at the stage," Walker says.

"That's too far away. I need something up close," Dean says.

"Since when are you nearsighted?" Walker asks.

"I like tits in my face. That a crime?" He looks down at Kristen. "What do you think? You want a dance?"

"Maybe." Her attention stays on the round stage. A pink babydoll hits the ground. The pigtailed blonde kicks it aside with her black heels. Rolls at the waist to show the crowd her ass.

Slowly, she lowers herself onto the floor, crawls around the stage and thrusts her pussy into some guy's face—inches from his face.

He tucks a bill into her garter.

"What about you, babe?" Dean raises a brow. "You willing to offer a show."

Ryan is still staring at the curtain.

He's not here.

He's not mine.

Is he ever going to be mine?

"What do you think?" I rest my palm on his thigh. "Should I?"

Finally, he looks at me.

"I can drag you to that back room. Give you an excuse to spy on her."

"That's not—"

"Or I could strip right here." I play with the hem of my dress. "Let everyone watch me grind against you."

He just stares.

Words rise in my throat without stopping in my brain. "Would you even care if I was naked in your lap?"

His brow furrows with confusion.

"What do you say, Ryan? Let's go. Right here." I climb onto his lap. Hike my dress up my thighs.

His hands go to my hips. "What are you doing?"

"We're at a strip club."

"Stop."

"Am I that repulsive—"

"You know that's not it."

"No. I don't know anything."

He pushes me off his lap.

I stumble backwards. Land on my ass.

Fuck. That hurts.

I push myself to my feet. Pull my purse from the table. "Excuse me. I've had enough of tonight." I spin on my heels. Move to the exit as quickly as possible.

But I'm not getting any closer to privacy.

He's coming after me.

27

LEIGHTON

I t's a breezy summer night, but my blood is boiling.

The freeway overpass roars with a steady stream of cars.

I turn toward the quiet street—what the hell is a strip club doing on such a quiet street?—and let the click-clack of my heels fill my ears.

Ryan's steady footsteps overpower them.

His fingers curl around my upper arm.

The possessive gesture undoes me. How can he be so fucking blind? How can he not see how badly I want to be his? How much I need him to be mine?

"What the fuck, Leigh?"

"Now you want to touch me?"

He makes that *what the hell* noise.

I pull my arm to my side, but it's not satisfying. It only rubs salt in the wound.

I keep my back to him. Take another step toward the streetlight. Not that it helps. We're in West LA, but we're still two miles from my apartment and these heels aren't made for walking.

Ryan follows, one pace behind me. "You promised, Leigh."

"What the fuck did I promise?"

"You'd tell me if I'm about to lose you."

"You're not." But that isn't true. Or maybe it is. I don't know. I only know I can't be here anymore. "I'm going home."

"I'll take you."

"Your car is at her place."

"I'll Lyft with you." His fingers curl around my upper arm —the left this time. He moves closer. Presses his crotch against my ass, his chest against my back.

It's not a sexual gesture.

It's a protective one.

I swallow hard. "I don't know if that's a good idea."

"Why?" Frustration drips into his voice.

He doesn't see this.

He's such a smart guy. How can he not see someone so obvious?

"It's just not." I hug my purse to my stomach. I tap my toes together.

He presses his body against mine. "Explain it."

"I want to be alone."

"I need to make sure you get home okay."

"I get home okay every day. I don't need your help."

"Let me take care of you, Leigh." His fingers dig into my skin.

That's what I want.

That's everything I want.

"Fine. But you're not coming in." I swallow hard. I want him taking me home, walking me to the door, escorting me to my bed.

Joining me.

Fucking my brains out.

Usually I'm okay with some of that. But not right now.

I need all of it. All of him. All his love and affection and tenderness.

He has so much to give.

I know it.

Even if he doesn't.

I keep my back to him as he pulls out his cell and calls a ride share.

"Three minutes." His voice is soft. "You're shivering."

I shake my head. Maybe it's cool this late, but I don't feel it. Not with my heart pounding against my chest. Not with him this close.

He slides his jacket off his shoulders then drapes it over mine.

I force myself to turn, but I can't bring myself to look him in the eyes.

He brushes a stray hair behind my ear then he wraps his arms around my waist and pulls me into a close, tight hug.

We stay like that for all three minutes. Until a car stops and a voice calls out, "Ryan?"

Ryan pulls away to nod. He opens the backseat for me. Motions *after you*.

I slide inside. Ryan follows. Seatbelts click. The door locks. The driver double-checks the address. Ryan confirms.

The driver laughs. "Must have been a fun night."

"Yeah." Ryan's voice is matter-of-fact.

I stare out the window to my right. Watch restaurants and office buildings blur together.

Night in Southern California is the same everywhere. The sky is a soft blue. Fluorescent yellow casts highlights and shadows over the expanse of beige sidewalks, charcoal pavement, green lawns, taupe Eucalypti branches.

Light, barely there stars.

Bright silver moon.

A sliver today. Almost nothing.

Would it be better if it was nothing? If the sky was dark?

What if I had to choose between a sliver and nothing?

My eyelids press together. My forehead sinks into the window's cool glass. The car glides over the empty road. Slows as it turns into my neighborhood.

Stops in front of my apartment complex.

Ryan's seatbelt clicks. His door opens.

No. I can't let him walk me to my place. I can't let him look at me.

I'm about to burst at the seams and I can't even explain it to myself.

Or maybe I can.

It's not that complicated.

I'm crazy about him.

And I'm painfully jealous of the hold Penny still has on him.

He opens my door and offers his hand.

I undo my seatbelt, grab my purse, and take it.

"Thanks." He nods to the driver.

The drivers returns the gesture. He says something, but I haven't got a clue what it is.

My nails scrape Ryan's fingertips as my feet hit the pavement.

He slides his arm around my waist as he walks me to the sidewalk, up the stairs, all the way to my apartment.

I press my back against the door.

"Leigh." His fingers skim my shoulder. "What the fuck is wrong?"

I shake my head.

"Talk to me."

"You pushed me away."

"You were trying to give me a lap dance."

I blink back a tear. "Exactly."

"What the fuck?"

248

I unzip my purse. Fumble for my keys.

"You're in love with someone else."

"No, I'm not."

His blue eyes bore into mine. "Then why does Dean—"

"It's not Dean." There. I wrap my fingers around my key.

His brow knits with frustration. "Who the fuck is it?"

"How can you not see this?"

"You know anything about me?" That same frustration drips into his voice. "I can't see shit."

"This has nothing to do with Penny."

"Doesn't it?"

"You still love her."

His hair falls in front of his eyes as he shakes his head.

"You were staring at that curtain like you were desperate to be the one with her—"

"Because I couldn't believe she wanted a lap dance."

"No." I shake my head.

"You know how I feel?"

"You're in love with her."

"No." His fingers curl around my right wrist. He pins my arm to the door. "Not anymore."

My body betrays me. It crumbles under his touch. It begs for his hands *everywhere*. I freeze, unable to do anything but stare back at him.

"What if I was?" He stares back at me. "Who the fuck are you to call me on that?"

"You don't love her anymore?"

"No."

"At all?"

"Leigh, what the fuck?"

"Answer the question!"

His eyes go to my wrist. He stares at his hand like he's not sure how it got there. Releases me. Takes a half step backward. "There's a part of me wrapped up in her, but it's shrinking."

"But you—"

"Don't give me shit about this. You're in love with someone else."

"No, I'm not."

"Yeah, you—"

"No, Ryan." I stare into his eyes. "I'm not losing sleep over Dean, or Brendon, or Walker. Or any other guy I know. It's you."

His eyes go wide.

"You're Mr. Powers." I swallow hard. "You're the guy I can't get out of my head."

RYAN

You're the guy I can't get out of my head.
The words bounce around my brain.
It's me.
The guy who has her heart, who doesn't want her back, who's such a fucking idiot he doesn't see what's right in front of his face—

That's me.

My fingers curl around her wrist. I can't let her leave. Not now. Not until I wrap my head around this. "What?"

"It's you." Vulnerability fills her eyes. "It's always been you."

"But—"

"You're my favorite part of every day." Her fingers brush my neck. "You're my favorite person in the world."

"But Dean—"

"Is an idiot."

"Yeah, but—"

"We're only friends. Ryan, I'd tell you if there was anything between us. If there'd ever been anything between us." She stares into my eyes. "There hasn't."

"It's me?"

"Is that really surprising?"

Yeah. It's incomprehensible. "You let me believe it was him."

"I told you it wasn't a million times."

"You let me believe it was someone else."

"I wasn't ready to risk losing you."

"You'd never—"

"Yeah, I would. If you'd known, you would have locked me out. To help me get over you." Her hand knots in my hair.

She's right.

I'd do anything to protect Leighton.

Even something as awful as backing away from our friendship.

"You, um…" She presses her lips together. "You aren't saying anything."

"It's really me?"

"Yeah."

"For how long?"

"Since the day we met. But that was a crush. Now that I actually know you…" Her eyes bore into mine. "Are you really over her?"

"Almost all the way."

"Do you think about me?"

"I try not to."

"But you do anyway?"

My nod is heavy. "You?"

"All the time." Her eyelids press together. "You need to kiss me now."

My eyelids flutter closed. I pull her closer. Let my lips brush hers.

It's soft. Slow. Sweet.

Then it's harder.

She tugs at my hair.

I pin her to the wall.

She parts her lips.

I slip my tongue into her mouth.

Two years.

She's wanted me for two years.

And all this—

Fuck, my head is spinning. I don't know what to say. How to handle this.

Leighton wants me.

It makes no sense.

And it makes every lick of sense in the world.

She sighs as she pulls back. "Inside. Now."

I shift my hips backward to release her.

Her ass brushes my crotch as she turns and unlocks the door. She slides it open and steps inside.

I follow her, locking the door behind me.

She shrugs my suit jacket off her shoulders and hangs it over the side of the couch.

Her eyes find mine.

They beg for love, trust, satisfaction.

I still don't know shit about the first two.

But I can make her come.

I need to make her come.

Now.

I press my lips to hers. Soak up every ounce of her need. Home in on every place she hurts.

I want to be her salve.

The key that unlocks her.

The puzzle piece that makes everything click together.

Is that love?

I don't know.

I don't know what to tell her.

Only that I need her.

Fuck, how I need her.

I peel her dress up her thighs. Over her ass.

She groans as my fingers curl into her lace panties. "Ryan."

I pin her with my hips. Grind my hard-on against her pelvis.

Her fingers fumble over my belt. "Too many clothes."

I peel her panties to her thighs.

"Ryan…"

My lips skim her neck.

She groans as she undoes my belt. My button. My zipper. "Mmm." Her palm brushes my cock. "I love that you go commando."

"Leigh." Fuck, that feels good.

Her other hand knots in my hair. She holds my head against hers as she brings her lips to mine.

I kiss her hard.

My tongue dances with hers.

My need pours into her.

And hers pours into me.

I'm kissing Leighton. I'm kissing my best friend.

My brain can't comprehend it.

She wraps her fingers around me. Strokes me harder.

I drag my fingertips up her thigh.

She groans against my lips as they get closer, closer, closer—

There.

She nips at my bottom lip as she strokes me.

I rub her harder.

Her groan vibrates down my neck.

I draw circles on her clit. Soft. Slow. Hard. Fast. Right. Left. There—

"Fuck." Her blue-green eyes fill with pleasure.

She looks so fucking beautiful like this.

I watch pleasure spread over her face as I rub her.

Her eyelids press together.

Her lips part with a sigh.

Her hands fall to her sides.

I have to pin her with my hips to keep her upright.

"Ryan." She slides her hand into my hair. "Fuck."

I rub her with those same perfect circles.

Her neck tilts backward. Her head presses against the wall. Her thighs spread wider.

She's inviting me into her body.

Opening herself to me.

It's everything I want.

Leighton is everything I want—her heart, her head, her body.

I still don't know shit about the first two.

And this—

Fuck, it's been awhile.

I need to know her. Every inch of her. Every place that makes her purr.

She groans against my mouth as I tease her with one finger.

Two.

Three.

"Fuck." She throws her head back. Leans her weight against the wall.

Her teeth sink into her lip as I slide three fingers inside her.

"Fuck, you're wet." I drive my fingers deeper.

"Ryan." Her breath is as heavy as her nod. "More. Now."

I bring my thumb to her clit. Rub her as I fuck her with my fingers.

Her lips find mine.

She groans against my mouth, rocking her hips to grind against my thumb.

It feels so fucking right, bringing her all this pleasure.

She feels so fucking mine.

I need her to be mine.

She pulls back with a heavy sigh. "Fuck. Ryan. Oh God."

"Louder."

"Ryan." She turns her head to one side as she groans my name again and again.

She pulses against my fingers as she comes.

When she's finished, I release her. Bring my hand to my lips. Suck the taste of her from my fingertips.

She stares at me in a trance. Lust or love or need, I don't know. But I know I need it.

All of it.

"Take off your dress," I demand.

"Take off your suit."

"Come here."

She moves closer. Undoes the knot of my tie and tosses it aside. Fumbles over my buttons. Pushes my shirt off my shoulders.

I kick off my shoes. Step out of my slacks.

Her eyes stay glued to mine as she undoes the zipper of her dress.

She pulls it over her head and lets it fall to the floor. "Bed now."

Her apartment is tiny. It's a dozen steps to her bed. I fall backward onto it. Take her hands. Pull her body on top of mine.

She stares down at me with every ounce of affection in the world.

I drag my fingertips up her stomach. Over her breasts, collarbones, shoulders.

I cup her over her bra.

She reaches behind her back to unhook the black lace then slides it off her shoulders.

"Fuck." I bring my thumb to her nipple. "So much better than I imagined."

She groans as I draw circles around her nipple. "I'm safe. And I'm on the pill. If you're—"

"I am. You sure?"

"A hundred percent." She plants her palms on my chest and slings her leg over my hip. "I feel like I'm in a dream."

"You are my dream." I press my palm against her back to pull her closer.

She gasps as I bring her nipple to my mouth. "Fuck."

I suck softly. Then harder. She tastes so fucking good.

And the way she's responding to me—

Fuck.

I bring one hand to her hip. Guide her body over mine.

My tip strains against her.

Then it's one inch at a time.

Fuck.

I suck harder on her nipple.

"Ryan." She knots her hand in my hair. "Oh God."

Her groan is exactly what I need.

It's everything I need.

She stares down at me as she rocks against me.

That's Leighton on top of me.

That's her soft, sweet cunt wrapped around me.

That's her groan filling the room.

I toy with her nipples as she fucks me. Watch her brow knit with pleasure. Watch her lips part with groan after groan.

She reaches to her hair, pulls out the pins, lets it fall over her cheeks. "You feel so fucking good." She digs the heel of her hand into my chest. Uses it for leverage to lift her hips then drive down on me.

My last conscious thought flees my brain.

My world is a blur of Leighton. Her purple hair falling in

front of her blue-green eyes. Her red lips curling in pleasure. Her nails digging into my chest. Her cunt pulling me deeper.

Her groans run together.

They get higher.

Needier.

I bring my thumb to her clit. Rub her as she drives down on me.

"Ryan, fuck." A groan falls off her lips. Another. Another.

She drives through her orgasm, rocking her hips against me, grinding against my cock and fingers.

I flip her onto her back. Pry her thighs apart. Plant my hands outside her shoulders.

With one hard thrust, I drive into her.

She wraps her hands around my back to pull me closer.

My body sinks into hers.

Her legs wrap around my thighs.

My lips find hers.

I thrust into her with steady strokes. I savor every soft, wet inch of her. Every groan. Every gasp.

Every fucking part of her.

We stay pressed together, limbs tangled, tongues dancing together until I'm there.

Pleasure spreads out from my pelvis.

My cock pulses as I come inside her.

Fuck.

I rock through my orgasm. Once I've spilled every drop, I collapse next to Leighton and wrap my arms around her.

She looks up at me with a hazy smile.

I pull her closer.

And I hold her like I'm never going to let her go.

29

LEIGHTON

L ight bounces off the hardwood floors. It's soft. White. Morning light. *It's way too early to be awake light.*

But there isn't a single part of me that wants to stay asleep.

The apartment is warm. The air smells like coffee. And Ryan is sitting at my dining table wearing nothing but a smile.

Soft light falls over his hard body. My fingers itch to trace the lines of his muscles. His ink. His smile. The soft tuft of hair just beneath his belly button—

"My eyes are up here." He stands.

With me lying down, his cock is right at eye level.

I...

Uh...

"You're objectifying me." He reaches for something on the table. Brings it to his lips. Really, above the waist it's all a blur.

"Was that ever a question?" I prop myself on my elbow. Force myself to stare into his piercing blue eyes.

They're wide with enthusiasm, joy, satisfaction.

He's still smiling.

There isn't a single hint of frustration in his expression.

Ryan's happiness is the best thing I've ever seen.

Okay, it's second to watching him come. But that's not a fair competition.

"I'm more than a beautiful face." He offers me his mug of coffee.

The sheets fall to my chest as I push myself up. "Your body is also amazing."

My fingers brush his as I take the cup. It's good coffee. Dark. Strong. Just enough half-and-half and Sugar in the Raw to make it sweet and creamy.

"Mmm. Amazing." I try to hand it back.

He shakes his head *keep it.*

"Thanks." I revel in my second sip.

"You don't have any food."

"I never have food."

"I'm gonna change that."

"You're going to stock my fridge for me?"

"Yeah." Light falls over his side and torso as he sits next to me on the bed. "You got a problem with that?"

"Will you cook it for me too?"

"Try and stop me."

My smile spreads over my cheeks. I scoot closer to him. Until my thigh is pressed against his. And my shoulder is against his. And I can feel all the warmth of his skin against mine.

His fingers brush my thigh. He draws circles over my skin, a mindless gesture that screams *I love you.*

My fingers skim his temples. "You already put in your contacts?"

He nods.

"I don't get Ryan in glasses?"

His brow rises with surprise. "You like them?"

"Of course." My voice gets dreamy. "I love them."

"Don't have them on me."

"Will you wear them at your place?"

"You like them that much?"

My nod is the definition of enthusiasm.

He brushes a stray hair behind my ear. "I don't know. Can you convince me?"

My sex clenches. Yes. I should convince him. I should drop this coffee and convince him right now.

I restrain myself.

Take a long sip. Offer him the mug.

He shakes his head. "It's yours."

"I think I love you." My cheeks flush. "I mean, um, it's just an expression."

"I know."

I hide behind my mug.

"Do you?"

I do. And I'm pretty sure he knows. But I'm not ready to say it yet. Not so straightforwardly. "I have a strict policy. No declarations of affection for twenty-four hours after sex."

"The oxytocin fucks with your judgment."

I nod. "Mmm. I do like an educated man."

He chuckles. "College had its uses."

"There is the oxytocin. But it's more that it's easy to love someone who's making you come." I slide off the bed. Leave the cup on the table. Spin on my heels so I'm eye to eye with Ryan. "Usually, it's twelve hours. But I had to double it on account of how great the sex was."

His smile spreads over his face.

My cheeks flush. This is weird. Amazing, but weird. I'm a giggly schoolgirl again. I'm on a fucking cloud. I'm floating.

My hand finds his hip. God, will I ever get tired of touching him? Soft skin. Hard muscles. All those lines of ink.

And it's Ryan.

My best friend.

My favorite person in the entire world.

The guy I've been lusting after for two years is still naked in my apartment.

I've died and gone to heaven. Really, I have.

"This is surreal," I whisper.

"Good surreal." His lips skim my neck. "We're due at work in two hours."

"Can we ditch? Stay in bed all day?"

"You can, yeah. I have appointments."

"Have Dean do them."

He shakes his head in horror.

"Kidding."

"I know." He releases me as he takes a step backward. "Let's go out. I'll buy you breakfast."

"What about your car?"

"Dean moved it into our parents' driveway. I'll get it tonight."

"He has your keys?"

"Parents have a spare."

"What do they think of Penny?"

"They don't know why it ended. Think I was an idiot to leave her." He shrugs. "They'll get over it."

Have you? Are you all the way there yet? I bite my lip. I can't bring myself to ask. I don't want to hear the answer. I don't want to think about her.

Right now, everything is perfect.

I want to float on that for a while. "Dean's been trying to help me. I think."

"Help you do what?"

"Get in your pants."

"Dean helping someone get laid isn't weird."

"But it's more—"

"I know."

"He warned me not to hurt you."

He raises a brow. "That's ridiculous. You wouldn't—"

"I know. But I did."

He nods. "Yeah. But it wasn't you. It's me."

No. It was my lie of omission. But why retread ugly things?

He grabs his slacks-currently hanging over a chair—and steps into them.

"Do we have to get dressed?"

"Fuck no."

"We could—" My stomach interrupts me with a low growl.

Ryan laughs. "We will. After."

"But work-"

"After that."

I pout.

His chuckle fills the room. "Get ready. We'll eat. I'll make you come later."

"You promise?"

"You're gonna have to beg me to stop."

"Two." Ryan smiles at the hostess. *Yeah, I wore this last night. What's it to you?*

She giggles as she hugs two menus to her chest. "Right this way, sir."

He's still wearing his suit. I'm in a casual dress and wedge sandals and he's in a suit.

God, he wears that suit.

How can he look so good in everything? And nothing?

He presses his palm into my lower back to lead me to our table.

The hostess arranges our menus then motions to our seats. "Your server will be with your shortly." She shoots Ryan another nervous smile then gives me one of those *is she really competition* once-overs.

He catches her staring. Wraps his arms around my waist. Pulls me into a long, deep kiss.

The possessiveness of the gesture sets me on fire.

Does he want that as badly as I do?

He must.

I sigh as he pulls back. My knees knock together. I press my palm into the table to steady myself, but it's not enough.

Ryan brings his hands to my hips. He helps me onto the bench seat then slides in next to me.

My heartbeat picks up.

I'm all thumbs again. I can barely open my menu.

Ryan runs his fingers over the hem of my dress. "You all right?"

I nod.

"You really get your first three clients last week?"

"Yeah."

"That's amazing, Leigh."

"Thanks."

"You start work on them?"

I nod.

"Can I see?"

"Of course." I pull up my cloud storage app and find the designs. The first—a historical romance with a woman in a glorious dress—is done. The second two, both smutty covers with shirtless models showing off their six-packs, are works in progress.

I hand the phone to Ryan.

He studies each image like it's something going on his body.

The waitress stops by. We order. He continues staring.

She drops off our coffees.

He continues staring.

I down my entire mug in three long sips.

He continues staring.

Finally, he hands my cell back. His knee brushes mine as he turns toward me.

He stares into my eyes. "Fucking amazing."

My blush spreads to my chest. There's so much earnestness in his voice, his eyes, his smile. Praise from Ryan is rare. And it's always earned. "Thank you."

"I mean it."

"I know." I want to believe it, that I'm good enough to do this on my own. That I'm skilled enough to deserve Ryan's praise. "You're my biggest fan."

"I am." He runs his fingertips over my chin. "We didn't celebrate your class finishing."

"We weren't talking."

"You weren't talking to me."

"You apologized for kissing me."

"I thought you were in love with Dean."

"I know." I lean into his touch as he runs his fingertips down my neck.

"If I'd know it was me—" He traces the neckline of my dress. "Fuck. I don't know what I would have done. I can barely comprehend it now."

"Really?"

"Yeah." He leans in to press his lips to mine.

It's a soft, slow kiss.

It isn't enough.

But then nothing is enough.

He pulls back with a needy sigh. "Hold on." He leans in for another kiss. This time, his teeth scrape against my bottom lip. His tongue dances with mine. His groans vibrate down my throat.

The kiss is a promise.

I want you. I need you. I'm going to make you come until you pass out.

He pushes himself from his seat and disappears around the corner.

I take a minute to check my makeup with my cell phone camera. Winged eyeliner, under eye concealer, bronzer, brows, berry lipstick. I look awake and badass and over the fucking moon.

But I don't need the camera to tell me that.

Ryan slides back into the booth. His leg nudges mine. His fingers brush my thigh.

They go higher, higher, higher.

Then they slide under my dress.

I press my forehead to his chin. "Fuck, Ryan."

"Yeah?" He drags his fingers higher.

Higher.

Higher.

His fingertips skim my panties. The soft fabric brushes against my sex. It's too much friction. And it's not enough.

I need his hands on me. "Please."

"Here?"

"Yeah."

"We'll get arrested." He rubs me over my panties.

"I don't care." My breath hitches in my throat.

"At the shop."

"*At* the shop?"

"Yeah." His index finger finds my clit. He rubs harder, pressing cotton into my tender flesh. "I'm gonna wait until everyone's gone, then I'm gonna set you on the counter, tear off these panties, and lick you until you're screaming my name."

"Ryan—"

"Yeah, baby?"

266

The term of endearment sets me on fire. It isn't the first time he's used that pet name, but it's the first time it's been for *me*. "Say it again."

"Say what again, baby?"

"Mmm."

He rubs me harder.

"Please."

"You can beg all you want. You're still gonna wait."

My eyelids press together. My fingers dig into my knees. Then into his. It's too much. I'm too close. I need to come. I need him. I need—

"I hear we're celebrating something." The waitress's voice snaps me out of my lust.

I press my knees together and slide into the booth, breaking his touch.

Fuck, every part of me is buzzing.

I can barely see straight. The waitress is setting down something. A plate of blueberry pancakes. Only there's a lit candle in the stack.

She smiles as she drops off Ryan's house omelet, refills our coffees, takes her leave.

Candle.

Pancakes.

Breakfast.

Oh.

He waits until she's out of earshot to motion to the plate. "We need to celebrate you finishing your class."

"My what doing what?"

"You all right, Leigh? You look—"

"Like I need to come."

His smile gets cocky. It should be obnoxious, but it's not. It's so fucking hot, him reveling in how desperately I'm wound around his finger. "Yeah."

"Ryan—"

"Yeah, baby?"

My groan isn't even close to a word.

He brushes his lips against my check then nips at my earlobe. "This is accomplishment, Leigh."

That sounds reasonable. Maybe. My body is still screaming for his touch.

"And getting your first clients. It's fucking amazing."

I suck a breath between my teeth. Let out a heavy exhale.

My nerves settle enough for me to grasp what we're doing here.

There's a candle on my pancakes. To celebrate my class ending. It's weird and cheesy and sweet as sin.

"Grades in?" he asks.

I nod.

"What'd you get?"

"An A."

"You're on your way." He motions to the plate of pancakes. "Blow it out."

"Do you really make a wish for this?"

"Yeah."

"Says who?"

"Me."

"Fair enough."

God, the pride in his eyes. It does something to me.

It makes the world into a beautiful place.

I let my eyelids flutter together, I lean in, and I make a wish.

I want to have him forever.

I blow the candle out.

"I know you're gonna leave soon." He hands me my fork. "And, fuck, I'm gonna miss you. It's gonna suck not seeing you all day. But I'm happy for you."

"Not that soon."

"Where'd you find time to do all those designs?"

"I wasn't exactly sleeping."

"And now?"

I shake my head. "I can't. Not yet." I cut off a slice of pancake and bring it to my lips. Mmm. Sweet, fluffy, fruity perfection. "Inked Hearts is the only place that's ever felt like home."

He nods *I get that*.

But his eyes scream *you need to move on.*

30

LEIGHTON

Dean launches into a slow clap.

His eyes find mine as I step inside. He raises a brow. *How was it?*

I nod to Ryan. *What do you think?*

He shrugs *who knows*. His attention turns to Walker—who's standing at the counter next to him. They share one of those best friend looks.

Walker fights a chuckle, but he doesn't make it.

He laughs as he joins Dean's slow clap.

Then Brendon steps out from his suite—what is he doing here this early?—and surveys the scene. He shoots me his usual paternal look. "These idiots bothering you?"

"No." I fight my smile. This is sweet in a Dean kind of way, but it's so not his business. "They're just confused. They don't know what a satisfied woman looks like."

Walker mimes rolling up his sleeves. "Those would be fighting words if I thought you meant them."

"I mean Dean." I laugh.

Walker nods. "It's new for him. You'll have to give him a minute."

Dean jumps—actually jumps—onto the counter. Continues his slow clap. "Sorry, babe, but that is not a satisfied woman." He looks to his brother. "Tell me you didn't skimp on the manual—"

Ryan cuts him off. "I'll tell you to get the fuck to work."

"I'm not working today," Dean says.

"Go fuck with someone else." Ryan feigns irritation, but his smile breaks through.

Brendon shoots me that same paternal look. "You and Ryan?"

"Yeah." I brush my hair behind my ear. "Does anyone else have an opinion?"

"No. It's good." He offers me a hug.

I lean into the gesture.

He whispers in my ear. "You sure you know what you're getting into?"

"You know how it is when you can't get over someone." I pull back. Turn to Dean. It's impressive how obnoxious he is standing up there clapping. "You're gonna hurt yourself."

"Or get your ass kicked." Walker motions to Brendon and Ryan. "He's overdue."

"I'm a loveable scamp," Dean says.

"A what?" Walker asks.

"A rogue," Dean says.

"Where'd you learn a D&D class?" Walker asks.

"Nerds don't own the word." He jumps off the counter and turns to Ryan. "Why'd you leave your girl hanging?"

Ryan shakes his head *you're insane if you think I'm answering that.*

Dean turns to me. "Come on, Leigh. You'll give me the dirt."

"Nope." I take my spot behind the counter. Set up.

"Are you dating now?" Walker runs his hand through his wavy hair. "Or is this—"

"He's wearing last night's clothes," Dean says.

Walker nods.

"And he smells like pussy," Dean says.

Walker nods *obviously*.

"You two fucked," Dean says.

"Everybody got that." Brendon returns to his suite. "You don't have to spell it out."

"Yeah, I do." He turns, winks at me. "How good was it?"

"Why? You place a bet on that?" I ask.

"I would have if anyone would have taken it." He laughs.

"Nobody would bet against Ryan? You guys." I press my hand to my heart. "You're so supportive."

Dean motions *give me the juicy details*. "Let's hear the dirt now. How many times did you come?"

I flip him off.

He laughs. "Can't be good if you have all that hostility."

Walker shakes his head. "Just 'cause she's on edge now doesn't mean she didn't come plenty last night."

"Sex tips from the Master Tease." Dean laughs. "Fuck, Leigh. You better hope Ryan isn't listening. We've seen Iris panting enough times to know Walker isn't fucking around."

My cheeks flush. That's exactly it. Ryan is a tease. A cruel, evil, horrible, wonderful tease.

"Shit. Look at her face." Dean's eyes go wide. "Right on the money."

Walker chuckles. "If she's already wanting, you're being cruel."

"And when you're on the verge of fucking your girlfriend all night?" Dean asks.

Walker's smile gets wicked. "Don't look if you don't like it."

"He likes it too much. He goes home and fucks himself to that shit," Ryan says.

Dean shrugs *so what if I do?*

273

Ryan shoots Dean a knowing look. "You ever gonna focus on your life?"

"My life's exactly how I want it," Dean says.

Ryan shakes his head *whatever you want to believe.*

"I have work." I turn on the computer and log in. "If you're done—"

"Where's the play-by-play?" Dean asks.

I flip him off and pull up the shop's Facebook account.

"Fill me in." Dean turns to Ryan. "She as kinky as she looks?"

"You trying to get your ass kicked?" Walker asks. "'Cause my money's on Ryan in that fight."

"I can bench twice what he can." Dean feigns indignant.

"He does karate," Walker says.

"Aikido," Ryan corrects.

"He's got a fire. That gets you far." Walker looks to me. "What do you think?"

"Who wins in a fight—Dean or Ryan?" I ask.

Walker nods *exactly.*

"Ryan. He's fighting to defend my honor. He's motivated." I catch his gaze. Try to figure out exactly what he's thinking.

But I can't. I'm too lost in those baby blues.

"You want me to kick his ass?" Ryan's voice is playful.

I shake my head. "Maybe later."

"My girl doesn't want me risking my hands." Ryan adopts a *don't fuck with me* stance, but his smile stays wide. "Drop it."

"She's your girl?" Dean asks.

"Of course." Ryan's eyes go to the clock—twenty minutes until we open. "What are you three doing here this early?"

Walker laughs. "Dean said we wouldn't want to miss it."

"You're an asshole," I say.

"'Cause I wanted to celebrate my brother finally getting laid?" Dean feigns offense.

Ryan ignores him. "Leighton's starting a design business. It's new, but it's growing fast. She'll be full time at it soon."

"That's happening?" Walker asks.

"Yeah." I press my lips together.

"That's fucking amazing," Walker says.

After a round of congratulatory hugs, the guys take their usual positions—Brendon leaning against the half wall to his suite, Dean and Walker at the counter, Ryan in front of his suite, leading the meeting.

"I am going to leave." My lips curl into a frown. "But not yet. Not for a while." Not until I'm sure I can do this. Even if that takes six months. Or three years. "I'll give you two weeks notice. Promise."

———

WORK TAKES OVER. I LOSE MYSELF IN ADMIN, CHECK OUT customers, break for lunch at the taco truck around the corner, fill my afternoon with a mix of coffee and social media.

Sometime around four, I run out of Inked Hearts work.

I boot up my laptop and pour myself into finishing the mock-up. It feels good getting it done, even if I still have another half a dozen rounds of small changes to go.

I love designing covers.

It fills me in some place that's usually empty. Scratches an itch that's in desperate need of attention.

I love building my site's social media.

It's a million times more engaging than flirting as I thrust my chest in the air *yes, that's so interesting, the tips are here. Oh, most people leave thirty percent, but the really generous guys leave fifty percent.*

Design is my future.

It's what I want.

But running a business all by myself is still terrifying.

Leaving Inked Hearts is still terrifying.

Staying for a while isn't just cowardice. It's smart. I need to pad my savings. To make sure I can actually find enough design work to pay my rent and put food in my fridge.

But it's a matter of time.

If I really want this to work, I have to devote more hours to it.

I have to say goodbye to the only place where I belong.

I try to focus on my cover, but it's impossible. There's a neon sign in my head flashing *THIS IS THE END*.

Ryan finishes with his client. He stands and shakes the guy's hand. His t-shirt—he changed in the bathroom after the meeting—pulls up his stomach as he stretches his arms over his head.

He smiles as he catches me staring. Motions *my eyes are up here*. Runs a hand through his wavy hair.

The client—a tall guy with a nervous smile—whispers something to Ryan.

Ryan nods and motions to the counter.

They cross the room to me. It's all routine. Flattery, price quote, credit card, receipt, flirting, tip, smile, wave goodbye.

The bell rings as the guy takes his leave.

Ryan plants his palms on the black plastic. Leans over the counter to press his lips to mine.

Mmm. He tastes so good.

I sigh as I pull back. Everyone's attention is turned toward us. They're watching. Figuring out what this is.

Ryan ignores them. "You working on a design?"

"Are you asking as my boyfriend or my boss?"

His smile spreads over his cheeks. "I'm your boyfriend?"

"Aren't you?"

He intertwines his fingers with mine. "Of course."

"Okay. Good." I slide off my stool. Press my thighs against the counter. "So who's asking?"

"Boyfriend."

"Yeah. I ran out of Inked Hearts stuff."

"Boss doesn't care either."

"Bullshit."

"No. We have the same agreement. You do your Inked Hearts shit, you can do whatever you want with the rest of your time."

"Okay."

"You know how much longer you want to stay?"

"A lot longer."

He brushes a hair behind my ear. "You're gonna be great, Leigh. You're gonna soar. Being here forty hours a week is clipping your wings."

"I know. But they're my wings. I'll leave when I'm ready. You don't get a say."

"I'm being pushy?"

"You know you're being pushy. But I do appreciate that you have my best interests in mind."

"I'll drop it."

"You promise?"

"Yeah. For a while."

"Until after the wedding. At the very earliest."

"It's soon."

"We leave in a week and a half," I say.

"You ready for that?"

"Yeah. I think so." It's still at the back of my mind: *what if he's still in love with her?* Most of me believes him when he says he's over her. But there's this ugly, jealous part of me that doesn't believe it.

Walker emerges from his suite and swings his backpack over one shoulder. "Clean up after."

My cheeks flush.

Ryan shrugs *maybe I will, maybe I won't.*

"Damn. Ryan's still smiling." Walker winks at me. "You must be fucking amazing, Leighton."

My blush spreads to my chest.

Ryan turns back to Walker. "You have no idea."

Walker chuckles as he nods goodbye.

The door swings shut.

But the room is still buzzing with Dean's gun.

Dammit, are we ever going to be alone?

Ryan moves behind the counter. Stands next to me. "Show me what you're working on."

"Are you going to do this forever?"

"Yeah." His fingertips brush the hem of my dress. "But I can switch to stalking you on social media if you prefer that."

"No. It's sweet." I lean into his touch. "I can work here sometimes. So, we're still—"

"You should."

"You get annoyed when Kay does that."

"I don't want to make Kay come on the counter."

"Oh."

"You're fucking adorable nervous."

"I don't get nervous."

"Yeah, you do."

Dean's gun turns off. He stands. Stretches. Looks to us. "You really waiting for me to leave for the show?"

Ryan nods.

"Cruel." He motions to us then turns to his customer. "What would you pay to watch that?"

The guy chuckles. "How come you're not constantly walking around with a black eye?"

"Lightning fast reflexes." He weaves to the right, dodging an invisible punch.

He takes forever cleaning the guy up.

Bringing him to the counter.

Checking out.

Packing up.

God, he's still here.

Ryan leans in to whisper. "I'll get rid of him."

Yes. Now.

He motions to the bathroom. "Meet me here in ten minutes."

I nod.

"Without your panties."

31

LEIGHTON

I leave the door open a crack, but it isn't enough. The air conditioning drowns out Dean and Ryan's conversation.

I shouldn't spy. Even if I'm desperate for more insight into Ryan's thoughts.

We're still carrying on with this ruse even though it's true. We're still going to his ex-girlfriend's wedding. We're still proving some point about how over her he is.

But he is over her. Almost.

And he's obliged to go. His parents are close with her parents. His parents are going to be there. I think. We haven't exactly talked about that. More about how heinous she is. How much I want her to suffer.

But I want her happy and far away so much more.

I take a deep breath and exhale slowly. There's no sense in getting jealous. Ryan is honest with me.

He tells me what he's thinking.

He tells me what he wants.

Right now, he wants to throw me on the counter and fuck me senseless.

Penny's wedding is an excuse to enjoy paradise with my boyfriend. That's all.

"You do realize there's closed circuit security here." Dean's voice flows through the crack in the door.

Ryan chuckles.

"Okay, I'm leaving. But Leighton, you should know anybody can access that footage with the password."

He's right—we have a security camera. But no one checks the footage. And I have the password too. I can easily erase the half an hour in question.

My heartbeat picks up as footsteps move toward the door.

The bell rings.

The door slams into the frame.

I push aside my friends' commentary. I push aside the five foot three, raven-haired, honey-eyed elephant in the room. I push aside everything besides the desire pooling between my legs.

Dean is gone.

It's just me and Ryan.

We've been alone at Inked Hearts a million times. But not like this. Never like this.

After a deep breath, I turn the handle and step into the main room.

The window shades block the sunset. Pink and red string lights glow in the dim room. The hearts shine like stars in a dark sky.

Ryan is leaning against the counter, the picture of patience. His pupils dilate as I unfurl my fist to show off my black panties.

Fuck, it feels so good having every ounce of his attention.

Having him wrapped around *my* finger.

It's half a dozen steps to him. As soon as his fingers brush my palm, I crumble. I lose any sort of upper hand. But then I don't care about being the one in control.

He takes my panties and slides them into his pocket.

I back into the counter. My palms hit the plastic. Slowly, I push myself up.

I stare into his eyes as I spread my legs.

God, the intensity in those baby blues. Like he's going to devour me. Like he's going to drive me out of my damn mind. No, that isn't a like.

It's exactly what he's going to do.

His fingertips curl into my skin as he places himself between my legs. "You're nervous."

"Not for this."

"Yeah for this."

I hold up my thumb and forefinger. *A little*. "To leave the shop. To lose my family here." To go to Hawaii and face the possibility of losing him.

"You won't lose me."

"Easy to say when you're about to fuck me."

"I'm not about to fuck you. It's gonna be an eternity before I fuck you."

I swallow hard.

He looks up at me with every ounce of affection in the world. "You won't lose me." He plants a soft, slow kiss on my lips. "*This* is everything I want."

"But Penny—"

"I don't give a fuck about Penny."

"Then why are we—"

"You want to call it off? Say the word. I'll cancel our flights right now."

"No zip lines?"

"We can find some here."

"No crystal blue Hawaiian waters?"

"Afraid I can't find those here."

"You're that over her."

"Yeah. But it's like your rule—" He hikes my dress up my thighs. "Easy to say when I'm about to dive between your legs. I don't blame you for doubting me. Fuck, I doubt me all the time."

"You'll tell me if you realize you still have feelings for her?"

"If you want to talk, I'll back off."

No. I need to feel our connection. "I want to not talk."

He nods. "Whatever you want to know, I'll tell you." He pushes my dress another inch up my thighs. Drags his fingertips over my skin.

"Ryan—" my breath hitches in my throat. "I… please…"

"Please what?"

"Touch me."

"Close your eyes."

I do.

He slides one arm around my waist and uses it to hold me in place. His other hand stays between my legs.

His thumb traces a line up and down my inner thigh. Higher, higher, higher, almost—

Then down again.

"You have no idea how much I think of you." Up, up, up. "How badly I want you." Almost—"You're everything."

"Ryan?"

"Yeah, baby?"

"Keep saying sweet things."

"No." His voice drops to something low and demanding. Mine squeaks. "No?"

"No, Leigh. We're done with sweet today." He switches to his index finger. Drags it up my inner thigh with the lightest touch in the world. "I have a million dirty thoughts of you. I want you to hear them." His fingertip skims my skin.

A groan rolls off my lips.

He traces that line with his middle finger. His ring finger. His pinkie. Then he works his way back again. Ring. Middle. Index. Thumb.

My eyelids press together.

My sex clenches.

My toes curl into my sandals.

He does it again—all five digits in both directions.

Every brush of his fingers sends heat right to my sex.

"Look at me, baby."

His eyes are filled with this intoxicating mix of lust and control.

Ryan is an evil tease.

He's a fucking sex god.

Fourteen months without and he's still a fucking sex god.

"You have any fucking idea what it does to me, seeing you here all day?" He plants a hard kiss on my lips.

"You have any idea what it does to me?" My hands dig into his hair. I hold his head against mine and kiss him hard.

I suck on his top lip.

He scrapes his teeth against my bottom lip.

Then his tongue is sliding in my mouth. And all my words are floating away.

Words seem so much less important than this.

Everything seems so much less important than this.

It's like every single molecule in my body is a neon sign flashing *Ryan Ryan Ryan*.

He pulls back with a needy sigh.

His fingers curl into my inner thighs. His eyes bore into mine. "You drive me out of my fucking mind, Leigh. I see you flirting with guys and I start thinking about throwing them out of the fucking shop."

"What else?"

"Fuck. With the way you dress?" He presses his lips to my

neck. "I spend half my time trying to get thoughts of stripping you to nothing out of my head."

"For how long?"

"Too long."

"When you're doing a tattoo?"

"Sometimes." He pushes the strap of my sundress off my shoulder. His hand goes to my chest. He cups my breast over my bra.

Then his thumb is dipping beneath the nylon.

Brushing against my nipple.

"Fuck." I wrap my legs around his hips and squeeze as tightly as I can. "What else?"

"Your tits in my hands." He draws circles around my nipple with his thumb. "Or around my cock." He nips at my neck. "Or those dark lips around my cock."

My yes isn't even close to a word.

"But all fucking day there's only been one thing on my mind." He rubs me harder.

I dig my fingers into the counter. Squeeze my thighs against his lips. "What?"

"The taste of your cunt." He presses his lips to my collarbone.

His fingers curl into my bra strap.

I reach around my back to unhook the thing. It's messy, but I manage to get it off my shoulders.

It falls onto the counter behind me.

Ryan wraps his arms around me. He holds me in place as he brings his lips to my nipple.

He sucks softly. Then harder. Harder. Fuck—

"Ryan—" My fingers curl into his hair.

"You need to come on my face now." He kisses a line down my torso.

His lips brush my belly button.

Slowly, he lowers himself onto his knees.

His fingers curl into my thighs.

I tug at my dress. Barely manage to get it over my head and on the floor.

I'm naked on the Inked Hearts counter.

He's completely clothed. Kneeling in front of me. About to dive between my legs.

Fuck.

He stares up at me as he pries my legs apart.

My outer thighs hit the counter.

His lips brush the inside of my knee. "You have no fucking idea what you do to me, Leigh." He drags his lips higher.

Higher.

Almost—

He nips at the skin of my inner thigh.

He does it again and again.

He gets so, so close, then he moves to my other leg, plants a kiss on my inner knee, and works his way up my thigh.

My body buzzes with anticipation.

Conscious thought flees my brain with every brush of his lips.

He gets higher, higher, higher—

His teeth scrape against my tender flesh.

They do it again and again.

There—

His lips brush my clit. It's so soft I can barely feel it, but that only makes it more intense.

Then his fingers are curling into my inner thighs, and he's pinning me to the counter, and he's licking me from top to bottom.

Fuck.

My knees buckle as he does it again.

He pulls back to groan against my inner thigh. Looks up at me a mess of wavy hair and control and need.

There's a promise in his eyes. That he'll satisfy me as long as I trust him with my body.

And I do.

Fuck, how I do.

But can I trust him with my heart?

Does it matter if I *can*? It's already his. I'm crazy fucking in love with him and there's no coming back from that.

He pins me to the counter as he dives between my legs. He licks me with long, soft strokes. Then long, hard ones. Then short, fast ones. He goes harder, softer, left, right, up, down, there—

I tug at his hair. "Don't stop."

He groans against my sex.

Then he licks me just how I need him, just where I need him.

My back arches. My sweaty hand slips, but I catch myself.

I stay upright, my thighs pressed against his cheeks, my heels digging into his back.

These are heavy shoes. It must hurt. But I don't fucking care. I don't care about anything but his soft, wet tongue against me.

His nails dig into my thighs.

My hand knots in his hair.

"Fuck. Ryan." A groan rolls off my lips. I squeeze my thighs against him.

Every flick of his tongue winds me up.

It takes me higher, higher, higher.

With his next lick, I unwind. All that tension unfurls in a wave of bliss. My sex pulses. Pleasure spreads through my pelvis, down my legs, up my torso, all the way to my fingers and toes.

Every part of me feels good.

Spent.

Alive.

He pulls back to nip at my thigh. "So much better than I imagined."

"Ryan—"

"Come here." He drags his lips up my thigh. My pelvis. My stomach. His hands go to my hips.

I tug his t-shirt over his head.

He unbuckles his belt, unzips his jeans, pushes the damn things off his hips.

And there's Ryan. All of him. And it's mine.

I wrap my hand around his cock. Bring my lips to his.

He tastes like me. There's something intoxicating about it. I need more of him. All of him.

My thumb brushes his tip.

He groans against my mouth.

"Leg's around me." His fingers dig into my hips.

I hold onto his shoulders for balance as I wrap my legs around his waist.

He guides me into position, tilting my pelvis until my sex brushes his cock.

Fuck.

He teases me with his tip.

Again.

Again.

Again.

There—

Once inch at a time, he fills me.

I arch my hips to take him deeper.

My nails dig into his skin.

He brings his hand to my ass to guide my body over his.

I stare into his eyes as he drives into me.

He stares back.

The intimacy is almost too much to take. But it's not. It's Ryan.

He holds me in place as he shifts his hips. He pulls back, until I've only got his tip, then he thrusts into me full force.

His eyelids press together.

His nails dig into my skin.

He fills me with long, slow thrusts.

I arch my back to meet him. I claw at his skin. Nip at his shoulder. His neck. His ear.

He groans as my lips close around his earlobe.

His head turns to the other side. His nails sink into my skin.

I suck on his lobe until his groans fill the room.

He wraps an arm around my waist. Guides my body over his as he fill me with hard thrusts.

Pleasure pools in my sex.

My body buzzes. I need to come, yeah, but I need his bliss more. I need his *everything*.

My nails dig into his skin. I try to fight my orgasm, but I can't. It feels too good.

"Fuck. Ryan. Don't stop." I let go of my breath.

My hips move of their own accord. They drive him deeper again and again and again—

There.

I groan his name as I come. The world goes white, nothing but pure, blinding light.

Then he's there, groaning my name into my neck. His cock pulses as he comes. He thrusts through his orgasm, spilling inside me.

When he's finished, he wraps his arms around me.

I collapse against his chest.

Slowly, my thoughts find their way into my brain.

But my head is still blinking *Ryan Ryan Ryan*.

I still need every fucking drop of him.

3 2

RYAN

The sun falls over the tiny apartment.

The breeze blows between the windows. It ruffles her hair. Raises goose bumps on her skin.

She rolls onto her back. Stretches her arms over her head as she stirs.

Her eyes blink open. Fix on mine. "You were watching me sleep."

"A little."

"How creepy."

"I prefer romantic."

Her lips curl into a smile. "You would."

"You never watch me?"

She makes a show of crossing her fingers. "Never."

"Believable."

She laughs. "Thanks." She pushes herself onto her elbows. Turns to check the time on the microwave. "It's not really ten. Tell me it isn't ten."

I slide off the bed. Grab my cell from the dining table. "It is."

She lets out one of those *I want to sleep forever* groans.

"You're off today. Go back to bed."

"You're not?"

"I'm working later."

"How much later?"

"One."

"That's only three hours."

"Still plenty of time." I offer my hand. "I'll buy you breakfast."

She smooths her loose tank top. Adjusts her cotton panties. Both are white. Sheer. Inviting as fuck. "I'm not going anywhere until I take care of this travesty." She twirls a silver-purple strand around her finger.

"Travesty?"

"I don't have a stronger word." She slides off the bed. Tugs at the drawstrings of my pajama pants. "Can I destroy these?"

"I have more."

"And those too?"

"You want me naked, ask."

She bites her lip as she gives me a long, slow once-over. When other women look at me like this, I get irritated. But there's something about the delight in Leighton's eyes.

It's intoxicating.

"Tempting." She drags her fingertips over my stomach. "But something tells me I won't get my hair done if you're naked."

"Something?"

"Experience." She rises to her toes to press her lips to my forehead. "I'm going to get ready. We can have breakfast here. Hang until you need to leave."

"I'll make coffee."

She blows me a kiss, spins on her heels, moves into the bathroom.

There's actual food in her fridge—I dragged her to Trader

Joe's last night. She deserves all of it. She deserves a feast. I settle on scrambled eggs.

I scoop coffee into the French press, set the electric kettle to boil, gather the ingredients for breakfast.

Steam fills the air.

I pour hot water over coffee.

The smell of java fills the room as I chop. Then it's tomatoes and bell peppers. Eggs.

Leighton's footsteps move closer. "I'm going to have to kidnap you at this rate."

I shoot her my best *don't fuck with me* look. "You want to throw down?"

"No. But you can throw me down. On the bed." She laughs. "That was bad. I must be caffeine deprived."

"You got your point across."

She brushes against me as she moves to the coffee maker. Fills two mugs. Fixes mine light on the cream and sugar, hers heavy on it. "Mmm. You're too good at this." She slides onto the counter behind me. "It's too bad my place is so small. I can't bribe you to move in."

"You can't?"

"Well... I'm sure I can think of something. But with the lack of air conditioning—it's really hot, huh?"

"A little." The ocean breeze is enough to cool us off. With her sitting there smiling, it's hard to complain about a room a few degrees too hot. "I can ice that coffee."

"It won't be strong enough." She takes a long sip. Lets out a low moan.

My cock stirs.

I love that sound.

I know what buttons to push to get her naked. Fuck, the thought of pinning her to the counter and driving into her—

I will.

But not yet.

Not until she's panting.

I turn the pan off. Scoop eggs onto ceramic plates. Bring them to the dining table.

Leighton joins me with the coffees. "Would you want that?"

I arch a brow.

"To live together?"

"One day."

"Really?"

"Of course." But it's still hard to believe this is real. That she wants me that badly. That she'll stick around.

She's beautiful, smart, charming.

She could have her pick of any of the guys who come into the shop.

I know I'm a catch in all the superficial ways. In others too. But it's not like I take care of her to win points. It's what I want.

I want her happy, healthy, well fed.

I want her coming until she can't take it anymore.

I want her fucking beaming.

Yeah, I'm letting go of Penny's hold on me, but the baggage is there.

It's hard for me to believe I'll be enough for someone.

That I'll be able to trust someone.

That they'll trust me.

It's fucking everything knowing Leighton wants me like this.

But there's still that voice in the back of my head, nagging at me, asking me if I can believe this is real.

I will get over it.

But it's not gonna be fast. Not if my history of getting over shit is any indication.

"You sure you can handle an all black apartment?" I tease.

She laughs. "We'll have to compromise."

"Fuck. This might be a deal breaker."

Her smile spreads over her cheeks. "What's with the black sheets? I've only ever seen black sheets on guy's beds when they're goth."

"You've seen that many?"

"Shut the fuck up." She blushes. "I was never a Dean, but I... I had fun."

"Was it fun?"

She stares into my eyes, assessing my intentions. She must decide I'm worth trusting, because she nods. "When I was bartending, yeah. That was a solid four years, I guess, of being careful with guys. I only dated guys who seemed like a good time. I made it clear I wasn't interested in anything serious. I didn't get invested."

"Didn't that get lonely?"

"Sometimes. But that was better than the alternative." She stabs a red pepper and brings it to her mouth.

"Getting hurt?"

"Yeah." She scoops eggs into her mouth, chews, swallows. "I did enough of that in high school. Fell for the whole *I love you, honey. Let's make love* bullshit. Let guys treat me like crap because I believed they'd change. Before I gave up on my mom, I still believed people could change."

"And now?"

"I don't know. You've changed."

"You have too."

"Maybe."

"You're starting your own business."

"Eventually." She finishes her last sip of coffee. "In a long, long time."

"It will come up fast."

She sets her mug down. Traces its rim. "I know. But I don't want to talk about leaving."

Fair enough. I nod. Inhale my food. She worked me hard last night. I'm starving.

"I guess I gave up on guys long before I gave up on my mom. There wasn't really anything notable. Just a long string of shitty boyfriends. One day, I was at work, crying in the bathroom because I'd just gotten dumped via text, again, and I decided I was done. I was done choosing the wrong men."

"Did it work?"

"Sorta. I kept choosing guys who weren't boyfriend material, but I stopped trying to make them my boyfriend. I stayed in control. I missed that feeling of intimacy, believing I could trust someone. But it was better that way. Easier."

"Why'd you stop?"

"Sleeping around?"

"Yeah."

"It doesn't bother you?"

"I don't like thinking about you with other guys."

She chews on her bottom lip. Her blue-green eyes flare with concern.

"But, no, I don't care that you used to sleep around. It doesn't matter how many people you've been with before."

"It's not that many."

"It could be a thousand or one. Wouldn't matter to me either way."

"Really?"

"Really." I know her well enough to know she's telling the truth. Those guys didn't matter to her. They had her body, yeah, but they never had her head or her heart.

And the ones who did, who manipulated that younger, more trusting version of Leighton—

If I ever meet any of them, I'll punch their douchebag faces.

"That's incredibly evolved of you," she says.

"Learned from you."

She shakes her head. "No. I'm not there. I get sick thinking about you and Penny."

"Still?"

"Yeah." She finishes her last bite. Pushes her plate away. "But I'm getting better. Thinking about it less."

"Me too."

She pushes herself to her feet. "I want to shower. But I have to do my hair first. And I don't want to waste our time together."

"I'll help."

She raises a brow. "I don't know."

"You think I'm not capable."

She moves closer. Reaches down to run three fingers through my locks. "Tell me these are natural."

"Natural?"

"That you're not doing at home perms?"

"At home whats?"

"Perms!" She makes that *ugh* noise. "Men have it so easy. No makeup. No chemical treatments. No high heels."

"You don't need any of that shit. You look fucking amazing right now."

Her cheeks flush. "Thank you. But I like that shit."

"Then don't complain."

She flips me off.

I grab her wrist, bring her finger to my lips, suck on her fingertip.

Her knees press together. "I will do my hair before I fuck you."

"While you fuck me?"

She shakes my head. "In my shower cap? No. Wait." She giggles as she pulls her finger back. "I'm skipping too many steps. You can't see me in a shower cap."

"I bet you look fucking amazing?"

She shakes her head.

"Twenty bucks."

"Who are you, Dean?"

I shudder. "Never say that again."

"Or?"

"Or I'll punish you."

"You're not doing a good job convincing me."

I take my last bite, chew, swallow. "Or I won't punish you."

She laughs. "That's better."

"What if I wear one too."

She brushes my hair up my head, first the right side, then the left. "Hmm. I think you'll look more ridiculous than I will."

"I wore a cap on swim team."

"You did not."

"I did."

"You have pictures?"

"I was twelve, you perv."

She laughs. "How about you recreate it for me later?"

"Sure." I press my lips to hers. "In Hawaii."

Her lips curl into a frown. It's a quick thing. A second, and she's smiling again. "Okay. Come with me."

I follow her to the bathroom.

She places the lid on the toilet seat, motions for me to sit.

I slide my arms around her waist instead.

She leans into my touch. "I will send you home."

"You won't."

"Are you testing me?"

"I need a reason to hold you?"

In the mirror, her eyes catch mine. "Okay. Stay there. One step back. Be good."

I release her. Step backward. "Good?"

"No funny business." She reaches for the hem of her tank top, bends her arms to pull it over her head.

"This is entrapment, baby."

She shrugs *is it?* "I don't want to startle you. But I'm about to put on something even sexier?"

"Than you topless?"

She folds her arms over her chest. Her expression gets shy.

It's fucking adorable.

God, there's something about seeing *take no prisoners, I get off on showing off my tits* Leighton shy.

It's hot.

And sweet.

I'm not sure whether I want to fuck her or hold her.

Her ass brushes against my crotch as she bends at the waist.

That answers that question.

My fingers curl into her hips.

"After." She swallows hard. Her breath gets erratic as she opens the cabinet, pulls a shoe box from it. She rolls from her hips to rise. Sets the box on the counter.

"You'd turn me down?"

She bites her lip. "I had this idea."

"Yeah?"

She pulls the lid from the box, finds an old Inked Hearts t-shirt stained with half a dozen different colors, dons it. "I never got to give you that lap dance."

My cock stirs.

"I thought we could do that after."

Conscious thought flees my brain.

"If you're into it."

"Yeah."

"It's not too trashy?"

"Isn't that the appeal?"

"Well... I guess it's obvious I like showing off my body."

I nod.

"You could try to look surprised."

My thoughts return with my laugh. I wrap my arms around her. Plant a kiss on her neck. "Does it turn you on, the thought of being my personal stripper?"

Her nod is heavy.

"Then I fucking love it."

"Okay." Her blush spreads to her chest. "What do you want me to wear?"

"Same shit you always wear."

She arches a brow. "Not a schoolgirl outfit or something?"

"No."

"But isn't that the fantasy?"

"How many times do I have to tell you, Leigh? You are my fantasy."

33

LEIGHTON

My hair is dyed and blow dried.

My makeup is perfect.

Ryan is waiting for me on the couch.

Nerves rise up in my throat. I curse my past self for her suggestion. Stripping before sex is one thing.

Announcing an intention to put on a show is another.

Yes, I want to erase the ugly memory of Ryan pushing me off his lap.

I want to watch his eyes go wide with pleasure as I tease him mercilessly.

But I also want to live to see tomorrow.

My heart thuds against my chest.

My breath catches in my throat.

I'm still wrapped in a towel, in another room, and my stomach is all butterflies.

Can I really do this?

I suck a breath between my teeth. Exhale slowly. I have to. I want to, yes, but I also have to.

I have to prove to myself that I can.

I have to have him under my trance.

It feels so fucking good, being with Ryan. Whatever we're doing—eating breakfast, dying my hair, taking shower cap selfies, trashing a shitty TV thriller while we wait for the dye to set—I'm where I belong. I'm happy. Satisfied. At ease.

But now that I'm putting on a show…

I hang my towel on the rack. Slide into my sexiest thong —a lacy black thing. Pull on a black mini skirt and that tight white crop top he loves.

Not that he's ever told me he loves it.

More that he stares at my tits enough I know he loves it.

My nipples peek through the sheer fabric.

It's sexy as hell.

I look good. But then that's never really been a question. I have the occasional moment of insecurity. What girl doesn't? But I'm happy with my appearance. I may not be the most gorgeous girl in the world, but I'm in shape. I take care of myself. I work my angles.

Deep breath.

I slide on my black slingback pumps and I step into the main room.

The curtains are down. The string lights twinkle in shades of red and pink.

Ryan's eyes go wide as he takes me in. "You look amazing, baby."

"Thanks." My gait is unsteady. "Could you get the Bluetooth speakers?"

He nods. Reaches for the speaker to turn it on.

It's three steps to the dining table. I pick up my phone. Stream the first song that comes to mind.

My favorite band. The one with the breathy, tortured singer. I introduced Ryan. He constantly teases me about just how broken the lyricist is, but he can't hide how much he loves it.

They're our band.

A heavy guitar riff fills the air.

Then it's the singer's breathy vocals.

I can't remember what he's saying. But there's no ignoring how much he sounds like he's in the middle of a fuck.

Ryan's eyes meet mine. "Perfect."

I nod as I take a step forward. With the lights off and the music blaring, my tiny apartment feels like a private room in some club.

At least if I keep my eyes on Ryan.

I swing my hips, strutting slowly as I approach him.

His gaze travels up my body. From my shiny heels, to my short skirt, over my bare midriff and my low-cut white top, to my red lips.

To my eyes.

There.

My knees brush his legs. His jeans are rough against my skin.

I stare back at him as I slide into his lap.

My hands go to his shoulders.

I use them for leverage to grind against his crotch.

He stares up at me.

His pupils dilate.

His cock hardens.

Fuck, that feels good.

I bring my hand to his cheek. Run my fingertips along his jaw. Slide the pad of my thumb into his mouth.

Rock my hips in figure eights.

He sucks on my digit as I rub against him.

Fuck, the friction of his jeans against my lace panties—

I'm on fire.

I'm buzzing.

Every part of me wants every part of him.

This is supposed to be to tease him. But, fuck, I don't have a single hint of upper hand.

I need to tear off my clothes.

I need to come.

And make him come.

I bring my hand back to his shoulder. Push myself up.

Slowly, I peel my top over my breasts.

Ryan brings his hand to my side. Slides it over the curve of my waist. Over my breast.

He rubs his thumb over my nipple in time with the music.

My eyelids flutter closed.

I pull my top over my head and toss it aside.

He stares into my eyes as he toys with my nipple.

Fuck, he's so in control.

I love it, but I need to be the one leading this.

I wrap my hand around his wrist and bring his other hand to my chest.

Slowly, I lower myself onto his crotch.

I circle my hips, grinding against him as he toys with me.

His blue eyes fill with need.

When I can't take it anymore, I shift off him. I spin on my heels.

Fuck.

My full-length mirror is set up at the wall.

My reflection stares back in her fuck me heels and her impossibly short skirt.

His eyes connect with mine through the mirror.

I look back at Ryan as I unzip my skirt and push it off my hips.

It falls at my feet.

I kick it away.

Then I back myself onto his lap.

I stare at our reflection as I grind against him.

As his hands go to my hips.

I spread my legs wider.

His hand knots in my hair. He pulls my head back until my neck is pressed against his lips.

"Fuck, Leigh." He nips at my neck. "You're gonna make me come."

My sex clenches. I want to make him come. But not yet.

I rock my hips, rubbing my ass against his crotch. I'm in his lap in a thong. He's naked under his jeans.

But there's still way too much fabric in the way.

I bring his hands to my chest.

He sucks on my neck, toying with my nipples as I grind against him.

I get lost in our reflection.

My hair falls over my ears.

His locks fall over his face as he sucks on my neck.

He works me with those expert hands.

My thighs are light against his dark jeans.

Watching is too intense. I have to close my eyes. My body hums with electricity. My sex aches. My nipples throb.

I need more.

I need everything.

Still, I grind against him until the song shifts to the next.

This one is heavier, harder.

I take his hands and pin them to the couch.

Slowly, I stand.

I watch him through the mirror as I slide my panties off my ass.

I keep them around my thighs as I roll at my hips.

There. My fingers touch the ground.

I'm on display for him.

He lets out a low, appreciative groan. "Come here."

I rise. Step out of my panties. Turn and slide onto his lap.

I grind against him.

Only his jeans in the way.

And, fuck, the friction of the denim against my clit—

"Mmm." My hand knots in his hair. I stare into his eyes as I draw figure eights with my hips.

He stares back, as needy and desperate as I am. "How long is this dance?"

"Three songs."

He shakes his head.

I nod. It feels so good, torturing him, pushing him to the edge.

Watching desire fill his eyes.

His hand goes to my inner thigh.

Fuck, I want that.

But not yet.

I take his wrists. Bring both hands to my chest. Lean down to whisper in his ear. "Watch." I motion to the mirror as I turn.

He does.

He stares at our reflection as I grind against him.

As he toys with my nipples.

As he pushes me to the brink of what I can take.

The song shifts into the next. It's softer. Slower.

I match its pace, but it's torture.

My sex screams for attention. For him.

He's so fucking hard.

The chorus fades into the verse.

Into the next chorus.

My eyelids flutter closed.

He rolls my nipple between his thumb and forefinger, sending a pang to my sex.

He does it again.

Verse.

Again and again.

Breakdown.

I open my eyes. Turn to face him. Stare at him as I grind against him.

This is my dance.

I'm still in control.

I plant a slow, deep kiss on his lips.

Then I shift off his lap.

Onto my knees.

I unbutton and unzip his jeans.

Fuck.

I brush my lips against his cock. But the tease isn't enough. I need him coming. I need release.

I take him into my mouth.

His hand knots in my hair.

His gaze goes to the mirror.

Mine follows. God, he's a genius, setting that thing up at a forty-five-degree angle.

I watch his cock strain my dark lips.

Watch his hand knot in my purple hair.

I'm naked, on my knees for him.

And it's so fucking hot.

Feminine power fills me. He's mine. He's under my spell. Under my control.

God, I need him to be mine.

I take him as deep as I can then I pull back and do it again and again.

Ryan tugs at my hair, pulling me off him. "I'm coming inside you."

My sex clenches.

"On the couch. On your back."

We're on the next song, but I still want my control.

I crawl onto the couch, but I don't get onto my back. I plant on my hands and knees. "Fuck me. Now."

"Not until I taste your cunt."

His fingers curl around my thighs. "Ass up."

I raise my hips. Lower my shoulders.

He holds onto my legs as he brings his mouth to me.

I watch him plant a long, slow lick on my clit.

It's weird and intoxicating, watching him work me.

Tension builds in my sex as he licks me.

His nails curl into my thighs.

He goes harder. Faster.

"Fuck." I rock my hips, pressing my sex against him. "Fuck me. I want to come with you. Please."

"Fuck, Leigh." He nips at my inner thigh.

My sex aches from emptiness. "Please."

His groan is low. Heavy.

He pushes himself onto his knees.

His hands go to my hips.

Slowly, he pulls my body onto his.

I stare at our reflection, watching his cock fill my cunt.

He drives into me with deep, steady thrusts.

My tits bounce.

His hand knots in my hair.

The other slides between my legs.

He strokes me as he fucks me.

Pleasure builds quickly. It's intense watching our bodies join.

A few more thrusts and I'm there.

"Fuck. Ryan." I squeeze the fabric of the couch, but it does nothing to stave off my orgasm.

With his next thrust, I go over the edge.

My sex pulses as I come.

I groan his name again and again.

Then he's there.

His cock pulses.

He thrusts through his orgasm, groaning my name as he comes.

When he's finished, he untangles our bodies and pulls me into his lap.

"You're fucking amazing." He presses his lips to my neck. "I ever tell you that?"

"Yeah, but I don't mind hearing it again."

"Don't go anywhere."

"I live here."

"No, Leigh." He wraps his arms around me. "Don't leave."

34

RYAN

The next few days are paradise.

I see Leighton every break at work.

Spend every night at her place.

Sunday, she finishes work early and laces up her running shoes. I can't join her—I'm stuck finishing this sleeve—but I promise to work her hard after.

She begs for the mercy of my air conditioning.

I offer her my spare key.

Somehow, I manage to focus on work even with my client teasing me about my relationship with the hot purple-haired chick.

I manage to get to my car, drive home, park.

My thoughts turn dirty the second I step inside.

Leighton is sitting on my couch in nothing but a black towel.

Fuck. That's a *welcome home*.

She tugs at the soft cotton. "You have to admit this is overboard."

"What about it?"

She points to the black couch. The black dining table. The black coffee maker. The black frames.

"Should I get red frames?"

"Purple."

"Buy them. I'll put them up."

"You'll let me decorate your apartment?"

"You have good taste."

Her dark lips—her makeup and hair are as perfect as always—press into a smile. "What if I adorn the walls in posters of hot rock stars?"

"Not gonna find anyone hotter than I am."

Her smile widens. "Is that right?"

"Yeah." I kick the door closed. Click the lock. "You disagree?"

"No. Just glad you see it." She reaches for something on the black coffee table—my spare key. She holds it up, offering it to me. "You need this back?"

"Keep it."

"You sure?"

"Yeah." There aren't many things I'm sure of. Leighton being in my life is a no-brainer.

"Okay." She picks her pink, gem-stone shaped purse off the floor and carefully tucks the key into a hidden zipper.

"Where do you find that shit?"

"Shit?"

I motion to the shiny purse.

"I assume you mean amazing clothes and accessories."

"Of course."

"You really need to work on your sweet talk."

"Where do you find that amazing shit?"

She laughs. "Internet. Where else?"

"You think I'm carefully cultivating my t-shirt collection?"

She stands and cinches the towel. "Of course." Her teeth

sink into her lip as she drops the towel. "You have to find just the right shade of black."

I can't help but chuckle.

She motions *come here*.

I do.

Her fingers curl into my belt loop. She tugs at my jeans, pulling my body against hers.

There's only one layer between my skin and hers. I need to have her. Now.

"Your jeans always hug your ass just so." Her fingers skim my stomach. "That doesn't happen by accident."

"And?"

"Your hair—nobody rolls out of bed with perfect waves."

I can't help but smile. "What if I do?"

"I'll hate you forever."

"You don't already?"

She shakes her head. Tugs at my belt loop as she takes a step backward. "You can admit you try."

"Can I?"

Her nod is heavy.

"Can I be honest with you, Leigh?"

She looks behind her to turn the hallway corner backward. "Of course."

"Don't have a fucking clue what we're talking about."

"Your jeans."

I bring my hand to her ass and hold her body against mine.

She groans as my hard-on brushes her stomach. "You're too good at this."

"You complaining?"

"No." She takes another step backward. Kicks the bedroom door open. "I just…" She steps into my bedroom. "I had this epic plan of winding you up and leaving you wanting."

"Now?"

She shakes her head. "Take off your pants."

"What if I like your plan?"

Her groan is agony.

"What if I want you on edge all fucking night?"

"Ryan—"

"Yeah, baby?"

"You're evil."

"I know."

She slides her hand under my t-shirt. Presses her palm flat against my stomach. "You're supposed to be desperate."

"I am."

"But you're so—" She looks up at me, her blue eyes wide with lust. "In control."

"Don't tell me you don't like it."

Her purple hair falls in front of her eyes as she shakes her head.

"That a yes or a no?"

She backs herself onto my bed. "I fucking love it." Her lips press together. She lies on her side, draping herself over my black sheets as she pats the spot next to her.

She looks like a centerfold.

She's fucking perfect.

But this is all wrong.

This is so fucking wrong.

There hasn't been a naked woman in my bed since—

Fuck.

My head fills with that awful mental image. Penny under Frank. His name rolling off her lips. Her nails digging into his back. Her honey eyes filling with relief.

I can't fuck Leighton in my bed.

I can't even fuck myself in my bed.

Leighton pulls the sheets against her chest. The same way Penny did.

The same fucking—

"Ryan?" Her voice gets soft.

"I can't. Not here."

"Oh." Her blue-green eyes turn down. Her lips press together. "Did I do something?"

"No, Leigh. It's me."

"I thought you were over…" Her voice trails to a whisper. Her brow furrows. She can't bear to finish her sentence. She can't bear my bullshit.

"Me too."

"So you're still…"

I nod to the hallway. "Let's go to the couch."

She shakes her head. "No, uh… I… I'm gonna get dressed." She stares into my eyes.

She's asking for something.

But I don't have a fucking clue what it is.

She must not find it, because she looks away with a frown.

Slowly, she slides off the bed, pulls the mirrored closet door open, and dives into the top drawer of the black dresser —her drawer.

"Could you give me a minute?" She hugs the black sheets to her chest.

"It's not you, Leigh."

"I believe you."

But she doesn't. It's written all over her face.

"It's just not… I don't want to think about her either." She swallows hard. "It's okay. Really. I'm starving anyway."

"I'll make you something."

"No." Her voice drops to a whisper. "I should probably—"

"Stay."

"Maybe."

"Let's get street tacos."

Her voice perks. "Yeah?"

"Your pick. You can school me on how to make them."

"You didn't add any cilantro last time."

"I'm a monster."

She nods, but there's no enthusiasm in it.

She's pulling away.

I can't let that happen.

I need to fix this.

But that means fixing my head.

And I don't have a fucking clue how to do that.

RYAN

Leighton shifts her weight between her heels. She taps her grey jeans with her silver fingernails. Adjusts the lacing on her tank top.

Fuck. It's like she's wearing this shit to make some point about what an idiot I am for not taking her against the wall.

No arguments here.

I'd kill to turn off the part of my brain that throws up the brakes. That part that's still tied to my ex-girlfriend.

I'd kill to pry that last bit of my heart from Penny's French manicured grasp.

The couple in front of us rises to their tiptoes to order at the window. The guy wraps his arms around the girl. Laughs at some joke as he hands over a twenty-dollar bill.

Leighton taps her cork sandal against the pavement. "I'll order."

"I know."

"I'll get it too. You can find us someplace to sit."

"We can go back to the apartment."

"I don't want to be there."

I bite my tongue. She's pissed. I get that. I deserve it.

If she needs time to deal with that, fine.

But I need to know.

She motions to another couple sitting on the curb. "Let's grab that spot."

"All right." I'm being a hypocrite—holding onto all this instead of explaining it to her. But I don't know how to put it into my words. I don't know how to make her understand.

It's not that I still love Penny.

It's not that I want her.

It's the scar tissue. I don't know how to heal it. I don't know if it's possible to heal it.

Am I going to walk around struggling to trust people for the rest of my life?

Wondering if I'll ever be enough for a woman?

Looking for evidence in every sigh or frown?

I find an empty spot on the curb a block away. Watch Leighton turn on the charm as she orders and pays.

She's magnetic. Nobody can resist her smile. Or her laugh. Or the way she curls her hair around her finger in that *I'm thinking about you naked* way.

She steps aside. Joins the dozen people waiting in front of a closed furniture shop.

Her hips sway as she shifts her weight between her heels. Her nervous gestures stay the same. She keeps tapping her nails against her thighs. She keeps avoiding my gaze.

A short guy picks up his order. Drowns a burrito in red salsa.

A tall guy squeezes lime on his tacos.

A curvy woman adorns an enchilada plate with cilantro.

Leighton turns to me. Her eyes meet mine. They're still asking for something. And I still don't know what it is.

We stare like that forever.

Until the happy couple steps in front of her to grab their

takeout order. They laugh like they're the first people to discover love.

I want to hate them, but I can't. I remember that feeling. I don't miss Penny, but I miss the intoxication. I miss being able to let my guard down. Being able to love someone without wondering when the other shoe is gonna drop.

Leighton knows my head is a mess.

But that's different than living in it.

I need to explain this to her. Or convince her it doesn't matter.

But it does.

And I don't know when I'll feel normal.

If I'll ever feel normal.

She taps her heels together as the guy calls her name. Her eyes fix on me. She motions *come here*.

That defeats the purpose of us splitting up, but I do it anyway.

The taco truck casts yellow light over the beige pavement. It turns her purple hair pink. Bounces off her white tank-top.

A million things flit through my head. *Come back to my place. Spend the night in my bed. Let's replace that ugly memory.*

But I can't ask that.

'Cause I can't offer it. Not yet.

She turns to the window. Smiles as the woman in the truck hands her two plates of tacos.

I take the bottles of water.

Leighton turns to me and nods to the salsa bar. "Watch and learn."

"I'm studying under the master."

"You'd like to be under me, wouldn't you?" The joke doesn't land. Her smile stays sad.

She shakes it off as she sets the plates on the silver bar. She picks up the tongs and grabs slices of limes two at a time.

"Chicken is perfect with citrus." She stacks eight slices on the plate.

"That great?"

"Yes. That great." She grabs a green container of salsa. "Traditional salsa verde is perfect." She drowns the plate in salsa.

"It's gonna be a mess."

"Life is a mess. Grab a fork if you can't handle it."

I do. And napkins.

She laughs. "That was a dare."

"What if I need my hands clean?"

She presses her lips together. For a second, her eyes meet mine. Then they're on the second plate. "I went easy on you. Steak and chicken. No tongue. Not even chorizo."

"You're kind."

"Thank you, I know." She grabs an orange-red salsa. "Chipotle brings out the flavor best. Trust me. I've tested it." She drowns these tacos in the orange-red sauce. "But we need a little of this—" She grabs a different green salsa. "Avocado salsa. The nectar of the gods."

"That why you use so much?"

"Don't hate until you've tried it." She uses tongs to shower the plates in cilantro. "Now, they're perfect. Trust me. You'll be begging for seconds."

"Guess you'll still get me begging."

Her eyes go to the concrete. "Ryan. Can we... Let's just eat, okay?"

"Yeah." Hunger doesn't exactly make conversation easier.

She follows me down the street. Past my previous spot. "Where are you going?"

"It's a surprise." I lead her around the corner.

It's a dozen blocks to the nearest park. We walk them in silence.

The air between us stays heavy.

We step under the yellow glow of a streetlight. Take seats on an empty concrete bench.

Leighton sets the plate between us.

I hand over her water bottle.

Her fingers brush mine as she takes it. "I forgot about this place."

"I run here sometimes."

"It's small." She looks at the empty basketball court. It's late enough the lights are off. Kids are home.

No one is here but us.

The world is ours.

But, right now, there isn't an *our*. There's her and me and a million walls between us.

"I want to explain this to you," I say.

"You don't have to." She grabs a chicken taco and brings it to her lips. "I understand."

"You don't."

"You walked in on your girlfriend fucking another guy in your bed. Of course you're gonna feel weird about the bed." She picks up a lime, squeezes it over her taco, does it again. "I'm sure you're more tired of thinking about her than I am."

"Yeah."

"So let's eat."

She doesn't want to talk about this.

But I've only got two ways to convince her. And it's not like things are gonna go different if I take her back to my bed a second time.

I *can* fuck her in my bed. I don't have any problem getting hard.

But there's no way I'm fucking Leighton with that image in my head.

And there's no way to erase it.

Leighton groans as she licks salsa from her fingers. "Perfect. Right?"

I take my first bite. Soft tortilla. Tender chicken. Tangy salsa. Just enough cilantro. "It is."

"If you don't eat faster, I'll finish yours."

"You can."

She shakes her head. "The whole point of this is teaching you how to enjoy Mexican cuisine."

"So I can pick up takeout when you're busy?"

"Well, if you insist." She grabs a steak taco. Bites off half. Chews. Swallows. "But I doubt you'll give up the chance to cook me dinner."

"You don't think I'll get over it?"

"Not with how obsessed you are."

"You don't worry I'll stop wanting to take care of you?"

She licks cilantro from her finger. "No. I..." Her eyes go to the ground. "I worry you're going to get to the wedding, see her walking down the aisle, and snap. Do a Dustin Hoffman."

"Huh?"

"*The Graduate.* He's lusting after the girl next door all summer. While he's sleeping with her mom. He shows up at her wedding and whisks her away. Then they get on a bus."

Oh. That movie. "And the camera stays on them. It goes from romantic to awkward. They realize they made a mistake."

"You know it?"

"It's a famous scene."

"You don't watch movies."

"We watch three a week."

"I guess..." She taps her nail against her thigh. "You can't have sex in your bed, Ryan. The place where you've slept every night for the last year. I get that it would be confusing. But you've had a year. Why not get a new bed?"

"That wouldn't—"

"Or a new apartment? Why not erase those memories from your life?"

It's a fair point. Even if—"I have rent control."

"If you were broke, that would explain it. But you have plenty." She takes another bite. Chews. Swallows. "I get it. Change is hard."

"I want shit to change. The last year, I've grown more than I did the eight years before. I figured out what the fuck I liked to do. I figured out what I wanted."

"What do you want?"

"I want to run the shop until the day I die. I want to take care of someone I love. Start a family."

"You do?"

"Yeah. I always saw that with her. But now I just see it."

"You want kids?"

I nod. "They'll rebel by getting MBAs and wearing Abercrombie."

She laughs. "God, could you imagine the two of us for parents?"

"How would you have felt if your mom approved of your pink hair?"

"Mortified." She picks up a chicken taco. "It was awful enough that she got over it fast. She was complimenting me by week two."

"Yeah?"

"Yeah. She thought I was 'so creative' for the way I expressed myself through my clothes. Even when my boobs were about to pop out."

"Like that?"

Sadness returns to her smile. "I guess I wanted to... It was petty. Stupid."

"Worked."

"You're thinking about me naked?"

"Now, yeah." My gaze settles on her chest. Fuck. Her tits

defy description. "You're making me lose my train of thought."

"Take some personal responsibility."

"I'll buy you a new top when I destroy that one."

"Ryan." Her laugh lifts to a giggle. "Don't tease me. Not after that."

"What's the tease?"

"You'd go here?"

"It's empty." I stare into her blue-green eyes. "Unless you're chicken."

"It's a crowded area."

"Should I make a back-ay noise?"

"You just did." She picks up another taco. "Besides, you're bluffing."

"Try me."

She shakes her head. "Another time. I need to nurse my ego."

That's fair.

She takes a bite. Chews. Swallows. "I want a family too. But I don't know if I'd be any good at it." She finishes her taco, plants her hands on the concrete, and leans back to look up at the stars. "I don't exactly have a worthy role model."

"You can learn."

"Maybe."

"You can talk about it."

"Another time. I've had enough baggage for tonight."

"You can still spend the night."

"I know."

But she doesn't.

She doesn't know how much I need her. How much I want to be all hers. How much I want to fix this.

There's some way to prove it to her.

I just need to figure it out.

3 6

RYAN

When I wake at three a.m., she's gone. But yesterday's clothes are still on my bedroom floor.

She isn't running away.

Not completely.

I brush my teeth, wash my face, take out my contacts.

My bed isn't an inviting place to sleep. It's a fucking curse. She's right. I've had a year to get rid of this fucking thing. To replace the frame and the mattress instead of just the sheets.

I thought getting rid of it meant Penny had some power over me. But she still does, whether I admit it or not.

I might as well move on with my life.

When sunrise creeps through the curtains, I give up on sleep.

I can't replace the bed at the moment. But I can do this.

I slide on my glasses and spend an hour rearranging the room.

There.

The bed no longer mocks me.

It's not much, but it's a start.

———

My eleven o'clock is a woman getting a Latin quote on her ribs. I'm careful about every line, but my thoughts stay on Leighton. The frustration in her brow. The hurt in her eyes. The words inked onto her side.

I finish the quote. Turn off the gun. "Done."

The woman jumps to her feet and stares at her new ink in the mirror. Her eyes go wide with wonder.

I see this expression a few times a day, but it never gets old.

This is where I belong. I'm lucky to have that. "Sit down." The demand in my voice covers my irritation.

The woman perks. Her brown eyes fix on mine. Her soft lips press into a smile. "Ryan, this is amazing."

"It was all your idea."

She shakes her head. "You designed it."

Yeah, I added the rain drops. The umbrella. The clouds. But it was all her. Talking to her. Seeing what made her eyes light up or her lips curl into a smile.

I found what was in her soul.

Not what was in mine.

Even so, I accept her praise. "Thanks."

"No. Thank you. It's amazing."

She squirms as I clean her up.

"You're done."

She jumps to her feet and throws her arms around me.

I step backward. Shift my weight into my heel. I never get used to this either.

"Thank you so much." She squeezes me tightly.

"My pleasure."

She releases me. Grabs her hoodie from the chair, slides it on, zips it until it's covering her taped on tube top.

I lead her to the counter. Give her my usual aftercare routine. Ring her up myself.

It's easy enough, but it's not the same without Leighton.

There's something missing from my goodbye.

There's just something missing.

The thought of not seeing her at work every day steals my oxygen. It's what's best for her. It's inevitable. But it's fucking terrible.

The thought of not seeing her, period?

My stomach churns.

I grab my sketchbook, take a seat behind the counter, work on a mock-up—a colorful ocean inspired sleeve. I'm halfway through a rough sketch when the bell rings.

Dean steps inside. Stretches his arms over his head.

He surveys the room—it's just Brendon finishing a shoulder tattoo—then turns to me. "How was it?"

"How was what?"

He motions to the counter.

Oh. How was fucking Leighton on the counter? Amazing. But it's not exactly front of mind. "None of your business."

"You're moody for someone who got laid as much as you did in the last two days."

"I'm always moody."

He makes that *kinda* noise. Moves to the Keurig in the corner and starts fixing a cup.

"You don't drink coffee."

"I'm aware of that."

"What are you doing?"

"Something nice for my brother. That okay with you?"

I run my hand through my hair. What the hell is up with him? "Yeah. Sure. Thanks."

"You're welcome."

The smell of coffee and the *drip drip drip* of the machine fill the room.

I turn my attention back to my sketchbook. Draw an octopus breaking a ship with its legs.

Dean's footsteps move closer.

He sets the coffee on the desk. Stares at my drawing. Chuckles. "Freudian."

"Is it?"

"Worried you're gonna break between someone's legs?"

Fuck, when did he get so perceptive? "You that desperate for details on me and Leighton?"

"Fuck yeah. But that's not what I'm getting at."

"What are you getting at?"

"Why aren't you reveling in afterglow?"

"Been at work all morning."

"Still." He studies my expression. "What happened?"

"Nothing."

He shakes his head. "Something."

"Why do you think I'm gonna tell you?"

"It ever occur to you that I love you and want you to be happy?"

"No."

"I do."

"You're being earnest."

"I'm not gonna admit this again, but I want you both to be happy."

"You knew she was into me?"

"Everybody but you knew she was into you."

"Why didn't you tell me?"

"Not mine to tell." He turns, moves into his suite, starts setting up. "I don't know what you did. Or what she did. But get over it. Or apologize. She's the best thing that ever happened to you."

"I know."

"Don't fuck it up."

"Trying not to."

"You need to do better than that"

"Tell me something I don't know."

"I didn't fuck Kristen."

I can't help but chuckle. I would have bet a lot of money Dean took Kristen home. "That's shocking."

"Yeah. She was begging for it too."

"That an excuse to brag?"

He laughs. "No. She was. I wanted to. But all I could think was *this girl stood by Penny as she fucked over my brother.* Couldn't do it."

"Fuck. You have feelings."

"Don't tell anyone."

"I won't."

"You ditching her wedding yet?"

"No."

"Whatever's wrong with you and Leigh, I bet you a hundred bucks the wedding is gonna make it worse."

"Maybe."

He holds out his palm. *Pay up.*

"You still owe me two hundred bucks."

He laughs. "Double or nothing."

"I'll think about it."

He turns back to his suite. "Do me a favor, Ryan."

"Yeah?"

"Don't scare her off."

Don't scare her off.

It's good advice, even if it's hard to put into action.

This is the best I've got.

I hope it's good enough.

I slide the bag off my shoulder as I knock.

Footsteps move toward the door. "Yeah?"

"It's me."

"Ryan?" Leighton pulls the door open. Her blue-green eyes fill with surprise. "What are you—"

"Making you dinner."

"Okay…"

I step inside. Close the door behind me. Click the lock.

"You know I don't have food."

I hold up the blue Trader Joe's bag.

"You're insane."

"I prefer devoted."

Her lips curl into a half smile.

I move into the kitchen. Set the bag on the counter next to the fridge. Motion *come here.*

She crosses the room. "I'm sorry I bailed this morning. I needed to think."

"About?"

"I haven't figured it out yet."

"You want to talk about it?"

"No."

"Me either." My fingers skim the bottom of her tank top. It's the same thing she was wearing last night—tight, white, with lacing crisscrossed over her cleavage.

I bring my other hand to the straps. Undo the bow holding them together.

"Ryan." She looks up at me. "What are you…?"

I loosen the lacing. "Feeling you up." I back her into the counter.

She arches her hips, brushing her crotch against mine. "You're not gonna freak out?"

"Not today."

"You promise?"

"Yeah." I push her tank top off her right shoulder. Then the left. "You're the only fucking thing I can see right now."

Her breath hitches in her throat.

"Turn around."

Her ass brushes my crotch as she spins on her heels.

"Put your hands on the counter."

She plants one palm on the counter. Then the other. "What about dinner?"

"Bag's insulated."

"Oh."

"Unless you'd rather eat first."

Her hair falls over her cheeks as she shakes her head.

"I need you, Leigh. I need you to know that." I trace a line down her spine, from the base of her skull to the waistband of her shorts, then back up again. "I'm not good with words. I can't explain how I feel about you. But I can show you."

Her nod is heavy.

"I thought about you all fucking day." I unhook her bra and slide it off her shoulders. "I'm gonna be fucking miserable without you around."

"I won't go anywhere."

"You swear?"

"Yeah. But I'm not sure my word is any good at the moment." She groans as she rocks her hips against mine. "I need you to touch me."

"I need you."

"Ryan. Please."

"I want these shorts at your knees." I trace a line around their high waist. "I want them binding your legs while I fuck you."

"Mmm."

"I want you at my mercy, baby." I cup her breast with one hand. Toy with her nipple with my thumb.

Her groan is a mess of consonants.

"Tell me you want that."

"Please."

"It's gonna be hard."

"Yes."

"I'm gonna split you in half."

"Mmm."

I pin her to the counter as I toy with her breasts.

Her groan fills the room. "Fuck me."

"Not yet." I draw circles around her nipples.

She grinds against my ass. "Now."

I want to.

But not yet.

I need to push her to the edge. I need to be sure I'm the only thought in her head.

Fuck knows she's the only one in mine.

This makes sense.

I bring my lips to her neck, suck on her soft skin as I play with her tits.

She groans as my touch gets harder.

I roll her nipple between my thumb and index finger. Harder. Tighter. Until the bud is a deep pink and her groan is half agony, half ecstasy.

"Fuck." She rocks her hips against me. "Don't stop."

I toy with her other nipple. Watch it darken. Listen as her breath hitches. "I love the way you respond to me."

Her fingers dig into the counter.

"I want every inch of you, Leigh. I want you every way I can have you."

"You mean—"

"Yeah."

"Now?"

"No." I unbutton her shorts, roll them down her torso, over her ass, down her thighs. "I want your cunt wrapped around me today."

She groans.

"But soon."

"How are you so good at this?"

"It's you, baby. It's how you respond to me." I toy with her breast with one hand. Run the other over the waistband of her panties.

She arches her back, lifting her ass into the air.

I trace the waist of her panties over her lower back. My fingers skim her spine.

I trace a line over her ass, along her cunt, across her clit.

She's wet. I can feel her through her panties.

My balls tighten.

My cock begs me to move faster. To tear her clothes off and dive inside her.

Soon.

Very fucking soon.

Slowly, I roll her panties over her ass and down her thighs.

"Ryan." She leans onto the counter, bringing her ass into the air. "Please."

"Please what, baby?"

"Touch me."

"Yeah?" I brush the back of my hand against her cunt.

She's wet and she smells so fucking good. It takes everything I have to keep my pace.

She needs to stay on the edge.

I need to stay the center of her universe.

We need to be here—this beautiful place where everything makes sense.

We fit together. Belong together.

I don't have words for it.

But I do have this.

I tease her with one finger.

She lets out a heavy sigh.

Two.

"Ryan."

Three.

"Fuck."

I do it again. Again. Again.

With one hard motion, I slide two fingers inside her.

She arches her hips, driving her cunt over my fingers.

Her legs strain against her shorts. She stumbles.

I catch her. Wrap my arm around her waist to hold her in place.

She straightens herself. Presses her palms into the counter to keep her balance.

I bring my free hand to her chest. Toy with her nipple as I fuck her with my fingers.

Her breath hitches in her throat.

Her fingers dig into the counter.

She's almost there.

And, fuck, I need her there. I need her groan. I need her bliss.

She was right. I would move the stars for her. I will. I'll do whatever the fuck it takes.

I'll do anything for Leigh.

But, right now, I need to make her come.

I keep a steady pace, driving two fingers into her slick cunt as I roll her nipple between my thumb and forefinger.

"Ryan. Fuck." Her head tilts to the right. Her eyelids flutter closed.

With the next thrust of my fingers, she comes.

Her cunt pulses around me.

Her groans run together.

Her legs shake against her shorts.

"Please." Her breath stays heavy with need. "Fuck me."

I unzip my jeans. Let them fall to my knees. "Come here." I peel her body off the counter. Hold it against mine.

She groans as her back sinks into my chest.

I move her to the right. Press her against the wall. Toss my t-shirt over my head. "Hands above you."

Her palms go flat against the wall.

I bring my hands to her hips. Hold her in place as I drive into her with one steady thrust.

Fuck.

She feels good.

Like home.

"Ryan." She arches her back to drive me deeper.

I wrap my arm around her shoulders. Hold her body against mine as I pin her to the wall.

She cushions her head with her arms. Turns toward me. "Kiss me."

I do.

She sucks on my top lip.

I scrape my teeth against her bottom lip.

My tongue slides into her mouth. Dances with hers.

I kiss her hard and deep. Claim her mouth as I'm claiming her cunt.

She pulls back with a sigh. Turns to the wall. "Fuck me."

It feels so fucking good just being inside her. I want to stay like this forever. I want to die like this.

I take my sweet, sweet time pulling almost all the way out of her.

I fill her with slow, deep thrusts. I feel every fucking inch of her. Then I do it again.

Again.

Again.

Her toes squeeze the hardwood.

Her groans fill the room.

"Harder," she breathes.

My fingers dig into her hips.

I hold her in place as I thrust harder.

"Fuck," she groans. "Don't stop."

Like hell.

I fill her with steady strokes.

She rocks her hips to meet me.

We fall into a rhythm. I guide her cunt over my cock as I drive into her.

My body takes over.

I move faster. Harder.

My nails dig into her skin.

A groan falls off my lips. "Leighton. Fuck."

"Come for me." She rises onto her tiptoes, arching her back, driving me deeper. "Come inside me."

Fuck.

The need in her voice pushes me over the edge.

With my next thrust, I come.

My cock pulses as I fill her.

I thrust through my orgasm, spilling every drop.

Pleasure overtakes me. Every molecule of my body feels good. Every molecule of my body is tuned to her.

Relaxation washes over me. But I'm not finished. No matter how spent I am.

I slide my hand between her legs. Rub her clit with my index finger.

"Mmm. Ryan." She reaches back. Her palm plants on my ass. Her nails dig into my skin.

"Say it again."

She groans my name a little louder.

I find the spot where she needs me and I rub her harder.

Her eyelids press together.

Her teeth sink into her lip.

A few more brushes of my hand and she's there.

I rub her through her orgasm, reveling in the way she groans my name as she comes.

Reveling in the way her breath hitches and her nails sink into my skin.

When she's spent, she collapses.

I wrap my arms around her, carry her to the bed, lay her down.

She looks up at me with a dreamy smile. Pats the spot next to her.

This time I climb in next to her.

I lose myself in her arms.

3 7

LEIGHTON

Our night is easy. After dinner and work and a perfect 90s romantic comedy, we crawl into my bed. Fall asleep pressed a tangled mess of limbs and breath.

I wake before him. Dress in my workout gear. Put on sunscreen.

Even with my sunglasses, it's bright outside. I walk the path to the sidewalk.

When my foot hits the pavement, I pick up my pace. I run the two miles to the beach, take in the sight of the deep blue ocean rolling into the soft sand, turn, run back.

Heat rises. Sweat drips from my pores. My hair sticks to my cheeks and forehead.

Clarity eludes me.

I'm buzzing with endorphins when I get back to my apartment.

It's enough to convince me this is okay.

He freaked out about his ex while I was naked on his bed. I can deal with that.

He didn't even freak out. He asked to change locations.

It's a completely reasonable request. Even if it's been a year. Even if there's no way to convince myself it means he isn't over her.

All right.

It's not okay.

But I'll get to it being okay. Somehow.

I unlock the door. Step inside. The ocean breeze blows between the windows. But that does nothing to cool me down.

Ryan is sitting at my dining table in his glasses.

Only his glasses.

Mmm.

My worries fade. I forget I'm leaving the shop. I forget he's *something* with his ex. I forget he isn't all mine.

He smiles. "We're both off today."

"Are we?" I ask.

He nods. "How do you feel about being fucked so thoroughly you can't walk straight?"

My cheeks flush. "I can live with that."

"I need a better yes than that, baby."

"Yes, please."

His lips press into a wicked smile. "Come here."

"I'm a sweaty mess."

"I like it." He motions *come here* again.

I do.

And he makes good on his word.

―――――――

FOR THREE DAYS, EVERYTHING IS PERFECT.

Ryan and I laugh at work. We spend our evenings running together then designing side by side—covers for me, tattoo mock-ups for him. We fall asleep watching movies on his couch.

We sleep in his bed.

I barely think about how Penny used to sleep in it.

I barely think about our Thursday morning flight to Hawaii.

Or her Sunday at sunset ceremony.

Until we pack and drive to the airport and get through LAX's typical hellish security line.

And it's the only thing on my mind.

The *Hawaiian Airlines* logo might as well say *Penny still owns his heart.*

FIRST CLASS IS AMAZING. PLUSH LEATHER SEATS. PLENTY OF leg room. The quiet that comes only with people who are too rich to bother with small talk.

Ryan leans back in his seat. Intertwines his fingers with mine.

I squeeze his hand. "How much did this cost?"

"Less than you'd think."

I shake my head. "Rich people talk."

His laugh lights up his piercing blue eyes. "Yeah. What's it to you?"

"I have to readjust my mental image of you if you're rich."

"Why? I'm still me."

"Your parents have that huge house in Beverly Hills." I lean to the left—I have the window seat—until I'm pressed against the arm rest. I want to forget all the ugly thoughts in my head—it's only two days until Penny's rehearsal dinner, until I might lose him. I want to be lost in the moment with him. "That's already one strike against you."

"Most women consider wealth an upside."

"Most guys want lap dances from busy strippers." I run my fingers through his hair. "Most doesn't matter."

341

He nods *true*.

"How much do you make?"

His wavy hair falls in front of his eyes as he shakes his head. "Not going there."

"Guesstimate it for me."

"What about *not going there* makes you think I will?"

"The look in your eyes."

"I'm thinking about you in a bikini."

My lips curl into a smile. "Yeah?"

"No." His fingertips brush my wrist. He draws those same lazy circles. "I'm thinking about making you come under." He nods to the blanket tucked into the seatback pocket.

My cheeks flush. My body begs me to call his bluff. But I can't.

There's no way I can stay quiet.

There's no way I can relax enough to feel it.

That awful scene—Ryan standing up as Penny walks down the aisle, shooting her that *it's me* look, and whisking her into the sunset—is still playing in my head.

Those are nerves.

There's no way that's happening.

There's no way I'm letting my fear of losing him keep me from paradise.

"What are you thinking?" He draws a heart on my forearm.

I love you. I need you to tell me you love me. I'm not sure I can do this if I don't know you love me. "Nothing important."

"Bullshit."

"Is it that much?"

He arches a brow.

"Your salary."

"Don't have a salary. I make a quarter what the shop makes."

"I know what the shop makes."

"I know."

"That is a lot."

He laughs. "I guess arguing won't help my case. My parents don't think they're rich either."

"Business degree paid off."

"They'll be proud."

"Are they?"

"I don't know. Maybe." His eyes fix on mine. "Your mom?"

"I don't know. Maybe she follows me on Instagram. But then what would she be proud of?"

"You mostly post your hair and makeup."

"And boobs."

"Do you get creepy messages?"

"Sometimes."

"Like what?"

"Oh baby, come to my place. I'm not like those boys you've been with. I know how to handle a real woman." I drop the put-on voice. "I assume that's something about how I'm old. Or curvy. Or both." I drift back into my creepy-PMer impression. *"I'm gonna come on those gorgeous tits."*

"Not bad."

I shoot him my best side-eye.

He laughs. "Just saying. Guy's got game."

"Why do I care that he's gonna come?"

"Where's your generosity?"

"Oh my God. Don't even—"

"What if I pinned you to that chair and whispered—" He leans over the arm rest. Plants his hands on my shoulders. Brings his lips to my ear. "On your knees, baby. I'm gonna come on those gorgeous tits."

Uh…

His chuckle flows into my ears.

"I, uh… that's different."

"How?"

"It's you."

The flight attendant stops in front of us. Clears her throat. "Seatbelts on, please." She points to the fasten seatbelt sign.

Ryan flashes her a million-dollar smile.

She blushes, but shakes it off. Walks away with a *mmm, if only he was single* sigh.

"She wants to fuck you," I say.

"Who doesn't?"

"I like confident Ryan."

"I've never doubted my fuckability."

"Even when you lost all that weight?"

He laughs, but there's a sadness to it. "You got something against skinny guys?"

"No. But... you're..."

"You wouldn't have fucked me twenty pounds lighter?"

"No. I just... You know what women are like. We don't want to feel bigger than a guy."

"Shallow."

"Look at you."

"Look at me?"

"You're dating me."

He laughs. "You're actually admitting your gorgeous?"

"No. That my tits are amazing."

"That idiot on Instagram wasn't enough to convince you?"

I shake my head.

He leans in to brush his lips against my neck. "All of you is amazing, Leigh." He nips at my skin. Moves higher. Higher. Higher. His lips close around my earlobe. "I am gonna come on your tits."

"Here?"

"No. In the hotel."

"Oh."

"Unless that's a problem."

"Not at all."

"Good." He shifts into his seat just in time for the beverage tray to reach our row.

The flight attendant smiles at Ryan. "Anything to drink?"

"Water." He looks to me. "You?"

"Vodka."

He shoots me some serious side-eye. "It's noon."

"So?"

He shrugs *fine*. "Your body."

I turn to the flight attendant. "And water." Yes, he has a point about my tendency to drink my feelings. And about how I probably should be stricter about avoiding that, what with my genetic predisposition to alcoholism.

But it's still my body.

The flight attendant hands my drinks over first.

Ryan pulls down his tray table. Arranges everything then hands over my water.

The flight attendant moves onto the next row.

"Would you?" I ask.

"Would I what?"

I motion to her.

"If I don't want lap dances from strippers, you really think I want a one-night stand with a stranger?"

"It sounds so reasonable when you explain it."

"It is reasonable."

"So you say." I wrap my fingers around my water. Take a long sip. "We have all day today."

He nods.

"And tomorrow."

"Most of Saturday. Until the rehearsal dinner."

My stomach twists. Reality is ugly. It's much better hanging out in some fantasy world where Ryan and I are going to Hawaii to celebrate how much we enjoy fucking each other.

"We can skip it."

I shake my head.

"We can skip the fucking wedding if you want."

"No." I can handle it. In theory. "Your parents will be there."

"So?"

"They hate me already."

He brings his plastic cup to his lips. Takes a long sip of his ice water. "They'll love you."

"You sure?"

"When they see how happy you make me, yeah."

My lips curl into a smile. "You really think that?"

"Of course." He downs the last drop from his cup. Pops an ice cube in his mouth and sucks hard. It muffles his words. "You're my silver lining, Leigh."

I stare into his piercing blue eyes.

I want to believe him.

I really, really want to believe him.

My water fails to wash away my worries. The vodka is right there, all shiny and clear and inhibition erasing.

I can't think about this.

Not anymore.

But I'm not going to drink it away.

I don't *need* that.

I need to stop drowning my feelings.

I reach for the first distraction I can find. "I've been thinking about a date."

His eyes fix on mine.

"For my last day. Officially."

"Already?"

"Yeah." I take another long sip. Swallow hard. The water is freezing against my lips, tongue, throat. It cools me down.

Brings me back to reality. "The end of September. I know that's almost two months away, but—"

"That's so fucking soon."

"Yeah."

"I'm gonna miss you."

"You are?"

"Of course." He rest his palm on my cheek. Runs his thumb over my temple. "Seeing you is the best part of my day."

"More than doing tattoos?"

"Yeah."

Warmth spreads through my chest. "But that's your favorite thing in the world."

He shakes his head. "Making you come is my favorite thing in the world."

"That's cheesy."

"I don't care. It's true." He holds up the mini bottle of vodka and unscrews the cap. Booze spills over melting ice. "To you soaring." He raises his glass.

Does this count as drowning my feelings? I don't know. It's a celebration. And it's only half a shot. "If this is a toast, both of us should have a drink."

"Fair." He motions to my cup. *Give it to me.*

I take my last sip of water and hand it over.

He pours half the drink into my cup and hands it back.

His eyes fix on mine as he raises his glass. "To you."

I bite my lip. "I can't toast to me."

"Too bad." He taps his glass against mine then brings the cup to his lips.

I take a long sip. It's good vodka. Crisp. Clear. Smooth. I swallow it in three gulps.

Ryan follows suit. "You've gotta be careful getting me drunk."

"Oh?"

"I might do something stupid."

Like admit you're still in love with her? "Like what?"

"Try to fuck you in that bathroom."

My nose scrunches in distaste.

"Baby, that hurts."

"Not in a bathroom."

"Right here." He motions to the blanket again.

"When we get in."

"You sure you can wait that long?"

Hell no. I offer him a coy smile anyway.

He laughs. "That's bullshit."

"Maybe." I drop my cup on his tray. Slink into my seat and rest my head on his shoulder.

He runs his fingers through my hair. "I tell you how proud of you I am?"

"Once or twice."

"I'm being obnoxious, huh?"

"No. It's sweet." My eyelids press together. Being with him, doing nothing, feels so right. Why can't it always be this easy? "But I'm terrified."

"That's normal."

"I hate that I won't see you every day."

"You can."

"Every single day?"

"Of course."

"You move fast for a guy who isn't over his ex."

"Leigh."

"You know what I mean."

Frustration drips into his voice. "No. I don't. You're my favorite person in the world." He leans down. Presses his lips to my forehead. "When I think about losing you... it makes me sick. It steals my oxygen. I need you, Leigh."

I love you. Tell me you love me. Please. I need to know. I need to feel it.

348

The words climb into my throat.
But I swallow them down.
I can't say that yet.
Not until this is over.
Not until I'm sure he's really mine.

38

LEIGHTON

A winding pool wraps around a lush garden.

Behind it, the sun casts a sparkly glow over the azure ocean.

The guy at the counter smiles as he takes Ryan's credit card and presents us with orchid leis. Actual orchid leis made out of actual flowers.

Ryan's smile widens as he picks up a lei and hangs it around my neck.

I do the same to him.

He slides his arm around my waist. Laughs at the attendant's joke.

His fingers curl around the set of keys.

Mine curl around my giant pink suitcase's handle.

Ryan presses his palm against my lower back to lead me through the hotel lobby, past the cafe that smells of coffee, the gift shop overflowing with sarongs, the wide courtyard glowing in the sun.

The elevators are to the right.

Shiny silver doors pull apart. Three kids in swimsuits run

onto the concrete. A middle-aged dad chases after them. He's wearing a wedding ring. He's happy.

I step inside the elevator. Lean against the mirrored wall.

Ryan follows.

The doors slide together.

The rest of the world disappears as his lips meet mine. He sucks on my bottom lip. Soft. Then harder. Then he's scraping his teeth against my flesh.

He shifts his hips to pin me to the wall.

My fingers curl into his t-shirt. I tug at the cotton. Pull him closer. Kiss him deeper.

Yes. I need this. I need his love and affection pouring into me. He can't say it. But I can feel it.

When he kisses me like this, I can feel it.

He keeps me pinned to the wall as his tongue slips into my mouth.

I groan against his lips. Bring my other hand to his hair to hold his head against mine.

He kisses me until the elevator dings.

The doors pull open.

Ryan releases me.

My knees knock together. I nearly crumble onto the floor. I need him so badly. I need this—the two of us, in our own world—so badly.

I need to believe in that.

In him being mine.

He takes my hand as he leads me into the hallway, around the corner, to the third door on the right.

He slides the keycard into the lock.

The door flashes green. Ryan turns the handle and motions *after you.*

I step inside.

The room is gorgeous. And huge.

An orange and teal pineapple print comforter adorns the

massive king bed. A matching blanket hangs over the teal sofa. Sheer white curtains fall over the sliding doors to the balcony.

I kick off my sandals. Sink into the scratchy carpet.

It's half a dozen steps to the balcony. I pull the curtain aside, unlock the door, push it open.

Warm, sticky air greets me. Bright blue sky bleeds into the cerulean Pacific. The hotel pool is to the right. The freeway and the town beyond it are to the left.

It's like something out of a postcard.

Hello from paradise.

Ryan's footsteps move closer. He slides his arms around my waist. Brings his lips to my neck. "You look fucking adorable all contemplative."

"Yeah?"

"Yeah." He mumbles into my skin. "But it's worrying me."

"I'm just thinking."

"About?"

Things I want to forget. "It's beautiful here."

"Paradise."

"It really is. When it's just the two of us and the rest of the world is far away, everything is perfect. I want that."

"It is just the two of us."

It is.

But the world isn't far away.

It's infecting my thoughts.

I press my lips together. There's nothing to say. He's been forthright about his feelings. It's just, his feelings aren't moving fast enough for me.

How can I be upset about that?

He warned me his head was a mess.

I knew his head was a mess.

The whole point of this exercise is bringing him closure.

We're almost there. Three days, and we'll be there. He'll be mine. Or he'll still be hers.

But I'll know for sure.

I swallow hard. "I want to go to the pool."

"Of course you do." He brings his hands to my hips. Holds my body against his. "You're part mermaid."

"My hair is too short."

"Why can't mermaids have short hair?" He plants a soft kiss on my neck. "Why are you putting them in that box?"

"If mermaids were real, they'd be hairless and scaly. They're basically porn for sailors."

"They don't have cunts."

"Sailors love blow job."

He chuckles. "Do they?"

"Yeah. Everyone knows that."

"You're full of shit."

"Maybe. But it's true."

"Uh-huh."

"Find me a sailor who's anti-fellatio. I dare you."

His hands go to his sides as he takes a step backward. "Can't say I give a fuck on anyone else's opinions about fellatio."

"Did you really just say fellatio?"

He laughs. "You said it first." His smile spreads over his cheeks.

He looks happy.

Why can't I feel that?

Why can't I get over this mental image?

Why do I feel the same way I did as when I ran home to show off my report card and Mom's *I'm proud of you, honey* was so slurred it was hollow?

His expression shifts to something dirty and demanding. "You want to suck me off."

My cheeks flush. "Yes."

"After."

"You're cruel."

"I take that as a compliment."

"I know."

He motions to my hot pink suitcase. "I want to strip you out of that bikini before I come on your tits."

My sex clenches.

"I want you fucking desperate."

I step inside the hotel room. Pull the sliding door closed. Press my ass against the cold glass.

It's not enough to cool me down.

My stupid dress is in the way.

Ryan turns, sets his suitcase on the bed, starts unpacking. He's effortlessly casual. Like he didn't just promise to come on my chest.

I go to the bathroom—it's as teal as the rest of the room—fill a glass with water, swallow it in one go.

It does nothing to dampen the heat racing through me.

But then I don't want to cool off.

The buzz of desire is chasing away all the ugly thoughts in my head.

I strip to nothing in the bathroom. Saunter into the main room. Make a show of bending to unzip my suitcase and dig for my bikini.

Ryan drinks me in as I step into my swimsuit. His tongue slides over his lips. His pupils dilate. His cock strains against his jeans.

But he's still effortless about stripping to nothing and stepping into his Speedo.

He's actually wearing his Speedo.

God help me.

WARM WATER RUSHES OVER MY SKIN AS I JUMP INTO THE POOL.

I pull my arms to my sides to surface.

Blue sky fills my view. This pool is huge. And this part of it—the shallow end—is crowded. That's no good.

I take Ryan's hand and guide him into the tiny tunnel to our right. The air goes cold as the sun disappears. We pass the swim up bar—who sits at a bar when they could frolic around the pool—then come up to the back of a waterfall.

"On three?" I offer.

He chuckles as he presses his palm into my lower back. "You first."

"Chicken?"

"I'm here for the view."

My cheeks flush. The heat of his gaze makes my heart race.

I grab onto everything that makes sense. He wants me and I want him and we're half naked in paradise.

My hips sway as I step under the waterfall.

Cool water pounds my head and shoulders. My hair sticks to my forehead. My bikini threatens to come undone.

Still, I stay under the waterfall.

I hold my hand over my eyes and look out at the other side of the pool. The deep end. It's surrounded by people with books and cocktails, but the pool itself is empty.

Which means it's ours.

The world is ours. Right now, I feel it. I need to hold onto that.

I turn around. I can only barely see Ryan through the blur of running water. He's all hair and light skin and black fabric.

Barely any fabric. But still too much.

I bring my fingers to my lips, blow him a kiss, and fall backward in the water.

Fuck, this pool feels good.

I push off the bottom. Glide toward the deep end. Three long, slow underwater strokes and I emerge.

The deep end is a huge circle twenty feet wide. Lawn chairs line one side. Fake rocks and plants line the other. They make an almost-natural jungle gym, with high spots and nooks and baby waterfalls.

I spin in the middle of the pool. Watch Ryan swim toward me.

God, the way his shoulders flex and relax. The lines of ink running down his back. The sunlight casting him in a soft glow.

He's a good swimmer, but I'm better. I dive under the water and glide to the waterfall behind me.

I surface in front of the blur of white-blue.

Water pounds my head as I enter. The world gets darker, more diffuse. Blue sky and sunlight filter through the running water, breaking into fragments of light and color.

Someone moves closer.

The illusion breaks as Ryan glides past the running water.

There's just enough space for both of us.

I scoot backward, find a seat on a curved section of the wall.

He moves closer.

Closer.

Until he's pinning me against the wall. "You're fucking brilliant."

I nod.

"Fuck, you have no idea what I want to do to you right now." His fingers trace a line down my neck. Over the strap of my bikini.

He traces its line into the water, over my triangle top, over my breastbone, along the other triangle.

Slowly, he pushes one triangle aside, exposing me.

No one can see—you can't see anything past the running water—but I still feel like I'm on display.

My sex clenches from the exhibition of it.

He cups my breast with his palm. Drags his thumb against my nipple. It's different in the water. Smoother and harder at the same time.

He watches as he pulls the other triangle aside.

My breast spills from my bikini.

I'm topless in a pool packed with a hundred people.

My thoughts dissolve as he covers me with his palm. Teases my nipples with his thumbs.

"Fuck." I bite my lip. Try to wrap my legs around him.

He plants one hand on the curved wall beneath me. But he stays floating. He's right there, but his body isn't connecting with mine.

The water is between us.

I bring my hands to his ass. Pull him closer.

There.

His crotch brushes mine.

He's hard.

I want that. I want it here. I don't care that someone could see. That I won't be able to keep quiet. That I'll probably get arrested.

I only care about getting my fill of Ryan.

He slides his arm around me. Uses it to hold himself in place as he toys with my breasts.

"You're fucking perfect." He presses his lips to my neck. "I ever tell you that?"

I shake my head.

"Fuck." He presses his lips to my neck as he pulls one triangle over my breast, covering me. "I'm gonna come if I keep this up."

"That isn't a problem."

"Yeah, it is." He adjusts my swimsuit, returning it to its

rightful place. "I'm not coming until I get those pretty red lips around my cock.

He pushes back, through the waterfall, to the massive pool.

I take back the control I can. Lead him to the steps then push off them. Back to the deep end.

He chases me around the pool, under the water, through the tiny tunnel, back to the packed shallow end.

He wraps his arms around me.

Holds my body against his as he brings his lips to my ears. "I'm gonna get you back for that, baby."

"I know."

He shakes his head. "No, Leigh. You have no fucking idea."

LEIGHTON

B y the time we're alone in the elevator, I'm not sure which of us is torturing the other.

He tugs at the towel wrapped around my chest. Watches as it hits the floor with a thud.

His eyes trace my body. He does it slowly, like I'm a work of art. Like it's the first time. Like he's memorizing every line.

But is that because he needs every ounce of me?

Or because he knows this might be the last time?

No. We have another day and a half until the dinner. There's no way we'll make it a day and a half without stripping to nothing.

But then maybe he—

My thoughts dissolve as he brings his lips to mine. His kiss is hard, hungry. Like he's claiming me. Like he's desperate for every drop of me.

I try to rise to my tiptoes, but I slip on the slick floor.

There.

My feet find the towel. Still, it's too slippery. I can't move. I can't get closer. Or break our embrace.

I want both. And neither. I want to tell him I love him. And I want to run a million miles away from anything that might hurt.

How can I let myself fall harder?

How can I stop myself?

It's Ryan.

He's everything.

The elevator dings. He shifts his hips, releasing me. He bends to scoop my towel and drapes it over his arm.

He steps into the hallway. Turns to me with a smug smile as he unwraps his towel and drapes it over mine.

He's just as beautiful with soft orange wall paper and fluorescent light surrounding him.

His wet hair sticks to his forehead.

A bead of water drips off his chin. It traces a line down his chest and stomach. Beneath his belly button. Past that soft tuft of hair. All the way to the waistband of his swimsuit.

I swallow hard.

He takes my hand. Leads me to our hotel room. It's only a few dozen feet, but it feels like a million miles. I need him. I need the world disappearing again. I need to lose myself in my lust.

He stops at the door.

Oh. I have the key.

I slide it into the lock. Watch it flash green. Turn the handle.

I step inside.

He follows.

The door slams shut.

Sunlight streams through the sheer curtains.

We're alone again. And I feel it. I feel that the world is ours.

I move into the room. Into the wide-open space between the couch and the balcony.

Ryan places his body behind mine, his chest against my back, his crotch against my ass.

His breath warms my ear. "You like being on display, baby?"

"Yes."

His voice drops to something low and demanding. "Pull the curtains."

My sex clenches. My feet sink into the carpet as I move to the sliding door. There. I grab the plastic rod and pull it all the way to the right.

The room gets brighter.

The light gets harsher.

It bounces off the glass with a glare.

It casts highlights over Ryan's hair, shoulders, stomach.

Casts shadows behind him.

It means something, shadows being behind him, but I can't connect the dots. Not with my brain screaming *need Ryan now*.

"Come here," he demands.

It's three steps to him.

His fingertips skim my hips. He traces a line over my hips, up my side and chest, along my shoulder, up my neck, along my chin.

He catches my lower lip with the pad of his thumb.

Slowly, he slides the digit into my mouth.

My eyelids press together as my lips close around him. I suck the taste of chlorine off his finger. Until it's just Ryan's skin.

But it's not enough.

A thumb isn't enough.

I need *him* in my mouth.

My eyelids blink open. Find his. He's in that same trance of lust, but there's something else in his expression. This sense of control. Like he knows exactly how to work me.

He's like this with everything he does—an in-control perfectionist.

And, fuck, he really is good at this.

He drags the fleshy pad of his thumb across my lip. Over my chin. Down my neck and chest.

He takes his time tracing the outline of my triangle top.

His touch is light. His fingers slide along my slick skin with barely any friction.

I'm ready to beg him to touch me properly when he drags his fingertips down my stomach.

He traces the waist of my bikini bottom.

His fingers curl into the straps. They toy with the bow holding the right side together.

Then the left.

Then he's brushing his fingers against my sex, pressing the wet Lycra against me.

I need it gone.

I need his hands on my skin.

I need him as desperate as I am.

Slowly, he drags his fingertips up my stomach. He traces a triangle to its tip, follows the halter strap.

He tugs the bow undone.

Peels my bikini top from my skin.

His pupils dilate as he brings his hands to my chest.

He toys with my nipples. It's different than it was in the water. Less smooth. More intense.

He draws circles around my tender buds. It starts soft—I can barely feel it—then gets harder.

Desire pools between my legs. This feels so fucking good, but I need more.

I shimmy out of my bikini bottoms then kick them aside.

I move closer.

My hands skim his hips. I trace the waist of his speedo. Cup him over the swimsuit.

He's hard. I need that. I need him out of his fucking mind.

His hands curl around my wrists. "Not yet."

My sigh is a whine. Now. I need him now.

He releases my right wrist. Brings his hand to my breast. Toys with my nipple again and again.

My eyelids press together.

My sex clenches.

Every brush of his fingers winds me up. The tension in my sex builds. It gets higher, deeper, tighter.

My body buzzes with desire.

And all from his hands on my chest.

"Fuck." I reach for him. Get his chest. Dig my fingers into his firm flesh. "Ryan."

He moves to my other breast. Teases it just as mercilessly.

Finally, he releases his grip on my wrist.

Both hands go to my chest.

His rolls my nipples between his thumb and index finger. It sends a pang straight to my sex.

He does it harder.

Harder.

"Fuck." It's the only word I have. The only way to explain what he does to me.

He toys with me again and again.

Winds me up.

Gets me panting.

Fuck. I'm aching with desire.

"Open your eyes, baby," he demands.

I do.

He wraps his fingers around my wrist and brings my hand to his cock. I cup him over his swimsuit. Rub the soft, wet fabric against his hard flesh.

His lips part with a groan.

His eyelids press together.

His brow furrows and softens.

Mmm. He looks so fucking good wracked with pleasure.

I need more. But I need to stay in this trance too.

To feel like I'm under his spell.

I rub him over his swimsuit. Watch pleasure spill over his expression.

His eyes blink open.

He stares back at me. Stares into me. Into some part no one else sees.

He brings his palm to my cheek. Runs his thumb along my lower lip.

He pulls his hand back. Rests his thumb on my chin. "On your knees, baby."

Yes.

My body cries with relief.

I need his pleasure. More than I need mine. More than I need to come.

And I really fucking need to come.

I bring my hands to his hips. Use them for support to lower myself onto my knees.

He leans down to slide his thumb between my lips.

I stare into his eyes as I suck on the digit.

Fuck, he tastes so good. And I'm so close to being exactly where I need to be.

He pulls his thumb from my lips.

His hands go to his swimsuit.

He pushes it from his hips.

The scrap of black fabric falls to his ankles.

He steps out of it, one foot at a time, and kicks it aside.

And there's Ryan. All of him, hard and ready for me.

Fuck, he's big this close.

My tongue slides over my lips. I look up at him, begging him with my eyes.

He stares back at me. "Suck me off."

Fuck. Yes.

My fingers dig into his hips as I lean forward. Brush my lips against his tip.

He shudders from the soft touch.

I do it again. Again. Again.

It feels so fucking good, making him shake. But it's not enough.

I need more than a tease.

I need him groaning my name as he comes.

I wrap my fingers around his firm flesh. Hold him in place as I bring my lips to his cock.

My tongue slides around his tip. He tastes good. Like chlorine and like Ryan.

I do it again, softer.

Then harder.

His hand knots in my hair.

His groans spur me on.

I look up at him as I take him into my mouth.

Wet waves fall over his piercing blue eyes. But it's not enough to hide the bliss in his expression.

Right now, he's wrapped around my finger.

Right now, I'm the only thing he wants.

Feminine power courses through my veins. He's at my mercy. I'm still at his mercy, but I don't care.

It feels so fucking good.

I suck on his tip until I can only taste Ryan.

Then I take him deeper.

Deeper.

His palm presses against the back of my head. He pushes me farther. To the brink of what I can take.

I swallow to relax my throat.

Take him as deep as I can. Wrap my fingers around the base of his cock so I have all of him.

Slowly, I pull back.

Then I do it again.

Again.

Again.

My eyelids press together as he nudges me with his palm. I surrender to his guidance, taking him deeper then pulling back to suck on his tip, then doing it again.

His free hand goes to my breast. He toys with my nipple as I suck on him.

My sex clenches.

Desire courses through my body.

I feel so good I can barely move.

But I need this. Need him.

I move faster.

Suck harder.

Flick my tongue against his tip.

He lets out a low groan.

There. That's it. I flick my tongue against him again. Softer. Longer. Harder. Shorter.

He tugs at my hair.

I pull back to groan. "Do that again." I wrap my lips around him. Savor the taste of him.

He tugs at my hair as I flick my tongue against him.

I do it again. Again. Again.

"Fuck, Leigh." His breath hitches.

His thighs shake.

He tugs harder.

He's almost there.

I need him there.

I swirl my tongue around his tip. Watch his eyes fill with ecstasy.

His palm nudges against the back of my head.

He stares down at me, asking for permission.

I nod. Groan a yes into his flesh.

His other hand goes to my head.

He tugs at my hair as he holds me in place.

His hips shift as he thrusts into my mouth.

I relax my throat as he rocks into me again and again.

He goes faster. Harder. Deeper.

I swallow so I don't gag.

I stare up at him.

Watch his eyelids press together, his brow soften, his teeth sink into his lip.

There.

"Fuck, Leigh." He tugs at my hair, pulling me backward.

His cock pulses.

His spills over my chest as he comes.

His eyelids blink open.

He stares at me like I'm heaven sent.

Like I'm everything he wants.

The only thing he wants.

RYAN

L eighton steps out of the bathroom in a slinky silver dress. She kicks, showing off the mid-thigh slit.

My eyes trace a line from her toes to the gap in her dress.

That thing was made for her. "You look like a spy." Like a gorgeous, too hot for this world spy.

Her hair is pulled back the way it was the first night we fucked.

Silver makeup brings out the green in her eyes.

Purple-pink lipstick draws my gaze to her mouth.

A flashy pendant hangs between her breasts.

"Who says I'm not?" She presses her back against the wall and places her hands in the shape of a gun. "What is your mission, Maddox?"

"Making you come."

"Hmm." She blows smoke from her imaginary pistol. "I may be able to work with you."

"May?"

"It's a vague promise. Is that one orgasm? Two? Three?"

"Until you beg me to stop."

"Hmm." She sets her imaginary gun on the dresser. "And how will you do this?"

"How will I make you come?"

She nods.

"How do you want it, baby?"

"Mr. Maddox, I'm not sure if these pleasantries are appropriate for our relationship."

"What should I call you?"

"Ms. Black."

"That's awfully formal, Ms. Black. Do you really want to scream *Maddox* when you come?"

She breaks character with a laugh. It's quick, a second, then she shakes it off.

Back to the aloof spy.

"I don't wish to scream anything when I come. Screaming will alert our enemies to our location." She scrapes the carpet with her toes.

"We should be quiet?"

"Of course. Discretion is of primary importance."

"How much time do we have?"

Her eyes go to the alarm clock on the nightstand. "Not much. My mission commences at the top of the hour."

"Your mission?"

"I'm afraid that's classified."

"But we're here together. There must be some reason for that."

"Our missions are aligned?"

I nod.

"Still. I can't be sure."

"But you have twenty minutes?"

"At best."

I cross the room to her. Wrap my fingers around her wrists. Pin her to the wall with my hips.

Fuck, I want her so badly.

We've had two perfect days in Paradise. We've done every single fucking thing I wanted to do here. She completely ignored my attempts to teach her to surf. Insisted she knew what she was doing, even when she fell down for the fifteenth time. She squealed with delight as she glided down a zip line. We danced under the fucking moonlight.

I press my lips to her neck. "Any weapons I should know about?"

"Besides my wit?"

I break character with a chuckle. "And your charm."

"What do you think?"

My fingers find the edge of her dress. I trace the slit up her thigh. Then down, over her skin.

She arches her back, shifting her hips against mine.

"A thigh-holster." My palm curls around her leg. I bring it higher, higher, higher.

"No." Her breath hitches in her throat. "Not at the moment."

"How can I trust you?"

"All I have is my word, Mr. Maddox."

"How do I know that's any good?" Higher.

"You don't."

"It's a good thing I want my hands on your thighs."

"Yes. It's—" Her words fade into a moan. "Fuck." Her nails dig into my shoulders as my fingers skim her cunt.

My balls tighten. "You're naked under here."

She drops character with a heavy nod.

I forget all about the game we're playing. "That for me?"

"Yeah."

"And this?" I bring my other hand to her chest. Slide it under her tight dress. Toy with her nipple.

"It's all for you." Her teeth sink into her bottom lip. "It's always for you."

My thumb finds her clit. It's instinct. I need her body pressed against mine. I need her lost in ecstasy.

Everything has been fucking perfect. But that's about to end.

Tonight is Penny's rehearsal dinner.

Who knows what the fuck that will bring?

"Ryan." She tugs at my suit jacket. "You… I… Harder."

I rub her harder.

Tease her with one finger.

Two.

Her eyelids press together.

Her tongue slides over her lips.

She's lost in me, but that isn't enough.

I bring my lips to hers.

She arches into me, opening her mouth to make way for my tongue, parting her legs to invite my hand.

I rub her until she's groaning against my mouth.

Then I pull my hand to her thigh and drag my lips over her cheek.

I plant a soft kiss on her collarbone.

Then lower, just above the neckline of her dress.

Her hand knots in my hair. She nods a *yes*. A *please*. A *now*.

My hands go to her hips. I pull her body onto mine as I walk backward. It's a messy path to the bed, but we get there.

I push her onto the mattress.

Her eyes find mine as she scoots up the bed. She hikes her dress to her waist. Pries her thighs apart.

Fuck, she's beautiful.

I climb onto the bed. Place myself between her legs.

She shudders as I drag my lips up her inner thigh.

I go higher and higher and higher.

Her hand knots in my hair as I bring my lips to her cunt.

She's already wet and she's so fucking sweet.

I lick her from top to bottom. Then from bottom to top.

I do it a little faster.

A little harder.

I take my time tasting every inch of her. Then I bring my lips to her left labia and suck hard.

"Fuck." She groans as I scrape my teeth against her flesh.

I move to her right and do it again.

Her heel digs into my back.

My jacket gets too fucking heavy. Even with the AC turned up high, I'm burning up in this thing.

But that doesn't fucking matter.

Making her come matters.

It's all that matters.

Still, I revel in her pleasure. I suck on her lips. I scrape my teeth against her. I plunge my tongue inside her.

She unfolds for me. She spreads wider, digs her heel into my back, tugs at my hair.

"Ryan." She tugs harder. "Please. Make me come. Please."

My cock pulses. She's so fucking sexy like this.

She groans as I bring my mouth to her clit.

I brush my lips against her as lightly as I can.

I do it again.

I do it until she's panting.

Then I take her clit between my lips and I suck hard.

"Fuck." She squeezes me with her thighs. Her knees wobble.

I bring my hands to her ass and hold her in place.

Then I suck on her clit until her groans are running together. Until she's pulsing as she comes on my lips.

She gets wetter. Sweeter. Louder.

I pull back to nip at her thigh.

She stares down at me, her blue-green eyes hazy with lust. Slowly, she nods.

I dive between her legs.

Flick my tongue against her clit. I start soft and slow. Then I go harder. Faster.

There.

She tugs at my hair as I hit just the right speed, just the right pressure.

A few flicks of my tongue and she's there.

She groans my name as she comes.

Her hand finds my suit jacket. She tugs at it, tugging me up her body. "Fuck, Ryan."

I press my lips to hers.

Her hand curls into my hair. She holds my head against hers as she kisses me hard and deep.

I keep her pinned to the bed.

Keep my mouth against hers.

Fuck, she tastes good everywhere.

Her hands find my belt. She pulls it from the loop. Undoes the buckle.

Then she stops.

Fuck.

Someone's knocking on the door.

They're still knocking on the door.

My brother's voice flows through the wood. "You miss me?"

"Tell him to fuck off," she breathes.

I could.

I want to.

But I want her like this. I want her on the edge. I want her aching for me.

I shake my head. "We should go." I bring my hand to my lips. Suck the taste of her from my thumb.

Her gaze goes to my crotch. "You *want* to go?"

"I want to make you wait."

"But you..." Her eyes nearly bug out of her head. "You do?"

I nod.

"Why?"

"It turns me on."

"But you're already—"

"It's better when you draw it out."

"Okay." Her eyes find mine. "Are you sure?"

"A hundred percent."

"What if I demand you fuck me?"

"I'm not gonna deny you."

She presses her lips together, assessing her options. Finally, she nods an *okay*. "I'll get the door. You should—" she nods to the bathroom.

"Wipe the taste of your cunt from my lips?"

"Say one more thing like that and I will fuck you in front of Dean."

"Good to know." It's a tempting offer.

She adjusts her dress and checks her reflection—perfect, as always.

I move into the bathroom. Wash my hands and face. Ask myself if I'm fucking crazy for making her wait.

We could ditch this stupid dinner.

Stay in and fuck like rabbits instead.

I could be inside her.

But the thought of her fighting her arousal as she laughs with Dean—

Fuck. Thinking about this shit isn't the way to get my cock to cool it.

She *is* laughing at something Dean's saying.

And he's chuckling in that shit-stirring way of his.

I wipe my hands and face. Move into the main room.

Dean nods to Leighton. "Damn. He cleans up nice."

"Tell me something I don't know." She motions *come here*. When I do, she brings her hands to my tie. Adjusts the knot. "You look amazing."

"You look sexy as fuck."

"Thank you." She rises to her tiptoes to press her lips to mine. "Shoes."

They're sitting by the dresser. I take three steps backward, bend to pick them up.

She smiles. "I can do that."

"But I can look up your dress if I do it." I motion to the bed.

She takes a seat.

I drop to my knees between her legs.

"This is familiar." Her gaze flits to Dean then it's on me. "What would you do if I jumped you now?"

"Now?" My fingers skim her ankle as I slide her right shoe onto her foot and secure the clasp. "Let him watch."

"Hmm." She chews on her bottom lip as she considers it.

My cock whines for attention.

I ignore it as I slide her other shoe on and secure the clasp.

She leans down and offers me her hands.

I take them, let her help me up.

Dean laughs. "You're a disgustingly cute couple." Earnesty drips into his voice.

It's weird.

Leighton stands. Smooths her dress. Slides her arm around my waist. "Thank you."

"You guys eat?" He laughs. "Besides—I'm not even gonna make that joke."

"You're growing up." She laughs. "Wait. Why would we eat?"

"Dinner was family only. We're invited for dessert and cocktails," he says. "You didn't know?"

I shake my head. "Let's stop somewhere first."

"No. It's fine. I want to get back to the room as soon as

possible." She slides her hand under my jacket. Rests her palm on my side.

Dean chuckles. "He's that merciless?"

She shrugs, playing coy, but it's written all over her face. She needs me inside her.

My heartbeat slows as we make our way down the hall.

The elevator is crowded with a mix of people in swimsuits and casual clothes. We stick out like sore thumbs.

Hawaii is the land of laid back attire. Nobody wears suits or *fuck me, I'm a spy* cocktail dresses.

A tall woman eyes us curiously. I guess it's strange, two guys accompanying one girl. Especially when the girl is somehow satisfied and wanting at the same time.

I intertwine my fingers with Leighton's as the elevator doors slide open.

We wait for the families and couples to pour onto the concrete. I motion *after you* to Dean. Then I lead Leighton through the hallway.

The restaurant is here. At the hotel.

It's right there. On our left.

The chatter of conversation fills the air as Dean pulls the door open.

His eyes meet mine. He raises a brow. *You okay?*

I nod, but, honestly, I don't fucking know.

One way or another, tonight is the beginning of the end.

41

RYAN

There are a hundred people crammed into a space meant for two dozen. It's Penny's party on steroids. Twice the guys in suits. Twice the Dockers-wearing crew. Twice the expectations.

Leighton's fingers curl into my side. Even with my suit jacket and my shirt in the way, her touch is hard.

The easiness of the day is gone.

She shakes off the furrow in her brow. Presses her lips into a perfect smile.

But it doesn't fool me.

She doesn't want to be here.

Her gaze moves over the room. The restaurant is all open space at the moment. It curves around a man-made lake. A mesh fence keeps out bugs and birds. It does nothing to block the sunset.

The sun sinks into the deep blue ocean. It casts an orange glow over the beige sand. It's gorgeous, but it's nothing compared to Leighton.

"Oh my God, you're here!" A bouncy voice flows into my

ears. Kristen. She steps through a group of older women to greet us. Her cheeks flush as she nods *hello* to Dean. "Hey."

"Hey." He nods back.

She bites her lip as she looks him up and down. He said he rejected her, but not how. He must have made some excuse. Some promise of *another time*. She's got that look in her eyes—*let me cash in on the other time now*.

His expression screws with confusion. This might be the first time he's ever asked a woman to wait. He's not exactly—

He's a manwhore.

It makes him happy. He's safe. It's not my business and I like to keep it that way.

Leighton spares us from their awkward stare. "Your dress is cute. Is that the bridesmaid's dress?"

Kristen twirls. Corral chiffon twirls with her. "No. That's tomorrow. But it's not terrible. Penny was specific about the color, but the rest was up to me."

"Can I see?" Leighton asks.

Kristen shakes her head. "Sworn to secrecy."

"And the color?" Leighton asks.

Kristen points to the baby pink bouquet lining the buffet table. She winks at Leighton. "Our secret."

The soft pink flowers are gorgeous.

But they're the kind of thing Penny hated. Does she still hate them or is this one of the million ways she's changed?

I don't know.

And I'm not sure I want to.

"Your dress is great." Kristen's gaze fixes on Leighton's chest. "Bold."

"Slutty." Leighton laughs. "I know. Probably not appropriate for this kind of event, but I had to have it when I saw it, and I haven't had a chance to wear it."

"It could be good for some role play." Kristen looks to me curiously, like she's assessing whether or not I'd be into role play. "I can see it now. James Bond and the femme fatale."

"Austin Powers," I say.

Kristen's nose scrunches with confusion. "Huh. I guess that's different."

Leighton laughs. "Inside joke."

"Oh." She turns to Dean. "How have you been? Busy?"

"Yeah." He shoots her a *fuck me* smile. "But I'm free tonight." His gaze goes to me. "In theory."

"Worried Ryan's going to cry over Penny?" Kristen's dark eyes fill with regret as she realizes her words. "I mean... Uh... It could happen."

"Yeah." Leighton pulls her hand to her side. "It could."

"I'm sure he's happier with you. Really, you're a much better fit than he and Penny were. She was always talking about how it wasn't right anymore. I mean. Not always. But toward the end." Kristen's voice is encouraging. She's completely unaware she's saying tactless shit.

Dean laughs. "Should we get a drink?"

"Yeah. Okay." Her eyes light up. "You know. I'm free tonight too." She takes his hand, ready to head to the bar.

But Leighton stops her. "Did you ever get that lap dance?"

"Oh. Yeah. I guess you and Ryan left before that. Whatever happened? You seemed upset?" Kristen asked.

"I fucked her senseless," I say.

Kristen blushes. "Oh. Good. That's always good."

"What happened to your boyfriend?" I ask.

She frowns. "Well... I don't actually... I just said that so you wouldn't get jealous."

"So you got the dance?" Leighton asks.

Kristen nods. "Yeah. A little after you left. Your friends— the girl with the short hair and the hot guy. They left. And so it was just me and Dean and Penny and Frank. And this dancer came over in this amazing strappy black outfit. When she offered us a dance, I just had to say yes. It was out of this world."

"She was fucking jazzed to dance for a woman," Dean says. "Barely looked at me the whole time."

"No. She was good about giving both of us attention. It was amazing. I was transfixed. But when it ended, she walked away, and I felt sort of... dirty, I guess. Used, maybe. It was obvious how fake it was. Like a bad porno." She turns to Dean. "You think?"

He nods. "I only watch amateur stuff."

Leighton rolls her eyes. "You bring that up five times a day."

"The world has to know. Homemade or bust." They share a look. He must decide she's okay, because he turns and whispers something in Kristen's ear.

She waves a goodbye then follows him to the bar.

I slide my arm around Leighton's waist. She leans into my touch, but her gaze stays fuzzy.

I bring my lips to her ear. "Let's ditch this party. Go back to our room."

She shakes her head. "I need to show off my dress." She turns, bringing her neck to my lips.

I nip at her skin.

She tugs at my suit-jacket.

For a moment, everything makes sense. She wants me. I want her. The rest of the world doesn't matter.

Then that familiar voice floats into my ear. "I hope I'm not interrupting." Penny clears her throat.

Leighton turns to my ex-girlfriend. Her eyes narrow to something protective. "It's all the swimming. I keep seeing him in his speedo. It's making me insatiable."

"You still have that?" Penny laughs. "I didn't think his mom would talk him into the summer league swim team."

Leighton taps her heels together. She's thinking something, hurting over something, but I can't put the pieces together. She doesn't want to be here. She doesn't want to leave.

Does she want me to prove I'm over Penny?

Or does she want me to run a million miles away?

I don't have a fucking clue.

I turn back to my ex-girlfriend. "No. It's a new one."

Leighton laughs. "You intentionally bought a Speedo?"

"You saying it's not flattering?" I tease.

She shakes her head. "Absolutely not." Her gaze fixes on Penny. On the rock around her ring finger. "Where's Frank?"

"He had to see his parents to their hotel room. His mom isn't well. He's going to stay with her." Penny digs her nail into the pad of her thumb. "He's a gentleman."

Leighton nods *of course*. She turns to me. Studies my expression like I'm a design she can't figure out. "Excuse me. I'm going to get a drink."

"Of course." Penny points to the bar behind us. "It's an open bar."

"Of course." Leighton parrots her tone.

"Stay." My fingers curl into her side.

She shakes her head. "I'm sure you need to talk."

My body goes cold as she slips from my grasp. She spins on her heels and disappears into the crowd.

Penny stays put. "Is she okay?"

"Do you care?"

"Of course. I want the best for you."

Leighton's dress strains against her ass as she leans over the bar. She points to a bottle on a high shelf.

The bartender laughs. His gaze goes right to her tits. He turns away like he can't bear looking at anything besides her cleavage.

Not that I blame the guy.

Her tits are fucking amazing.

But my fingers are still curling into fists. Who the fuck does this guy think he is flirting with my girlfriend?

Who the fuck does Penny think she is asking if Leighton is okay?

"Really, Ryan. You're a great guy. You deserve to be happy." She rests her palm on my forearm.

I pull my arm away. Brush my hair from my eyes. "Thanks."

"I'm sorry if I'm overstepping. I'm not sure where the lines are, right now. I feel like I'm in the Twilight Zone." She looks around the room and shakes her head. "This doesn't feel like the night before my wedding."

"What's that supposed to feel like?"

"I'm not sure anymore." Her lips curl into a frown. "Frank bailed so quickly. I know his mom is sick. But I hate doing these things alone."

"If he's good to her, he'll be good to you."

"He is." She bites her lip. "I just… it's nice to see you. I swear, you're the only person here who really knows me."

"I don't really know you."

"Of course you do."

I nod to the pink flowers at the buffet table. "That isn't you."

"I know. This whole thing isn't me. But it's already done. The only way I can change any of this is if I run away tonight."

"You're nervous. It's normal."

"I hope you're right." Her eyes fix on mine. They bore into mine. She's asking for something.

I don't know what she wants.

But then I don't care.

Not when Leighton is drinking her feelings at the bar. "Congrats, Pen. Really. You'll be great tomorrow."

"Thanks."

I nod goodbye, turn, make my way to the bar. It's crowded with guys in suits. Dean and Kristen are nowhere to be seen.

But Leighton is still sitting on the stool on the left.

She brings her glass to her lips and takes a long sip.

"Hey." I slide between the stools. Place my body next to hers.

She looks up at me. "Hey." She downs what's left of her drink in one gulp, slams it on the bar, motions *hit me* to the bartender.

He leers at her tits as he pours.

"You want something?" She turns toward the bartender. "My boyfriend drinks bourbon."

He frowns at the word *boyfriend*. "I'll hook you up, buddy."

"Thanks." She spins on her stool, so she's facing me. "How's Penny?"

"Nervous." I unpeel her fingers from her glass. "How many is that?"

"Three."

"Maybe you should slow down."

"Maybe you should drop the condescending tone."

"You only get one liver."

"My liver." She picks up her glass. Takes a long sip. Makes a show of sighing with pleasure. "Perfect."

My stomach sinks. Something is wrong. But what the fuck is it? "Talk to me, Leigh."

"What about?"

"Why you're frowning."

"I don't drink that much. You should mind your own business."

"You're my business."

"You wouldn't say that shit if you didn't know my mom's a drunk."

"I do know." I run my fingers along her jawline. "I fucking love that I know. I love when you let me in."

Her brow softens. The frustration in her eyes fades to affection. "Ryan, I…"

"Best shit we got." The bartender interrupts with my bourbon.

She presses her lips together. Swallows whatever she was about to say. Holds up her glass. "Now we can toast."

"What to?"

"The end of this."

I lift my glass. Clink it against hers. Drink.

It's good bourbon, but it doesn't go down easy. It burns my throat. Twists my stomach. Sends my thoughts to ugly places.

"You think Dean took Kristen home?" she asks.

"He told me he didn't fuck her."

"What?" She arches a brow. "No way."

"Said he couldn't get over how she stood by Penny."

"Damn." She takes a long sip. "He's admitting he has feelings again. This is an alarming trend."

"Probably good for him."

She nods *yeah*. "She's still looking at you." Leighton motions to Penny, in the middle of the room, talking to her dad and—

Fuck. That's my mom.

He catches us staring. Waves.

"Fuck." I down the rest of my bourbon.

Leighton turns to me with a curious expression. "Huh?"

"That's my mom."

"Oh." She stares at the conversation. "It is."

Mom waves. She turn and makes her way toward us.

Leighton laughs. "You're nervous."

"Yeah." I set my glass on the bar. "Another when you get a second."

The bartender nods *sure thing*. He stares at Leighton's tits as he refills me. "You need one too, sweetheart?"

She stares at her glass like it's the hardest question she's ever heard. "Yeah. Sure." She throws her head back to finish her drink then sets it on the bar.

He smiles as he refills her. He's practically screaming *get rid of this loser and come home with me.*

I slide my arms around her reflexively.

My lips go to her ear. "Talk to me, baby."

"Not here."

"Ryan. You look great." Mom taps me on the shoulder. "This must be your girlfriend."

I release Leighton. "Leighton, yeah. You two have met."

"Of course." Mom smiles as she opens her arms for a hug. "What a dress! I wish I could pull off something like that."

Leighton shoots me an *is she for real* look then goes to hug my mom. "Thank you, Mrs. Maddox."

"Please. It's Amelia." She smiles. "It's sweet of you to come."

"Is it?" She wraps her fingers around her drink. "I couldn't let Ryan come alone."

"No. I suppose you couldn't." Mom turns to me. "Tell me the truth, honey. Was she the one who got you into this suit?"

"Yeah." I slide my arm around her waist. "She's the one who opened up my entire world."

Leighton shakes her head. "That's more credit than I deserve."

"No. It's less." I pull her closer. "You're my silver lining."

Mom rests her hand on her heart. "How sweet. You two work together, yes?"

"For a little longer. I'm leaving to start my own graphic design studio," Leighton says.

"She's amazing. Better than I am," I say.

"Really? That's quite an accomplishment. Ryan is talented," Mom says.

Huh?

"He really is. But then he never doubts that. He knows he's a great designer. He knows he's hot. But he doubts everything else," Leighton says.

"We all have our insecurities." Mom's expression gets concerned.

"I know what you're thinking. She's drunk. It's true. I'm a little drunk. I have a bad habit of downing vodka when I'm nervous. Like about the way Penny keeps flirting with Ryan. And the way he keeps looking at her like he's trying to figure out if she's what's missing from his life." She takes a long sip of her vodka. "I get it. My mom's a drunk. It's what gave me all these intimacy issues that make it hard to believe Ryan's going to be mine. But I am working on it. The drinking."

Mom's brow scrunches with confusion.

"Let me take you back to the room, baby." I help her off the stool.

She shakes her head. "No. I just need some air. And I need to stop causing a scene. Excuse me." She cuts past me before I can answer.

I reach for her, but she's already gone.

Flashes of silver and purple move through the crowd. Out the door.

"Ryan, is that true?" Mom asks.

"Which part?"

"Are you still in love with Penelope?"

"No. But..." I can't explain it. Whatever I am, it's not enough for Leighton.

Fuck.

This is the same shit again.

"It must be hard, figuring out how to love someone after the way you and Penelope ended." Mom places her hand on

390

my shoulder. "The same thing happened to me when I was young. Before your father."

"What are you talking about?"

"Dean explained it. Don't be mad at your brother. He loves you—"

"He told you she cheated?"

"Not in lurid detail."

"It's Dean."

"With more detail than we needed, yes. We were defending her. Asking why you'd do something so foolish. He was right to explain."

"It was mine to explain."

"No. He cares about you. That's what happens when you love someone. Their business becomes your business."

I bite my tongue.

"You know your brother looks up to you. He always has."

"Maybe."

"He's been following in your footsteps since he could walk."

Maybe.

"Forgive Dean. He's only trying to help." Mom's eyes fill with pity. "And her too. Leighton seems good for you."

"She seems like a drunk mess." I shake my head. "She is that sometimes. But she's more. She's everything."

"I can tell you love her."

Why can't I tell?

It's not fucking fair.

Why is it all these other people know how I feel?

Mom's lips curl into a frown. "You shouldn't be here Ryan. Your father convinced me I shouldn't talk you out of coming, but that was a mistake. You shouldn't be spending your time and energy on someone who did that to you."

"I'm not here for Penny." My gaze goes to the restaurant's front door. Leighton isn't coming back. Which means I need to leave. "It feels good wanting this for Pen. Being happy for her."

"Are you sure that's it?"

Almost.

But there's still a part of me that hates it.

"Listen, Mom, I have to—"

"Go."

I cut through the restaurant. Push out the door.

But there's no sign of Leighton.

42

RYAN

Leighton isn't in the lobby.

She isn't in our room.

She's not lounging on a deck chair by the pool. Or strolling along the garden path. Or sucking sugar syrup from a shaved ice.

My dress shoes sink onto the sand as I step off the concrete path.

There.

Moonlight bounces off a silver dress.

She's sitting on the beach, her legs pulled into her chest, her gaze on the starry sky.

I move closer.

The fear in her eyes comes into focus.

She pulls her hands to her sides. Lets them sink into the dry sand. "It's beautiful here."

"Yeah."

"More stars than I've ever seen."

There are, but it's hard to see it as beautiful at the moment. Not with my stomach sinking like a stone.

"I'm sorry about your mom. I—"

"It's okay. She gets it."

She pats the spot next to her.

I drop to the sand.

She turns toward me with a soft smile. "You're fucking up your suit."

"I don't care."

"I do. I like it." She shifts, straddling me.

She's warm. Soft. Everything.

But is she mine?

I don't fucking know anymore.

Her eyelids flutter closed as she kisses me.

I scrape my teeth against her bottom lip.

I kiss her hard.

I kiss her like the fucking ship is going down.

'Cause it might be.

She pulls back with a sigh. "I had to be sure."

I reach up, rest my palm against her cheek, rub her temple with my thumb. She's so fucking beautiful. So perfect. So everything.

It needs to stay like this.

We need to stay like this.

"Leigh…"

Her voice is a whisper. "I am sure."

"Of what?" The words are heavy on my tongue.

She stares into my eyes.

She stares into my goddamn soul.

"I love you." Her voice is steady. "I love you so fucking much."

I stare back at her.

"You're my first thought when I wake up. My last thought before I fall asleep. When I see my future, I see you. I see us. Until it gets messed up and I see her. I see you loving her forever."

"I don't love her anymore."

"But you're not over her?"

"I'm almost there."

"Almost." Her eyes turn down. "Do you love me?"

I swallow hard. I can't tell her what she wants to hear.

But I can't lie to her.

I could never lie to her.

I run my thumb over her temple.

She closes her eyes. Turns to lean into the touch. "Please say yes. Ryan. Please. Please tell me you love me."

"I want to."

Her eyelids blink open.

"I want to so fucking badly."

A tear catches on her lashes. "But you can't." It's not a question.

I answer anyway. "I'm not sure what that feels like."

She nods, accepting my explanation.

Deeming it inadequate.

A tear rolls down her cheek. Catches on my thumb.

She blinks and her lashes are curtained with them.

I wrap my arms around her. Pull her closer. Breathe in every ounce of her.

That coconut shampoo.

And something distinctly Leighton.

She sinks into my touch.

She cries onto my suit jacket.

Waves crash onto the beach. Moonlight bounces off the ocean. Stars shine against the dark sky.

"I know I said I'd be patient. But I can't." Her voice is a whisper. A promise. A plea. "I'm sorry, Ryan. But I can't do this anymore."

"Leigh…"

"I want to be okay with it. Really, I do. But I'm not."

She leans down and presses her lips to mine. It's a long, slow kiss. It's everything she has.

It's everything I have.

But it isn't enough.

43

LEIGHTON

The pineapple print bedspread mocks me. *You're in paradise and you're crying? Are you ever going to be happy? Is anything ever going to be enough for you?*

Try putting down the vodka for once.

Or womaning the fuck up.

It's been two weeks. So what if he's confused. Give the guy a little time.

Stop putting your intimacy issues on him.

You knew he was fucked-up when this started. Now you're leaving him for it? That's entrapment, honey.

Did you ask him to open his heart just to tear it from his chest?

Did you offer yours just to take it away?

You call that love?

I try to reason with the goddamn comforter. It's my body and my life. I can ruin it if I want. I can leave my favorite person in the world if I want.

I can run away from the rejection that awaits me tomorrow if I want.

Yeah, I'm second best again.

But at least this time I know it.

This time I'm not spending ten years crossing my fingers, praying he'll change.

I find my suitcase in the closet. Toss it on top of that stupid pineapple bedspread. Pour my entire underwear drawer into it.

My dress tugs at my hips.

The right strap slips off my shoulder.

This is not how I'm supposed to undress.

This is not how I'm supposed to end tonight.

This is not how I'm supposed to lose Ryan.

Is it really him?

Or is it something about me—some quality I'm lacking?

A sob rises in my throat. I do nothing to choke it back.

Ryan doesn't love me. And I'm tipsy in our hotel room, unable to pack because my dress is too tight.

Unable to leave because I can't pack.

Unable to figure out what the fuck all the hurt in his eyes means.

He wants to love me. I know he does.

But I also know that isn't enough.

My heels sink into the carpet as I cross the room. Then they're tap-taping against the tile.

I fill a glass with water and drink it in three gulps.

It soothes my throat, but it fails to soothe my heart.

No, I'm making this complicated when it's simple.

He doesn't love me.

What else do I need to know?

I slide out of my dress. Fold it at the bottom of my suitcase. Find panties, shorts, a t-shirt, and a bra in the dresser and change.

But now I look ridiculous. Who wears shorts with heels?

I sit on the bed the way I did earlier, when Ryan was looking up at me, sliding my heel on like I was Cinderella.

Fuck these shoes.

I undo the right strap. The left. I kick them halfway across the room.

They bounce off the wall with a thud.

It fails to satisfy me.

He doesn't love me.

How could anything possibly satisfy me?

44

RYAN

The stars keep shining.
    The waves keep crashing.
    My head keeps spinning.
It's like the first time we kissed.
It makes no fucking sense.
And every lick of sense in the world.
I'm not enough for her.
I thought things were different. That we were different.
I thought I was okay with my destiny.
No, I was.
Until Leigh.
Until she showed me every scar.
Until she made me realize how badly I wanted to let my walls down.
To love somebody and let them love me.
I love you.
The words still feel like a weapon. They're poison in the humid air.
I can't say it.
Can't think it.

I certainly can't feel it.

How the fuck do you love somebody?

I don't know.

Will I ever?

Will I ever be enough for someone?

For her?

Questions bounce around my head as I walk the winding concrete path.

The hotels are alive. Bright. Romantic.

The world is couples. Two people sharing mai tais at the bar, leaning over the candlelight, staring into each other's eyes.

Jumping in the pool.

Kissing under the moonlight.

I walk until the trail ends.

A cliff hangs over the beach in imposing browns. It screams *climb me, I dare you. You won't survive. I'll throw you into the ocean, drown you, smash your body to pieces against the rocks.*

It's gorgeous.

Dangerous.

Intoxicating.

The shining stars promise hope.

But they're bullshit.

It's all bullshit.

It's not enough that she loves me.

It's not enough unless I love her back.

I want to.

Fuck, maybe I do.

But that word…

It's still a knife in my chest.

Penny and I traded *I love you*s every day, without fail. That last year, when she was done with me, she still stared into my eyes and cooed *I love you.*

And I whispered it back.

But it was bullshit.

She didn't love me.

And I... did I still love her?

I know what *that* feels like, that twisted, rote *I love you*, but the real thing?

I don't have a fucking clue.

Is it the couple walking hand in hand along the beach, laughing as they dip their toes in the surf, kissing under the moonlight?

Is turning over every little detail? The berry shade she wears on her lips. Her purple hair twirling around her finger. The chipped silver polish on her nails.

The sound of my name on her lips.

The sound of hers on mine.

Is it the hole in my gut, thinking about waking up without her tomorrow and every day after?

Love is supposed to be a good thing.

But it feels more like a weapon.

I'm sorry, but I don't love you anymore.

I'm sorry. I love you. I need more.

I love you.

I loved you.

That's why I'm hurting you.

I'm sorry, but I have to twist that knife.

I have to pry your heart open.

And tear it to shreds.

I love you too much to leave it alone.

None of it makes sense.

The walk back to the hotel fails to help.

Leighton is gone. There's no sign of her in the room. Nothing but the smell of her coconut shampoo on the sheets.

It goes right to my bones.

It tears a hole in my gut.

Is that love—the aching feeling in my chest that begs for her?

I don't know. But I know love shouldn't be defined in negatives.

I'm on a fucking cloud when she's here.

I want to wake up next to her.

I want to fucking dream about her.

I practice the words in my head. *I love you, Leighton.*

They're not toxic when they're about her.

They're effervescent.

It takes forever, but they find a way to my lips.

I love you, Leighton.

They dissolve into the air.

They hit me someplace deep.

It feels good on my tongue. Like a dirty demand.

Like her name.

But I'm still not sure what the fuck that means.

I pull out my cell and text her.

Ryan: Let me know you're okay.

She texts back immediately.

Leighton: I'm safe.

Ryan: Where are you?

Leighton: Safe.

She isn't gonna tell me. I know her that well.

Or maybe I don't. Maybe Leighton wants me to ignore her boundaries. To fight her no. Plead for a yes. Beg her to change her mind.

But I respect her too much for that.

Ryan: I'll be here if you want to talk. All night.

Nothing.

I stare at my cell for ten minutes, but it fails to blink with a notification. The humid air—the AC is off—gets warmer.

My suit sticks to my skin. My tie strangles my throat.

Layer by layer, I shed my suit.

I leave it a mess on the floor—what does it matter how I look tomorrow?—and step into the shower.

The hot water washing away the sand and the salt, but it does nothing to erase the day.

When I close my eyes, I see her. The hurt in her blue-green eyes. The tremble of her lip. The heave of her chest as she mustered up the courage to spill those three little words.

My eyes get itchy. Tired. I shampoo, condition, soap, scrub, rinse.

When I'm done, I step out of the shower, wrap myself in a towel, take out my contacts.

My eyes relax behind my thick lenses. The world isn't quite as sharp. But then it's not like I can see any of the shit in front of me.

She left because I wasn't enough.

How the fuck do I deal with that?

Leigh is my best friend. My silver lining. My favorite part of every day.

Losing her as a partner is one thing. But this...

She doesn't want to see me again.

She wants to run a million miles away.

That's what she does when someone hurts her. She burns the bridge to the ground.

Unless—

There's a knock on the door.

My heart thuds against my chest.

My veins buzz with nervous energy.

I close my eyes. *Please be here, Leigh. Please come back. Please be mine.*

I need a little more time to put the pieces together.

That's all.

I pull the door open, but Leighton isn't the person standing in the frame.

It's Penny.

45

LEIGHTON

Palm trees and storefronts blur into the deep blue sky. Dean stops at a red light. He taps his fingers against the dash in time with the song.

Hawaii's local rock station is fond of grunge. Eddie Vedder mumbles agonizing poetry over a heavy guitar riff.

Does Ryan hate Pearl Jam as much as he hates Nirvana? Not that Ryan really hates Nirvana. He taps his toe along to *Smells Like Teen Spirit* whenever it comes on at Inked Hearts.

Which is whenever Dean has say over the music. He's Mr. Guitar Rock. It's a bit much for me—how can anyone who did this much heroin be this miserable?—but it's better than Walker with the metal.

Only I'm not going to stroll into Inked Hearts Tuesday and torture Ryan (and Brendon, if I'm really lucky) with my favorite pop-punk albums.

He isn't going to tease me about how I can find all these pathetic guys appealing. *I know that song was popular when you were in middle school. Not like I missed it. But come on. The guy is begging his ex-girlfriend to fuck him like it's an insult. It's pathetic. Does he really think that lowly of his sexual abilities?*

I'm not going to say anything about how he should understand how men are always obsessed with who their ex is fucking. Because isn't he?

Because he is.

He's the guy in the song who can't get out of his own way.

And I'm Gwen Fucking Stefani, singing about how I always knew he'd end up my ex-boyfriend.

The song fades into a commercial for the local Honda dealer.

Dean turns to me. Shakes his head with disapproval.

"What?"

He shrugs like he isn't judging me with his eyes.

Finally, the light turns green.

Dean taps the gas. Drives slightly faster than a snail.

"Maybe you should drive slower. So you can be sure I miss my flight," I say.

"You know I could be getting laid right now." He blows air up from his lips, blowing his messy hair from his eyes.

"You know I offered to take a cab five times." I came close to insisting. But, even with his attitude, I'm glad I didn't. I'm coming apart at the seams.

The familiarity of my obnoxious, intimacy avoiding friend in the driver's seat is the only thing holding me together.

Dean Maddox is holding me together.

What a terrifying thought.

"You know Ryan is going to kill me," he says.

"He's not. He's gonna thank you for taking care of me." That's the kind of guy he is.

Dean chuckles. "Yeah. He is. You like that?"

"That he's considerate? Why wouldn't I?"

"You broke his heart. He shouldn't give a fuck."

"We're still friends." In theory. One day.

"You're gonna be his friend?"

The apprehension in his voice tugs at my heart. I can't imagine my life without Ryan. But Dean is right. I can't be his friend right now. Not after that second-choice slap in the face. "I promised I would."

"But you're not."

"Not right away."

"You'll ghost all four of us."

"I wouldn't do that."

"Yeah, you would." He shakes his head. "You forget how well I know you."

I shrug, playing coy.

"Please, Leigh. I watched you ghost too many guys."

"Not that many."

"That many."

"I couldn't disappear on guys who knew where I worked."

"Which is why you stopped dating guys you met at the bar."

He's right.

It's terrifying how well Dean knows me. But I guess we've been friendly for a long time now. Four years. And good friends for half that.

I want to disappear. I want to forget about the last two years.

I want to do whatever it takes to make this hurt less.

But I can't run anymore.

I ran from every guy who ever hurt me.

I ran from my mom's drinking.

I ran from every design setback.

This… I'm not running from this.

Dean continues. "You know—"

"Whatever it is, I'm sure I know."

"I heard you and Ryan."

"You—"

"You didn't know that."

"You did not."

"Yeah. I did. I was coming to your room to pick you up. Could hear it all the way in the hallway. You're fucking loud, Leigh."

My sex clenches. My stomach twists. My veins buzz with some horrible mix of misery and desire. "Your point?"

"You begged him to fuck you."

"I did not beg."

"Yeah, you did. It was hot."

"I don't need to hear that." Fuck, I already miss him so badly. My pulse is weak. My breath is shallow. My head is a mess.

"Might fuck myself to it later."

"That's your brother." I turn to face him. Try to find the genuine emotion hiding in his playful expression. It's not desire. It's concern. Which only adds to the dread in my stomach. "You're full of shit."

"Not gonna think about him. Mostly gonna think about your tits in that dress. Fuck, that might be all I need."

"And my ass?"

"Of course. You looked like a spy in a porno."

"You know—"

"I do." He parrots my tone. "Whatever it is, I know."

"If I really thought you were masturbating to me, I wouldn't talk to you."

"Believe what you want."

"I will." I sink into my seat. Set my purse in my lap. Stare at my text from Ryan.

Ryan: I'll be here if you want to talk. All night.

I do.

I want to be there so badly.

I want to collapse in his arms as he whispers *I love you* in my ear.

But that isn't going to happen.

He isn't going to be mine.

Not when his fucking ex-girlfriend owns his head.

"Still think I can talk you out of this." Dean motions to the other side of the divided street. "Not too late to make a u-turn."

My heart thuds against my chest. It's tempting. God, how it's tempting. Some of Ryan is better than none. That's what I decided a long time ago.

And it was.

But it's not anymore.

I need all of him.

I'm not sure when it changed, but it did.

"You can't." My fingers trace Ryan's words. *I'm here if you want to talk. All night.*

"He text you again?"

"No."

"Uh uh. No way he let 'safe' slide."

"He did." Sort of. He knows I'm a scared little bird, that I have to be coaxed into opening up.

He knows exactly how to play me.

Even when I'm running away from him.

"Bullshit."

"He said we can talk."

"Let's go back to the hotel. Talk."

"I should have taken a cab." Even if this conversation is the only thing holding me together.

Dean cares. About me and about Ryan.

It's on the surface today. There's no façade. Just concern.

It's fucking terrifying—Dean is never serious—but it's comforting too. He's a good friend. He'll make sure I'm okay.

I stare at my cell as commercials fade into music. A Foo Fighters song. It's familiar. A song the LA rock station plays every hour.

My fingers glide over my cell.

Leighton: Did you realize you love me?

The words are even more pathetic in digital form.

He's made it clear he doesn't love me.

I'm not going to beg him.

I deserve a scrap of dignity.

Dean turns. Studies my cell. Shakes his head. "You know it's more than that."

"It isn't."

He turns back to the road. "He's an idiot."

"Not my type. Unfortunately for you."

"You think I'd take Ryan's sloppy seconds?"

"No, I don't think you'd sleep with someone your brother is… whatever this is."

He shrugs, playing cool, effortless, soulless. "Still not too late to turn around."

"I spent a fortune on this flight."

"I'll reimburse you."

"That's sad. Paying me to give your brother a chance."

"Paying you to get your head out of your ass."

Those are strong words coming from Dean.

I sink into my chair. Stare out the window. Let my phone rest on my thigh.

My breath stays shallow.

My pulse stays weak.

My cell stays silent.

"You have another flight in thirty-six hours." He hits a fork in the road, turns left, toward the airport. "You'll be fine if you miss it."

"A flight next to Ryan."

"Gives you time to talk."

I shake my head.

"He has time to make this one."

My eyes go to the clock. He doesn't. I'm barely going to make this flight and it's the last one out of Maui. At least, the last direct flight to LAX. "There's no way he's missing the wedding."

"Want to bet?"

"Not everything needs to be a bet."

Dean laughs. "That's where your wrong."

"Okay, fine. I bet. Twenty bucks."

He shakes his head. "If you're wrong, you stay at Inked Hearts."

"I'm leaving in a month." The words are heavy on my tongue. It's different now that it means no more Ryan. And that means no more Dean or Walker or Brendon. Or even Emma or Kaylee.

No more laughing at my friend's stupid jokes.

No more studying Ryan's work.

No more taunting him with miserable music. Or teasing him about being serious. Or eating the lunches he makes me. Or fixing his coffee. Or fucking him on the counter.

No more Ryan.

Forever.

It's warm in here—the AC is off, the windows are down—but I'm freezing.

Without Ryan, my future is an ugly, grey place.

My life is dull and empty.

I have Iris. But all my other friends are *ours*. All my hobbies are wrong. Running is ours. Movies are ours. Swimming is ours. Romance novels—

Fuck romance novels.

"So stay the month." Dean's bouncy voices fills the car. Pulls me back to the moment. "If you're that sure."

"What do I get?"

"Whatever you want."

Maybe there's some way he can convince Ryan to love me. They are brothers. They share something…

I swallow hard. Think of something that might give me

the tiniest hint of satisfaction. "I want you to go a month without sex."

Horror spreads over his expression.

But it does nothing to thrill me. Teasing Dean is usually fun. But this isn't. All I see when I look at him is Ryan's eyes. They're a little darker. A little deeper.

Still, I play along. "Including masturbation."

"Did it for six fucking weeks after I got my cock pierced."

"I try not to think about your cock."

He nods. "You're on."

I shake his hand, but there's no enthusiasm in it.

I'm out of enthusiasm.

46

RYAN

Penny wraps her fingers around her glass of bourbon. She holds it up to toast. "I'm not sure what I should say."

I'm not sure why she's here. The ten minutes I bought myself changing in the bathroom did nothing to illuminate her motivations.

I should probably tell her to go fuck herself.

But there's this doubt lingering in my gut.

I need to be sure.

I clink my glass with hers. "To commitment."

She lets out a nervous laugh. "To forever." She brings her glass to her lips and downs half of it.

It's good bourbon. Three hundred dollar a bottle top-shelf shit. Rich. Oak. Leather.

It might as well scream *the manliest fucking drink around*.

That was why I got into it. Seemed like a man's drink. Like most seventeen-year-old boys, I was desperate to prove I was a man.

Penny sits on the couch and crosses her legs.

She smooths her ivory dress.

She looks every bit the bride to be. Glowing, nervous, happy.

But she's in my hotel room.

That's not a good fucking sign

Her honey eyes fix on mine. They fill with nostalgia. "You remember the first time we snuck some of Daddy's bourbon?"

"I said I loved it, chugged a glass, spent the night throwing up." Fuck, that was miserable.

She laughs. "You made it half an hour."

"You still went out with me."

"I liked you."

"Was it the dry heaving that did it?"

"No. It was you. All those things that are still you. The intensity in your eyes. The way I can always tell you're thinking something deep and meaningful. The way you never give up on what you want. You're principled and uncompromising to a fault. And you're... You were everything I wanted then."

What the hell is she getting it?

"Sorry. I'm getting nervous." She takes a long sip. "Only twenty hours to go now."

"It must be scary."

She nods.

"Frank is good for you."

Her expression gets contemplative. She stares into her glass like it contains all the secrets to the universe.

I take a seat next to her.

She turns toward me. Finishes her bourbon and drinks me in instead. "Where's Leighton?"

I try to find a lie and come up blank.

Penny's gaze darts around the room. The clean dresser. The sparse floor. The utter lack of Leighton's bright pink suitcase. She studies my expression, looking for cracks.

"She left."

"She's just—"

"Is it over?"

"I don't know."

"Because of me?"

"Is that what you want?"

Her brow furrows. "Of course not."

"Then what the fuck are you doing?"

Her fingers brush my thigh. It's a quick thing. Then it's not. She rests her entire hand on my thigh. "Ryan, I…"

I freeze.

"I miss you." Her eyelids press together. She leans in. She leans close enough to kiss me.

I wrap my fingers around her wrist. Pull her hand back.

She jumps back. "Oh. I'm sorry." Hurt flares in her expression. "That was… I… I don't know."

Bullshit.

"I wasn't—"

"You were."

Her cheeks flush. It's not a blush of desire. It's embarrassment. "Don't tell Frank."

"I don't give a fuck about Frank."

"But—"

"You do this a lot?"

"No. Never."

I believe her. Somehow, I can tell she's being honest. She learned her lesson destroying me. Decided not to do it again.

Maybe I should be bitter.

But I'm not.

"You're scared. You're panicking. But I'm not gonna help you run away from your fiancé," I say. "If that's what you want, find someone else."

"I don't."

"You sure?"

"No. What if I'm wrong? What if he isn't enough? If I'm not enough?"

"How do you feel now, when you think about him?"

"Happy."

"When you think about celebrating your ten-year anniversary?"

Her lips curl into a smile.

"Seeing kids in boat shoes and Dockers playing soccer on the weekends."

"They're playing soccer in their boat shoes?"

"Yeah. They want to dress like daddy."

She laughs. "The Dockers too?"

"Of course."

"How are they running?"

"They aren't. They suck. But they're eight. They're gonna suck no matter what."

Her laugh gets louder. "That's absurd. But I see it."

"You love him?"

"Of course."

"What else do you need to know?"

She stares at her empty glass. "You're right. God, I'm sorry." She stands, moves to the counter, wraps her fingers around the bottle. "I told myself I was coming here to make things right between us. But I guess I was—"

"You wanted validation."

Her lips curl into a frown. "How is it so obvious to you?"

"I know you."

"I don't deserve you."

"You don't have me."

"You're here."

"This is my room."

She laughs. "True." She turns and stares into my eyes. "What happened with Leigh?"

"We're not there, Pen."

"You two—"

"No, me and you. We're not there and we're never gonna be there. I'm always gonna love you. But I can't be this person for you. I can't be your friend. I'm glad I'm here. I'm happy for you. Really, I am. I want you and Frank to have a big, beautiful life together. I want you to soar." My shoulders relax. "But I don't want anything to do with it."

The words hit me someplace deep.

I want her to light up when she whispers *I do*.

I want her and Frank to make a billion babies.

And I don't want a fucking thing to do with it.

Those French-manicured nails release my heart.

I'm done with Penny.

And not in some *I'm better off without her* break up song kind of way.

I don't want her to die in a fire.

I want her to burn bright with passion and love and joy.

I can see her big, beautiful life and it makes me feel good.

I don't want her anymore.

I don't miss her anymore.

I don't need a single part of her.

"I gotta go, Pen." I stand. Move closer. Plant a goodbye kiss on her cheek. "Congratulations, really."

Her smile gets sad. "Thank you."

I walk her to the door. "You deserve it."

"You really mean that?"

Yeah, I do.

She tore my fucking heart out.

But it's still beating. I'm still here. I'm still alive.

And I feel so much fucking better wanting the two of them happy.

"Are you and Leigh gonna be okay?" she asks.

"I don't know." I close the door behind us. "I hope so."

"Me too."

I walk Penny to the elevator.

I say goodbye to her.

To her hold on me.

To this whole fucking phase of my life.

This is it. The end of the *Penny* chapter.

I just hope it's the beginning of the *Leighton* one.

No.

Hope isn't enough.

Hope hasn't ever done shit for me.

Somehow, I'm going to make this right.

4 7

LEIGHTON

The automatic check-in machine spits out my ticket with a loud whir.

The air conditioning hums.

A middle-aged couple hugs a twenty-something guy goodbye. They linger in their embraces, exchanging promises and *I'll miss you*s and love.

Dean taps his foot against the tile. "It's not too late."

I wave my ticket.

"So?"

"I asked you to drop me off."

"You really think that was gonna happen?"

No. But not for the reasons Dean is suggesting. Not because he's an asshole who lives to cause trouble.

He is. But he's staying to see me off.

To make sure I get to security without crumbling into a million pieces.

My cell buzzes against the pocket of my shorts. Again. This must be Ryan's fourth call. Or maybe it's the fifth.

I can't bring myself to look at my phone to find out.

"What is that?" Dean nods to my pocket.

"My crotch."

He makes a show of laughing. "Is that a call you're getting or you just packing your vibrator with you?"

"My vibrator is too big to fit in my pocket."

"Go on…"

"In your dreams."

Again, he motions to my pocket. "It's buzzing."

It is. "It's nothing."

"Nothing, really?"

"Yeah. An alarm," I lie.

He shakes his head *you're so full of shit*. His sandals squeak against the tile as he takes a step toward me. "Then let me see."

"I have to go."

"Am I holding you down?"

"You're into that?"

His grin gets mischievous. "Maybe I am, maybe I'm not. I'll fill you in if you let me see."

"I don't care."

"Bullshit."

"Even if I did." I really don't. "You'll fill me in either way." I should go. I should turn and run to security. But I can't leave. This is normal. It's easy. It's family.

As soon as I leave, that's gone.

Hell, this might be the last time I see Dean for a while.

Or ever.

My entire life revolves around Ryan.

There's nothing to go back to in Los Angeles. I want to crawl into my bed and cry. I want to fall apart in my apartment. I want to be home.

But without Ryan, I don't have a home.

I don't belong anywhere.

My damn cell buzzes again.

Dean stays teasing. He motions *hand it over*.

I do.

I need to be here.

I need him screening the message.

I need someone making this okay.

The call ends. Right away, the screen flashes with a text.

Ryan: Penny

That's all I see.

Her name.

Penny is naked in my bed.

Penny told me she's in love with me.

Penny is dead to me.

I don't have a clue what it is.

Dean unlocks my cell with the password.

I raise a brow.

He shrugs. "Like you don't know mine."

I know everyone at the shop's passwords. But I never use them. Even when it's tempting. "I plead the fifth."

He reads from a text. "Penny came by my room." His eyes go wide. "Wait. Shit."

"See." My heart sinks like a stone. She came by his room. God knows what they did after.

I don't get a say.

I ended this.

I broke up with him.

I have no right to hurt over him fucking Penny.

But he's better than this.

He deserves more than this.

He deserves everything.

That's why I feel this in my bones. Because everything *should* be right. We're good together. We're happy together. He wants to love me. He just can't.

"No." Dean's voice goes dead serious. "He talked her out of her cold feet then told her to get lost. But, fuck, maybe he should have led with that. It's like he's trying to lose you."

My shoulders soften. "They didn't have sex?"

"Fuck no. He kicked her to the curb."

"Does it actually say that?"

"Ryan isn't smooth. You have to let me translate."

My chest warms. "He really isn't." But the warmth hurts. I'm staring at a bright, shiny memory of what I used to have.

I want it so badly.

But I can't have it.

"You like that?" Dean asks.

"Yeah. He's honest. He doesn't try to charm me the way you do."

Dean adopts his mega-watt smile. He shoots me an *I know you want to fuck me* look. "Charm is enjoyable for the charmed as much as the charmer."

"Is that right?" I know Dean well enough to know he's full of shit, but his smile is chipping away at the ice around my heart. It feels good, being the center of his attention, letting his radiance light up my sky.

It needs it.

The decorations are all bright, tropical hues, but they feel ugly and grey.

"You don't laugh at my jokes?" Dean teases.

"I'm not in the mood."

"'Cause you're cock hungry."

I can't help but laugh. He's right. The ache between my legs is not helping matters any.

My body is still singing for Ryan's.

My thoughts are still turning to his eyes, his hands, his lips, his cock.

Fuck, I want him pinning me against the wall.

I want him whispering *come for me, baby* in my ear.

I want him splitting me in half.

"Really fucking cock hungry." He shakes his head. "If you

weren't Ryan's main squeeze, I'd drag you to the bathroom to satisfy you."

I laugh so hard I double over. Okay, his stupidity is helping. I almost feel normal.

The phone buzzes. *I felt it*. "Fuck." Dean's eyes bug out of his head.

It's bad. It has to be bad. "Let me see that."

"No. I'll read it." His voice is steady. Reassuring. Completely unlike Dean. "There's no way he felt her. I saw him leave looking for you."

"And?"

"He was worried."

"He's always worried."

"When it's about you, yeah. Why do you figure it is you tie him in knots?"

"Why am I standing here when I could be going through security?"

"'Cause I'll call Ryan and get him on your plane if you leave."

Yeah, he will. Somehow, he'll defy the laws of physics to do it.

I stare into Dean's mischievous blue eyes. "Weren't you with Kristen?"

"Yeah, I was with Kristen. At the party. Talking. I am capable."

"You like her?"

"She's fun. And hot. But not like that, no. I'm not gonna fuck some chick who screwed over my brother."

"She didn't—"

"The friend of my enemy is my enemy."

"Still. Ryan wouldn't care."

"I have standards."

"You do?" My voice isn't quite teasing. It's more confused.

But I can't help it. The world is a confusing mess at the moment.

"You think I'm gonna leave when one of you two might need me?"

"Yeah... Of course."

He shrugs. "Yeah. Guess I would." His voice is effortless, but it does nothing to hide the concern in his expression.

Fuck, Dean is struggling to bullshit.

This must be tragic.

It feels all wrong. But standing here, talking to him, is enough to make me forget. I'm wrapped up in Dean's stupidity instead of in my loneliness.

Right now, it feels like it's going to be okay.

As soon as I say goodbye...

"There's plenty of hot chicks here. I'll bang one back at the hotel. Tell you all about it tomorrow morning."

"Tomorrow morning?"

"Take you back to the hotel—"

I shake my head.

"All right. Tuesday at work."

I press my lips together.

"Leigh. A bet is a bet."

"And if he doesn't show?"

"Then I'll be by your place as soon as I get off."

"And?"

"And I'll annoy you into coming back."

I want to be there. I want to be under the heart string lights. I want to hear the bell ring and the tattoo guns hum and the guys laugh. I want all of it. But not with this space between me and Ryan.

"I can't. I'll get Em to fill in. Teach her what I know. She's been asking me to go over shop admin forever. She really wants to have a hand in running it." I motion *give it back*. "I can't text her like this."

426

"Agree to come."

"You know I can lie now."

"You wouldn't. You have honor."

"I'm gonna miss my flight."

He hands my text over. "Only giving you this 'cause you're gonna like what Ryan said."

Ryan: I'm here if you want to talk. All night.

Ryan: Penny came by my room. She had a bottle of bourbon and a 'you can fuck me if you want smile.' I could have. She offered, more or less. But I didn't want to.

Ryan: I'm not telling you this to win points. I'm telling you there wasn't a single part of me that wanted that. I didn't want her body or her affection or her love. I didn't even want her apology. I told her what I really thought. I told her she and Frank are right together. That I'm happy for them. That I want the best for them.

Ryan: I felt it.

Ryan: As soon as I told her, I felt it. I'm done with her. Over her. Completely. It's so much more fucking obvious right now, because I can feel a gaping hole in my gut. That's you being gone, Leigh. Maybe that isn't enough for you. Maybe it's not enough that I want to be the person who cooks you dinner every night and wakes up next to you every day. Maybe it's not enough that I want to watch your design company take off, and teach you to surf, and race you around the park. Maybe it's not enough that you're my favorite fucking person in the world. But you are. And I want all that. When I see my life, you're in it. You are it. There are only three things I want. I want to do ink, I want to see the world, and I want you.

"Ryan said something good." Dean's voice brightens.

"No." I bite my lip.

"You have a look."

"I do not."

"Like you're thinking about going back."

"No." Kind of. I... I want to talk to him. I want to wrap my arms around him. I want to collapse in his bed.

Our bed.

I want everything to be ours again.

But I *need* him to be mine.

"You sure?" Dean asks. "You look like it."

I want to, but I can't. I need to be home. I need to be safe. I need Ryan to love me. I can't have the latter. So I'll have to take the first two. "I'm exhausted."

"So crawl into bed, whisper *I love you, I'm sorry*, and collapse."

I shake my head.

"He loves you, Leigh. You two are the only people who don't see it."

"How do you see it?"

"How do I not? It's everywhere. He cooks you lunch every day. He gushes about you nonstop. He looks at you like you hang the sun."

I bite my lip.

"He's fucking obnoxious. Like Walker."

I shake my head.

"He is. He does love you. Trust me. The guy's my brother. I've known him for twenty-five years now."

"I can't."

"Leigh—"

"I have to go home." I have to be alone, in my apartment, away from everything that confuses me. And right now, everything confuses me.

I hug Dean goodbye.

"You sure?" he asks.

I nod.

"Let me know when you get in."

"Let me know he's okay."

"He's not. I guarantee it."

"Let me know he's alive." I hug my purse to my shoulder. Wrap my fingers around my suitcase.

He stares at me like he's going to ask me to stay again.

But he doesn't.

It's a good thing.

I'm not sure I have another no in me.

48

RYAN

fter an hour of silence, my cell sings with a text from Leighton.

Leighton: Are you still going to the wedding?

My exhaustion fades into nervous energy. There's a right answer to that question. But I'm so fucking past not going to Penny's wedding.

I need to make her understand that.

Ryan: No. Where are you?

Leighton: Going home.

Ryan: I'll come.

Leighton: You should stay. The hotel is nice. You paid for two more nights.

Ryan: I don't give a fuck about that.

Leighton: You have to see Penny off.

Ryan: I have to talk to you.

Leighton: This is the last flight to LAX. The first one tomorrow is around six a.m.

Ryan: Are you asking me to chase you or telling me not to?

Leighton: I don't know.

Ryan: What do you want?

Leighton: You know what I want.

Moonlight streams through the sheer curtains. It's the only thing illuminating the dark room.

It's beautiful, peaceful, serene.

It's mocking me.

She wants me to love her.

The words are easier, but are they right?

Leighton: I have to go. We're about to take off. I'm sorry I made such a mess of this.

Ryan: You didn't.

Leighton: I did. But, you know what? I'm not sorry. I'll never be sorry for falling in love with you. Enjoy paradise, Ryan.

There's no way I can enjoy shit without her.

I'm sure she's telling the truth about her flight taking off. But just in case—

I call Dean.

"Who is this?" he answers in his usual shit-stirring tone.

"She just get on a plane?"

"Sounds right. She went through security half an hour ago."

"You're still at the airport?"

"Yeah."

"You couldn't stop her?"

"I tried." His voice gets serious. "She's too hurt right now. Once she nurses her wounds, she'll see it."

"See what?"

"That you love her."

Fuck, Dean being insightful is weird. Disarming.

For a second, I forget all the ugly shit surrounding us.

Then I blink and it all comes flooding back.

I want the easiness back. "You drove her instead of getting laid?"

"I don't have a shortage of pussy."

"You're getting soft on me."

He laughs. "Never had that problem. You'll have to explain it."

I laugh too. The familiarity of my brother's teasing is comforting. Hell, his concern is comforting.

That hole in my gut is wide open.

I *need* Leigh. I need to make this right.

But there's this freedom surrounding me.

I'm done with Penny.

I don't give a fuck that she's getting married tomorrow.

And not in that *the lady doth protest too much* kind of way.

It means nothing to me.

I'm letting go of my baggage.

I can have everything I want.

And I want Leigh.

"I gotta go, Dean." I end the call before he can respond and I buy tomorrow's first flight out of Maui.

Then I text Brendon to see if I can make the rest of this happen.

Of course it's the middle of the night in California.

My phone stays quiet.

But I know he's good for it.

Whether or not this works…

That's anybody's guess.

49

LEIGHTON

I sleep in fits. When I do, I dream about Ryan. When I press my eyelids together in an attempt to end my consciousness, I think about Ryan.

The hurt in his blue eyes.

The weight of his body on top of mine.

The feel of his palm against my lower back.

The promise in text message form.

When we start our descent into LAX, I give up on sleep. Read his text over and over again instead.

As soon as I told her, I felt it. I'm done with her. Over her. Completely. It's so much more fucking obvious right now, because I can feel a gaping hole in my gut. That's you being gone, Leigh. Maybe that isn't enough for you. Maybe it's not enough that I want to be the person who cooks you dinner every night and wakes up next to you every day. Maybe it's not enough that I want to watch your design company take off, and teach you to surf, and race you around the park. Maybe it's not enough that you're my favorite fucking person in the world. But you are. And I want all that. When I see my life, you're in it. You are it. There are only three

435

things I want. I want to do ink, I want to see the world, and I want you.

If love is the sum of its parts, that's love.

But is it enough?

I'm way too tired to put those pieces together.

We land. Taxi. Stand. I'm a zombie as I grab my carry-on and walk off the plane. Familiarity takes me through the maze of LAX. Past the stores, along the hallway, down the escalator to baggage claim.

But I'm not destined to climb into a ride share.

Iris is standing in front of the sliding doors.

She runs to greet me. Throws her arms around me and squeezes tightly. "You okay?"

I shake my head.

"I'm sorry." She releases me. "Ryan asked me to pick you up."

"Of course."

"He's sweet."

"Even when he…" I don't know how to end the sentence. My thoughts are too slow. My heart is too heavy. "It's early."

"That's how much I love you." She takes my suitcase and motions to the door. "Come on. I'm parked in the garage. I'll buy you breakfast."

I shake my head.

"Coffee."

"You convinced me."

THIS IS A BAIT AND SWITCH—WE'RE AT A RESTAURANT, NOT A coffee shop—but the java is too good for me to complain.

I down my second cup. Revel in the dark, nutty, creamy, sweet deliciousness.

Iris offers a slice of bacon. "You should eat something."

I motion to the empty cup of cream between us.

"That's drinking."

"I'm not hungry."

"What if it's chocolate?"

"I'm not a monster."

She hails the server.

He stops at our table with a smile. "Yes?" Guys are always so sweet when you're with another cute girl.

"More coffee and cream. Please." I trace the outline of my mug.

"Do you have chocolate chip pancakes?" she asks.

"It's not on the menu, but I'm sure I can make it happen," he says.

"Great. We'll take an order. Thank you." She smiles *you are eating, dammit.*

I wait for the server to leave. "Do chocolate chip pancakes have any nutritional value?"

"Flour and eggs?"

"I might as well pour the sugar straight into my coffee."

"Fine. Don't eat them. Just look at them." She takes a long sip of her coffee. Lets out a soft moan. "Mmm. I see the merits to filling up on this."

"Right?"

"Ryan said you haven't eaten since lunch yesterday?"

"Maybe. I don't know." It sounds right, but the last twenty-four hours are a blur of hurt and rejection. I really can't remember.

The server refills our coffee and drops off a new cup of cream.

Iris shoots him a sweet smile. She fixes her coffee and takes a small sip. "You want to talk about it yet?"

"Maybe." My java is a caramel color, plenty sweet and creamy, but nothing compared to Iris's half sugar and milk, half coffee concoction. "I guess it's simple. I told him I loved him and he looked at me like I ripped his heart out."

"You did."

"Is it really asking too much, wanting him to love me back?"

"It's been two weeks."

I ignore her reasonable statement.

"You were okay with it then."

"It's different now."

"How?"

"It just is."

"Ryan has always been—"

"Hurt?"

She nods. "You knew he was hung up on his ex."

"Yeah. But he's not. Not anymore. At least, that's what he says."

Her eyes go wide. "He's not?"

"He didn't tell you?"

"He just asked me to pick you up. Offered to pay for our breakfast."

"Of course." He's considerate about cushioning the blow of his rejection.

Only it might not be…

Fuck, my head hurts.

Downing half my coffee does nothing to help.

Iris leans back in her seat, but there's nothing relaxed about her posture. Her gaze stays fixed on me.

At least the cafe is quiet. It's a small place with a dozen tables and a cute, artsy vibe. The kind of place I'd take Ryan just to hear him insult the mass-produced paintings on the walls (they really are generic. Is the Eiffel Tower supposed to make me feel like this cafe really is Parisian?)

"You can't drop a bomb like 'he's over his ex' and not

explain." She snaps her bacon in half, offers it to me. When I shake my head, she takes a bite.

"He said he isn't going to the wedding."

"He's coming after you."

"Maybe." The thought warms my chest. Sends the clouds packing. Makes the air sweeter. I want it to be true. I need it to be true. I need it too badly.

I can't get my hopes up.

Her voice gets soft. "You were ready to be patient before."

"It changed."

"Why?"

"I thought, once we were together…"

"You thought you had a magic pussy?"

I can't help but laugh. "I guess so."

"Don't we all."

"You kind of do."

She tilts her head to one side. "Uh-huh."

The server interrupts us to drop off a plate of giant chocolate chip pancakes.

They smell amazing.

And there's this beautiful cup of maple syrup.

I pick up a fork, take a slice, dip it in maple.

It dissolves on my tongue. Mmm. Sugar. Chocolate. Flour. I take another bite, chew, swallow.

Iris smiles, victorious.

"You do have a magic pussy," I say. "You should have seen the way Walker plowed through women before you."

"That's my boyfriend."

"You know he's a slut."

"Still. I don't want to hear about it."

"Isn't there something about taming him?"

"Maybe. Mostly just having him." Her gaze softens as her expression gets dreamy. She sighs that *I'm madly, passionately in love* sigh. "Sorry. I'm sure that's obnoxious"

"It's sweet."

"I love him so much. It's crazy."

"I love him so much. It's crazy." I take another bite. Let the sugar chase away my thoughts.

I hate admitting she's right, but I feel better with food in my stomach.

Like maybe there's some way to fix this.

"Do you love him enough to wait for him?" she asks.

The words wash over me. They make so much sense, but they feel so far away. "Why do you say it in that tone?"

She finishes her coffee. "That tone is your mind knowing I'm right."

Maybe. I pry a chocolate chip from a pancake, let it melt on my tongue. "Can you shrink me and fix it?"

"No. You're my friend. And I'm not gonna be that kind of shrink. But it probably does have something to do with your mom being a drunk."

"Alcoholic."

"Choosing booze over you."

"Yeah."

"And you were scared Ryan was going to choose her over you."

"Maybe." Definitely. Even I know I'm walking around with a mountain of baggage over my mom. Even I know I left because I was afraid of getting rejected again.

But it feels more obvious on her tongue.

I run away when I get scared.

When I get hurt.

It was the right call with guys who didn't treat me well. With shitty jobs. With my mom.

But with Ryan—

I need to be strong enough to stand and feel this.

To listen to him.

To give him time to love me.

I think.

My brain is running on too little sleep for this to make sense.

I finish a pancake and a half and the rest of my coffee. "Can you take me home? I need to sleep."

"Sure." She hails the server for the check. "Are you're going to be okay?"

"I'm not sure, but I think so."

50

RYAN

Wheels screech as the plane touches down at LAX.

The older woman sitting next to me stretches her arms over her head as she yawns. Her hand taps my shoulder. She smiles, apologetic. "I'm sorry."

"It's fine."

"Your first red eye?"

"I guess it is."

"You get used to them."

I nod. Turn my cell off airplane mode. The time refreshes, but my texts and emails stay silent.

"Why were you in Hawaii?"

"A wedding."

"How sweet?"

"No." I slide my cell into my pocket. Better not to look at messages. I already got a yes from Brendon. I can't let anything talk me out of this. "It's today."

"Oh."

"I had to... my girlfriend needs me."

She rests her hand on her heart. Makes that *oh, how sweet* noise. "Will you two be next?"

"I don't know. Probably not. We're new."

"But you love her?"

I stare back at this woman. She's a stranger, but she seems kind. Loving. She's wearing a wedding ring. She must have some fucking insight. "How can you know for sure?"

"You feel it."

"How did you know?"

"I thought about my future, about what I looked forward to. I asked myself if I wanted to wake up next to him every day. I did."

"That's it?"

"What's more loving than staying in someone's life?"

"How long have you been married?"

"Thirty years."

"Congratulations."

"Thank you."

The plane stops at the gate. The fasten seatbelts sign turns off. The intercom whirs with something about how we can now stand.

The woman smiles. "I hope things work out with her."

"Me too."

LEIGHTON

I t's afternoon when I wake. Even with the breeze blowing between my windows, my apartment is hot.

But the heat isn't irritating. The familiarity of it is comforting. This place is home. Its quirks and flaws are home too.

A glass of ice water cools me down. As does shedding my pajamas.

It's way too hot for a run, but I need to clear my mind too badly to care.

I change into my workout gear, lace up my sneakers, fill my reusable water with a mix of ice and water.

Then I slide my keys into the hidden pocket in my shorts, step outside, and take off.

The sun beats down on my chest and shoulders, but it feels good. Warming, not oppressive.

A breeze blows over my arms.

The air cools as I pass Eleventh.

But the view of the ocean crashing into the sand doesn't offer the clarity it usually does. It sends my thoughts back to

Maui. To climbing into Ryan's lap and kissing him and *knowing* I loved him more than anything.

Maybe even enough to wait for him.

I try to push my thoughts away as I hit Ocean, turn, run back toward my apartment.

Slowly, the dust in my brain settles.

Things come into focus.

But there's no time to make sense of them.

Ryan is sitting on my stoop. Staring at me like I'm an angel sent from heaven.

Like I'm the only thing he's ever wanted.

5 2

LEIGHTON

My pulse pounds in my ear.

My heartbeat is the only thing I can hear. It's loud, fast, steady.

He's here.

He's not at the wedding.

He's not in Hawaii.

He's here.

"Hey." He rises to his feet.

"Hey." The words stumble on my tongue. My stomach flutters. My limbs get light.

Ryan is here.

He's really here.

He offers his hand. "You want to talk inside?"

"It's hotter inside."

"That's okay."

I pop the cap of my reusable bottle. Suck down my last drop of water. It's still cold, but it does nothing to cool me down.

I'm buzzing from his proximity.

My body shares none of my caution. It screams for Ryan. For his lips, his touch, his cock.

For every single thing he can give me.

No, that's my head.

Or maybe my heart.

All of me wants all of him.

My fingertips skim his palm. "Okay. Inside." If this is good, and we're inside, then my body can get what it wants. I can get what I want.

If it's bad, and we're inside, then I can fall apart without prying eyes.

But if it's bad…

It doesn't matter where I am.

I punch the code into the gate.

The door buzzes. I turn the knob, hold it open for Ryan.

He nods as politely as he always does.

I follow him up the steps, down the hall, to my apartment door.

The key is lodged into that tiny pocket. I fish it out, slide it into my lock, turn it. This is familiar. Like the night I explained everything.

Like a million nights I let Ryan in.

Then *let Ryan in.*

I want that so badly.

I want him so badly.

Please be here to kiss and make up.

Please say you love me too.

Because I really don't know what I'll do if you don't.

I push the door open and step inside. "Come in."

He does. His sandals squeak against the tile floor. He slides them off, leaves them in a neat row by the door.

I step out of my sneakers and socks. Leave them in a messy pile.

He presses the door shut. Clicks the lock. Turns to face me. "Your flight okay?"

I nod.

"Iris picked you up?"

"Yeah. Thanks… I think."

"You eat something?"

"Were you behind the chocolate chip pancakes?"

He shakes his head. "That was all her."

"Oh. She's a good friend."

"Yeah."

"I'm lucky."

His blue eyes bore into mine.

I stare back at him. Words crawl into my throat and dissolve on my tongue. None are quite right.

But I can't keep up this staring contest forever.

I have to say something.

I *want* to say something.

"I, uh, I kind of freaked out." My heels plant on the hardwood as I take a step backward. "I'm sorry."

"Don't be."

"I didn't need to give you an ultimatum. I could have waited. But I was scared. And hurt. And I didn't know what else to do but run."

He nods. "I'm glad you did."

"What?" My brow furrows. He's glad. I… He… That doesn't make any sense.

He closes the distance between us in three steps.

His hand skims my hip. His palm goes flat on my lower back. He pulls my body into his.

I look up at him.

I stare into those beautiful baby blues. "What is this?"

"Give me a minute to put this together."

"Okay." My fingers curl into his soft cotton shirt. I press the fabric into his shoulders. They're hard. Warm. Familiar.

449

But are they mine?

I need them to be mine.

He brushes a stray hair behind my ear. "I felt it."

"Felt what?"

"All night, it got worse, this gaping hole in my gut. The only thing that filled it was thinking about you."

I stare back at him.

"I think I needed that. I needed to realize I might lose you. That I would lose you if I didn't figure it out."

"No, I, we… I was too harsh. Too impatient."

"It killed me watching you walk away."

"It killed me too."

"But I needed it." His voice is steady. Sure. "I thought about my future. And I see you, Leigh. I see myself waking up next to you. Arguing about whether we should have medium roast or French roast. I see you teasing me about wearing nothing but black. And I see you standing in our bathroom, perfecting your makeup, rolling your eyes when I insist you look great without it. I see us getting our own place. Getting married. Having a family."

"Ryan…"

"I love you, Leighton."

My heart thuds against my chest.

He rests his palm on my cheek. Rubs my temple with his thumb. "I love you so fucking much, it hurts."

"I love you too."

"I'm sorry I didn't see it. The word felt like a weapon or a wound. And you were the opposite of that, baby. You are. You're an angel. You're my salvation. You're everything."

"I…"

He turns to his side and rolls his jeans down his hip.

It's there, in big, bold letters.

Leighton

With wings on each side.

It's still wrapped in plastic.

His skin is still raised, red, raw.

"When?" I stare at the ink.

"When I got in. Then I came here."

"Ryan…"

"You like it."

"I love it." I stare into his eyes. "I… I love you."

"I love you too."

He brings his lips to mine. His kiss is soft, sweet. It's every ounce of love and affection in the world.

It's mine.

He pulls back with a sigh. "I'm not gonna lie. I'm never gonna be normal. I'm done with Penny, but those scars aren't going anywhere. I'm gonna worry I'm not enough for you. I'm gonna wonder if you're looking elsewhere. I'm gonna turn over bad moods and quiet days and every time you get home late. But I'm gonna tell you what I'm thinking. I'm gonna ask you for the reassurance I need."

"Okay."

"I'm gonna need it all the fucking time."

"That's okay. I will too. I'll worry I'm second choice. And I'll want to run when you hurt me. Or when I get scared. And I might. But I'll come back. I promise."

I slide my hands into his hair and I kiss him hard. "Say it again, please."

"I love you, Leighton."

"I love you, Ryan."

And I kiss him like I'm never going to let go.

Because I won't.

EPILOGUE

RYAN

Leighton slides off her stool. A yawn escapes her berry lips as she stretches her arms over her head.

Her blue-green eyes meet mine.

They light up as her lips curl into a smile.

That's all it takes for me too. I see her, and I'm happy.

I feel like a different person.

Not that she'd agree.

According to my girlfriend, I'm still plenty moody and difficult. I'm sure she's right. I still work too much, run miles at a time, spar until I drop. I still obsess over cooking her dinners, making her smile, making her come—

Fuck, I'm getting distracted.

Her snug black sweater does nothing to help matters. Its low neckline shows off the lace of her black bra.

She catches me staring and tugs the sweater lower.

My tongue slides over my lips.

My thoughts get dirty. I want to strip her out of those clothes, place her on the counter, and spread her legs.

She looks hot as hell.

And it's the perfect distraction from the thought racing around my head.

What if she says no?

She smooths her black mini-skirt as she presses her laptop closed.

I turn back to my client. As soon as I check him out, I'm done with work. And that means I'm taking her there. And I'm asking.

My voice is quiet. Nervous. "You need a minute?"

He shakes his head *no way*. Stands. Continues admiring his work—a Storm Trooper ready to shoot—in the mirror.

It looks good, though I can't say I appreciate the subject matter. "Still in love?"

His eyes go wide. His smile goes wider. "It's so fucking cool." He stays hazy as he follows me to the counter.

Leighton taps her nails—hot pink today—against the black counter. She winks at me. I know that look. It's *can I check him out, please, for old time's sake?*

Not that it's really old time. She stayed through September, as promised. Then she struck out on her own. For two months now, she's been busy. She's been working nonstop. She's been fucking amazing.

But it's been torture, not seeing her every day.

We spend most nights together, at my place or hers. I still cook her dinner as often as I can. And drop packed lunches in her fridge.

But I only see her at the Inked Hearts counter once a week.

She spends her Fridays working here.

Which means I spend my Fridays distracted by whatever tight outfit she's wearing.

Thinking about fucking her senseless.

And holding her all night.

And never letting go.

Her tits nearly spill out of her top as she leans over the counter. "That looks amazing."

My client's laugh is so high-pitched it's nearly a giggle.

I've seen this a million times—a guy simultaneously flattered and intimidated by her.

It used to make my fingers curl into fists.

But now that she's mine, that I know she's doing it for a reaction…

It's thrilling.

It's a game we play.

Foreplay by flirting with other people.

"You must love *Star Wars*." She bats her eyelashes. Presses her lips into a soft smile. "They're amazing movies, aren't they?"

"Uh-huh." He nods as he pulls out his credit card and hands it to her.

She brushes her fingers against his palm as she takes it. "Who's your favorite character?"

"Uh…" He turns to show off the tattoo of Luke Skywalker on his right arm. "How about you?"

"Hard to say." She runs his credit card. Watches the machine spit out a receipt, hands it over. "Can I confess something to you?"

He leans in. Nods with enthusiasm.

She stages whispers. "My heart is devoted to Austin Powers."

"No way," he whispers. "Really?"

We share a look. It's our secret. The whole world is our secret.

It's ours.

She turns to my client. "I love a guy who makes me laugh."

He scribbles a tip, signs, hands over the receipt.

I shake his hand and walk him to the door.

He nearly skips down the street.

I can't blame him.

She has the same effect on me.

"Funny guys, huh?" Walker crosses the room to the counter. He motions to Dean, who's currently in his suite, showing Chloe his water color technique. He's concentrating. Serious. It's weird. "You might have a chance."

My brother snaps back to his usual trouble making bullshit. "I think we all know how Leigh feels about me." He winks.

Chloe rolls her eyes. She rises to her feet. Her combat boots pad the hardwood as she moves to the backroom.

"You're a charmer." Walker laughs. "You trying to get her to quit."

"She quits, I quit." I hired Chloe as an assistant/apprentice a while ago. She should be a perfect fit here—she's talented, serious, quiet—but Dean keeps giving her shit. The two of them hate each other.

They think nobody notices that they alternate between trading *I hate your guts* looks and *I want to fuck you senseless* looks.

But it's obvious.

I just hope he keeps it in his pants for once.

She's good for Inked Hearts.

"I'm not gonna steal my brother's girl." Dean stands. Stretches his arms over his head. "You know how much shit our parents would give me?"

"Why you still hanging here, Leighton?" Walker catches the yawn. "Your boyfriend not giving you enough?"

"Never." She twirls a purple strand—she's kept her hair purple forever now. Says she's sticking with it long term. That she adores looking in the mirror and seeing the girl I fell in love with.

"He's cruel," Walker says.

"You have no idea." She nods.

He raises a brow.

Dean motions *go on*.

Leighton rolls her eyes. "You're not getting any info on my sex life." She slides her laptop into her messenger bag. Slings it over her shoulder. "But I'm flattered by your obsession."

"What did you do to Chloe?" Emma steps into the main room. She brushes her dark hair behind her ears. Shoots Dean a glare. "I will kick your ass if you keep fucking with her."

"I'll help," Walker offers.

"Oooh, can I too?" Leighton presses her hands together. "Pretty please." She steps out from behind the counter. Nods a goodbye to Emma. "I'll get out of your way."

"You'll leave me with these idiots? All by myself?" Emma feigns horror. She's been working at the shop since Leighton left.

She's only here part time, but it's nice having her around. She's known us forever. She doesn't let the guys get away with shit. She knows her older brother well enough not to flirt when he's around.

But when he's not…

Let's just say she makes Leighton proud.

"I'll be back next Friday." She hugs Emma goodbye. Whispers something in her ear.

"You promise?" Emma releases her.

She nods.

They share a laugh.

Then she's all mine.

She takes my hand, wraps her arms around me, holds me like she'll never let go. "I missed you."

"I missed you too." I've barely seen her all week. She's been working too hard to leave her apartment.

But that isn't gonna matter soon.

Fuck, I hope that isn't gonna matter soon.

I brush her short hair behind her ear. "Should we get out of here?"

"Thought you'd never ask." She turns to our friends. Waves goodbye. "We don't need the audience."

"Baby, you wound me." Dean blows her a kiss.

She feigns disgust.

But she can't hide her smile.

She loves being here, at Inked Hearts, bantering with everyone.

I press my palm into her lower back to lead her out the door.

The orange glow of sunset fills our view. The street is incredibly California. Beach cottages, palm trees, the smell of salt mixing with the smell of gasoline.

"You miss working at Inked Hearts?" I intertwine my fingers with hers. I need to lead her here without making it obvious. I need it to be a surprise.

"Every day." She looks to the ocean, some five blocks away. Watches the sun sink into the horizon. "But I love design more."

"You can work here more often."

"No. I can't." Her eyes fill with affection as she looks up at me. "You're too distracting."

"I can wear baggy clothes."

She shakes her head.

"Cut off my hair?"

"Over my dead body."

"Really? You'd die for my hair?"

She reaches up, runs her fingers through my waves. Address my locks. "I'm sorry he's trying to hurt you. I promise I won't let him."

My laugh dissolves the tension in my shoulders.

But the relaxation is short lived.

This is still happening.

I need her to say yes.

I need it so fucking badly.

I wrap my arms around her waist, pull her body into mine. "All right. No haircuts."

"Promise?"

"For a while." I press my lips to hers.

She groans against my mouth. "Did I already say I missed you?"

"Yeah." I plant another kiss on her lips. "I missed you too." It's only been two days since she last fell asleep in my bed, but neither of us brings that up. Two days is plenty of time. It's an eternity.

But after this…

Fuck, I need a yes.

I need it like I need oxygen.

———

At Eleventh, I turn right instead of going straight.

"Ryan." Leighton squeezes my hand. "Did you forget where you live?"

"No."

"So, we're…" The cross sign flashes white. She follows me into the intersection.

"It's a surprise."

"A good surprise?"

I hope so. "Great."

"Does it involve dinner? I'm starving."

My stomach is in knots. Fuck, I can't remember the last time I was this nervous. Being with Leighton is everything. But the possibility of living with her?

Of waking up next to her every morning, fixing her

breakfast, designing side by side, arguing about what we'll watch, falling asleep next to her every night…

"Ryan?" She steps onto the sidewalk. Turns so she's staring into my eyes. "Are you sure you're okay?"

No, but I will be. If she says yes. I nod.

She offers her hands. When I take them, she pulls me into the sidewalk with her. "You're worrying me."

"It's good. I promise."

She looks up at me, staring into my eyes, looking for meaning.

We've been here so many times.

I never get tired of it.

"Come here." I bring my hands to her waist. Lean down. Press my lips to hers.

She arches into me, opening her lips to make way for my tongue, groaning against my mouth.

I want to take her right here on the sidewalk.

It's a good way to put off asking.

But I have to do this.

I have to get a yes.

She pulls back with a sigh. "Lead the way."

I nod as I take her hand.

We walk the two blocks to the apartment hand in hand. This place is closer to the beach, but it's farther into a residential area. The city sounds drop to a murmur. The streets fill with trees. There are lawns and parked cars everywhere.

There.

I push the gate open for her.

She looks up at me. "Ryan… are you…?"

"Yeah."

"And you want to…"

"Let me show you before you say anything."

"You don't have to."

"Yeah, I do." I take her hand. Lead her into the complex.

Past the small courtyard. Up the steps. To our new place. Apartment 205.

Her eyes go wide as I slide a key into the lock. "You already—"

I nod.

"But you didn't ask me—"

"It's time for me to live somewhere else." Somewhere Penny's never been.

Not because she haunts my memories.

But I'm done with that part of my life.

And I need Leighton to know how fucking sure I am.

I push the door open. Motion *after you*.

She steps inside. Flips a switch.

Florescent light bounces off the sleek white walls.

Leighton's heeled boots tap the hardwood floors as she walks down the hallway. She takes in the new, stainless steel kitchen. "It's you."

"Yeah?"

"Of course." She turns to the room on the left. Her eyes go wide as she takes it in. "That's a view of the ocean."

I nod.

"From our apartment?"

"It is."

"Can we really afford this?"

"It's cheaper than living apart."

"By how much?"

Not as much as I'd like. But—"I have plenty, baby. Don't worry. I'm set on living here. I've paid first and last. I've put the deposit down."

"Oh."

"It's okay if you aren't ready. I can afford it on my own." I slide my arms around her waist. Bring my lips to her neck. "But, fuck, Leigh, I want to wake up next to you so fucking badly."

She leans into my touch. "I want that too."

"Let me show you something."

"Okay."

I take her hand. Lead her to the other room.

Her jaw drops as she takes it in. "You got a new bed."

"It was time."

"It's huge."

"You don't like that?"

"What if I don't?"

"I'll convince you otherwise."

She turns to me. "How?"

"I'll strip."

"You could do that now." She closes the distance between us. "Right here." She plants her hands on my chest. Her fingers curl into the fabric of my hoodie.

"Do this?" Slowly, I undo the zipper of my hoodie. I shrug it off my arms. Stare into her eyes as the fabric hits the ground.

"Yes." Her fingers curl into my t-shirt. "Do that."

"Uh-uh." I shake my head. "This first." My fingers go to the hem of her cropped sweater. I peel it over her chest.

She raises her hands so I can get it over her shoulders and arms.

I drop it on the floor.

"Now this." She tugs my t-shirt over my head.

"And this." I undo the clasp of her lacy bra.

She stares into my eyes as she peels it off her chest.

Fuck, she has amazing tits.

I need my hands around them.

I need her legs wrapped around my hips.

I need her screaming my name.

Still, I continue her game. I kick off my shoes. Peel off my socks. Drop to my feet to undo the zipper of her boots.

The right.

Then the left.

She steps out of both. Kicks them aside. "Your turn."

I undo the button of my jeans. Push them off my hips.

Her eyes go wide. "Fuck. Have I told you how much I love that you go commando?"

"Yeah." I reach under her skirt. Find the waistband of her black tights and peel them, and her panties, over her ass.

They collect at her thighs.

Her hand knots in my hair. "Bed. Now."

I back her onto it. Drop to my knees between her legs. Peel her tights off her right leg. Then the left.

She squirms as I drag my lips up the inside of her calf. Her knee. Her thigh.

My fingers curl into her soft skin.

I pin her legs to the bed as I bring my mouth to her.

Fuck, she tastes good.

I lick her from up and down again and again.

I tease her until she's groaning.

Until she's tugging at my hair.

"Fuck, Ryan." She groans as my nails curl into her thighs.

I hold her in place as I bring my tongue to her clit.

I can't tease her anymore today. I need her bliss. I need her coming. I need her screaming my name.

Her breath hitches as I hit the speed she likes.

I go a little faster.

A little harder.

Up.

Right.

"Don't stop." She tugs at my hair. "Fuck."

I lick her just how she needs me.

Her thighs fight my hands.

Her groans bounce around the room.

Around our room.

I'm eating out my girlfriend on our bed.

It's everything.

She's everything.

I pin her harder.

Lick her faster.

A few more flicks of my tongue and she's there.

"Ryan." Her nails find my back. Sink into my skin.

She claws at me as she comes on my lips. I can feel her orgasm in the way she pulses. Taste it in the way she gets sweeter. Hear it in the way her groans run together.

"Fuck me. Now," she demands.

I pull back. Plant a kiss on her pelvis. Push her skirt to her waist as I climb up her body.

Her eyes find mine as I plant my hands outside her shoulders.

She wraps her legs around my hips.

Fuck.

Pleasure floods my senses as my tip strains against her. She feels so fucking good. Warm. Wet. Mine.

It echoes though my thoughts.

Around the room.

Around the entire apartment.

Our apartment.

Our fucking universe.

No teasing today.

I drive into her with a steady stroke.

Her nails sink into my back.

Her other hand finds my hair.

She pulls me into a long, deep kiss.

Lifts her hips to take me deeper.

I sink into her. Claim her mouth. Her cunt. Her soul.

We stay locked like that, moving together, breathing together until she's there.

She groans against my mouth as she comes.

Her pulses pushing me over the edge.

I wrap my arms around her.

Fill her with steady thrusts.

Pleasure floods my body as I come.

Once I've spilled every drop, I collapse next to her.

"I love you so much." She nestles into my chest.

"You saying that 'cause I made you come?"

"No. But it doesn't hurt."

"I love you too."

She looks up at me like she's exactly where she wants to be.

I brush a hair behind her ear.

I stare into her eyes until her lids flutter closed.

She kisses me hard and deep.

She kisses me like she's claiming me.

No, she is claiming me.

But she doesn't have to.

I'm already hers.

Wherever life takes us, I'm hers.

And she's mine.

And that's fucking everything.

AUTHOR'S NOTE

I fell in love with Ryan back in *Tempting*, when he first glared at Brendon and muttered something about everyone getting to work. At the time, I wasn't sure what I wanted to do with his heartbreak. Would he get back together with his ex? Would he be the hero perfect for the moody second chance romance idea I had way back when? Or did he need to let go of the idea of the one who got away?

Writing a series is a funny thing. The side characters shape themselves. It's some kind of magic. Honestly, I can't explain it. Book one is impossible. I curse the written word. I find every excuse I can to hide from the blank page. But, by the end, I know who Hero Two is, what he wants, who he needs, exactly how I need to torture him to force him to change. By the time I finished *Playing*, I knew Ryan needed to end up with Leighton. And I knew he would struggle to get over the idea of himself belonging with his ex.

At its heart, that's what this book is about: it's about throwing away your idea of who you are and what you're supposed to feel so you can look in the mirror and see who that person really is. It was so much fun diving into Ryan's damaged head (I love the broody ones). But what was really fun was pushing him out of his comfort zone, forcing him to confront the ideas that were no longer serving him.

This book was a treat. It was so much fun poking Ryan's bruises, watching him fail to see what was right in front of his face, reveling in Dean torturing his brother. I hope you love Ryan as much as I do. As always, I hope to see you for the next Inked Hearts book. Dean's story is a treat—everything you expect from him and so much more (and so much banter).

Thanks for reading.

Love,

Crystal

ACKNOWLEDGEMENTS

My first thanks goes to my husband, for his support when I'm lost in bookland and for generally being the sun in my sky. Sweetheart, you're better than all the broken bad boys in the world.

The second goes to my father, for insisting I go to the best film school in the country, everything else be damned. I wouldn't love movies, writing, or storytelling half as much if not for all our afternoon trips to the bookstore and week-ends at the movies. You've always been supportive of my goals, and that means the world to me.

A big shout out to all my beta readers. You helped give me the confidence to put out a book a little more heartbreaking than usual. And also to my ARC readers for helping spread the word to everyone else in the world.

A special thanks to my fellow pop-punk addict, Molle, for fangirling over music with me, for talking me through my business decisions, and for reminding me that loving my work matters as much as all the marketing money in the world.

Athena Wright, you are the best author friend a girl could

ask for. Thank you for your feedback, for being my chat buddy, and for always being there to give me the perspective I need. And thank you for mocking me when I deserve it and telling me no when I need to hear it.

Thanks so much to my editor Marla, my designer's Tash and Gel, and to all my beta readers.

As always, my biggest thanks goes to my readers. Thank you for picking up *Pretend You're Mine.* I hope you'll be back for *Loving You, Hating You* (Dean's book), coming this June.

STAY IN TOUCH

Sign up for my mailing list to get an exclusive extended epilogue (if you're already subscribed you'll get this soon).

You can also join my Facebook group, like my page on Facebook, or friend me on Facebook.

More books about the men of Inked Hearts are coming soon.

Dean's book is coming soon. Turn the page for a teaser!

HATING YOU, LOVING YOU

SPECIAL TEASER

CHLOE

Sign up for my mailing list to be notified as soon as *Hating You, Loving You* is live.

Please note: This text has not yet been edited.

W hy do so people drink?

This stuff tastes awful.

I force myself to swallow another mouthful of orange juice and vodka.

My throat burns.

My head spins.

I reach for something to hold onto. Find the white banister. It's a smooth, ornate, pure money.

This entire house is pure money. Pristine carpet. Glass tables. Three thousand dollar leather upholstery.

Six dollar Trader Joe's vodka.

The cheap booze ruins the aesthetic. It clashes with the sky lights, the sliding glass doors, the glowing aqua pool.

Not that anyone notices. My classmates are used to expensive furniture and two million dollar mansions.

But cheap vodka and an empty upstairs?

That thrills them.

I've heard enough rumors to know the drill. Rich kids. Nice house. Cheap booze. Parents out of town. *I heard Dean fucked Judy...*

Not that it's always Dean.

It's just those are the only rumors I pay attention to.

A giggle cuts through the big, white room. It bounces off the high ceilings. It bounces right into my ears.

There's Judy, all blonde hair and long limbs, standing at the table, running her red nails over Dean's forearm.

His smile lights up his blue eyes eyes. They're bright. Full of energy and life and lust for torturing me.

He raises a brow. Runs his strong hand through his shaggy dirty blond hair.

Shrugs his broad shoulders. Those are swimmer's shoulders. He has a swimmer's everything. I've seen him in a Speedo enough times to know—the guys practice a few lanes over.

He's more than a hot body too. He's handsome. Charming. Funny.

Evil.

My head knows better. My head despises the cocky playboy. For calling me sunshine. For taking nothing seriously. For throwing people away.

But my heart?

My body?

It's impossible to get over a guy you see shirtless five times a week. That's a scientific fact.

He laughs at Judy's joke. Shoots her that trademarked Dean million dollar smile as he blows her a kiss.

She paws at his chest.

He shrugs *maybe, maybe not.*

He's indifferent. Effortless. Aloof.

He has so much female attention he could give or take a knockout in fuck me heels.

That doesn't give a nobody in combat boots much of a chance.

I force myself to look away.

Watch Alan—this is his place—pound his red solo cup. He finishes. Crushes the cup. Watches it fall onto the pristine white carpet.

Drops of brown liquor catch on the fibers.

He shrugs like he doesn't care, but the worry in his eyes betrays him. The jocks around him laugh. Pound their drinks. Whisper some secret.

There are a dozen people here. Half in that circle. The rest on the couch or in the airy, stainless steel kitchen.

Everyone here is casual. Comfortable. Used to parties. To money. To cheap booze in plastic cups.

I...

This is way out of my comfort zone.

My gaze shifts back to Dean.

His eyes lock with mine. He raises his glass. Smiles.

My combat boots tap together. My hands go to my tank top. I play with its edge. Try to figure out what the hell that means.

Dean and I have shared two classes a day, every day, for the last three years.

He spends most of his free time teasing me.

Calling me sunshine.

Mocking how seriously I take art, math, and science.

Mocking my all black clothes, my thermos of tea, my tendency to gush about cartoons.

He turns to Alan. Whispers something.

Alan laughs.

Dean nods *hell yeah*. "Everybody come here." His playful voice bounces around the room.

Everyone turns his way.

Looks at him.

Hangs on his words.

Dean commands attention, friendship, respect. All he does is smile and a dozen girls fall over themselves trying to claim him.

A dozen guys want to be his friend.

The world is his oyster.

"Why should I listen to anything you say, Maddox?" Alan teases back.

Dean's shrug is effortless. *Why should I bother exerting a single ounce of energy on anything?* "If you don't want me to blow your mind, go ahead. Leave."

"Maddox, I don't want you blowing anything." Alan laughs.

I roll my eyes. How original.

Dean's eyes catch mine. He shakes his head *not great, huh?*

I fight my smile.

Every day this year, he turned our art class from my happy place to my *deal with Dean's constant teasing* place.

He doesn't get a smile now.

Even if my body is buzzing with nervous energy.

Even if my limbs are light and airy.

Even if my sex is aching.

I must be blushing, because he's smiling wider. Knowingly. Like he's sure I'm eating out of the palm of his hand.

He turns back to the group. "Truth or date."

"I'm not fourteen," someone says.

"Sounds like you're chicken." Dean turns to me. "What do you think, Chloe? Are you chicken?"

"No." My heart thuds against my chest.

My head fills with ideas. Every dirty dare he could offer me.

His hands in my hair.

His groan in my ears.

His lips against mine.

God, those soft lips.

I want to slap them for all the stupid shit he says. For not giving a fuck about the classes his parents pay a fortune for. For calling me sunshine every three seconds.

But he's calling me Chloe.

He...

I...

My heart pounds so hard I'm sure it's going to break out of my chest.

It doesn't.

But a deep breath does nothing to help me calm down.

For three years I've been smitten. Ever since our first day in geometry, when he turned to me and asked to borrow my protractor. Then promised to make it worth my while with a wink and smile.

Calm eludes me.

Sense eludes me.

Everything but a fangirl voice screaming *Dean Maddox* eludes me.

His lips curl into a smile. He holds out his arm. Motions *come here*.

My knees knock together.

Lightness spreads into my chest, neck, head. I'm dizzy. Like I'm going to faint.

Who knew swooning was a real thing? I thought Gia made it up.

My feet move of their own accord.

My combat boots sink into the plush carpet.

My hands slip from my pockets.

One finds his palm.

He wraps his fingers around my hand. Rubs the space between my thumb and forefinger with his thumb.

He looks down at me—he has to, he has a foot on me—like I'm the only thing he needs.

Like I'm *everything* he needs.

His voice is soft. Sweet. "Nice of you to join, sunshine."

The nickname breaks my trance.

Dean doesn't need me. He needs to push my buttons.

Gia insists he's teasing because he likes me, but what does Gia know about guys like Dean? She met her boyfriend at a comics shop. They read *Spider-Man* and play video games together.

Gia doesn't know Dean, but I do.

With him, you have to bite back.

I shoot him my best *fuck you* smile. "Nice to see you, Dick Face."

He chuckles. "You know I take that as a compliment."

I shrug *do you?* People mill closer. Take seats on the couch, at the table, on the ground.

"If you'd seen my dick, you'd know why." He steps forward to let someone pass. His hand brushes my arm. His chest brushes my shoulder. His crotch brushes my outer thigh.

My body responds with gusto.

Any sense of calm, of upper hand, of any hand, dissipates.

My body goes into overdrive. Every molecule screams the same thing: *more Dean please.*

A jock's voice pulls me from my thoughts. "Damn, Maddox. Stop bragging. We're playing a game here." He pats a spot on the the packed couch. It's all designer jeans and BCBG dresses and pretty girls in hot guy's laps.

I take a step backwards, but there's nowhere to go. My ass hits the glass table.

Dean turns to his friend. "Should I whip it out instead?"

A girl sitting on the couch claps with glee. "Hell yeah!"

The five girls sitting on the ground clap with her.

"There's a demand." Dean shrugs, effortless. He reaches for his jeans. Pretends to undo his button. "I can't let my fans down."

"Save it for the game," the friend says.

A dozen *awwws* and *no fairs* bounce around the room.

Dean turns to me. Winks. "Fair is fair." He offers his hand. "Sit with me, sunshine."

He leads me to the couch. Rests his ass on its arm.

I stand next to him. Shift my weight between my feet. Tap my toes together. Listen to the hollow sound the synthetic leather makes.

His hand brushes my hip.

My body responds immediately.

My pulse races. My nipples perk. My sex clenches.

I want him touching me. I think about it all the time. Too much.

He's everything I hate.

He's someone I hate.

But I still want him touching me.

I still stroke myself to orgasm thinking about him every fucking night.

"Why don't you start, romeo," Dean's friend calls.

Ooohs and *ahhs* bounce around the room with *do its* and *Oh my gods!*

The room wants Dean.

The entire world wants Dean.

He wants…

How knows what the hell the manwhore wants.

He smiles, reveling in the attention. "With pleasure." He turns to me. "Chloe, truth or dare."

My head fills with ideas.

A dare to kiss him.

To flash him.

To touch him.

God, I want to touch him.

And to slap the smarmy smile from his face.

He did call me by my name.

Maybe there's some shred of decency behind his party boy facade.

Or maybe that's my hormones talking.

Either way.

I adopt his aloof posture. Watch clouds roll over the skylight. Watch the wavy lines of the pool bounce off the sliding glass door. Watch a dozen people turn their attention to me.

Deep breath. Slow exhale. "Truth."

His blue eyes sparkle as his smile spreads over his cheeks. "Are you a virgin?"

My cheeks flush.

My chest too.

Fuck Dean.

He must know I am.

Everyone at school knows.

I'm the weird loner who spends lunch drawing in her sketchbook.

Guys aren't interested.

Not that any guys appeal. The guy who tortures me is the only one I want.

Why am I here?

I step backwards. Dig my heel into the soft carpet. My instincts scream *leave*, but I can't do that.

I'm not embarrassed of my inexperience.

I'm not letting him rattle me.

I'm not letting his friends think I'm some loser ashamed of her decisions.

"Yes." I shoot Dean my most serene smile. "I have standards. I'm sure that's hard for you to imagine."

He scratches his head. "Standards. Never heard of those."

His friends laugh.

Someone calls out, "It's when you need more than a pulse and two legs."

"Two legs? Look who's Mr. Picky." A jock laughs.

"I'd never discriminate against a woman with one leg. Or no legs." Dean's eyes find mine. "I don't need a smile either. A million dollar scowl is better."

I fight my scowl. I'm playing Dean's game. Indifference. Aloofness. Utter coolness. "Unfortunately for you, I do have standards."

Someone makes that *ooh, burn* sound.

The girls on the floor giggle. Whisper something. No doubt it's *who does she think she is? No way Dean wants her.* But I don't care about them.

They're seniors. They're graduating. In two weeks, they'll be out of my life forever.

Dean looks up at me with a wicked smile. "Your turn."

Oh. So it is. I scan the room.

Fuck the girls trading rumors.

Fuck the guys looking at me like they're deciding if I meet their standards.

Fuck this whole party.

My gut churns. Why did I let Gia talk me into this? Why did I think an invite from Dean could lead to anything but teasing and embarrassment?

I need to get out of here. Fast.

I look to Alan. He's a wannabe Dean. Not quite as cute or tall or blonde. Not as funny or charming or attention grabbing. "Alan, truth or dare."

Everyone turns to him.

He leans back in his black chair. Revels in the attention. "Dare."

I have to fight fire with fire. "I dare you to streak around the neighborhood."

Alan jumps to his feet. Holds up his hand in salute. "I hope you ladies are in for a show." He sends winks in every direction. Even mine.

Then he marches over the carpet, the white tile foyer, the mat. All the way out the door.

It slams shut with a thud.

"Let's set up on the porch." Dean motions to the door. Leans in to whisper something to the girl next to him.

Even though she's sitting on some guy's lap, she giggles at Dean. "Sure."

She slides off her boy-toy's lap. "Follow me." Her red heels sink into the carpet, then they click against the tile.

She turns back. Motions *let's go*.

And everyone does.

One by one, people stand. File out of the room.

Someone, a guy about Dean's height, with a Letterman jacket and dark hair, whispers something in Dean's ear.

Dean shakes his forehead. "Got something else to do."

The friend laughs.

Dean watches him leave.

It's just us in this giant house.

I move to the table. Fill my glass with more orange juice and vodka. Pray for it to erase that *you don't belong here* voice completely.

This is supposed to be the best time of my life. Parties. Boys. Fun.

I'm having fun, dammit.

Dean follows me to the table. "You don't want to watch?"

"Alan isn't my type."

"What is?"

"Smart guys." I take a long sip of my drink. "You know any?"

"Not one. But I can help with that drink." His hand brushes mine. Slowly, he peels my fingers from my cup.

"Grenadine." He picks up a bottle of candy red liquid. Pours it into my glass. "Goes does smoother."

"Thanks." My stomach flutters as he hands the glass back. This is intentional.

He's touching me on purpose.

He's helping me on purpose.

He's alone with me on purpose.

He fills his cup with Jack and Coke then lifts it to toast.

"To?" I ask.

"Good friendships."

"We're good friends?"

"Of course." His voice is earnest. Honest.

"I hate you."

"I know."

"That doesn't bother you?"

"Fuck no. It's what I like about you." He clinks his glass with mine. Takes a long sip. Lets out a low sigh of pleasure. "You keep me on my toes."

"You live on your toes."

"Should take up ballet." He makes a show of rising to his tip toes. It's nowhere close to a ballet move. But it's Dean all the same.

Charming *and* irritating.

Gia says he reminds her of Han Solo.

But Gia isn't the one taking his constant insults. (And Gia needs to lean that *Star Wars* isn't the answer to all of life's questions).

"I do like you, sunshine." His eyes find mine. "Have for awhile."

"So that virgin question?"

"I wanted to know something. So I asked."

"What did you want to know?"

He moves closer. Until I can feel the heat of his body. Smell his cologne. "If I'd be your first."

What? My cheeks flame. There's no way he...

There's no...

I...

"Chloe?" His fingers brush the inside of my wrist.

"Huh?"

"I want to fuck you."

"But—"

"Let's go upstairs. I'll show you the night of your life."

My defenses crumble.

Dean wants me.

He's offering to fuck me.

He...

How is this possible?

My heart screams for him. My body aches for him. My head— it's still reasonable.

I throw up the only defense I know—sarcasm. "Of my entire life?"

"Yeah."

"Doesn't speak well for your future performances."

"You already thinking about round two?"

"No. I..." My cheeks flame. "I meant—"

"I know what you meant, sunshine. Round two will be just as good. But nothing is as special as your first time."

"Yours?"

He shrugs, effortless. "Wasn't lucky enough to have someone like me showing me the ropes."

"You're going to show me the ropes?"

He nods. "Yeah." His fingers trace circles over my skin. "If that's what you want."

"Judy offered to fuck you."

"And?"

"Why me over her?"

"I told you, sunshine. I like you. It's that simple."

"You're about to graduate."

"You will next year."

"But you're… you're leaving."

He shakes his head. "Not going anywhere."

"Where will you be?"

"Ryan is gonna get me a gig as an apprentice."

"Yeah?" I bite back my enthusiasm. Dean's older brother is a tattoo artist. It's the coolest thing ever.

"Yeah." He nods. "Just got this one." He pulls his shirt up his torso, showing off inches of taught abs.

He pulls it higher.

All the way to his side.

He turns to show off a tattoo on his ribs—the state of California, adorned with grey and red roses.

"How much did that hurt?" I ask.

"Like a bitch."

"Guys usually say it doesn't hurt."

"Liars."

"Can I?"

"Of course."

My fingers go to his skin. It's soft, but he's bone and muscle beneath it.

God, the feel of him against my fingertips…

My knees knock together.

"Didn't think you were the ink type," he says.

Words dissolve on my tongue. He's so close. And so undressed. And so hot.

My hand knows what it wants.

It traces his ink again and again.

I look up at him. He's so tall. I'm short, yeah, but he's on some other plane of height.

"Can you keep a secret?" I ask.

He pulls an imaginary zipper over his lips in a *my lips are sealed* gesture.

"I got one last month." I roll my jeans over my right hip to show off my new tattoo. A star. It's a little lopsided, but it's mine.

"Bad ass." He flashes me that million dollar smile. "I have another one to show you." He offers his hand. "Upstairs."

There's weight in the word.

Upstairs isn't for conversation. It's for what I've been dreaming about for the last three years.

"Okay." I down half my drink. Pray for the liquid courage I hear so much about. "Upstairs."

I take his hand and follow him to the bedroom.

***

Dean presses his lips to mine.

He strips me out of my clothes.

He lays me on the bed and warms me up.

Pulls a condom from his jeans. Tears it open. Slides it on.

Then he's on top of me, easing into me, whispering dirty promises in my ear.

It hurts, but not as badly as Gia told me it would.

The pain fades to discomfort.

To pleasure.

To the thrill of knowing that Dean and I are one.

He takes care of me. Makes sure I come.

It feels like we go forever.

We finish. He helps me dress. Promises to stay in touch.

Never does.

He doesn't text, or call, or email, or IM.

The next week, he graduates.

And I spend seven years without hearing a peep from Dean Maddox.

Sign up for my mailing list to be notified as soon as *Hating You, Loving You* is live.

ALSO BY CRYSTAL KASWELL

Dangerous Noise

Dangerous Kiss - Ethan

Dangerous Crush – Kit

Dangerous Rock – Joel

Dangerous Fling – Mal

Dangerous Encore - series sequel

Sinful Serenade

Sing Your Heart Out - Miles

Strum Your Heart Out - Drew

Rock Your Heart Out - Tom

Play Your Heart Out - Pete

Sinful Ever After – series sequel

Inked Hearts

Tempting - Brendon

Playing - Walker

Pretend You're Mine - Ryan

Hating You, Loving You - Dean - coming summer 2018

Emma - coming summer 2018

Sign up for the Crystal Kaswell mailing list

Printed in Great Britain
by Amazon